THE HIGHEST-RANKING MEMBER OF THE KGB IN NORTH AMERICA STARED AT CORBETT WITH STEEL GRAY EYES.

"A million dollars is a lot of money, Gyorgi . . ." he said, hesitating.

Corbett exploded. "We have no choice, General! Without Waxman's vote, I'm dead. With it, there's a good chance I'll be Fed chairman, and when I'm chairman, I shall then be able to engineer the downfall of Imperial America!"

Peabody stood motionless. Then he opened a drawer in his workbench and took out a key with a red plastic end. "Kennedy Airport, South Terminal, Locker 3341—near Gate 44. In two hours' time your one million dollars will be there. I expect results. And so does Moscow Central. Understood?"

"I will hand you America's head on a platter, General, an apple in its mouth."

Peabody dropped the key into Corbett's palm. "If you don't, it may be your head on that platter, Gyorgi."

ACTION ADVENTURE

SILENT WARRIORS   (1675, $3.95)
by Richard P. Henrick

The Red Star, Russia's newest, most technologically advanced submarine, outclasses anything in the U.S. fleet. But when the captain opens his sealed orders 24 hours early, he's staggered to read that he's to spearhead a massive nuclear first strike against the Americans!

THE PHOENIX ODYSSEY   (1789, $3.95)
by Richard P. Henrick

All communications to the USS *Phoenix* suddenly and mysteriously vanish. Even the urgent message from the president cancelling the War Alert is not received. In six short hours the *Phoenix* will unleash its nuclear arsenal against the Russian mainland.

COUNTERFORCE   (2013, $3.95)
Richard P. Henrick

In the silent deep, the chase is on to save a world from destruction. A single Russian Sub moves on a silent and sinister course for American shores. The men aboard the U.S.S. *Triton* must search for and destroy the Soviet killer Sub as an unsuspecting world races for the apocalypse.

EAGLE DOWN   (1644, $3.75)
by William Mason

To western eyes, the Russian Bear appears to be in hibernation — but half a world away, a plot is unfolding that will unleash it awesome, deadly power. When the Russian Bear rises up, God help the Eagle.

THE OASIS PROJECT   (1296, $3.50)
by William Mason

The President had a plan — a plan that by all rights should not exist. And it would be carried out by the ASP, a second generation space shuttle that would transport the laser weapons into positions — before the Red Tide hit U.S. shores.

Available wherever paperbacks are sold, or order direct from the Publisher. Send cover price plus 50¢ per copy for mailing and handling to Zebra Books, Dept. 2068, 475 Park Avenue South, New York, N.Y. 10016. Residents of New York, New Jersey and Pennsylvania must include sales tax. DO NOT SEND CASH.

USSA

A NOVEL BY
JAMES N. FREY

ZEBRA BOOKS
KENSINGTON PUBLISHING CORP.

ZEBRA BOOKS

are published by

Kensington Publishing Corp.
475 Park Avenue South
New York, NY 10016

First printing: May 1987

Printed in the United States of America

In memoriam
Jacob Ernest Frey

The best way to destroy capitalism is to debauch the currency.

—Lenin

BOOK I

ONE

George Corbett, investment banker, financier, financial wizard *par excellence*, paced about nervously in his lavish office high up in the Sullivan Building on Fifth Avenue, in midtown Manhattan. He was waiting for the damn phone to ring. It was almost five o'clock in the afternoon and he'd been waiting for over an hour.

The meeting in Washington, where he was to be picked as the President's choice to be the next chairman of the Federal Reserve, had been scheduled to start at two-thirty which meant, he figured, it probably had started at about a quarter to three. The only thing on the agenda was his nomination, and he knew he had the votes to get approval without debate. Okay, so they would be sociable for a few minutes, talk about the weather, what they were going to do over the coming Labor Day weekend, the recent dip in the prime rate, maybe even talk about him for a few minutes, then have the vote. Forty-five minutes tops. By three-thirty they should have been out of there. He should have heard something by now, which meant something was definitely wrong.

He stopped pacing suddenly and sat down heavily in his high-backed swivel chair and nervously fingered his gold-plated letter opener. He had put a Brahms string quartet on his quadraphonic stereo system, hoping it would have a salutary effect on his nerves. It didn't. He looked out the window at the gloomy Manhattan skyline. The sky was grayish-brown with a late-summer haze that sat over the city like a pall.

What could possibly have happened?

Until now, his campaign to have himself appointed chairman of the Federal Reserve Board had been going exactly as planned. The previous spring, he'd managed to get an editorial planted in two very prestigious financial weeklies extolling his virtues, both saying he'd be the ideal man to be the next Fed chairman. He had won the support of Vernon Storkweather, the outgoing chairman. During a weekend with Storkweather in the Bahamas, George had promised to see that his son, a Harvard Law graduate but nevertheless an idiot, was given a place on the board of First Atlantic and Pacific Bank, where George was the principal stockholder. He'd have given a great deal more, but Storkweather was in some ways a timid man and, in George's view, stupid—when it came to looking out for number one.

George had, of course, lined up most of the New York banking community on his side. He was one of them, after all. He let them know that they could rely on him to run the Federal Reserve pretty much to their advantage. George Corbett was *their* man.

The final decision as to who would be nominated was up to the President of the United States, Jerome Hustead. But in the past Hustead had relied on his Council of Economic Advisers, which included the secretary of the treasury, the President's chief economist, White House chief of staff, the budget director, a senator, and a congresswoman. George had made sure throughout the summer that each of them knew his qualifications and connections. He was sure of two of them, somewhat sure of two others, and one was wavering. Only Ernest Ramsey, the budget director, was

10

openly opposed to him.

The door to George's office opened; his secretary, Marla Crane, came in and said if there was nothing else she was leaving for the evening. She was a plain woman, even-tempered, efficient. Minded her own business. He told her to have a nice holiday. She reminded him to turn off the coffeepot. Whenever he stayed late he always forgot the coffeepot, she said. "Yes, yes," George said, "I won't forget. Good night." She left with a wave. He got up and started pacing again.

George Corbett was fifty-four, but looked younger. He was five feet nine and weighed 175 pounds, with a barrel chest and a thick neck and wide shoulders. He had been lifting weights three times a week for thirty years. His tailors had problems making his suits hang correctly on such a muscular frame. But he paid fifteen hundred a suit and they fit perfectly. He wore striped ties, a vest with a gold watch chain, and his shoes were handmade in Italy of the most exquisite leather. He had a military bearing and walked with a side-to-side swaying motion common to weight lifters. The skin on his face was uncommonly smooth with a ruddy glow of health. He used tint to cover the gray in his thick brown hair, which he combed straight back. He had thick eyebrows. Once his eyes were narrow, almost Oriental, common among the Slavic races, but he'd had them "rounded" by a plastic surgeon long before he ever came to America and became George Corbett. No one who knew him as George Corbett the investment banker was aware that he had been born Gyorgi Vlahovich in Yazykov, a small town in the Caucasus in southern Russia.

His office was as large as most living rooms, and richly appointed. The furniture—a large desk, eight chairs, a bookcase—were hand-crafted of solid mahogany. The chairs were upholstered in authentic red Moroccan leather and the floor was covered with a Persian carpet George had bought for seven thousand in Teheran before the fall of the

11

shah and which was now worth twenty. It was an office worthy of a man of his stature, he thought. Everything was just as he wanted it, right down to the brass ring around the lip of the wastepaper basket, the lead crystal from Holland in his liquor cabinet, and the two Monet impressions of water lilies hanging on the wall. It was nothing short of magnificent. His office was the place where he did his best thinking, where he felt most in control of his destiny. Only, at the moment, he felt totally out of control.

At two minutes to five he called a friend in the Economics Department at Columbia University, Margo Yost-Konning, who he knew had connections in the Hustead administration. She had gone for the day. Then he called a reporter he knew on *The Wall Street Journal*. He was out of the office and wouldn't be back until Tuesday. He called home. His wife was out shopping, the maid said, and added that no one had called.

He poured a little cognac into his coffee cup. Ordinarily he didn't drink at the office—unless he was being sociable—but this was no ordinary day.

At ten after five the phone rang. "Hello," George said.

"Tim McAfee." McAfee was the secretary of the treasury, a member of the President's Council of Economic Advisers.

"I've been expecting your call, Tim. I won't kid you, I've been a little anxious. Am I in or out?"

"Still in limbo, I'm afraid."

"How so?"

"Ramsey said he's come up with a new prospect, he wants to present it to the Council on Tuesday. He's damn adamant. You know how much he's got the ear of the President. So we went along with him."

"Who is it, do you know?"

"Damian Carter."

"Damian Carter's a good man," George said evenly. He didn't let his tone betray his bitterness. "I think I'm a little

12

more qualified, but he'd be good, too."

"Damian Carter's too, well, gentlemanly for my tastes. I'm going to put up a fuss, George. I'm in your corner one hundred percent. I'll get back to you on Tuesday. Have a nice weekend."

"You, too, Tim. Best to Mary and the kids."

George hung up the phone and pounded his fists on his desk. "Damn! Damn! Damn!" He circled the desk once again, like an angry lion in a cage. So Ramsey wants Damian-the-blue-blood-Carter? What the hell did he think, that George Corbett would take this lying down?

He picked up the phone again and dialed the number for Embassy TV Network in Washington, D.C. When the operator answered, he asked for Carson Black. The line buzzed, then a man answered: "Carson Black's phone."

"This is George Corbett, from New York. Tell Carson I have to talk to her about the gathering we're having this weekend, we've had a little change in plans." There was no gathering. It was a code signal he'd worked out with her which meant he needed to talk to her right away. A moment later she came on the phone. "Hello, George, nice to hear from you."

"Carson, dear, how are you?"

"Fine. I've got a taping in about five minutes—something about this awful business in Cyprus—so you'll have to talk fast."

"Ramsey's pushing for Damian Carter all of a sudden. I'd wiped out all the others he'd been able to get, but Carter is at least in my league. A couple of the members on the council will vote with Ramsey because they know what a favorite he is with the President. We're going to need the vote of your friend. The one you said needed a little sweetening? Have you any idea what exactly he wants?"

"No, but I'll find out. How long do I have?"

"The meeting's Tuesday morning, but if something can be worked out, I'll need to know ahead of time. I have sixty

13

thousand on hand, see if he'll go for it. I'll be up at the lake. Let me know how it goes."

"I will, George. So nice to talk to you."

George hung up the phone feeling a burst of restored confidence. The "friend" they were talking about was the chairman of the Senate Finance Committee, Senator Harold Waxman. The sweetening they were talking about was money. The senator was for sale.

George knew he could trust Carson Black to handle the deal. She was not only an anchorwoman on the evening Embassy Network News, she was one of his oldest and closest friends. She was also a captain in the KGB, and an extraordinarily reliable agent.

Only a very few people in the United States knew she was an agent. He knew because he was her control. He had recruited and trained her, and helped her progress in her cover identity. When they'd met she was a graduate student at Stanford University with a rebellious soul and no direction. He gave her direction.

George put on his hat, laid his coat over his arm, and locked up his private office. A couple of his young assistants were still at work across the hall; they were diligent young men, devoted to their jobs. He asked one of them to see what they had in the computer and in the files on Damian Carter. The printout took about five minutes. What they had wasn't much, barely ten pages and a few dozen news clippings. They had collected data over the past two years on everyone he thought might be a potential competitor for the Fed chairman's job. He was glad now to have this. It was always best to know who you were up against in a head-to-head race.

"Don't forget to turn off the coffeepot when you leave," he told his two young assistants.

George planned to spend the three-day weekend with his

wife Linda and his son Rudolf at their summer place at Lake Cayuga in the Catskills. It was supposed to be relaxing. They had dinner at a Chinese restaurant in Yonkers and drove on to their cabin that night. It started raining about nine o'clock and continued heavily through Saturday. Linda and Rudolf spent the whole day fighting over rock and roll, how he wasted his summer by quitting summer school, and pot smoking. Rudolf, about to be a junior in high school, was a dull student and would always be a dull student. George had come to accept it. Why couldn't Linda? Not everyone was an Einstein. Certainly not Rudolf. Rudolf quit fighting openly with his mother sometime around Sunday morning and went into one of his terrible sulks. Linda then had a migraine, which made her unpleasant and witchy.

The material George read on Damian Carter troubled him, too.

There was nothing in the records to even hint there might be something to use against him. No kinky sex practices, no hanky-panky in his business dealings—at least none that had ever drifted up to the surface—no personal scandals. Damian Carter was from an old Boston family, very wealthy. Made money in lumber, canning, banking, and beer. He had gone to Yale where he was a star on the crew team, received a degree in International Finance, then went on to earn a doctorate in Economics from Harvard. There was a three-year interruption in his studies while he'd gone off to war in Korea, where he was awarded a Silver Star for bravery. He lived quietly, taught at various universities including Brown, Princeton, and Stanford, raced yachts, supported a home for unwed mothers. A regular all-American-boy type, as squeaky-clean as an eel.

He read on. Damian Carter had had a personal tragedy in his life about four years before. His wife and grown daughter were killed in a light plane crash in Montreal. For the last year or so he'd been romantically linked in the gossip columns to heiress Catlyn Cavanaugh. There were pictures of them together in the file, attending this or that charity function. She was perhaps thirty-five and, at least from her newsphotos, a truly beautiful woman. One of the clippings said she was originally from Houston, Texas.

George called his most resourceful and industrious research assistant from the cabin and told him to find out what he could about Catlyn Cavanaugh, and he didn't care how much money he had to spend doing it, or how many people he had to bother on a holiday weekend to get the information. There had to be a way of derailing Damian Carter.

At four o'clock Sunday afternoon Carson Black phoned.

"Hello, George."

"Carson, nice to hear from you."

"Having a party on the twenty-eight, can you make it?"

"Sure."

"See you then."

The conversation had been in code, just in case the phone was tapped. George regularly had all his phones checked for taps by very reliable people; nevertheless, if there was something sensitive to talk about, he didn't want to do it on his phone.

George put on his raincoat. Rudolf was on the front porch with a purple-haired girlfriend listening to rock and roll. Linda had taken the car to town. She had said she wanted to see a movie. George walked down the trail to the small grocery store near the public dock. It was just a half a mile and it took him exactly ten minutes. He got there twenty seconds before the pay phone in the booth next to the road rang.

"I'm here," he said.

Carson Black said, "Bad news, George. Senator Waxman will back you, but he wants one million dollars, in cash."

"Great joke, Carson. Just a million? Why not a billion?"

16

"No joke, George. He wants one *million* dollars. Says he needs to fill his swimming pool while he still has the schwack. He's leaving public office next year and doesn't want to live out his years poor. As you know, he has not been very wise or frugal with what he has made. He owns race horses. And anyone who isn't from Kentucky who owns race horses is a fool with money."

"Does he know who he's dealing with—I mean, does he know who we really are?"

"Of course not! He thinks you want the job so your Wall Street cronies can cash in big when interest rates rise and fall and that kind of mush. He thinks he's giving the Wall Streeters a bargain. The question is, even if you have his vote, will you win the nomination? Mr. Ramsey, it seems, has come up with a candidate everyone can live with."

"I think I can," George said.

"Then cough up the bread."

"There's no way I can get one million quickly."

"You could if you go to see the general."

"I think I'd rather chew razor blades."

"Maybe so, but he's got the cash, and you've got to have it if you're to have any chance at all. The good senator wants the money in his grubby little hands *before* the ten o'clock meeting on Tuesday."

"I didn't say I wouldn't go to the general. I just said I preferred not to. Will Waxman take part as a down payment? I could probably come up with a few hundred thousand in cash."

"He insists on having it all."

"Looks like I go to the general. In the meantime, ask Moscow Central and see if they have anything on Damian Carter in their files we might be able to use as leverage."

"Will do, George."

George hung up the phone and took a walk out onto the dock. No one fishing. No boats on the lake. The lake was calm and dreary, peppered with the raindrops. What a

17

dismal place when the weather was bad, he thought. He tried to think of a way to raise that much cash himself. He had a personal worth of fifteen million dollars, perhaps a little more. But if he sold off stock or cashed bonds, there would be inquiries from the IRS later. He had money in a Swiss trust for Rudolf, but he wouldn't touch that. Not ever. There was no way he could go to his American financial colleagues and borrow the money without raising suspicion. No one dealt in cash for anything legitimate. No, the only place he could go was to the general.

He went back to the phone and dialed a number in New York City. When a man answered, George said, "Need an appointment. This is Mr. Gibson."

"Today at eight-oh-one." The line went dead. The reply was in code; it meant a meeting was set for the next day at ten. The oh-one was the location—the Maxwell Building in midtown Manhattan.

George went back to the cabin and asked Rudolf to start loading up the car, they were heading back to the city.

"Can copy that," Rudolf said. George hoped that meant he'd do it.

The Maxwell Building was constructed in the thirties, and rows of ornate, stainless steel panels ran up the sides. Between the rows, the stones were grimy and weathered. It was Labor Day, and there were not many people on the street. George stepped into an alley and went in the side door on East Thirty-eighth Street. He stood in the entry-way for a few moments to make sure no one saw him go in. No one did. A white-haired couple got off the elevator and he got on; they didn't look at him. Under the elevator's control board was a small compartment marked "fire emergency," which contained a fire extinguisher. He opened the compartment's door and lifted a panel on the bottom, removing a key. He inserted the key into a slot on

18

the control board and turned it. The elevator door closed and the elevator descended into the basement.

The basement was damp and poorly lit. There were old file cabinets and office furniture stacked to the ceiling, covered with dust. The place smelled strongly of fuel oil. George stepped out of the elevator. The door closed behind him.

"Mr. Peabody? Are you here?"

A lumbering figure emerged from the shadows. "Right here, Gyorgi, this way." Peabody always called him "Gyorgi," in the Russian manner, with the accent on the first syllable. George liked the sound of it. It was the only thing about Peabody that he liked. Otherwise he found him often overly cautious and reluctant to make decisions.

Peabody was nearing seventy, a big man with stooping shoulders. His mussed hair was snow white. He was wearing a pair of weathered coveralls and an old plaid shirt. He had angular features and steel gray eyes, thoughtful at times, staring out behind a pair of square, wire-rimmed glasses. No one, meeting this man, would possibly guess, George thought, that he was the highest-ranking member of the KGB in North America.

"Watch your head now, Gyorgi."

George followed Peabody down a dark, dank hallway and into a workshop full of boiler parts in the process of being scrubbed with solvent. There was a single low-wattage light over a workbench which illuminated only a small portion of the workshop. Peabody wiped off a tall stool for George and gestured for him to sit on it.

"How have you been, Gyorgi?"

"I'm fine, Mr. Peabody."

Peabody lit a pipe and leaned against the workbench. George had always wondered whether he was a Russian or an American. Mr. Peaobdy always spoke English with a sort of New England nasal sound, so he guessed he was American, but there was no way to be sure. Since he was a

19

major general in the KGB, however, his nationality didn't matter.

"Cleaning the boilers," Peabody said, gesturing with the match he had used to light his pipe. "I do it every summer. We got a little behind, so I have to work the holiday."

George nodded. Peabody was always slow getting down to business. George said, "Looks like a tough job."

"It is." Peabody smiled. It was a paternalistic smile. George didn't like it.

"Nice suit, Gyorgi," Peabody said. He sucked on his pipe, blue smoke surrounding his head like a cloud around a mountain.

George said, "I was not nominated to the Fed as we anticipated."

Peabody's face was impassive. His eyes narrowed almost imperceptibly. "Is there some problem?"

"Ernest Ramsey has opposed me all along."

"The budget director?"

"Yes. He was not able to come up with anyone as remotely qualified as I am until the very last minute. Damian Carter."

"I've heard of him."

"So they're going to have another meeting on Tuesday. One or two of my votes may go over to Carter—he's a very popular person. It's possible I could lose out. One vote can be bought—Senator Waxman's."

"Is this why you wanted to see me?" His pipe had gone out; he relit it. "You need money for a bribe?"

"Yes."

"How much does he want?"

"One million dollars—in cash."

Peabody's face grew more serious. "One million. Will this guarantee us getting the nomination?"

"No. Nothing in these matters is ever guaranteed. The President makes the final decision. Two of the council members want me based on my qualifications. They know

20

me personally and we are on friendly terms. I have done things for them over the years. One is the President's chief economist, James A. Preston; the other is the treasury secretary, Timothy McAfee. I don't think they will change their minds. If we buy Waxman, we'll have three strong supports on the six-member council."

"And the other three?"

"Budget Director Ramsey is for anyone *but* me. Congresswoman Penelope Stecher is for me, but I don't consider her strongly committed. She's a close friend of a close friend of mine, Margo Yost-Konning—who has been working on her tirelessly. Chad Spense, the President's chief of staff—I think will go along with Ramsey. If we buy Waxman's vote, I should get the nomination."

"A million dollars is a lot of money, Gyorgi . . ." He was wavering. From long experience, George knew Peabody was a plodding thinker who hated being pushed. But George had to push him. An opportunity like this didn't come along every day.

George said, "The council meets with the President tomorrow morning. We have until three o'clock this afternoon to deliver the cash in Washington. Time is short. We cannot contact Moscow Central for an opinion; they could not get a committee together fast enough."

Peabody thought for a moment, then said, "Say you get the President to nominate you. How sure are you to get approved by Congress?"

"I'm very confident. I will have to go for some hearings and will be questioned extensively about economic matters, politics, and so on. The FBI will do a background check on me to see if I have ever been involved in anything illegal or shady—I mean in my cover business dealings."

"And have you, Gyorgi?" His eyebrows went up.

"No, never. They can look all they want and nothing suspicious will come up. There is no record of the real George Corbett's death in Australia."

21

"I'm not worried about your cover, I set that up myself. No, that's the least of our worries."

Peabody knocked the ash out of his pipe on the sole of his shoe. Then he reloaded and relit it. He seemed to be absorbed in the task, and in no particular hurry. George grew impatient, but didn't let it show.

Now Peabody got up and shuffled back and forth for a moment, stopping to lean against his workbench again. "I don't like it, Gyorgi. You give a man a million, you're asking for trouble. He's likely to spend it. People will start asking questions. We could get burned. A man with that much greed cannot be trusted."

"We have no choice, General! We have to risk it. Without Waxman's vote, I'm dead. With it, there's a good chance I'll be Fed chairman, and when I'm chairman, I shall then be able to engineer the downfall of Imperial America!"

"I read your position paper, I know what you intend. I see the strategy. I know how confident you are."

"What's troubling you then?"

"Among other things, *you* trouble me, Gyorgi."

George's face warmed. "What the hell do you mean by that?"

"I think you would be in a position of real power for the first time in your life and I don't know what you would do with that kind of power."

"You think I would break discipline? When have I ever broken discipline? Never! When have I been seriously in error? My economic forecasts have been more than satisfactory. My intelligence reporting, impeccable. In the '74 oil crisis, it was my planning more than anything else . . ."

Peabody held up his hand. "No one doubts your genius, Gyorgi."

"Then what is it? I've proven my loyalty to the Party and our historic cause over and over again."

"Perhaps I cannot quite put my finger on it, Gyorgi. There is something about you that is off the track. I want

22

you to know I'm keeping my eye on you."

George was wildly angry now. He did not like having his integrity questioned by an old janitor. He got down off his stool, clenching his fists, holding himself in. "Where can I get the money? I have no time to waste, the payoff will have to be coordinated."

As if he had listened to George's thoughts, the old man said, "I am a major general, Gyorgi, and you are a colonel." He stabbed his finger in George's direction. "Your cover is that of a capitalist and I am a maintenance man, but I outrank you and if you ever decide to take any independent actions you know the consequences."

"Such ideas have never entered my mind."

"See to it that they don't!"

George took a handkerchief out of his pocket and dusted off his shoes. "If you will not grant my request, I will have to report it to Moscow Central, and you will be to blame for my not winning the appointment. You will not be able to explain it away, they understand the importance of my mission."

The old man scowled. "You think you are so powerful, don't you, Gyorgi? The big shot. Stand at attention! Attention!"

George made a halfhearted attempt; he felt as if his skin would not contain his rage, but he didn't speak. His whole body shook. Peabody reached into a can and scooped out a handful of black bearing grease, walked over to George, opened his coat, and smeared the grease on his silk shirt.

George felt rage radiating from his face. His collar could barely contain his swollen neck. He wanted to ram his fist into the man's mouth, to pound him into the floor. But if he did, he would be recalled, and there would be no explaining it away in a tribunal in Moscow. His career and his life would be over.

"Stay at attention, Colonel," Peabody said sternly. "You are a member of the committee for State security, and I am your superior. We are successful because we are disciplined. Each of us obeys orders, any orders! If I say to you crawl on the floor, you are to crawl. It doesn't matter that you are such a big shot. You are only there because we put you there, and you stay there only as long as we say. Clear?"

"Quite."

"I am your superior officer. You are never to forget that even for one moment, do you understand?"

"Yes, sir!"

Peabody opened a drawer in his workbench and took out a key with a red plastic end. "Kennedy Airport, South Terminal, Locker 3341—near Gate 44. In two hours' time your one million dollars will be there." George reached for the key. Peabody said, "I expect results. And so does Moscow Central. Understood?"

"I will hand you America's head on a platter, General, an apple in its mouth."

Peabody dropped the key into his palm. "If you don't, it may be your head on that platter, Gyorgi."

TWO

George left the Maxwell Building by the side door and walked over to Fifth Avenue, making a couple of loops to make sure he hadn't been followed. He buttoned up his coat so the grease stain wouldn't show. He got some change from a flower vendor at the corner of Lexington and East Twenty-fourth and placed a long-distance person-to-person call to "Mr. Judd" in Washington, D.C., from a pay phone. A woman answered and said there was no "Mr. Judd" at that number, and never had been. George said, "Tell him noon." The woman said, "There's no Mr. Judd here," and hung up. That was the correct response. The call for Mr. Judd would alert the party at the other end to catch the eleven-thirty plane out of Washington. George then called a Brooklyn number; when someone at the other end picked up the phone, George said, "Site six, four," which meant LaGuardia Airport, noon. "Okay," a man's voice said. The voice belonged to Nicolai Stepanovitch Pogorny, one of George's operatives. He knew where to go at the airport, so there was no reason for George to tell him, especially not on the telephone. That was simply a matter of good security.

George then hailed a cab and took it to his office, where he changed his shirt. He threw the soiled one away. He didn't want to ever see it again. His research assistant was in the office, the one he had asked to check out Damian Carter's girlfriend. The assistant hadn't yet gotten a report back from Houston on Catlyn Cavanaugh. George told him to keep at it. At eleven he took a cab to LaGuardia Airport. When he got out of the cab in front of the Eastern terminal he saw Nicolai standing nearby. Nicolai was a trained agent, fit, an expert in both small arms tactics and unarmed combat. He could kill a man hundreds of different ways. George had rarely engaged in that kind of business; in fact, he found violence repugnant to his basically amiable nature. Nevertheless, he was happy to have such services available in an emergency. George brushed his hand through his hair, which was the signal for Nicolai to stand by for further instructions.

George opened the locker and found a large suede suitcase inside. He carried it across the hallway to a men's room, went into a stall, locked the door, and laid the suitcase across the seat of the commode. It had a combination lock set to George's birth date. He opened the suitcase and there it was: strings of sparkling gold kugerands in plastic strips and bundles of large bills. He didn't count it. He knew it added up to one million dollars. Peabody was a man who dotted i's and crossed t's; there was no need to double-check his arithmetic. George, in his business, was used to handling large sums of money, but to see one million at the end of a balance sheet was not the same as seeing it in a suitcase. The smell of it! What could compare!

He locked the suitcase and lugged it back to the locker. How heavy it was! A man could get a hernia! Nicolai was standing against the wall smoking a cigarette, smiling. He knew what was in the suitcase. George had a cup of coffee at the snack bar. Nicolai got himself a cup and stood near him, stirring a mountain of sugar into his coffee.

"Stay with the suitcase, Nicolai," George whispered.

26

"Keep it safe until our lady friend has it in her hands."

Nicolai made no response. He drifted away to a lounge chair and sat down.

George had only fifteen minutes to wait for the Eastern shuttle from Washington. He watched the passengers disembark. The one he was waiting for was wearing a felt hat and checkered suit, and the dull expression of a man who had lost his soul. His name was Peter Fenner. One of the few men George ever trusted at all. George had certain photos showing Fenner in compromising positions with young boys, along with affidavits, names, dates, places, which could put Mr. Fenner in penal servitude for an eternity. Fenner supported his mother, to whom he seemed to have an unnaturally strong attraction; for her to know her son was a homosexual pedophile would finish her off and Fenner knew it. Hence, Fenner was George's slave. Over the years Fenner had supplied some pretty good intelligence when he was working for the Army Adjutant General's office in Washington, but since he'd been transferred to Medical Records he wasn't of much use except as a leg man. But he was a good leg man who had carried out every assignment ever given to him to the letter. With his beloved mother's health at stake, could he do otherwise? There weren't many George Corbett would entrust with the payment of a million dollars. A million dollars could tempt Saint Francis of Assisi.

Fenner traveled under the name of Hiram Judd. George used the white courtesy telephone to have him paged. He watched Fenner as he picked up the phone.

"Welcome to New York, Mr. Judd."

"What have you got for me?" Fenner said. He had never seen George, of course, face to face.

"A simple task. If you will walk down the aisle and stop in the third phone booth from the end, I'll tell you all about it. How's your dear mother?"

"Cut the crap."

27

George chuckled and hung up the phone. He watched Fenner walk to the phone booth, step inside, and close the door. George waited a few moments before walking to another phone booth and calling the number on the phone in Fenner's booth. Fenner answered on the first ring.

George said, "Ah, here we are now."

"I'm here," Fenner said, "now what do you want?"

"Take a suitcase to Washington, put it into Locker A 104—as you have done a dozen times before—and go home to your mother. Nothing to it."

"Where do I get this here suitcase?"

"You will find a key in a magnetized case under the seat in your phone booth. Locker 3341. Buy a ticket on the next shuttle. A man will be following you, an athletic-looking man with a mustache in a checked sport coat. He's standing against the wall opposite you at this very moment. He's protecting the suitcase and will make sure no one else is following you. You see how we take precautions so that nothing will happen to you? Take a walk around the airport terminal before you pick up the suitcase."

"Okay."

"You can expect a little gratuity in the mail for this one, Mr. Judd."

"How about you give me back my life, that's all the gratuity I want."

"Now, now, Mr. Judd. We're building World Socialism for the good of mankind. You're a front-line soldier for the cause. Can't you look at things that way?"

There was no answer.

George said, "Well?"

"Don't ever let me know who you are, because if you do, you're dead."

George flared. "You just do what you're told, and do it right. You threaten me again, your mother gets an eyeful you won't believe. Got that, mister?"

"Yeah, I got it. I don't know what came over me."

"You've had your instructions, now carry them out."

"Yes, sir."

Nicolai watched George march off down the corridor, noting both the satisfaction and the apprehension on his face. Nicolai wondered what was so important as to bring the great Gyorgi Vlahovich to the airport in person. Usually routine errands were turned over to subordinates. Must be something big going down. And he, Nicolai Stepanovitch Pogorny, wouldn't be called in to watch a suitcase unless there was something in it worth watching. A lot of something. And they were using Judd as the bag man. He wasn't used for routine stuff. Judd was a straight-arrow American and a keep-to-himself kind of guy who was never under suspicion and, therefore, safe. So this was big. Nicolai felt a jolt of excitement go through him. At last, there might be some action on the way. Nicolai craved action. He'd been trained for it. He had even volunteered for Afghanistan, but his application had been denied because he was so entrenched in his deep cover as an American. It was his fate, he often lamented, to be a well-trained lap dog. The lap dog of a man who would rather buy an opponent off than make him disappear.

Nicolai had joined up to make revolution, not to run errands. But he would obey orders, and wait his turn. He believed it was his destiny to rise to the very highest ranks because he knew how to make use of every opportunity. If, just once, Gyorgi Vlahovich slipped, Nicolai was ready to take his place.

Nicolai stood right behind Judd in line when he bought his ticket. He didn't have the suitcase with him. Just before the passengers were called for the plane, Judd picked up the suitcase out of the locker and walked onto Eastern's commuter flight to Washington. Nicolai got a seat in the back of the plane where he could keep an eye on things. He had six acrylic throwing knives (which could not be detected by an airport metal detector) under his jacket in case of trouble. He watched everyone who got on the plane. No one seemed interested in Judd. There were a half dozen Japanese tourists jabbering at each other and snapping pictures, some bored-looking businessmen, a group of old people who all seemed to know each other. Nobody who looked like an agent.

On the flight Nicolai passed up the free drinks. When on a job, Nicolai Stepanovitch Pogorny liked to keep his wits about him. When it came to drinking, Nicolai boasted he could drink anyone but a fellow Cossack under the table, but when he was on assignment he was sober. He sat next to a black preacher who read his Bible the whole way. Nicolai thought Bible-reading was a waste for blacks; they were an oppressed people, they should get up off their knees and make a revolution.

The black preacher asked him if he read the Bible. "Every day," Nicolai told him.

"Are you born again?"

"Absolutely. More than anyone on this plane." He grinned at the preacher. The preacher didn't quite know what to make of Nicolai and went back to his Bible.

When the plane parked on the tarmac at National Airport, Judd was one of the first off the plane. Nicolai had to push his way down the aisle so as not to lose him. Nicolai had learned a long time ago that you can get away with anything in America if you just keep smiling and say, "Excuse me, so sorry, so sorry . . ."

Judd walked across the lobby to a long row of lockers and left the suitcase, then disappeared into a cocktail lounge. Nicolai sat down on a bench near the lockers and took a paperback book out of his pocket, a thriller. He didn't like it much. He thought the author had made all the Americans brave and resourceful and all the Russians stupid and deceitful, when in actual fact Nicolai had found it to be the

30

other way around.

After an hour of sitting he got up and stretched his legs. No one who was not in the spy business could possibly know how tiresome it could get doing surveillance, he thought. Once, he'd kept an eye on a parked car for four days. That was down in Baltimore the first year he'd been in America. A woman had come to pick up the car. He broke her neck with a single blow. That was the spy business: interminable boredom and brief moments of great excitement.

He ate a hot dog. He paced around a little. He went back to the book. It was nearly eight in the evening when somebody finally showed. A broad-shouldered man in a striped sport coat. He had white hair and ruddy cheeks and there was a bulge under his coat. Nicolai just kept his hand in his coat, pinching the blade of one of his throwing daggers. To anyone walking past, here was a man engrossed in a book. But inside, Nicolai Stepanovitch Pogorny was on fire with excitement. He figured if the guy went for the suitcase, he'd let him take it out of the locker and then get him with a dagger at the top of the escalator.

But the guy didn't go for the suitcase. He walked up and down, then went back the way he came. He returned a few minutes later with the woman that George had called "our lady." She was in her early thirties, dressed in a gray suit. She had a scarf pulled down over her head and was wearing dark glasses, same as the last time Nicolai had seen her. Her walk had a lot of style in it, a nice little swing to her bottom, a proud tilt to her head. She gave the key to the man, who unlocked the locker and took out the suitcase. Then the two of them left. Her ass, Nicolai thought, was magnificent.

Nicolai didn't follow them. His instructions had been to make sure she got the suitcase. She got it. Assignment over. Waiting for the plane back to New York, he was on his third margarita in a cocktail lounge idly watching a baseball game between the Orioles and the A's on television when they had one of those spot announcements for the news at eleven. The announcer was a woman with dark hair and eyes, and a resonant, firm voice. Something about her reminded him of the woman who picked up the suitcase. Was it possible this was the same woman?

Couldn't be, he told himself. Even the great Gyorgi Vlahovich could not have recruited such a star. He looked closer. Yes, yes! It was possible. Nicolai congratulated himself. Knowing this could someday be very helpful. He filed it away in his memory for possible future reference.

George came to breakfast the next morning, Tuesday, the day after Labor Day, in high spirits. It was seven minutes past eight. He had gotten the message late the previous night from Nicolai that the bundle had been delivered safely. So all systems were go! George was sitting at the table beaming when his wife came into the room and sat down opposite him.

"You look pleased this morning, George," she said, opening the *Times* to the theater section.

"A little investment turned out well," George said.

"I'm so pleased," she said. Linda Corbett was now forty-four and, though she had spread out a little where she sat, she was still, George thought, an exquisitely beautiful woman. She had lush blond hair which she wore tossed to one side the way George liked it. He also liked her impish little nose and sparkling blue eyes. George knew she was good at bewitching younger men. Not that she ever went too far, to the best of his knowledge, but she enjoyed the game and George enjoyed watching her play it.

Mattie, their black live-in maid and cook, asked Linda if she wanted anything.

"Just coffee."

"Be ready in a minute."

"How about you, Mr. Corbett? More coffee?"

"No, but you can clear away the dishes."

"I be getting to 'em," she said, without touching them. Mattie didn't have a sunny disposition, but she minded her own business and never took anything that didn't belong to her. And she was a superb cook. For George, that was enough. "Anything new on the appointment?" Linda asked idly.

"The appointment?"

"Come on, George! You've been talking about nothing else for months. Are you going to be the next chairman of the Federal Reserve or aren't you?"

"I suppose."

"Has something happened?"

"The council is meeting this morning."

"And?"

"It looks like I might get the nomination," he said offhandedly, suppressing a grin.

She didn't smile. She was looking at him with a neutral expression on her face. Mattie brought her coffee, then cleared away George's dishes.

"Aren't you pleased?" George asked.

"I don't know if I am or not. That would make you just about the second most powerful man in the country. I really don't know . . ."

He remembered what Peabody had said the day before: *There is something about you that is off the track.* Was there something others saw in him that he didn't see in himself? Some small flaw? Some problem with a bloated ego? Linda, of course, had no idea of his real identity. She thought his getting ahead in the financial world was due mostly to his skill and genius, and maybe some luck. She had no idea he had secret sources of information and a hidden stockpile of capital.

"Do you think having a lot of power would corrupt me?"

"Truthfully?" She had a sudden interest in the proposi-

33

tion. "Yes, George, in a way I do. I think you operate very well in your circle. You're on what? Four or five boards of directors of big banks, a trucking and storage company, two or three multinational conglomerates. You do a lot of wheeling and dealing. But I think this is totally different. This is not just money-making, which you are very good at. This is power. In a way, you'll be more powerful than the President. The President can do very little on his own. The chairman of the Federal Reserve can do a lot on his own, or so you've told me. I think the responsibility is awesome. You could make decisions which, if wrong, would put this country out of business."

George leaned back, looked out the window at the view of Central Park, and thought for a moment. Then he said, "There's a big difference between presidential power and the power of the chairman of the Federal Reserve. The chairman of the Federal Reserve is a slave to the numbers. He merely reacts to the numbers."

"Why do you even want it, George? That's the thing I don't understand. You'll have to put all your money in a blind trust. The press will abuse you. We've lived our life out of the public eye. Now, all of a sudden, you'll be a celebrity. I don't get it. It seems so unlike you."

George smiled. "All my life I've had a secret unfulfilled desire to be in the spotlight. Haven't you read Freud? I wanted to kill my father and sleep with my mother. Since I never got the chance to kill my father, I have to do this instead."

"I hope it makes you happy, Oedipus," she said with a sigh and went back to reading the paper.

His gaze drifted out over the park. He wondered what she'd say if he told her the real reason he wanted to be chairman of the Fed. He wondered what she'd say if he ever told her who he really was. When he'd met Linda, she was working in the antiwar movement. She was a screaming Marxist–Leninist—at least he'd thought so then. He mis-

34

took her Vassar sophomore New Left rantings for true revolutionary fervor. A common mistake of KGB agents at the time. Most of the so-called radicals of the sixties were not radicals at all. They were against the draft because they didn't want to get their ass shot off in a faraway war. Once the Vietnam thing was over the men shaved their beards, the women shaved their armpits, and they all became insurance salesmen and stock brokers. The yippies of the sixties were the yuppies of the eighties. Of course he did manage to recruit a few good agents who had hung on to their revolutionary principles. But Linda had become a housewife and a patron of the arts. In fact, her radical past was the only thing that might stand in his way of becoming chairman of the Fed. How ironic! But he was three-quarters certain the FBI investigators would soon find out she had only been a springtime radical and was now about as far left as Jerry Falwell. He even suspected she'd voted once for Ronald Reagan, the dragon of dragons himself.

Mattie stepped back in and said, "The Indian Chief is up." She was referring to Rudolf. It was his first day back at school. He came into the kitchen in his robe and slippers, yawning and blurry-eyed. George guessed he had been listening to music with his earphones half the night. Rudolf was a spindly lad, a little under six feet, with two earrings in his left ear. George was fond of the boy, but he had long known he had not been born with an excess of brains. And he didn't have the ambition of a cockroach. But what difference did it make? George had set aside a lot of money in trusts for the boy and, as long as he didn't make a pig of himself, he could live well and happily for the rest of his life. The trusts were safely in hard currencies and gold. If what he had in mind for America really came to pass, Swiss francs would rise, gold would soar, and Rudolf would be very well heeled indeed.

"Morning all," Rudolf said.

"Morning, Rudolf," George said.

"Better hurry," Linda said.

"What you be wanting for breakfast?" Mattie asked him.

He opened the refrigerator and took out a glass bottle of milk. "This ought to do her," he said.

"You gonna bind yourself up drinking that stuff with nothing in your stomach," Mattie said. She gave a shrug, sat down on a stool by the kitchen door, and picked up her newspaper. Rudolf went back to his bedroom.

"We've spoiled him terribly," Linda said.

"He's a good boy," George said.

"He's almost totally out of control. He has no self-discipline. He has terrible study habits, no ambition, no appreciation of anything. That's what gets me the most—no appreciation."

"So you've told me—thirty-two thousand times."

Mattie slipped off her stool and disappeared in the direction of the dining room. She could see a storm coming and wanted to get out of the way.

Linda said, "I found marijuana in his room again—smoked."

"It won't hurt him."

"It *is* hurting him."

"What do you want me to do?" George said with exasperation. "We're already sending him to the finest school in the city."

"He needs counseling."

"He wouldn't go."

Rudolf came back into the kitchen and put the milk bottle back in the refrigerator.

"Would you speak to him?" Linda said. "Please, George. If you won't, I will." She stared at him coldly.

George frowned, and finally nodded. "Rudolf? Son?"

"What is it, Dad?"

"Your mother and I—we'll—we'd appreciate it if you'd stop smoking dope in the house. We think it might interfere with your school work, son."

"I don't do weed, Dad. I told you."

Linda crossed her arms and glared at him. "I found it in your room, Rudolf, now don't deny it! I like a liar even less than a pot head!"

"A few hits, helps relax me. It ain't like I was getting stoned. When somebody does weed, I mean it becomes like their life. I use it just to come down when I got to come down, know what I mean? Therapeutic use, not, you know, nothing heavy. What's the big fucking deal?"

Linda shot up out of her chair: "How dare you use *that* word in *this* house!"

"Darling, please," George said. "There's no need to be emotional."

She swung around to him: "Why is it you always have to take his side?"

"I wasn't taking anyone's side, darling, I was merely—"

"You were merely what?" She threw down her newspaper and stormed out of the room.

Rudolf said, "Women, wow. Combustible, eh?"

"Just do your therapeutic pot smoking someplace else, okay, Rudolf? Let's have some peace in the family. Now go apologize to your mother."

Rudolf made a sour face. George said, "Go on now, Rudolf, please. Tell her you know she wants what's best for you."

"Do I gotta?"

"Yes, Rudolf. You have to."

Rudolf dragged himself back down the hallway.

George looked out the window at Central Park, but his mind had flown halfway around the world to the quiet dacha that was waiting for him on the Black Sea. Soft sea breezes. Plenty of Cuban cigars, good caviar. Mattie brought him back to Manhattan Island: "You wanted on the phone, Mr. Corbett. A Mr. Van Nuys."

"Thank you, Mattie, I'll take it in the study."

37

George went into his study and closed the door. Charles Vanderbilt Van Nuys was a fellow member of the board of directors of First Atlantic and Pacific Bank. George had known him for twenty-five years. For him to call before nine in the morning was odd indeed.

George said, "Yes, Charlie, good morning. What can I do for you?"

"Bad news, I'm afraid, George. The meeting this morning was called off. No reason given, and it wasn't rescheduled. Damian Carter is coming to the White House to meet with the President, I don't know when. It looks very bad at the moment, George."

Charlie Van Nuys of course had no idea there'd been a million-dollar bribe paid. George sat down heavily. "How do you know, Charlie?"

"I received a call this morning from Congresswoman Stecher. As you know, Ramsey wants anyone but you. He's not crazy about Damian Carter, but he'll support him because he's a tight money man. The President is still making up his mind and he may yet listen to the recommendation of the council, but, like I say, it doesn't look good. I'm sorry, George, I know how much you wanted it."

"I'll miss the challenge, but not the work load," George said, trying to sound lighthearted. "It would have been an interesting experience, but Damian Carter is a good man, he'll be a good chairman."

"He hasn't got your foresight or your acuity, George."

"But he'll be very good, and I'll get to continue playing in the fields of finance, which is my favorite sport. Thanks for telling me, Charlie."

"We gave it the old college try. We'll have lunch this week."

"I'll look forward to it."

George hung up and walked over to his liquor cabinet and poured an ounce of cognac into a shot glass and drank it down. He noticed his hand was shaking. When he turned around, Linda was standing in the doorway.

"What is it, George? You look positively gray about the gills."

"An employee of the bank . . . scandal . . ." was all he could manage. He managed a feeble grin. "One of those things, we'll handle it."

"Have you seen the pants your son wants to wear to school?"

"No, is the fly left open?"

"It might just as well be. They're purple!"

"Purple pants? Let's have a look."

Linda said nothing more about the phone call and asked no more questions about the supposedly dishonest employee. But in her report to Mr. Peabody that she wrote hastily on a cheap manual typewriter she kept in the bottom of her closet, she mentioned how pleased George—who she referred to as Subject K—had seemed that morning, and how shocked he was when he'd received the phone call from Charles Vanderbilt Van Nuys. She signed the note "C. D."

By the time George got to his office he was calmer. He'd come so close, so damn close! He couldn't miss out now. He couldn't let Damian Carter take away everything he'd been putting together for twenty years. Too much time, effort, and money had gone into it to be turned away at the gate. Besides, if he didn't succeed, there was a million dollars down the rathole. From then on, Moscow Central would never trust him again. All the hard work over the years making a reputation as the most reliable deep penetration agent in the West would go up in smoke. From then on he'd be running errands for the military types. He'd spend his days chasing after high-tech trinkets. It was a mania with them. Hadn't he engineered the 1974 oil crisis? If the Arabs had been pushed hard enough to raise the price of oil to one hundred dollars a barrel, the whole financial system of the West would have collapsed. But no, the boys in the Kremlin were satisfied to start selling oil themselves to make a few fast rubles and relieve the crisis rather than hold back. Brezhnev, he thought bitterly, was an idiot with the balls of a goldfish.

His secretary brought him his coffee and a doughnut and left him alone. She could see he was in no mood to make small talk. He told her to hold all his calls.

The first rule of espionage is: know the facts. The only one he knew who was likely to know the facts was his friend at Columbia, Margo Yost-Konning. He called her office and was told she was in class until eleven, then she would hold office hours till noon.

George did some pacing and thinking. He had to be absolutely certain that Damian Carter was going to be the one nominated. Once he was certain, he had to act quickly if he was going to sling any mud. Once the nomination was made it would be in the hands of the Senate. If something incriminating was found, there would be a complete investigation. But if the President hadn't as yet made it official, a little innuendo might be enough to shake his confidence. And if there was a little truth to it, just enough to make it plausible, it might just tip the scales away from Mr. Blue Blood Carter and toward George Corbett, the people's choice. George's one hope was Catlyn Cavanaugh.

At nine-thirty the young research assistant he'd called Sunday to find out what he could about Catlyn Cavanaugh came into his office. He stood in front of George's desk with a half-smile on his thin face. He said, "She's no heiress. Not by that name, not from Houston. But I had to use extraordinary means to find this out—she's set up a cover identity very well."

"Who is she?"

"Don't know. She's got ten grand limits on her credit cards, but doesn't owe any of them a penny. Owns some small shopping centers on Long Island. Has a bank balance of almost a million. She lives pretty well—has an apartment in the East Eighties—not that far from you, Mr. Corbett."

"Where's her money coming from?"

"No way to tell. She's never borrowed money, so she hasn't disclosed her income source to creditors. My guess is she married well some time or other and changed her name. Might be hard to trace."

"Is it possible she's into something illegal?"

"No indication of it."

"Remember the Mayflower Madam? Running a call girl ring out of her West Side apartment. Something like that would be good news."

"I doubt it, Mr. Corbett. One thing—she has a four-thousand-a-month payment to a bank out on Long Island."

"Maybe she supports her mother. Keep on it, see if you can turn up anything."

George paced around the room for a few minutes. His mind was in turmoil. Time was ticking away on him. He had to know what was going on with the President. He took a cab to Columbia University at noon to see his friend. He found her office door open.

"George! What a surprise!"

"Hello, Margo."

"What brings you uptown?"

"May I come in?"

"Do, please do!" She closed her office door behind him and moved some papers and books off her desk. Her office was stuffed with papers and books. On the wall were photos of her with a hundred fifty different celebrities. Margo Yost-Konning was a tall and raw-boned woman, homely, and intensely intellectual. She was also in President Hustead's so-called kitchen council of economic advisers. She

41

was pulling for George over Damian Carter, who she regarded as a nice fellow, bright and witty, but without the guts to be chairman of the Fed. She sat in the chair behind her desk and a slow smile came across her lips.

"I think I know why you're here," she said. "The appointment."

George nodded. "I heard this morning that Damian Carter's meeting the President."

"Where'd you hear that?"

"Can't divulge my source, Margo."

"Let me guess. Charlie Van Nuys?"

"You're a good guesser."

She patted him on the knee. "Let me make a few phone calls, George. I'll see what I can find out."

She made a call while he sat trying not to look anxious. All he heard was her ask for "Bill," then a moment later ask what was going on with the nomination for chairman of the Federal Reserve. She listened and nodded, and said, "I see, yes, yes . . . I see . . . yes . . ." for a few minutes, then thanked whoever it was she was talking to and hung up.

"Well?" George asked. "What's the verdict?"

"Damian Carter has been asked if he wants it. The President offered it to him, just like that." She snapped her fingers. "He said he would let the President know tomorrow."

George forced a smile, then a laugh. "I'm not disappointed, Margo, I'm relieved! The waiting and not knowing was getting to me. Now I can make some plans and get on with my life. Thank you so much."

"Listen, George Corbett, you owe me one. I'll be sending over my new book and I want you to read it and give me a nice blurb for the cover."

"I'll praise it to the sky."

"I also want your reaction to my theory of value."

"I'll look forward to reading it, Margo. And thanks."

George felt disgusted. Betrayed by the system. A million

42

dollars down the drain. Why the hell set up advisory councils if you weren't going to listen to them?

On the way back to midtown Manhattan in the cab, he sat in a gloomy silence. He knew now, of course, what had to be done. There was no other choice. He knew just the number to call.

THREE

At one-fifteen in the afternoon that Tuesday after Labor Day, Robert Park was having breakfast in an Eighth Avenue barroom called The Horned Toad. His breakfast consisted of beer with tomato juice, a Polish sausage, and pickled eggs. As he ate, he was thinking of the two things he loved most in the world: money and making women hurt. He'd been trying to decide which he liked best and how he could maybe combine his passions. He hadn't come to any firm conclusions when Harry the bartender told him he had a phone call.

"Bring the phone down here," Park said.

"Sure," Harry said.

Harry never argued with Park. Nobody at The Horned Toad ever argued with Park. Not if they had any sense. Park wasn't all that big and he was forty-six, a little old to be a tough guy, but he had a kind of look in his eyes. A savage look. He wasn't just tough, he was mean-tough. Most everybody avoided him.

Park had sharp features and curly gray hair and wore jeans and an old brown leather jacket. He had an anchor tattooed on the back of his right hand. He had that done when he was seventeen in the Marine Corps. They were the ones who taught him how to "stick." He was with the Third

Marine Division at Ben Lo Doc in 1971. He did a lot of sticking that day. Had a fuck of a time. He liked sticking almost as much as he liked money and making women hurt.

Later, a captain by the name of Shaw brought him up on charges. It was said then that maybe he liked sticking maybe even a little too much for a U. S. Marine. There were some peasants he slaughtered that were maybe just fishermen. And some of them were women and they weren't just killed, they were dissected. Alive. "War, man, that's the way it is," he'd said in his own defense. He looked Shaw right in the eye and told him he wasn't recruited into the Corps because he was squeamish. The thing with the peasants got hushed; the colonel in charge of that sector knew how to do those kinds of things. Park got an honorable discharge. He tried to fight it because he loved being a Marine, but, as he saw it, the fucking brass were chicken-shitting out of the war by then and he figured what the hell.

Into the phone Park said, "It's your nickel."

"This is your friend, Mr. Park. We haven't spoken in some time."

"Mr. Timberwolf?"

"Yes. I am Timberwolf. I have a deal for you. You should come to my office at three this afternoon."

"Gimme a number."

"Two hundred and fifteen."

"Okay, Timberwolf, see you at three."

"You remember the place?"

"Sure I remember."

Park hung up the phone and sipped his tomato beer. Already his heart was beating fast. He crammed the rest of the Polish sausage into his mouth. He hadn't heard from Timberwolf in almost three years. He liked doing business with him. Timberwolf always wanted the business done quickly and he always paid big. Maybe enough to last a year, living good. Park could go out to Aqueduct, play the ponies. Get himself a good whore for a week, one who got off on leather, chains, takin' it in the ass, shit like that. And he wouldn't have to do any scuz work for the loan sharks for a while. Not that he really minded breaking legs and knocking teeth out, but it was crude, and he figured he was meant for better things.

He was, after all, damn good at his work. A real craftsman, not just some slob who'll fucking knock any head for a buck. When Robert Park broke an arm, he did it on the end, smashing the wrist, too. It'd hurt a ton more, and took longer to heal. And when he'd beat a guy, he'd do a job on the kidneys and not just the balls. Any asshole could pound on balls. The kidneys were his specialty. The guy would piss blood for a month. Little touches like that made the difference.

He finished his breakfast and wiped his mouth with a napkin. "See ya, Harry."

"Okay, Park. Take her easy, eh?"

"That ain't my style," Park said, chuckling.

Park hailed a cab and told the driver to take him to Lexington and Twenty-third. He was grinning to himself. Soon he was going to be doing some sticking and he was going to be paid big money. Whooeeeee. Two out of three of the things he loved most.

The cab ride was four bucks. Park got out and went across the street to the sleazebag hotel on the corner. Two hundred and fifteen, Timberwolf had said. That meant that the room number was 430. That was the code he worked out with most of his clients. A couple of hookers gave him the eye as he went in. He told one of them "maybe later." She was, he thought, the cutest nigger chick he'd seen since he left Philly. Leggy. He liked them leggy.

He took the elevator to the fifth floor, got out, walked down the stairs to the fourth floor, and knocked on the door with the number 430 on it.

46

"The door is open."

Park went on in. It was the same as before. Timberwolf was behind a bright light so Park couldn't make out his face, something like the cops do when they question a suspect downtown, but hey, that was okay. This was a high-risk business. He wanted to work for careful people.

"How's things?" Park asked.

"Please have a seat, Mr. Park."

Park pulled up a chair. He didn't look into the light. He looked at the wall. He made a finger silhouette, a rabbit. "Yeah—what's up doc?" he said, sounding like Bugs Bunny. Park chuckled.

"I am a little pressed for time," Timberwolf said coldly. "I'll see a display of your other talents some other time."

"Sure." Park folded his arms across his chest. Timberwolf passed him a photo and said, "Do you recognize this man?"

Park took a look. The man was mid-fifties, thereabouts, but in real good shape. Tanned and healthy. Razor-cut hair. In the photo he was wearing a tennis outfit and had a blonde on his arm. The blonde looked real ritzy, nice little boobies.

"Never seen him—the cunt neither."

"His name is Damian Carter, does that ring any bells?"

"Nope. Should it?"

"I don't think so."

"He the hit?"

"I don't like that word."

"What word do you like?"

"Subject."

" 'Subject' then." Park smiled agreeably. Park was agreeable to almost anything the client wanted. He was running a client-centered business and knew it. The customer was always right, that was a motto he lived by. He said, "What do you want me to do to the subject? Teach him some manners? Get him to change girlfriends? Cut off

47

his dick?" Park chuckled again.

"Please don't be crude, I don't like it— Here, study these." Timberwolf handed him some more photos. Same guy, same tennis stuff, same lady friend.

Park said, "You want me to croak him?" The client seemed nervous, Park thought. Death made people nervous. Crunch somebody, clients get off on it. They loved to talk about their enemies suffering pain. Death always got nerves jangling. Park never did understand why. A crunch job left witnesses. Victims who might come get you. Yap at the cops. Dead bodies did not do bad things like that to you. Dead bodies were cool.

Park grinned and said, "Croaking him would be my pleasure."

"Let us use the language as God intended," Timberwolf said. "I want the subject killed."

"Fine," Park said irritably. "The price is twenty-five thousand dollars."

The client said, "I will not quibble with you on the price. That seems eminently fair. Two things. It must not look like a deliberate killing and it must be done today."

"Today?" Park stared into the light, his eyes wide open. All he could see beyond it was the hazy outline of a man. Thick build maybe. He said, "Fogging some guy ain't like delivering a bouquet of roses, you know."

"I'm sorry, but that's the way it has to be. Can you do it?"

He looked away from the light, toward the shadow on the wall. "Ten grand extra."

"Agreed."

Park nodded, thinking he should have asked for twenty. The client didn't seem to care how much, only when. Park said, "What did you mean it can't look like a deliberate killing?"

"I mean I want it to look like an accident."

"Jesus, man, in one day! You better make that twenty

grand extra."

He heard a sigh from the other side of the light. "I will pay you forty thousand, total, not a penny more."

"Done," Park said. He was pleased. Forty grand was the biggest payday he'd ever had. He took out a cigarette and lit it. Timberwolf was busy shuffling papers. After a moment he handed Park an envelope. "Here you are, Mr. Park, forty thousand dollars. Old bills. Untraceable."

"That's what I call class."

"You'll also find in that envelope a slip of paper. It gives you Damian Carter's address, where he works, his club, the places he usually dines, and the name and address of the woman in the photos—Catlyn Cavanaugh. The best I can do is tell you they are going out to dinner tonight sometime around nine o'clock. I don't know the restaurant. You'll have to take it from there. Damian Carter must be dead by eight o'clock tomorrow morning. Preferably sooner."

"You can buy the flowers for the funeral, Timberwolf. He's dead as dead right now. How about blondie? His girlfriend here. You want me to do her, too? No extra charge."

"I don't care about her one way or the other. Just make sure you get him. No mistakes. And no one is to know it's— a hit—as you call it. And it can't be a suicide, no one would believe that. Accident is the only way."

"That ain't going to be easy." He made a humming sound, then said, "Wait a minute—I got it, how about this?—I make it look like a old-fashioned mugging. Happens all the time. Rich guy bringing his date home. Nigger gets him."

Timberwolf made no sound. Park figured he was thinking it over. That was okay with Park, let him think. Clients usually weren't all that spontaneous. But they weren't pros. A pro could always answer in a flash. He took a couple of drags on his cigarette.

The client said, "All right, but make it good. I want no

suspicions that Damian Carter's murder was done for hire. That would make a mess of everything."

"You've paid me, Timberwolf, you got the best. This time tomorrow they'll be rounding up every nigger mugger in New York." He crushed his cigarette out on the rug. "See ya, Timberwolf."

After he was gone, George turned off the light and went over to the door and locked it. He wiped his brow. How he hated this kind of business. It wasn't that he was squeamish, he wasn't. He was a Marxist and totally committed. Marxism was at war with capitalism, it was that simple. He was an officer in that war. In war, men got killed.

What bothered him was that, as a tactic, murder lacked subtlety. The men you had to get to do such work were always suspect—even the best. They were mercenaries and mercenaries could not be trusted completely—ever. Mercenaries were loyal to their payment. He walked over to the window and watched Park get into a cab. He loathed men like Park. Men whose sole motivation was money. Men who had no philosophy to guide them, no larger vision of the world and of themselves. Park was nothing more or less than an animal. And not only that, he wasn't completely right in the head. But that was always the problem with such men.

He could have chosen Nicolai instead of Park, but with Nicolai there was another problem. Nicolai knew the setup. He knew George's cover ID, he knew where the skeletons were buried. Nicolai was a good man, George thought, but if he was caught and faced a lifetime in prison, even a good man, even a committed Marxist like Nicolai might not be able to keep faith. And then there was always the possibility of drugs. Anyone could be made to talk with Pentothal. No, he couldn't risk using Nicolai on an important job like this.

50

So he had chosen Park. Park had no idea who he was working for. There was no way humanly possible to connect Park with George Corbett. And, despite his obvious insanity, Park was good at doing what he got paid for doing. George had used him twice before. Once, to rid the world of a business rival who was trying to keep George from getting controlling interest in First North American Securities. He was a stubborn Jew and had taken a dislike to George—for what, George had no idea. The second hit was a woman. She was a file clerk in George's office who had overheard a delicate conversation—one of the few times in his life he'd ever slipped up—and she was threatening to expose him to the FBI unless he paid her $1,000. George paid Park $20,000 to get rid of her.

Park raped her and left her cut-up parts in a garbage can. Yes, she had left a note for her sister telling all, but she told Park where to get the note—from a bank safe deposit box—before she died. George managed to get the box. It took some doing, but he managed. George remembered how horrified he was when he had to go down to the coroner's and identify the remains. Horrified, yet delighted.

George took a couple of Tums and went out into the hall. He was wearing a false beard, which made him feel self-conscious, but he couldn't take the chance of being recognized coming out of such a place. He went downstairs and hailed a cab. Forty minutes later he was at his mistress's apartment having a hot bath, sniffing and sipping eighteen-year-old Napoleon brandy and listening to Shostakovich's Fifth Symphony.

Esther Tamac wasn't the usual kind of mistress. She was more "round," as George put it, than the American ideal. She wasn't nearly as attractive as Linda, his wife. But she was a great cook, had a kind, loving nature, and an even disposition. She'd been well trained by a Chinese madam in Hong Kong. Esther had nothing whatever to do with politics. She created a comfortable oasis for him where he could retreat from the cares of the world.

Robert Park lived in an upper flat on the Lower East Side over a pizza restaurant named Izzy's. He loved the smell that came up from below. Sometimes on Friday and Saturday nights the music got a little loud, but that was all right, it made the joint seem alive.

The apartment was a roomy two-bedroom place with high ceilings. It had an old-fashioned kitchen with cheap molded plastic panels glued to the outsides of the cupboards to spruce the place up a bit. He didn't have much furniture; he didn't need much since hardly anyone ever came there but himself. He slept on a mattress he rolled out of the way in one of the bedrooms. In the other bedroom he kept his barbells and exercise equipment. He had a pedicycle and a rowing machine, some weight machines, and a couple of punching bags. On the walls were huge posters of Marines doing tough stuff: fording a rushing creek, going up a hill into the teeth of enemy fire, taking a Jap from behind with a knife. He liked to look at the posters while he did his workout every morning, let his imagination run.

The living room was mostly empty. There was an old couch, an old table, a TV which he only used to relax with cartoons on Saturday morning, lots of old *Soldier of Fortune* magazines, and empty beer cans lying around. On one wall was a big poster of Snoopy with his World War I goggles on, flying his doghouse. He liked Snoopy okay. But his favorite was the Road Runner. He never missed the Road Runner. Someday he was planning to buy Road Runner wallpaper for his "cave"—that's what he called his other room.

On the walls of the cave were pictures he'd clipped out of library books—books he was always bringing home about his favorite subject. Nazis. Mostly the death camp shit. It gave him goose pimples to see that. The idea of putting people in showers and turning on gas, thousands and millions of them, gave him a strange rush. And digging big ditches and lining guys up and mowing them down. Now that was something to just boggle the mind.

He had a triple lock on his cave. He let himself in, closed the door, and locked it. This room was far different from the others. The window had been boarded over. It was paneled, had a low ceiling, and was air-conditioned. Along one wall was a row of glass gun cases. In the gun cases he had sawed-off shotguns, gas-driven automatic shotguns, two AK-47 assault rifles, two Uzi submachine guns, an Astra .357 mag chambered for hotloads, a Beretta 70S, a couple of old Colt Army .45's, a few dozen frontier show-case guns, a collection of throwing knives from around the world, and his prize: a Browning automatic rifle. All in firing order. All loaded. All ready to go to work. And he had mufflers for most of them.

On the other side of the room were file cabinets and cupboards, a couple of desks, and a theatrical dressing table. That's where Robert Park sat himself down and went to work. First he got out a half dozen pictures of his model. Then he laid face putty along the side of his nose, covered with thin latex strips, to make it look flatter. His nose was bent a fraction of an inch to the right from being broken a few times and it took him fifteen minutes to make it look straight. Then he put a couple of wire rings inside his nostrils to make them flare out.

He took a long look at himself in the mirror. He'd gone to night school for two years to learn theatrical makeup. Private school, too. Cost a fucking fortune, but it was worth it, he thought. He was damn good at it.

Okay, next was the bony part above the eyes. He carefully built up a ridge. Perfect. Then he got out the shoeblack and covered up the tattoo on the back of his right hand. He took off his shirt and started rubbing his neck and upper chest with dark lanolin face cream, then his hands and arms below the elbows. He started applying the same cream to his face, but he didn't think he had the right sheen. He mixed in a little furniture polish to correct the problem—an innovation of his own. After all, he wouldn't be on a stage or in front of a camera; he was playing the part for an audience that would be only a few feet away. He had to be careful to get it right. Dark and shiny on the face, ears, neck, and arms. Lighter on the palms. He was careful to apply the makeup cleanly and evenly. When he was done, he leaned back and grinned at the negroid face in the mirror. Man, like fucking amazing.

Now the hair. He got out a pair of scissors and cut his hair close to the scalp. Then he put on a wig, a tight Afro, thick as a black wool carpet. That did it. He admired himself in the mirror again. "Hey, bro, wha's hapnin'?" he grinned. "Gimme five, jive."

He went to the closet and got out some dark pants and a dark shirt, a white windbreaker, some running shoes, and a long raincoat, the cheap plastic kind. He wore no underwear. The labels had all been carefully cut off the coats, shirt, and pants. Not that it mattered, he thought, he'd gotten all this shit at the Salvation Army.

Next, the tools.

Nothing from the gun case. What nigger was gonna use an Uzi or a Browning automatic rifle? Naw, this was Saturday Night Special kind of stuff. He opened his drawer and took out a couple of old hunting knives. They had bone handles and the blades had been honed. They just didn't seem right. He rumaged a little deeper. Ah, there it was. A Sicilian switchblade, made in Brooklyn. He thought: Every nigger has to have one of these. He switched it open. Yeah, yeah. Sharp. But he still needed a gun. You go out on a hit, you had to take a little heat, even if you didn't plan to use it. Emergencies did arise. Sometimes nosy passersby had to be scared off. Sometimes you had to make a little noise to get a crowd to move out of your way.

For this he chose a cheap .38 snub-nose he had bought from a cabdriver for two hundred bucks. It was okay for close work. He knew it had been used in a bank robbery in Brooklyn. The robber was black and the gun had killed a guard. So when they traced the bullet, they just might put two and two together and come up with five. A pro was always doing things to throw off the scent. It was the little things that made the difference. Details, you had to pay attention to them. Yeah.

He put on a pair of glasses, the kind that show a mirror to the outside world but aren't shaded. He was all set. A nigger junkie out to score a little change, buy himself some dreams. He locked up the cave and hid the keys behind the refrigerator. Not that the locks would stop anybody that broke in. He kept the cave locked in case the landlord came by to check things out. He never had, but you never could tell.

Time to get down to business.

He had a cold Bud at the kitchen table and looked over the list Timberwolf had given him. Where to start, where to start? What time was it? Ten after five. Maybe the guy was still at work. He reached for his phone and dialed the office number. He asked for Mr. Carter. He said it low and soft, with a southern drawl.

"Who's calling?"

"Mr. Brown."

"May I ask what this is about?"

"A deal. Just tell him, Mr. Brown."

"One moment, please."

He was put on hold. Music played. Elevator music. He sipped his Bud and waited. The music clicked off. "I'm sorry, Mr. Brown, but Mr. Carter has gone home for the day. If you'd like to leave a message I'll be happy to have him call you in the morning."

"I'll call back, thank you, sweetheart."

He hung up the phone, smiling. Whenever they say, "I'll see if he's in," you know he's in. Nobody leaves the office without the secretary knowing he's gone. So he was still there. Park finished his beer. It took maybe four minutes. Then he called back, this time speaking in high-pitched squeal:

"This is 'Eastern Onion,' we got a singing telegram here for Mr. Damian Carter, can we bring them over tonight? From a Ms. Cav-an-augh. We can be there in fifteen minutes. Don't tell him—supposed to be a surprise."

"Mr. Carter will be here until six, but no later."

"Thank you, ma'am!"

Park shook his head. This was going to be sooooo easy. He had another beer. Then he got out a bottle of industrial cleaning solvent and put it in his pocket along with a rag and a body sponge. In case he had to be a white man again in a hurry. The gun was loaded. He had extra bullets. He had fifty bucks cash. Keys. Okay, all set.

Ready or not, Damian Carter, here comes Mr. Death.

FOUR

The last hand of a three-day poker game was dealt at 5:40 P.M.

There were three players left in the game. One was Ali el-Towik, an Egyptian national in the international diamond trade, reputed to be one of the ten richest men in the world. He was dark and slender, aloof but polite. The hundred fifty thousand dollars in the progressive pot in front of him was loose change, but he played to win as if it were his blood cells.

To the Egyptian's right was Sal Crupiano, Jr., third son of the Crupiano crime family don. Junior was thirty-four, spoiled, volatile, and had been losing steadily since the game started Sunday evening. Junior had heavy jowls, a belly like an overinflated tractor tire, and bad manners.

To the dealer Junior said, "Come on, deal. Get the fuck on with it."

The dealer was not a player. He was paid fifty dollars an hour and was often generously tipped by the winners. He always shuffled thoroughly and dealt cleanly, in a mechanical way. He could not be rushed. He finished shuffling and passed the deck to the player on the right to be cut. This player was Catlyn Cavanaugh. She cut the cards deep, with no expression on her face. Not much was known about her, except that she could be counted on to play whenever a big stakes game was promised. No one knew where her money came from. It was assumed she was being staked by her rich boyfriend, but she never talked about her personal life. She was rumored to be extraordinarily lucky, a player's player: calculating, bold, unpredictable.

The dealer started dealing the cards. The game was "California Poker," where a player must have a pair of jacks or better to open. The ante was ten thousand dollars. The white chips were one thousand each; the red, five thousand; the blue, ten thousand. Catlyn anted up. The Egyptian anted up. The son of the don anted up. The deal had gone around four times without any of the three players having openers. There was nearly two hundred thousand dollars in the pot, easily the biggest pot of the game. On Sunday they had started with six players with a five-hundred-dollar ante. The stakes had been slowly rising. Three players had quit the game: a touring golf pro, a top eye surgeon, and a Texas oil man. Of the three remaining players, two were ahead. The Egyptian and Catlyn Cavanaugh. The son of the don was down a hundred forty thousand dollars.

The Egyptian read each card as he picked it up. He jerked his head back as he slid each card into his hand. The son of the don grumbled and picked up his cards all at once and read them quickly. When he did not like his card, he squinted slightly. The squint was almost imperceptible except to the most acute observer. Catlyn saw it, and she thought the Egyptian did, too. The Egyptian, eyeing his cards, had a faint smile on his lips. It meant he had no openers, Catlyn knew. He was harder to read than the son of the don, but there were clues. Poker players call these clues "tells" and the better you are at reading the other players' tells and controlling your own, the better player you are. Catlyn had been tapping the small finger of her left hand whenever she was betting heavy with a strong hand, giving them a deliberate clue. She was hoping for the chance to steal a big pot with her false tell. Maybe this one was it.

She picked up her five cards. She fanned them in front of her eyes for a moment, then dropped them back down on the table. It was her turn to go first. "No openers," she said. During the past few hours she had been feeling dull. Fatigue was overcoming her, and it was a struggle to not let it show.

"No openers," the Egyptian said.

"Ain't got shit," the son of the don said, throwing his cards into the center of the table with disgust.

"The ante is ten thousand," the Egyptian said, dropping two red chips into the center of the table. Catlyn Cavanaugh pushed in one blue. Her stack wasn't what it had been. She was less than a hundred thousand dollars ahead. Now that the pots were bigger, most of the chips had been sliding back across the table in the Egyptian's direction. He was at least four hundred thousand ahead, she figured.

"Do you wish to ante?" the Egyptian said to the son of the don.

Junior was sweating. In the last hour he'd seen a large stack of chips melt in front of him, perhaps a week's take from his father's best brothel. The pile of chips was now pitifully small. "I'll give you my marker," he said. He wrote out an IOU on a slip of paper and handed it to the dealer. The dealer gave him twenty red chips. One hundred thousand dollars.

"Let's play," the son of the don said.

"It is nearly six," Catlyn said. "We agreed to quit at four. Let's make this the last game."

"Not losing your enthusiasm for sport, are you, Miss Cavanaugh?" the Egyptian said.

"Getting to where we're separating the men from the sheep, ain't we?" the son of the don said.

"My ante's in," she said. "I believe Mr. Crupiano has yet to ante up."

"Didn't I ante?" he said. "Sure I did."

The dealer said, "The pot is ten thousand short." He

looked at the son of the don.

"Must be me then," the son of the don said, dropping his money into the pot.

The dealer shuffled, the Egyptian cut. The dealer dealt. The three players looked at their cards. The son of the don licked his thick lips. His eyes were rheumy and swollen from lack of sleep. He looked barely half awake. He lit a cigarette. "I got openers," he said, dropping two red chips—ten thousand—into the pot.

Catlyn's eyes drifted over her cards. She had two fours, a six, an eight, a ten. Three clubs, a diamond, and a heart. Pretty much trash. No chance on the draw to hit a straight or a flush.

There was almost a quarter of a million dollars in that pot and she wanted it. The dullness in her head suddenly vanished. She looked at the Egyptian, who must have taken amphetamines: his pupils were pinpricks.

"I'll play," she said, putting in two red chips.

"So will I," the Egyptian said with a grin. "In fact I'll sweeten it up a little." He pushed two blue chips across the green felt of the tabletop. Twenty thousand dollars. The dealer cleared his throat and took a drink of water.

It was now up to the son of the don. He loosened his already loose tie and unbuttoned the second button of his shirt. Sweat glistened on the black hairs of his chest. He wiped his arm across his brow, then picked up four red chips and put them into the growing pile on the table. He took a deep drag on his cigarette and looked at Catlyn.

She studied her hand. There was maybe three hundred thousand in the pot and Catlyn was facing at least jacks or better and a man willing to raise ten thousand without even waiting to draw. She had a pair of fours. She could toss three cards and maybe get another four or another pair. That would be the most sensible thing to do. Or she could fold. She would still be ahead around fifty thousand dollars for the whole game. Not bad for a couple of days' work.

But then she took another look at the biggest pot she'd ever seen and decided what the hell, she came to gamble, didn't she?

She pushed a blue chip into the pot. "My daddy used to tell me this was no game for the faint-hearted."

"Fuckin'-A right," said the son of the don.

"How many?" the dealer asked the Egyptian. It was his turn to get the draw first.

"Three," the Egyptian said. Obviously the best he had was a pair, plus whatever he got on the draw. Catlyn knew that the Egyptian was a careful and calculating player. The pair in his hand must be better than the pair of jacks minimum needed to open, at least a pair of kings, probably aces. Catlyn watched his eyes as he looked at the first card. He had a way of shifting his eyes to his stack of chips when the card was good. The card was not good. His eyes looked over the top of his cards to the son of the don. He looked at his second card. His eyes made the same pattern. Not good. Then the third card. Not good. His eyes never went in the direction of his chips. He smiled, almost beamed. Catlyn knew it was Academy Award time.

"Tickets?" the dealer asked the son of the don.

"Three," Junior said. Since he opened the betting, he had to have a high pair. Jacks, queens, kings, or aces. She watched him look at his cards as they were dealt. When he picked up the third one he sighed almost imperceptibly and his ears turned a little pink—he had gotten at least one card that he wanted. So he had either three of a kind or two pair, Catlyn figured.

It was her turn. The dealer looked at her. "One," she said. She'd already decided what she was going to do. They would have to think that she was going for a straight or a flush, and would beat two pairs or three of a kind and she was going to have to bluff it. She looked at her card and stiffened, then let a small smile come to her lips. She looked neither toward the pot nor toward the players. Her eyes went up to the ceiling and then across to the dealer, as if she were trying to hide the fact that she'd just drawn a fabulous card. She put her cards facedown on the table.

"Well now," she said, "here we are."

It was up to the son of the don, since he'd opened. He lit a cigarette and studied the cards in his hand, then his pile of chips, then the other players. He said, "Let's make it interesting." He shoved two blues and two reds—thirty thousand dollars—into the pot.

Catlyn said, "That's fairly interesting." She counted out two blues and ten whites and added them to the pile. "I'll see your thirty and raise you thirty." She pushed in two blues and two reds. "Since this is the last hand and all, we might as well make it more interesting."

She had her hands resting on the table now, tapping with her little finger, just as she had been doing every time she had a powerful hand. The Egyptian was looking at it, but his expression was neutral.

"It's your bet," she said.

He looked again at his cards, then at the large stack of chips in the pot. A third of a million dollars sat before him. Certainly the largest poker pot he'd ever heard of and, from the look in his eyes, he wanted it. He glanced again at her little finger, which was telling him she had a straight or a flush. But she was out of chips. She hadn't started with that much, he remembered. He might be able to break her. He was pretty sure he had the son of the don's openers beat, and one of the first rules of poker he'd learned was if you had the openers beat you had to stay.

The Egyptian raised one hundred thousand dollars.

The son of the don looked at the pot, shaking his head. He put his hands over his ears. "Hooooooooly shit!" He quickly wrote out another marker and handed it to the dealer. The dealer gave him a stack of chips which he immediately pushed into the pot.

"I see you and raise you a hundred thousand." He turned

to Catlyn. "It's two hundred thousand to you. What do you want to do?"

She said to the dealer, "Make me out a marker for four hundred thousand." The dealer did. She signed it and dropped it into the pot. "I'm raising you two hundred thousand."

It was the Egyptian's turn. He looked at her coldly and she knew he was trying to decide whether she could be bought. He looked again at his hand. His eyebrows pinched together and she knew his small pair must be looking lonely and weak, vulnerable. True, he was one of the richest men in the world and could stand the loss. But like most rich men he loved money, and four hundred thousand dollars was not toilet paper. He sighed heavily and tossed his cards in the direction of the dealer. "Time to fold the tent and head for the next oasis."

He didn't leave the game. He wanted to see how it turned out. But his face relaxed, and he was able to smile now, naturally. He was a good-natured man and, when not playing poker, amiable.

The son of the don was still studying his cards. Catlyn could tell by his sour expression that his faith in them was dwindling. Two hundred thousand more. That would put him out half a million dollars in a single hand. He no doubt knew if he could take this pot they would be talking about it in Brooklyn forever and the son of the don would be famous in his own right. The biggest pot of the decade. But he'd noticed her finger tapping, too, and was nearly certain she had caught a flush or a straight. Catlyn noticed his slow eye movements, which showed how much he was vacillating. Two hundred grand was still two hundred grand. He had already handed in markers for more than he had if he liquidated everything he owned. Catlyn guessed he'd have to go to the old man, and the old man would make him replay every goddamn hand before he made the markers good. And he was going to have to answer for every wrong bet and every cop-out. Catlyn thought: Fold 'em! Come on, fold 'em!

But he didn't.

He called her. He wrote out another marker and put it in the pot. From the frightened look on his face he must have felt she had him, but he wasn't going to let her buy it. "Let's see that straight," he said. "All I got is two jacks."

"I've got fruit salad," she said, dropping her worthless cards on the table.

The Egyptian shot up out of his chair. "I had that pot won! I had aces!" His dark skin turned a burnt orange. He grabbed onto his hair. "I had it, I had it! I owned that pot!" He circled the room stomping his foot. "I would have bet my life savings on the fact that you had your flush—or at least a straight. At least a small straight!"

The son of the don scooped the pot up in front of him and slumped back in his chair, dazed. He took a drag on his cigarette and blew the smoke toward the ceiling. The biggest poker pot in the history of New York, maybe. And it was his!

"Well, gentlemen, it has been enjoyable," Catlyn said, standing up and stretching. "I'd love to sit and chat with you, but I have a dinner date."

The son of the don looked at her in amazement. "You just dumped maybe half a million, lady. You just almost bought one hell of a damn big pot and missed. Ain't you a little, you know, upset?"

"If you're going to let the game upset you, Mr. Crupiano, then poker is not for you."

The Egyptian said, "I have never seen the likes of you, Miss Cavanaugh, you bought me out. I was one thousand percent sure you had won your draw. I bow to you." He bowed.

"Thank you Mr. el-Towik, it was a pleasure to play with a gentleman. And good day to you, Mr. Crupiano."

"Hey, I'm the big winner here, ain't you guys going to

bow to me?"

"To your luck," she said, bowing low.

"To your courage and elan," said the Egyptian, also bowing to the son of the don.

The son of the don stood up and bowed so low to them his forehead touched the table. "Thank you, thank you, thank you. The blessings of the good Lord be upon youse."

On the way down in the elevator, alone, Catlyn gritted her teeth and kicked the wall of the elevator, hard, with the side of her foot.

It made a dent.

Robert Park didn't like standing on the corner in his nigger getup. He didn't like the way the white chicks averted their eyes. He didn't like the way people looked *through* him instead of *at* him. It was as if he was wearing a sign that said AIDS carrier. Fuck 'em, he thought. He wasn't going to be a nigger all that long.

He was standing across the street from Catlyn Cavanaugh's apartment building. He'd tried to pick up the hit at his office, but there were too many exits and so he figured to wait here. It was a nice evening, lots of traffic, lots of people on the street hurrying all over hell. Mostly white people. Not many blacks and Hispanics in the East Eighties. Maids, butlers, delivery drivers, cabbies, that was about it. But that was okay with him, people would more likely remember the black dude hanging out on the corner. It was about ten to seven when a cab pulled up in front of her apartment building. He looked to see whether the cab's passenger was the mark, Damian Carter, but it wasn't. It was his good-looking girlfriend that got out and hurried on inside. She was wearing a pantsuit and her hair was mussed up. Maybe, he thought, she was shacking with some guy. *Poon in the afternoon.* He chuckled to himself.

Twenty minutes later a black Mercedes drove up, a

white-haired guy in a white dinner jacket at the wheel. He parked double, got out, and went into the building. He looked fit and trim, about fifty-five. That's the mark, Park thought, gotta be. He took the photo of Damian Carter out of his pocket just to double check. He thought: The store's open for business.

Park crossed the street to where he'd parked his black Honda motorcycle, and started it up with a key. After five minutes the mark came out with the blonde. She was wearing an evening gown and her hair was done up pretty. Robert Park shook his head in admiration. And it didn't take more than half an hour.

The mark and the blonde got into the Mercedes and drove off down Fifth Avenue. Park took off after them on his Honda. He was already excited. As he heard a football player say once before a Superbowl, "It's like rockets going off in your brain!" That's how he felt every time he went stalking a mark. There was nothing like it.

The Mercedes went up the Avenue of the Americas, then turned and went across the park and down West Seventy-seventh Street and pulled up in front of Clemond's on Broadway. Damian Carter turned the keys over to the valet parking attendant. Park maneuvered his motorcycle into the space between two parked cars across the street and thought to himself: The condemned man ate a hearty meal . . .

Just before they went in through the doors Catlyn noticed Robert Park. She thought he might be the same man she had seen across the street from her apartment house when she'd gotten home from the poker game. But then she thought that lack of sleep will make the mind play tricks like that.

Clemond's was, Catlyn thought, in every way a five-star restaurant. The flatware was from Oneida Silversmiths; it

66

was heavy and ornate, solid silver, hand crafted. The patterned blue china was trimmed in gold. A crystal chandelier hung over every table. The waiters glided silently across the thick red carpet. A fresh orchid floated in a blue bowl in the center of the table. Four violinists from Austria serenaded the diners.

She ordered the duck flambé and he ordered the cornish game hen in white wine sauce. She selected the wine, a California Chablis, 1967.

"You look a little tired tonight," Damian said.

"Actually, I overslept this morning. I've just been very busy." She smiled. She wondered what he would say if she told him she'd had only five thirty-minute naps in the past seventy-two hours. She was planning to make up for it by sleeping from Wednesday through Friday. You play polo, you learn to ride a horse, she often told herself; you play poker, you learn to ride out your fatigue. At the moment, the fatigue had gone through a couple of stages and had arrived at the point where she was feeling almost a little drunk. The wine was making her tipsy.

Damian said, "What have you been up to?"

"Yesterday I attended a meeting of investment advisers. I'm afraid I made some inappropriate investments lately that have cost dearly. I won't say how much, it might spoil both our appetites."

"Tell me about it, I'd like to hear."

"Family business I'm afraid, Damian."

"In other words, don't snoop."

"I'm sorry, really I am."

"You certainly are a mystery wrapped in an enigma."

"I think that's what Churchill said about Russia."

"You and Russia, two mysteries wrapped in enigmas."

She laughed; it struck her as funny. She was giddy as a schoolgirl even without the wine. God, she thought, how pleasant just to sleep. One of life's truly great pleasures.

"I have some good news," Damian said.

"I could use some good news."

He leaned over and whispered, "It's official—even though it has not yet been made public—that I'm going to be appointed chairman of the Federal Reserve Board."

She thought: Oh good God, no! That would mean investigations, not only of Damian, but of his associates.

"Amazing, isn't it?" he said, smiling. "I'm about to be made the second most powerful man in the nation."

"I'm impressed," she said, trying to make it sound as if she really were.

"You don't seem quite so delighted as I thought you'd be."

"That means an extensive background check, doesn't it?"

"I'm clean. I have only very old money. My great grandfathers on both sides stole enough for their descendants for generations to come. I've multiplied it in only the most sanitary ways. I'm Snow White."

The waiter served them. She looked down at her duck flambé. She touched it with her fork. What were they going to think of her? Fed Chairman Loves Poker Queen—what a nice headline for the *New York Post*.

"Is something wrong, Cat? You look positively gray."

"I'm fine, really. See me smile?" She forced a happy smile.

"That's better." He poured her some more wine. "I've got more surprises, are you ready?"

"Go ahead," she said.

"I had the results of my physical last week. My lipids—or whatever you call them—are below normal, my cholesterol is below 160, and my blood pressure is holding steady at 120 over 80. In short, I'm the fittest fifty-five-year-old in New York. My doctor said he'd give that to you in writing if you wanted it."

"Why would I want it in writing?"

"Let me finish my sales pitch. I'm also solvent in the

extreme and in the Social Register. There is no insanity in my family—if you don't count cousin Jeremy. I'm a Harvard graduate, and if I'm going to be Fed chairman, I'll have steady employment for at least fourteen years. In short . . ." His eyes drifted over the room, as if he were making sure he wasn't being overheard. "In short, I want you to marry me." He reached into his pocket and produced a large diamond ring in a small black box. "I know this is horribly old-fashioned of me, but I'm a horribly old-fashioned guy. Well, Cat, what do you say?"

"You . . . I . . . we . . ." she stammered. She never stammered, not since she was maybe twelve years old. She tried it again: "You . . . I . . . we . . . ah?"

"You, I, we, what? That's rather an odd expression. Does that mean yes?"

"Damian, I, we . . . No—it doesn't mean yes. Not exactly. Listen Damian, I'm rather overwhelmed. Really and truly I never expected this."

"You must have known I'm extraordinarily fond of you. In fact, I'd even venture to say that I'm totally and hopelessly in love with you."

"That's very sweet, Damian."

"Sweet? Did you hear what I just said? I want you to be my wife."

"Yes, of course, but *marriage.*"

"That's what happens when you become husband and wife. You commit marriage. You say it like it's a bad word."

"No, it's not a bad word, it's a good word. It's a very good word, Damian. But I don't think you want to marry me. You hardly know me."

"We've been going out now for three-and-a-half years, Cat."

"Yes, I know, but I haven't told you anything about myself. No, Damian, you're Harvard and I'm . . . well, I'm not. It just wouldn't work. I don't want to hurt you. I am fond of you . . . God, Damian, you're going to wreck a damn good romance."

He looked at the ring, then at her. "Not wreck it, fulfill it."

A tear ran down her cheek. Where the hell did that come from? She wiped it away. The musicians were playing "Canadian Sunset" at the request of a lady with hair as blue as an Air Force uniform. Catlyn turned to Damian and said, "I can't marry you, Damian. It's impossible."

He took a deep breath and nodded. "I'm twenty years older than you are. There's no way to get around that with blood tests and a good tennis game. I understand." He put the diamond ring back in his pocket.

She reached out and touched his hand. "Your age has nothing to do with it. Honest. I think of you as being just a little older, just right older. I've nothing against that."

"I understand, Cat. It's okay. I knew it was a long shot. You're a beautiful, charming, intelligent woman of independent means, you can have any man you want."

"Listen, Damian. I can't marry you for the very best of reasons—believe me."

He took a sip of wine, twisting the glass around in his hand. "I could understand a lot better if you'd tell me what that reason is. Aren't we good enough friends that you can at least trust me with that?"

She took a big gulp of wine and thought it over for a moment. There didn't seem to be any other way. Finally she turned to him and said, "I can't marry you or anyone, Damian. You see, I'm already married."

He shook his head in disbelief.

She took her napkin from her lap and dropped it on the table. "Take me home, will you, please?"

FIVE

In the car Damian said, "Are you going to tell me about it?"

"About my husband?"

"Yes."

"It's a long, dreary story."

"I'd like to hear it."

She looked out the window. It was a bustling evening in Manhattan. They were driving along Fifth Avenue. It was pleasantly warm. Throngs of people on the streets. She'd looked for the black man she'd noticed as they entered the restaurant, but he wasn't there when they came out. She'd checked behind them a couple of times as they drove, but didn't see him.

She said, "I'm not who you think I am, Damian."

"Who do you think I think you are?"

"You think I've inherited money. You think I'm from Houston and went to Vassar. You think the reason I cover up my identity is because my father was involved in a scandal at the Chicago Board of Trade. I know because you had me checked out and whoever you had doing the checking that's what they would find. That's what I made sure was in all the files at banks and insurance companies. I hired a firm called Secrets Inc. to handle that for me.

71

They were outrageously expensive, but they do remarkable work."

He glanced over at her with his eyes wide, as if she'd suddenly turned into a giant lizard.

"Are you sure you want to hear this, Damian?"

"I want to hear it."

"I should have told you about myself a long time ago. But somehow I thought if you knew I was married, it would ruin our relationship. And you might not like making love to a married woman. Some men don't. It doesn't matter that the marriage is only a marriage on paper."

He was driving with his eyes forward, not looking from side to side. "I can't deny that making love to another man's wife is not something I much relish."

"You haven't done anything wrong, Damian. I have. But the wrong is in not telling you. I haven't seen my husband in years."

"Who is he? Where is he?"

She sighed. "Where to begin? Let's see . . . in the early eighties I first came to New York. I had just gotten my B.A. degree . . ."

"From where? If not Vassar."

"The State University of New York, Buffalo."

"Buffalo—" he said as if it were a dirty word. He waited for her to continue. Two cabs had smashed into each other in the middle of the next intersection and the traffic was at a dead standstill. He pushed the button for the window to go down, probably just to have something to do. Then he closed it again.

She said, "I majored in Business Administration. I came to New York to find my fame and fortune. And a husband. I really had stars in my eyes. Just like any other numbskull who comes to New York, I looked in the *Times* want ads for a job. There was this one: Find yourself in Saudi Arabia! Giant Multinational seeks recent grads for exciting careers in international finance. How could I resist?

72

"Three weeks later I was working for a small freight airline called *Air East* in Addi Saba and living in an apartment about the size of a breadbox. I had signed a three-year contract and stupid me didn't know there was a way out of it. I tried to learn the language, but since women there are regarded as less than dogs, I couldn't find a good tutor. I hated my job, my boss, the food, the heat, the political climate . . . and then I met Razim Karin Ali, the handsomest man I'd ever seen in my life.

"He had black eyes and almost golden skin, and silken manners. A Moslem prince so damn rich he had his own 727 to take him for skiing holidays to Switzerland. I was swept off my feet. I was dazzled. I didn't love him—I didn't even know what the word meant—but I married him. Why? I guess I wanted to get from where I was to someplace else and this looked like the ticket. The next thing I know I'm staying at the Hotel Louis XIV on the French Riviera, playing roulette in the casino, plunking down ten-thousand-franc chips on a single spin of the roulette wheel."

"What happened? Did you find out he had other wives as well?" His tone had a bitter edge. She'd never heard anything like it from him before. "Sorry, Cat," he said. "I'm a little out of sorts."

"Nothing that exotic," she said, feeling suddenly hurt for his hurt. "No, my dear husband, it seems, was not only into oil, he was into revolution. Palace politics, they play those games over there. He got himself arrested and he's now awaiting trial. He's been awaiting trial for years."

"You could divorce him. You said you didn't love him."

"How could I divorce him while he's languishing in jail? I'm just lucky his yacht was in Monaco when this happened, or I'd have been left broke. He'd put it in my name as a goodwill gesture when we were on our honeymoon. I managed to sell it for seven hundred thousand dollars, and that's all the money I have. The Saudis won't let me touch the rest of his fortune."

He was rubbing his forehead the way he always did when he was upset. He was upset, but he believed it. Good, she thought. She wouldn't have to tell him the real truth.

Finally, he said, "I'm glad you've told me this, Cat. It explains a great deal."

They were at her apartment building. He pulled up out in front.

"Would you like to come in for a drink, Damian?"

"Not tonight, Cat. I think I'll go home and lick my wounds. All this has been pretty devastating."

"I'm really sorry, Damian. I should have told you about Razim before, I know that now."

"I'll get over it. I grew up a rather spoiled and pampered child, I never learned how to handle disappointment well. But I'll get over it." He leaned over and kissed her on the cheek. "I've never met anyone like you, Cat. You're really something."

He got out of the car and came around to open the door for her. She was picking up her purse from the seat when she saw someone coming up behind Damian. She yelled. "Watch out! Behind you!"

Damian spun around, coming face to face with a black man.

"Your wallet, motherfucker! Gimme the fuckin' wallet!" He grabbed Damian by the shoulder and spun him around. Catlyn got out of the car. The black man was holding a knife at Damian's chest.

Damian looked paralyzed, his eyes fixed on the knife. The black man suddenly turned and grabbed for Catlyn's purse. She let him have it. Out of the corner of her eye Catlyn saw the doorman at her apartment building on the telephone.

"The wallet, motherfuck!"

Damian pulled his wallet out from his jacket pocket, but it spun out of his hand and dropped to the sidewalk.

"Pick it up, motherfuck."

Damian reached down for it. Catlyn thought: Could this really be happening here, on Park Avenue? She had her eyes on the holdup man now. He was jumping around, looking both ways. Her eyes were tracing his features, making a photographic plate in her mind: his Afro haircut, the ridge across the top of his eyebrows, the scar along the side of his flared nostrils, the kind of crazy look in his eye. Damian stood up and handed him the wallet. Damian glanced at Catlyn and gave her a faint smile as if to say everything was okay. The holdup man opened the wallet. "Where's the fuckin' money?"

"I use credit cards. Here, take my watch." He fumbled for a moment getting it off his wrist, then he handed it over.

As the holdup man slipped the watch into a pocket with one hand, he punched Damian in the chest with the other. Damian gulped, and a short gasp escaped from his mouth. It took Catlyn a moment to realize that the holdup man still had had the knife in his hand when he punched. Blood appeared on Damian's shirt. He clutched his chest and collapsed. The holdup man jumped back and let him fall. Then he lunged for Catlyn and stabbed her in the arm with a quick slash, and a smile passed his lips as he did it. Then he turned and ran.

She yelled, "An ambulance, get an ambulance!" The doorman blew his whistle. A crowd quickly gathered.

She leaned over Damian and opened his shirt. His eyes were distant. He mumbled something. Blood was pulsing out of a hole in the middle of his chest. Someone handed Catlyn a shirt to use as a bandage. She balled it up and put it over the hole and pressed down. She knew the knife had either pierced the heart or a major artery by the way the blood was gushing out.

"Breathe evenly, Damian," she said, "keep relaxed, you can make it. Breathe easy. Help is on the way. We'll have you in a hospital in ten minutes."

He nodded. She kissed him on the cheek. "I made up the story of the Arab prince, Damian, but it is true that I *am* married, but not in the conventional sense . . ."

He smiled at her, as if to say he knew it all along. And then his breathing stopped. "No, Damian! No!" She quickly tilted his head back and put her mouth over his, and started breathing air into him. Five, six times. She drew back and pressed her fingers into his throat. No pulse. She pushed on his chest and breathed some more into his mouth. When the ambulance came five minutes later he was already blue. The two medics kept trying to revive him, but even as they were working on him, they kept shaking their heads. She refused treatment for her wound, insisting they do whatever they could for Damian. She just let the blood run down her arm.

At the hospital they worked on Damian Carter for another forty minutes, but he was pronounced dead at 10:48 by a resident named Harris. He came into the treatment room and told Catlyn they had done everything they could. He had blue-green eyes, that was all she really noticed about him. *Pronounced dead.* The words hung in the air, like smoke, after he left the room.

Another young doctor finished probing the wound on her arm for foreign matter, then closed it up with twenty-two stitches. He gave her a tetanus shot in her left buttock. Someone knocked and then the door came open. "Police," the man said. Lt. Alfred Somers showed her his badge and a photo ID. He had unruly salt-and-pepper hair, a tired face, and dark brown eyes. His cheap gray suit was rumpled. Catlyn guessed the last name was Anglicized, that he was probably Greek or Italian. She figured he was in his late forties and had seen more murders for real than she had seen in the movies.

He said to the doctor, "You give her anything? Any

76

drugs?"

"I offered her a tranquilizer, she said she didn't want anything."

"Okay, good."

The doctor left them alone.

Somers said, "Full name?"

"Catlyn Jean-Ann Cavanaugh." She folded the skirt of her evening gown over to cover some of the bloodstains.

"That Catlyn with a 'C' or a 'K'?"

" 'C,' " she said.

He wanted her address, phone number, place of employment if any, She told him. She stated her occupation as "financial planner."

"Are you married?"

"Separated."

"Relationship to the deceased?"

"Friends."

"Just friends?"

"We were lovers."

He kept writing in his book. "Did you get a good look at the man who attacked you and Mr. Carter?"

"I did."

"Could you describe him, please, as best you can."

"He was five feet nine or ten, kinky hair in a short Afro. Age, perhaps mid-thirties, perhaps younger. It was hard to say. His weight I would put at one hundred forty pounds. He works out. He had a muscular neck and the skin on his face was drawn in. He was wearing a dark shirt with a white windbreaker, black pants, and Adidas running shoes, well worn. White socks. He had a dark spot on the back of his right hand. A small scar on his right cheek, vertical, along his nose. His skin was dark brown and he had Negro features. I don't think he was black, though."

"Why do you say that?"

"I smelled the very faint odor of something like furniture stain. There was something about him that wasn't quite right—I think he may have been disguised."

The detective made a face as if he didn't need any fantasies in his life. Catlyn knew what he was thinking. He wanted a nice and simple mugging/killing, no disguises. Disguises meant he was dealing with a professional, and that meant the professional was paid. So the investigation would have to go along the lines of who paid him? And that would mean asking a lot of questions of people in high places. No cop would want to do that. Damian knew a lot of people with a lot of connections, people who wouldn't want to be bothered with questions. Better to be looking for a doper with a knife.

Somers said, "Did he say anything?"

She told him exactly what the man had said.

"Just what a black junkie would say?"

"Yes," she said.

"You notice anything peculiar in the voice?"

"No."

"Would you say he spoke like a black man?"

"Yes."

"You think he might have been just imitating black speech? I mean, if he was wearing furniture polish."

"Yes, I'd say he was very good. Not polish—stain."

Somers rubbed his chin and looked her over again. "What are you trying to tell me?"

"I think this may have been a deliberate killing. I think I saw the same man across the street from my apartment building earlier, when Damian picked me up. He was standing near a motorcycle; it might have been his. I think he may have followed us to the restaurant, though I couldn't swear it."

"Anybody else see him?"

"Not that I know of."

"You mention it to anyone at the time?"

"No. There was something else about him—I think he stabbed me because he likes it. He had no reason to do anything to me. I was just standing there trying to help Damian. He should have run, but instead, instead he stabbed me. He didn't want to kill me, just hurt me. He liked it, too, I saw it in his face when he did it."

Somers looked at her as if he thought she had an overactive imagination. He shrugged and wrote something in his notebook. "You think it's okay to smoke in here?" he asked.

She pointed to the sign that said it was forbidden. He shrugged again. Then he said, "How long did you know Mr. Carter?"

"Four years."

"What did he do for a living?"

"He had independent means. He was on the board of directors of several banks, charitable organizations, his own foundation. He's considered—was considered—one of the leading economists in the country. He wrote several books, many articles, made a lot of speeches. For a while he was assistant ambassador to the United Nations—during the Reagan years."

Somers blew some air out. No doubt about it, he didn't like what he was hearing.

"You call reporters?" he asked.

"No, why would I do that?"

"I just asked." He looked again at the sign. "Excuse me for a minute, I got to make a phone call."

"Why don't you just break the rule and smoke in here. I won't tell on you."

He looked at her for a moment with mild surprise, then he checked at the door, looking up and down the hall, before shaking out a Camel, rapping the end on the back of his hand, and sticking it between his lips. He lit it with a Zippo lighter.

"We was where now?" he said, looking at his notes. "Okay—you said you were romantically involved with the victim?"

"I was."

"Forgive me for saying this, but I would expect a little tears or something."

"Hysterical female?"

"I didn't say that."

"Just get on with your questions. I want to go home and get damn good and drunk."

"Forgive me for asking, but since you intimated this might not be a simple case of mugging, can you give me some reason that somebody would like to kill Mr. Carter?"

"I cannot."

"Let me put it another way. Has he had any recent bitter disagreements?"

"No."

"Was he married?"

"Widower. His wife died in a plane crash four years ago."

"Children?"

"He has a son. Christopher. He's a sophomore at Harvard. Economics major. His daughter was killed in the crash that killed his wife."

"Any other close relatives?"

"A sister who lives in France. She's married to a duke. They live in a castle."

"Has he had any big changes in his life lately? Sell anything, buy anything, bankruptcy, lawsuit, an accident, something like that?"

"He thought he might be appointed head of the Federal Reserve Board in a few days. Storkweather is retiring because of bad health."

His eyebrows went up.

"Damian Carter was a big-time guy."

Somers took a couple more drags on his cigarette, then crushed it out on the floor. He looked at her strangely for a moment. "Can I ask you something? Listen. I've been doing this job since before Christ was a carpenter, and I have yet to run into very damn many people who can stand next to somebody getting knifed and later tell more than maybe one, two things about an assailant. Sometimes they aren't even sure if it was a human being."

"What's your question?"

"How do you keep your cool?"

"I'm made of stone."

"Sorry I asked."

"Can I go now?"

"We may be having a lineup. Don't take any trips unless you check with the Department. I'm not in, ask for the captain." He handed her his card. "Something like this, we got to tell the reporters. They'll be on you like lice on a camel. My advice is, tell them nothing but nothing. They will take anything you say and put it in a sausage grinder before it gets on the front page. It interferes with our work to have the populace riled up, know what I mean—okay? Take care of yourself."

"One thing, Lieutenant. Have you given any credence to what I said about the killer being in a disguise?"

He looked at the floor for a moment, then at the wall. Then he shook his head. "Would you, you were me?"

"No."

Somers said, "We got routines and procedures. We got what looks like a mugging. A pill-head got squirrely, that's what it looks like. We got to act on that first."

"I agree. I admit I'm not sure of myself. I'm talking mostly about feeling and impression. I just want you to know that sometimes I'm uncanny when it comes to sensing things. But I'm with you. We've got to go with the highest odds first."

He shuffled his feet and digested what she said for a long moment. "Let's stay friends," he said, looking at her with narrowed eyes.

She thought that was a strange thing for him to say. She said, "I won't let someone get away with murdering Damian."

81

"I figured that out already."

He asked her whether she'd like to come down to the station, have a police artist make a sketch of the guy. She said that wouldn't be necessary. "I can do it myself."

"The sooner the better—we'll get it out on the TV."

She borrowed some paper and a pencil from the nurse and drew the murderer. It took her seven minutes.

"The guy looks like this?" the lieutenant said.

"Pretty much."

"I'm impressed."

"You will call me if anything comes up."

"Sure."

"I want Damian's body autopsied by the best man around, even if I have to pay him."

"I'll see to it."

"Can I go now?"

"Any time you want. Call me tomorrow, we'll set something up to have you look at some pictures."

Before she left the hospital, she made a call to her lawyer, Martin Getsong.

"Martin? Catlyn. A terrible thing has happened. Damian was attacked and killed on the street tonight in what appears to be a mugging. I was there. I believe the chances of the police finding the murderer are one in about ten thousand. I'm going to do a little checking on my own. Here's what I want you to do: Find me an expert in these matters, someone streetwise and experienced. Offer him whatever it takes."

"I will, Cat. Are you all right?"

"You know me, Martin. I'm tough."

Her next call was to France. Damian's sister was in Africa on a safari, a servant told her. Catlyn's French was not good enough to find out how to get in touch with her. She then called Halperin Limousine Service and said she'd need a driver and a car at her place in two hours for a long drive. They would not be getting back until the next day.

Then she took a cab home.

She showered, changed into a dark blue suit, and called her lawyer again to ask him to get in touch with Damian's sister in Africa if he could and give her the news. Then she poured herself a large glass of Old Granddad, sat in the living room, and looked out on the lights of New York. She was exhausted and felt hollow inside. The tears started coming and she didn't try to stop them. Her body shook all over. She just let the tears come for almost an hour, when the doorman called to tell her that the limousine had arrived. She told the doorman to have the limousine wait, then she went to the bathroom and cleaned her face. She looked at herself in the mirror. "No more crying," she said. "Ruin your image."

She went down in the elevator, got into the limousine, and gave the driver the address of Damian's son, Christopher Carter, in Cambridge, Massachusetts.

SIX

George had felt numb all that evening.

He didn't like ordering a man's death and he didn't like the waiting for it to happen. And afterward he didn't like waiting around to see whether the police were able to piece it together and come calling at his door, however remote the possibility.

The family had a late dinner. Mattie had overcooked the pot roast and he'd raised his voice at her, which got Linda upset. Didn't he know how hard good servants were to find? He didn't try to defend himself. He apologized to Mattie and to Linda, and ate his overdone pot roast in silence.

After dinner George tried to get some tickets to a Neil Simon play—some inconsequential piece of fluff that Linda wanted to see—but even the scalpers were sold out. Linda didn't believe he couldn't get tickets; he could always get tickets when there was something *he* wanted to see. So he had to make a few more calls to satisfy her that he had done everything humanly possible.

Then Rudolf came home late, looking not at all clear-eyed, and his mother started on him. Rudolf retaliated by going to his room and locking the door, and refused to open it for anyone, including George, who even threatened to terminate his allowance. Finally he told Linda to just forget it, leave the boy alone. She headed for the bedroom, slamming the door behind her.

George retired to his study and opened a bottle of brandy. He sat in his robe and slippers and read Barron's for a while at his desk, then sat in his recliner in front of a small portable television and turned on the news when it came on at eleven. He hated watching the news. His beloved Russia was always painted so black! Didn't anyone ever ask why the Soviets had to build such a huge military? The motherland had been invaded by imperialists over and over again: the Germans twice in twenty-five years, the Americans and British after the Revolution, the Japanese in 1907. The Americans were always accusing the Soviets of lying in their news, yet American news was the biggest lie of all. America, the meddling bungler of the world, always portrayed as sincere peacemaker, do-gooder, savior to the Third World. What was America in fact? An oppressor, capitalist plunderer, militarist. It made him sick. And the aspirin and pantyhose commercials made him even sicker.

Finally it was time for the local news. His pulse quickened. The co-anchor, a Puerto Rican woman with a hairdo like a Viking helmet, was saying something about a noted economist attacked on Park Avenue, dead tonight at fifty-five. And there he was, Damian Carter, shown making a speech to the U.N. back in 1988, and at a celebrity golf match with Bob Hope in 1985, then a shot of the scene where it happened with the blood on the sidewalk. Next came the sketch of the mugger. Not even remotely close to Park, George thought. Expertly done!

Park might be a little insane, George thought, but his craftsmanship was raised to the level of fine art. George lit up a Cuban cigar, inhaled, and blew the smoke toward the ceiling. It was over and Park got away clean. They were looking for a black mugger. All was right with the world!

George had a sudden longing for Esther, his mistress.

But it was late, and he didn't want to have to go through the effort of making up a lie to tell Linda. Linda was getting to be such an inconvenience in life. Nothing to be done about it, one must take the good with the bad in this old world, he thought glumly. He poured himself a large brandy, puffed on the cigar, watched yet another pantyhose commercial, and dreamed of his dacha on the Black Sea.

George was still in good spirits the following morning. He got to the office early with his *Wall Street Journal* under his arm and made himself some coffee on the office coffee machine. It was a little strong, but he liked it that way, he told himself. He put in extra Coffeemate to disguise the taste. The report from his research assistant on Catlyn Cavanaugh was on his desk. He was amazed that she turned out to be a high-stakes poker player. How very interesting, he thought, but now it was totally useless information.

The only nagging, worrisome thing still bothering him was he wasn't sure whether suspicion would be thrown on him because of the timing of the thing. After all, a man is killed on the very night it's been decided he'll be the new Fed chairman. But Fed chairmen are not knocked off by their rivals. Who would suspect such a thing? Certainly not the police. He'd met some New York police officers, even the chief once, and he was frankly not impressed. No, no one would suspect it was a deliberate assassination. He was safe on that score. A black mugger had done it; the police would be looking for him. Random street violence, they called it. A daily thing in New York.

At a little after eight his secretary arrived and threw out the coffee he'd made and made another pot—decent enough for people to drink, she grumbled. A few minutes later a call came from Margo Yost-Konning, his friend at Columbia.

She said, "No doubt you've heard about Damian Carter, George."

"Yes, Margo, and I can't tell you how heartsick I am. It really makes you think, doesn't it? Just yesterday I was composing a letter of congratulations to him and now—I'm just devastated."

"I just got a call from Washington, George."

"Oh? I suppose they'll start the council process all over again."

"Not this time. They want to see you, George, tomorrow night. The President wants to meet you personally."

"President, ah, Hustead wants to meet, ah, me?" He felt his throat close up.

She laughed mildly. "Haven't you ever met?"

"Well, not to speak, I mean . . ."

"You'll be getting the call this afternoon from the President's appointment secretary. First a dinner, then you'll have some time with the President and some of his key advisers. They'll want to chat with you, feel you out on certain key points. How's that sound?"

"Fine. I'll look forward to it."

"Just remember, the President is a politician, not an economist. He believes economists can make prosperity out of air, anytime they want."

"I can handle it, Margo."

When he hung up the phone he called Linda and told her to buy a nice dress, something appropriate for dinner at the White House. She screamed in his ear: "The White House!"

"You're going to soon be the wife of the chairman of the Federal Reserve Board."

"For certain?"

"Ninety-nine percent."

"Dinner at the White House . . ." Her voice had a dreamy quality now. "The girls at the Club are going to be green, just green — Maybe your being Federal Reserve chairman won't be such a bad thing, George."

"Get your hair done, it'll be tomorrow night."

"I don't think I've ever been this excited."

"Take a Valium," he said, chuckling.

He called Charlie Van Nuys, his closest business associate. Maybe they could have lunch. Charlie said okay. George didn't tell him the good news; he figured to save it for dessert. Charlie liked the luncheon spread at a little restaurant on Fifty-fifth Street where they served big steaks, tender and bloody. George said he'd make the reservation.

Next, he handled a few business calls, talked to two clients who wanted his assistance in brokering a hundred million dollars in commercial paper, which he agreed to do, and listened to a sales pitch from a young lawyer who wanted George to serve on the board of directors of a new high-tech software company, which he didn't agree to, even though there was the promise of stock options and other juicy perks. He didn't like the way the man combed his hair—sort of a brush cut with a long lock in front, in a pompadour. The young man was trying to look modern, which in itself was no sin, but in George's judgment he had overdone it. The man obviously did not have good sense, so George told him "no deal." It was the little things that told about a man.

George usually had a hectic, almost frantic schedule, but with the maneuvering to get control of the Federal Reserve over the past few months he had been curtailing his business activities. He also had had a lot of planning to do and a lot of reading and thinking. Now that he was nearly there he decided he would slow down and take a few minutes each day for himself. He was entitled, he told himself. He was about to achieve what no man in history had ever achieved before—the crippling defeat of an enemy through espionage alone.

Not that he was going to do it alone, of course. It hadn't

88

been his idea originally. Not the concept. He would have to admit that when the time came. The idea actually belonged to the greatest man who had ever lived, Nikita Khruschev. But now he was in a position to make it happen. He, Gyorgi Vlahovich, was the key.

He wandered into a small bookshop and browsed through the new titles. Someday, he thought, there would be a book written about him. By then, of course, the U.S.A. would be the U.S.S.A.—Union of Soviet Socialist America—and he would be a hero. He would be up there with Washington and Lincoln. He'd be known as the man who destroyed for all time the vile monster of capitalism, the great slavemaster of the world.

As his eyes drifted over the book titles in the Political Science section—a biography of Reagan, a treatise on peace, another on the Mideast and the future of oil—he began to wonder how a book about him would begin. Surely not with his arrival in New York as a very green and frightened agent with barely three months' field experience.

No, the biography would have to run from the very beginning, from the time he was selected for training.

George was ten years old. He was attending primary school in Belyakov, near Kiev. He was a little better than average student except for his rather phenomenal memory. His mother was a concert violinist with the Moscow Symphony and had no use for him or his father. George realized later that his mother had always regarded her marriage as something of a mistake, and he was simply part of that mistake. He was not bitter toward her; in fact, he could barely remember her. The last he had heard of her she had had a stroke and could no longer play her violin. He believed the Fates had paid her back for her crimes committed against him.

His father was a spy in the military branch—the GRU.

This bit of luck, George always thought, amply compensated for having a mother who wanted to forget she was a mother. Not that George's father had much to do with him either. He had sent George away to live with distant relatives in a small village, out of sight and out of mind. He had only seen his father half a dozen times in his life that he could remember. A hard drinker and a pipe smoker, with a harsh laugh. But his father had managed—just before he was assassinated in West Berlin—to have George accepted to what was then called the Lenin School for Technical Training. The school was supposed to be outside of Leningrad. George never saw the Lenin School. He went to a secret place in the South called the Foreign Service Training Institute. Not to attend school but to go through a month-long assessment process.

He was tested for his ability to learn languages and to remember codes. He passed with high marks. Then he was given a tutor and his first year of study began. He stayed with the tutor, a witch of a woman with a scrawny neck, alone in a small stone house on the outskirts of Odessa and learned English, the kind spoken in upstate New York, with a flat, nasal "A". He hated this woman, and all he could think about day and night was how to get away from her. Her name was Natasha Segur, the embittered granddaughter of a Count Segur. She told him the sooner he learned what he had to learn, the sooner he would be rid of her. When she had him recite conjugations she'd hit him with a spoon whenever he made a mistake. Over and over she'd have him go through the "th" sounds, saying the, those, these, them, their, Martha, Samantha, Thurston . . . whacking him on the side of the head each time he got one wrong.

One day an official showed up at the house in a black limousine. He was tall, pale, and very stern, George remembered. He spoke to the witch on the porch for a few moments, then came in and asked George some questions in English. How old are you, son? What's your name? Tell me the story of the Three Bears, and things like that. Each time George would answer, he'd cock his head, as if trying to hear every syllable. Finally he nodded and patted George on the head and told him to pack his things. The witch, he remembered, gave him a hug when he left and kissed him on the cheek. It was a wet, sticky kiss. On the way out the door with his meager suitcase he managed to accidentally step on her foot. It gave him the solitary moment of joy he had experienced in that house.

That day he took his first ride in an airplane, a four-seater. It landed on a small airstrip in the foothills of the Caucasus Mountains. On the plane he was fed a sort of picnic lunch of roast pheasant and raw vegetables and was given two glasses of champagne to drink. The official told him that he was on his way to a very special school, where he would learn how to do great things when he became a man.

A limousine driven by a soldier picked them up at the airport. It was not far to the school. The first thing he noticed on going up the long circular drive was a small neat clump of bushes with a flagpole in the center. On the flagpole there flew an American flag. He asked, "Are we now in America?" He had no idea at that age of the size of the world, or how far the plane had flown in six hours. The official smiled and said, "It is America, yes, but just a little piece of it right here in the Motherland."

In the parking lot on the side of the main building there were strange-looking American cars. Inside, there was American furniture and pictures of Washington and Lincoln on the walls, just like in an American school. And he soon found those weren't the only similarities.

The curriculum consisted of English language studies, English and American literature, algebra, geometry, physics, chemistry, Latin, French, and civics. They used American textbooks, listened to rock and roll records, played football complete with cheerleaders, and dated girls from the small girls' school on the other side of the hill—duplicating perfectly the American prep school as closely as possible. They watched American television programs shown on film every weekend. George loved *Leave It to Beaver* and *The Ozzie and Harriet Show*. He knew it was all fake, that most American families were nothing like the Cleavers and the Nelsons, but he liked the shows anyway. They had copies of *Playboy* magazine, saw John Wayne movies, lost their virginity in the backseat of a '49 Mercury with sponge dice hanging from the rearview mirror.

Then, each evening after dinner, for two hours they met in study sessions held in Russian where they learned the truth, how America exploited the poor, how the capitalists plundered the Third World, how Wall Street made wars, famines, and caused economic crashes and disasters. They learned Hegelian dialectics, glorious Marxist-Leninism, and were taught the inevitability of the worldwide Marxist revolution. These studies were difficult, and the instructors severe. No dissension or monkey business was tolerated, as it was tolerated in the prep school in the daytime. George and his classmates were made to memorize the twelve points of the Young Communists program and to read *Das Kapital*, and most of Lenin's forty volumes. And they were taught how fortunate they were to be at the vanguard of history, chosen for an historic mission.

The dual nature of his schooling led to a curious duality in George's nature. He became two people. He was an American who attended a college prep high school in the hills of New Hampshire and learned that Lincoln returned overdue books to the library even though he had to walk miles through the snow, and that George Washington never told a lie. He learned by day that freedom and liberty were the most important political concepts in the history of the world, and in the evening was told that these were bourgeois concepts whose purpose it was to hoodwink the proletariat.

Lenin taught that the ruling classes of capitalism would not give up their power without a struggle, and the struggle would not occur during temporary surges of capitalistic revivals—prosperity. George and his classmates were told they would infiltrate the West to collect and gather military information and technological advancements; infiltrate the higher organs of business and government, especially the intelligence networks and political parties; to disrupt as much as possible the economies of the capitalist world in order to create the proper conditions for revolution; and to organize cells and cadres to provide leadership when the time of revolution came.

On graduation day Khruschev himself came for the ceremony. He was a round, bald little man with sparkling attentive eyes, who spoke with a coarse accent and had a hearty laugh. He had a dream, he said, and that dream was that Marxist-Leninism would triumph over capitalism, and that in his lifetime the flag with the hammer and sickle would fly over the whole world. There would be no more class warfare, nor imperialism, nor oppression of the masses. The capitalist encirclement of the Soviet empire would be ended. Communism would sweep the world, he promised, ensuring freedom, happiness, and peace for all the nations of the world. Marx and Engels proved, he said, through scientific analysis, that the destruction of capitalism could not be halted, and that socialism would inevitably replace it. Young men, he shouted, rejoice, rejoice, rejoice!

Even now, whenever George would think of that day, his heart would feel like bursting in his chest.

Then the premier touched the twenty-six graduates one by one and handed them their certificates. He looked deep into the eyes of each and said, "Will you swear to devote yourself to the cause of the Motherland and her great historic mission?" George remembered the shivers that ran up and down his spine when the great man touched him. "I swear, I swear!" George exclaimed. And Krushschev smiled and patted him on the cheek.

Afterward, George was required to spend two more years of advanced training at the KGB foreign service school in Leningrad, where he had more political indoctrination and an introduction to tradecraft before he was considered reliable and ready. It was here that he learned to shoot guns, make bombs, and communicate in code. At the time, he thought of himself as something of a James Bond. How vital and alive he felt, so full of fire!

George remembered he was happy there, too. He knew an older woman named Tanya, who had big breasts and loved to cuddle him in bed. Those were such good days. What dreams he had, of being in a position of power, of being the key man in a vast espionage operation.

And now, at last, the dreams were coming true.

SEVEN

E Tank was where they put the hard ones, the ones charged with violent or capital crimes. It was on the seventh floor at the end of a long row of tanks and cells. Along the hall there were four grill gates to go through where bored guards checked ID's. There was a lot of security on the seventh floor.

E Tank was just for blacks, because of the prison gangs, like the White Aryan Brotherhood and the Black Guerilla Family. When the races were housed together there was always killing, so they were separated on Rikers Island.

The tank itself was sixteen feet by sixteen feet, with three concrete block walls, a high ceiling, and, facing the hallway, a row of bars. The door was the sliding type, which could be opened either by a correctional officer's key or electronically by the men in the bulletproof control room at the end of the hall. Like everyplace else on Rikers Island, E Tank was overcrowded. It was originally designed to hold twelve prisoners. It now held forty-eight, the bunk beds stacked four high.

One of the forty-eight prisoners housed in E Tank was B. B. Hanson. He was a big man, powerfully built. Quiet, kept to himself. Wasn't going to give nobody trouble.

When he wasn't doing push-ups or jogging in place, he

was usually just sitting next to the wall minding his own business. Trying to keep what he thought of as a level frame of mind. Plenty of things in E Tank could drive a man across the line. A mind could get out of level quick.

The johns, as an example. E Tank had four of them. Two were stopped up and, since some of the men continued to piss in them, the air in E Tank was foul. The guards did nothing about it. The inmate plumbers would get to it when they got to it. On Rikers Island a lot of toilets were stopped up. Prisoners with a lot of hostility and no sense liked to pack the toilets full of everything from shit to T-shirts.

So there was the stink. And then there was the food. The morning meal: cold coffee, lumpy oatmeal, and a hard-boiled egg. Lunch: a sandwich made of white bread with a ground-up spread inside, a third-pint carton of milk, cold soup. Evening meal (served at three-thirty in the afternoon so there wouldn't have to be a separate kitchen staff): meatloaf or chili or maybe sloppy joes, a canned vegetable, watery mashed potatoes, bread, coffee. At least, B. B. thought, they *said* it was coffee. It tasted more like turpentine.

He'd get used to the stink, he told himself. And the food. And the crowding. He'd been crowded all his life, so what else was new? The worst part was being around guys like Marcus Rudd and Jo Boy Fisk. One had raped his own daughter and the other had beat his woman to death. B. B. was thinking since he was going to go down for fifteen to life, why not just beat the shit out of both of them for the hell of it. It would feel so good to mess 'em up.

But then he thought, what the hell, why bother? They were living in their own hell. A couple young bucks out on the roof during exercise had already kneed Rudd in the balls, and Fisk was spending all his time whining like a woman, scared as hell he was gonna get ass-fucked in the shower.

B. B. rolled a cigarette and lit it up. He just had to think survival, that was it. How to do the time with no hassle. You go bustin' guys up, the next thing you know some friend of the guy you busted up is shoving a shank into you. Or pissing on your lunch.

A cockroach crawled across his shoe. He didn't try to kill it. He just watched it head for the crack in the plumbing fixture. A bunch of guys playing cards suddenly started a shoving match with a lot of yelling. A correctional officer came running over to the door, but things calmed down before he gave an alarm.

B. B. just inhaled on his cigarette and kept staring at nothing. He'd already figured out that the one guy in the cell to watch was the young one that looked like a ball player, always smiling. Curtis something his name was. Supposed to be in for killing his old man. Curtis just lay on his bunk and smiled all the time, watching whatever was on the television set. B. B. figured he found out what killing was all about, and now he had a mission in life. B. B. figured he'd be real nice to Curtis.

E Tank was going to be his home for at least six months, he figured. The bail was set at two hundred thousand. That meant that he had to have twenty grand to make the bail and he was about nineteen-and-a-half grand short. His father was dead, his mama was in a Florida nursing home, and he didn't have many friends. None that had twenty grand. The public defender didn't want to plead him guilty to second-degree murder because there was no way the prosecution could make a jury buy murder one. The prosecutor refused to let him plead guilty to manslaughter. So they were going to trial and try to work the jury, and while everybody got ready for the show, here he was in E Tank.

He'd already made up his mind he was going to lie like hell to the jury, even though he was innocent. What he was really guilty of was pissing the cops off for the last ten years, telling people the truth, which was that the cops are making a fortune off crime and if you want protection you got to do it yourself. The fact that he had thrown a guy out a window and the guy landed on his head didn't make B. B. Hanson a murderer. The guy attacked him with a knife. So what the guy was five nine and a hundred-ninety pounds, and B. B. Hanson was six eight and almost three hundred. Was it a crime to be big?

The guy was a no-good goddamn pimp anyway and the city was better off without him. Only reason he got arrested is the damn whore he was trying to rescue from the pimp now claimed the pimp was no pimp at all, just a boyfriend, and Hanson was jealous. B. B. spat on the floor. Christ, and to think he thought he was in love with the cunt.

A correctional officer opened the door. All forty-eight guys looked to see who the lucky one might be. The officer said, "Hanson?"

"Yeah?"

"Company."

B. B. didn't ask who the company was. Only company he ever had was his lawyer or his friend Harvey, and it couldn't be Harvey, because he was in the can, too, for public drunk and disorderly. B. B. raised his bulk off the floor and followed the jailer down to the elevator, and they went down together to the first-floor visiting room. The jailer let him in and closed the door behind him. Inside, seated at the Formica-topped table, was a blond white woman, well dressed in a tan pantsuit, and a guy standing next to her in a gray three-piece suit, about forty. Well-trimmed hair, a little prissy, B. B. thought. Fag, maybe.

The guy in the three-piece suit put out his hand and said he was Martin Getsong, an attorney, and he introduced the woman as Catlyn Cavanaugh.

"Yo sure yo wants me?" B. B. said. "Roosevelt Hanson. They calls me B. B."

"We're sure," Getsong said. "Have a seat, won't you?"

98

B. B. eased his mass onto a chair and folded his hands in front of him.

"How would you like to get out of here?" Getsong said. He had circled around the table so he was standing opposite B. B., leaning against the far wall with a thumb tucked into the watch pocket of his vest. He was keeping his distance as if he'd suddenly been put in a cage with a gorilla. "You can be on the street in two hours."

B. B. smiled. "Ah only been here forty-seven days, Ah ain't hardly got to know the place. Lots of real nice company. Nightly entertainment. Sunnin' yo'self on the sun deck every afternoon. This place a nice hotel, what yo got to offer tha's better?"

He looked toward the woman. Her face showed nothing, no emotion, no fear, not even any particular curiosity. Most women who come to a place like Rikers Island look like they want to puke. She was just staring at him with the coolest green eyes he'd ever seen on a human being. Cool and calculating, and it gave him a little shiver.

Getsong said, "A man was killed on the street last night. His name was Damian Carter."

"Ah seen somethin' 'bout that on the news. We got a color TV, me and the fellas watch."

Getsong said, "Here is a drawing of the man who killed him." He handed B. B. a copy of the sketch Catlyn had made. B. B. glanced at it and handed it back. "Nice-lookin' young fella. Too bad he got hisself in trouble."

"Do you know him?"

"No."

"Maybe you should take a closer look."

"Ah don't knows the man, don't have to take a closer look. Yo gonna tell me what this about?"

Catlyn said, "Do you know who Mr. Getsong is, Mr. Hanson?"

"He say he a lawyer."

"He's a senior partner in the firm of Robbes and

Borland, which is just about the most high-powered firm in the city. I have asked Mr. Getsong to represent you in your present difficulties and to arrange for your immediate release on bail."

"Why yo do somethin' like that?"

"We believe in your innocence. We know, as an example, that you were protecting a prostitute from a pimp, trying to get the prostitute to straighten out, when the pimp came to your home, armed, and demanded you give her up."

"It's a clear case of justifiable homicide," Getsong said.

"And yo jez a couple of nice folks wanna see justice done."

"You help us, we help you," Catlyn said.

B. B. folded his arms, leaned back, grinned broadly, and looked at Getsong. "What comes next is gonna be the part tha's hard ta swallow."

Catlyn said, "Damian Carter was a close friend of mine. It's very simple. I want the man who sent him to the cemetery to be brought to justice."

"Tha's what they got police for, why yo need me?"

"Because you know the rocks to look under. We know, as an example, you have a reputation for being able to broker any kind of property that comes along. You have a network of contacts in the underworld."

B. B. thought it over for a few moments, then shook his head. "Jez ain't my thing, Ah got friends livin' under those rocks."

"All I want you to do is help me put a name on that face," she said.

"Sorry." He got up. "Thanks anyways," he said. "Ah doan work for the man, an' tha's it."

"Wait a minute," Catlyn said. "Perhaps you don't understand me. We're not asking you to inform on anyone. I need a bodyguard and a guide. I've already gone through dozens of police mug books and haven't been able to find him. Take me to the people who might know who this man is, please. I need an entry into the underworld, Mr. Hanson. Only a man like yourself can give it to me."

"How yo know Ah get outta here, Ah doan go south with the crows?"

"I'll trust you," she said. "You have a much better chance of beating this thing with Mr. Getsong than by fleeing."

He looked at Getsong and slowly nodded. Then he turned to Catlyn. "Where we be goin' yo gonna find some pretty bad dudes. Ah mean, we gonna have ta go inta some sewers."

"I'll go if you will."

He thought of the stopped-up toilets, the food, and the company waiting for him in E Tank. What the hell, what was life if not a long, dreary series of compromises? He smiled at her. "Yo got yo'self a tour guide."

Robert Park had been drinking Jack Daniels at The Horned Toad all afternoon. He was in a foul mood. The whore he'd had right after the kill was a cold-hearted nigger-bitch he had to swat around a little to get her to hold still while he tied her up. And she had no technique. All lips and no tongue on his dick. He cuffed her ears. And now he had to look at that picture on the tube all afternoon, and every time he saw it, it just made him madder and madder. It was exactly what he'd looked like the night of the killing. Exactly! He hadn't counted on that. That had never happened before. Before, the composite pictures had always been worthless.

He left The Horned Toad around four o'clock when the place started filling up with the after-work crowd. He walked up to Broadway, trying to clear his head. He went into a couple of bookstores and looked at some leather magazines. He just couldn't get turned on. That damned picture was bugging him. He took a cab to his apartment and sat around watching the cartoons on the tube, drinking beer, and thinking. Then a little after six he made a phone call.

"Shirley? Robert. You gonna be in in about an hour?"

"You want to come over, sugar?"

"Yeah."

"Nothing nasty. I ain't in the mood for no trouble. You been takin' anything?"

"A few beers. Jesus, you want company or not?"

"All right, Robert."

He took a subway to 103rd Street and got off and walked two blocks to a dilapidated brownstone, pushed the buzzer, then went on up. Shirley Dills met him at the door wearing a pink peignoir and her flaming red hair frizzed. "I just washed my hair," she said. "I must look like a sight." She was nearly fifty, and used up. With the lights on, he couldn't stand to look at her. Her skin was like chalk, and wrinkled like the treads on a tractor tire.

"What brings you here this early in the evening, sugar?"

"Just shut up and bring me a beer."

He turned off the lights in the living room and sat by the window in an overstuffed chair with doilies on the arms. He stared at the apartment across the street, second floor front. That's where Ambrose Poindexter lived. He was black, and it was his face that Park had used when he built his disguise.

Shirley came back into the room. "Don't you want a light on, sugar?"

"No."

She gave him the beer and a stein. "What you watching, Robert?"

"Never mind, and if anybody asks you, I was never here. Ever, you understand?"

"Sure, sugar. Sure."

"Now why don't you go make yourself pretty."

Four beers and an hour and a half later, Park watched

Ambrose Poindexter come out of his apartment building. It had started to rain and he was wearing a yellow raincoat. He walked to the corner, crossed the street, and headed up the block.

"Got to go, Shirley," Park said.

"Aren't you even going to tell me what the hell you been doing staring out that window all this time?"

"Don't ask about what you ain't supposed to know. Live longer that way, got me?"

"Sure, Robert, I got you."

He dropped three twenties on the table by the door. "Be seeing ya."

"Don't be a stranger, sugar."

Park didn't have to hurry, he knew where Ambrose was going: Stone's Pool Parlor on West 112th Street near Broadway. Ambrose went there two, three times a week. He wouldn't have been there when Damian Carter was murdered. It was too early. He never got there before ten. Park knew the man's habits well.

When he got to Stone's Pool Parlor, Park went up to the door and looked in. Mostly blacks, but there were some Puerto Ricans and a few whites. Twenty-five, thirty customers altogether. A couple of broads. The place was dimly lit, except for the low-hanging lights over the pool tables. Six tables. A shuffleboard. Park went in and bought himself a coke out of a machine and watched Ambrose play a little straight pool with an old gent who looked as if he knew his way around a stick. The kid was pretty good, too.

Park drank his Coke. At one point the kid ran eighteen balls straight. Real good.

Then a lanky Latino kid came in and said, "Hey, Ambrose, seen your picture on the front page of the *Post*."

Park froze.

A couple of guys laughed. Ambrose looked up and said, "I ought to sue, you know that? Even my mother ask me what I was doin' last night. Shit. Fucking jerk-ass cops. To

103

them, every black face is just a black face."

The Latino kid said, "I should turn you in for the reward, man."

"Motherfucker," Ambrose said. He missed his shot.

Park had heard enough. Panic rose in him. He knew there was no way for anyone to get to him, even if Ambrose was taken in for questioning. And Ambrose most likely couldn't prove he wasn't on Park Avenue sticking Damian Carter. He was probably working a purse-snatching scam downtown that time of day. But say he could prove he wasn't uptown knifing Carter? And then the cops started asking questions and maybe somebody had seen him following Ambrose. It was a long shot, Park figured, but it *could* happen.

He'd used Abrose Poindexter's face because he wanted to have somebody to pin it on, and it gave him a kick to do it to a black dude, but he now realized it was a mistake. Okay, he told himself, so it was a mistake. So don't cry over spilt milk, clean it up. The question was how?

There was really only one answer Robert Park could come up with.

B. B. Hanson didn't quite know what to make of Catlyn Cavanaugh. She had an uncanny ability to sleep for fifteen or twenty minutes at a time, in a cab, anyplace. She'd say "excuse me," turn her head to one side, and she'd be out. The cab would stop, she'd wake up. He'd heard about prize-fighters being able to do that. Never a broad.

And he'd never seen a broad so ballsy.

B. B. Hanson was a huge man with a missing canine tooth, which gave him a kind of vicious look. And his round face was scarred and rough. Existence on the planet Earth had not been easy for him, and his face was a map of the struggle. Most Park Avenue broads, he thought, would take one look at him and scream. In fact, they did. That, or look away. This one just looked deep into his eyes back there on Riker Island and seemed to say to herself, this dude's okay.

The first stop was Larry's Jewelers in midtown. Larry fenced only the finer things. He was a part-timer who couldn't resist a bargain. Catlyn had told him her story plain and simple, showed him a watch identical to the one taken from Damian Carter, then X-rayed the guy's head with her cool green eyes as he took a look. He shook his head. "Nope." That's all he said. She didn't ask him anything else. No wasted motion, no wasted time.

When they got back in the cab she said, "That man is a chiseler. If you ever fence anything, Mr. Hanson, take it elsewhere."

He said he knew Larry was like that and already told all his friends. The next fence was uptown—a flower shop. He only bought gold. Goldblatt, his name was. He'd give a few bucks more than anyone else for good stuff. It was doubtful the dude they were looking for would know about a high-class guy like the florist, B. B. knew, but he figured it was worth a shot. Same thing happened once they were inside. She told her story, showed him the watch, and never took her eyes off him. He swore an oath that he'd never seen a watch like it. Hand raised. She believed him, too.

In the cab, she told B. B. that Goldblatt was a worrier and not to trust him, either. If the cops got him, he'd talk and talk and talk.

"Figgered he would, tha's why Ah only do business with the wops, myself. The wops, they got this *Amuerta*—the code of silence—they never rat on nobody. You can deal with them."

She said she wanted to talk to them. If you had to fence a watch you took off a man you'd killed, you'd want to fence it someplace where they wouldn't talk. He had to admit she had a point there, but they wouldn't tell her nothing, no way, he said. She said she wanted to go anyway. She said it in such a manner that he knew there wasn't any way he was going to argue her out of it. Then she went to sleep.

She woke up with a start.

He said, "It be coming up here in a few blocks."

She sat up and looked out the window. The rain was pouring down steadily.

"Doan understan' why yo doin' this," he said.

"Why does it matter to you, Mr. Hanson?"

"Ah doan know, jez curious, Ah guess."

"Would you ask the same question if I were a man?"

"Guess not."

"Then don't ask."

They were in Brooklyn on Amstead Avenue, which ran along the old warehouses and crumbling piers by the river. The street was a maze of potholes, junk piles by the curb, abandoned cars along the sides.

"Nice neighborhood," she said.

"The Big Apple, they calls it. This the bruised part."

They pulled into the driveway between two warehouses. There was no one around. A few cars parked in the lot. They got out, carefully avoiding the puddles. The cabdriver nervously lit up a cigarette. "Don't take too long," he said.

"Hey, man, jez be cool," B. B. said. "Anybody hassles yo, yo give a honk, Ah comes out and shoos them away."

Catlyn and B. B. Hanson walked down the driveway with their coat collars turned up and went into a small doorway around in back. Once the door closed, a light came on inside automatically and they found themselves in a wide, carpeted hallway. At the end of the hallway was another door; beyond it an armed, pot-bellied security guard sat behind a desk.

"Long time no see, B. B. Who's this, Miss America?"

"Jez buzz me through, Charlie, we gotta see Mo."

The security guard pushed a button on the side of the desk and the wall behind him slid back. Inside was a small reception room with a counter. Tables on both sides of the room were piled high with furs, cameras, jewelry boxes, paintings, antiques. The counter man looked at B. B. over the top of his gold-rimmed glasses, then at Catlyn, then at B. B. again. He took his glasses off and wiped them, then put them back on. He had a small, round, serious face that looked as if it rarely wore a smile, but it was smiling now.

"Helloooo," he said, looking Catlyn up and down.

"Mo, this Miss Catlyn Cavanaugh," B. B. said. "She got something she want yo to take a look at."

Mo said to Catlyn, "You hang around with rabble like this, lady, you're going to get corrupted." He laughed. It came out like a smothered squeal.

She said, "Last night a close friend of mine was viciously attacked and killed on the street. The attacker was a young black man."

Mo nodded. "Yeah, it was on TV. What a shame." His pale skin reddened. He obviously didn't like thinking about the body count, only the booty.

Catlyn showed him a copy of the picture she had drawn. "You know him?" she asked.

He looked the picture over. As far as B. B. could tell, Mo showed nothing on his face at all. Mo shook his head. "Nope." He handed it back to Catlyn.

Then she showed Mo the watch. He looked at it. "We've had a couple like it, not recently."

"Thank you," she said.

On the way back to Manhattan she didn't nap, as B. B. thought she might. Instead, she looked out the window at the fog-blurred lights of the city for a long time, thinking. Then she turned to B. B. and said, "He knew him, I'm ninety-nine percent certain."

B. B. looked at her in the darkness of the cab and said nothing. How she knew, he had no idea. Witchcraft, maybe. He didn't believe in witchcraft. Anyway, a witch wouldn't look like this.

She said, "He hadn't seen the wristwatch, though. I'm

ninety-nine percent certain of that, too."

She didn't seem too pleased; B. B. thought that was a bit strange. She looked out the window again, rubbing her chin. Finally she said, "Is that place open all the time?"

"Eight at night to midnight."

"Can you get me some men to keep a watch on the place, to see if this man shows up?"

"What's it pay?"

"Whatever you think fair."

"Twenty bucks an hour, that'll do her. What yo want done, this turkey shows his face?"

"Have him followed. I want to know who he is, where he lives, his friends, everything."

"What about the police?"

"I said I wanted him brought to justice, Mr. Hanson, I didn't say I wanted him brought to the police."

B. B. nodded. A small shiver went up and down his spine as he wondered what she might have in mind for the dude. Make him into a toad maybe.

EIGHT

Catlyn got off the elevator and went out the front door of her apartment building. The doorman tipped his hat. "Morning, Miss Cavanaugh."

"Morning, Charles."

The rain was finally over. It was a bright and sunny morning, the air was clear, the streets full of people on their way to work. B. B. Hanson was waiting for her by the curb, smoking a cigarette and talking animatedly with a cab driver, a dark-skinned black with hair like white lambswool. The driver held the door open; Catlyn got in the back seat, and B. B. climbed in after her.

"Ah figures we head up to this fella Ah knows, runs this sort of halfway house where they still doin' a little trade. We could talk to some of the fellas, get an idea who might been workin' this area . . ."

"Just head for Central Park, driver," Catlyn said.

B. B. looked at her.

"I'm being followed," she said. "I went out for a jog about six-thirty. I think best when I'm jogging, it clears my head. I went to Fifth Avenue and over by the park. I took a rest and bought an orange juice from a street vendor. That's when I spotted him."

"Yo think he the guy who stuck yo friend Carter?"

"Couldn't be. The man following me was quite tall. I'd say six three, six four. Hard, bony features. Early to mid-thirties. I jogged down Fifth, running a little harder, then I doubled back. He was running parallel to me on the other side of the street, suit and tie, everything. He's awkward and gangly, but he could keep up with me. He was sitting in a blue car on the other side of the street when I came out just a moment ago."

B. B. rubbed his chin. "Yo sure 'bout this?"

"Damn it, Mr. Hanson, I'm not in the habit of imagining things!"

B. B. grinned. "I was only askin'." His hands went instinctively to his pockets for a weapon, but he wasn't carrying any. He suddenly realized they were about to make a stupid mistake. "Turn off," he said to the driver. "Head back downtown!"

"No, the park." Catlyn said.

The driver glanced back over his shoulder. "Well, what's it gonna be?"

B. B. said, "We get into the park, no weapons, we easy pickin'. Yo jez let me handle this, okay?"

"I thought we could get him isolated in the park," Catlyn said. "I want you to sit on him or something until he tells you what he's after."

"We gonna do a number on him, he gonna tell us all he know. Doan worry none."

Catlyn watched the slow, confident smile come over B. B.'s round face. "Okay," she said. "I want to talk to him and I don't want him hurt."

"We might bend him a little, but we won't break him . . . Let's take a ride over ta Walker's, my man," B. B. said to the driver. To Catlyn he said, "Yo gonna like Walker's."

They drove down Park to Fifty-seventh Street, then over to the West Side and then north, finally pulling up in front of a gym at Broadway and 121st. B. B. got out and held the door open for Catlyn. It was a slum neighborhood with

110

broken wine bottles in the gutters and a lot of black men hanging around leaning against walls or sitting on stoops. B. B. told the cabdriver to take the cab around the block. Catlyn and B. B. glanced back to see whether the Chevy was still following them. It was.

Catlyn and B. B. went up a flight of stairs to the second floor and through two swinging doors. Inside was a fair-sized gym: a boxing ring with two young blacks going at it with headgear; a half dozen others were punching bags and doing sit-ups and jumping rope. A few stopped what they were doing when Catlyn walked in. She nodded to them, but didn't smile. B. B. went over and talked to a couple of them; they seemed to agree with what he was saying. One laughed. B. B. gave them some money and came back over to Catlyn. "All set," he said.

"You going to tell me what this is all about?"

"Naw, spoil the surprise."

On the way down the stairs, B. B. said, "They say yo a pretty foxy chick."

"I'm glad they appreciate a fine piece of meat," she said. He didn't know quite what to make of that.

Their cab was waiting for them across the street. They got in and drove a few blocks, then turned into an alley and parked at the rear of the building. They were surrounded by high walls without windows. There was a lot of broken glass lying around and some tufts of grass were growing up through broken cement. A dead cat lay against a wall. They got out of the car and a moment later the blue Chevy drove in. One of the young blacks from the gym was driving, and the two others sat in the back on either side of the man who had been following Catlyn. They stopped and opened the door and pulled the man out. Blood ran down his nose and his head wobbled from side to side.

"Mr. Hanson, I said I didn't want him hurt. He just might be a policeman!"

The two young blacks who were holding him up dropped

him and ran off down the alley. They wanted no part of roughing up a cop. The third tossed B. B. the car keys and smiled. Catlyn figured he didn't mind roughing up a cop. In fact, by the wide smile on his face it looked as if he might have enjoyed it.

The cabdriver got back in the cab and turned his back on the whole proceeding. He wasn't involved in any way.

Catlyn bent over the injured man, who was kneeling on the cement trying to shake the cobwebs out of his head. She asked him whether he was all right. He shook his head. B. B. grabbed hold of him and lifted him to his feet as if he weighed no more than a sack of laundry.

"Now jez relax, man," B. B. said, patting him down for weapons. He didn't resist. Catlyn said to him, "Who are you and why are you following me?"

"My name is Maximilian Franks," he said feebly. "I'm a reporter—really a stringer—for the *Manhattan Business Times-Journal*." He wiped his nose with a handkerchief.

B. B. looked through his wallet. "Tha's what it say here," he said. He handed Catlyn a business card. "He got credit cards, pictures, membership cards to the Press Club . . . old airline ticket stub." He shoved the wallet back in Franks's pocket.

"Check the labels on his coat, Mr. Hanson."

B. B. took a look. "Nothin'."

"Why is that, Mr. Franks?"

"I never noticed, my cleaner must have removed the labels."

"What would a stringer for the *Manhattan Business Times-Journal* be doing following me around?"

He took a couple of deep breaths. Color returned to his cheeks. "I was going to do a story on Damian Carter. I started asking around a little, found out you were asking around a little, and thought there might be a story in it. You know, human interest kind of thing. Wealthy woman doesn't believe her friend was killed by a street criminal."

Catlyn was looking him over as he spoke. He had an honest look about him. His pupils didn't contract and he wasn't staring. Liars, she'd found, would often "look you in the eye" when they were telling the boldest of lies. This man wasn't doing that, and he was not avoiding her gaze, either—another common habit of liars. She concluded that if he was lying to her, he was damn good at it.

"Are you from Boston, Mr. Franks?"

"Don't tell me I've still got an accent."

"Just a trace. 'Cahtah,' you said. "Not 'Car*ter*.' Would you mind emptying all your pockets on the hood of the car please?"

"If you don't believe I am who I say I am, why don't you just call the *Manhattan Business Times-Journal* and ask them?"

"We will, but first, everything in your pockets, please."

He sighed and reached into his pockets and started walking toward the hood of the car. As he passed the young black, he shrugged, looked at the kid with a strange kind of smile and then suddenly, without warning, kicked him in the groin. The kick was square on target; the young man rolled over forward, exposing his neck. Franks brought a fist down on it hard and put the young black on the ground.

B. B. reacted swiftly for a big man; he charged Franks with both arms out, but Franks ducked, spun, and hit him on the side of the jaw. B. B. stumbled forward and bounced off the car, turning. Franks kicked him squarely in the face. The blow didn't seem to phase B. B., who shook his head and dove for Franks's midsection, but all he got was a knee in the face and a blow to the side of his head, dropping him to his knees.

"Keys please," Franks said to B. B., holding out his hand. B. B. reached into his pocket, retrieved the keys, and dropped them into Franks's hand.

"When I call the *Manhattan Business Times-Journal,*" Catlyn said, "are they going to know you?"

113

"Sure. It was a pleasure meeting you, Ms. Cavanaugh. I'm sorry it couldn't have been under more pleasant circumstances."

"Why don't we have dinner tomorrow night? How about Kosar's on Forty-fifth Street. Say, eightish?"

"Sorry," he said.

He brushed some of the dirt off his trousers and got in his car and drove off.

B. B. got to his feet, shaking his head. "He doan look like much, but he knew wha' he waz doin'. Nobody ever done me in quite so easy. He a professional fightin' man, believe-you-me."

"I believe you," Catlyn said.

B. B. and Catlyn helped the young black to his feet. "Gonna kill that son-a-bitch" was all he could say. He kept saying it over and over. They loaded him into the cab. The cabdriver said, "Never seen nothin' like it, and Ah been in New York twenty-eight years and Ah thought Ah'd seen it all."

B. B. said, "Yo never seen nothin', hear?"

"No, sir, B. B., Ah didn't see a God-blessed thing."

Catlyn told the driver to head for the nearest emergency hospital. On the way, she said, "He was sort of awkward until he made his move, and then he was like a ballet dancer."

B. B. said, "Yo want ta get yo'self another bodyguard, Ah ready to go back to the can."

"I'm sure you're more than adequate. This man was obviously trained in Oriental martial arts and took you by surprise, which would never happen again."

"Ah be watchin' out, that for sure." After a moment he said, "Wonder who he was. He sure weren't no newspaper man."

"I was just wondering that myself, Mr. Hanson."

* * *

114

George didn't tell Linda, but he thought her hair looked like a chicken caught in a hurricane.

And the dress she bought, he thought, would be suitable for giving at a Salvation Army collection box. It looked like a scaly orange peel and bulged in all the wrong places. But he knew if he said anything, the woman would go into one of her typical spoiled-American-housewife tantrums.

The protocol office from the White House had called first thing in the morning and told him that his black evening wear would be appropriate, so all he had to do was get new shoes, which squeaked sometimes and were a little pinched. Even though he didn't need it, he had stopped for a trim down at his barber's. Before lunch he went to the gym, where he overdid it just a little, but he felt great. They'd flown down to Washington early in the afternoon and took a suite at the Hilton.

A White House limousine picked them up at precisely eight o'clock. A servant came down the steps and opened the door for them. A sudden feeling of triumph washed over George. He felt keenly aware that he was in control of his own destiny. He was ready, he thought, as few men have ever been ready for an historic moment. His wife squeezed his hand and gave him one of those secret smiles that sometimes pass between husbands and wives. It said, "We're doing just fine, aren't we?"

For a brief moment he flashed back to the old days when they'd first met and how much he wanted her. And how he had her the first time after an antiwar rally. He had taken her into a pine grove in Regency Park where they drank cheap apple wine and she took him in her standing up, leaning against a pine tree, while he was trying to talk some damn sense into her.

Now here she was, the same woman, going into the White House to meet the President of the United States. He looked over at her and her smile made him forget the orange dress and the awful hairdo and, for a moment at least, he was totally in love with her again. ~

The First Lady greeted them in the foyer. "Please call me Janine, won't you?" she said. She was from Illinois, George knew, had been a schoolteacher, and was well known for her folksy charm. Her dress was yellow and as shapeless as his wife's and George breathed an invisible sigh of relief. The First Lady said, "The President had some last-minute business—very urgent—and he swore to me he would be down just the minute he could get away. But I know how you men are, women are supposed to love to gab, but it's really the men who once they get gabbing, they can't stop. Come, I want you to meet everyone. I think you know Senator Peters from California . . ."

There were thirty-two people seated for dinner. The President arrived late, jocular as usual, making a comic excuse about always having to avert World War III at the most inconvenient times. Everyone laughed.

The President was in his early sixties, with a round, friendly face, a ready smile, and a midwestern down-homeness in his speech. He called the voters "friends," pretended to be a farm boy, and gave the military everything they wanted. He was a political middle-of-the-roader, and read the polls before making up his mind about anything, including whether it was safe to like *Playboy* magazine.

George had read the KGB file on the man, and knew he watched porno films in private and had had a string of affairs with starlets, while all the time pandering to the stupid Moral Majority.

George was seated at the long dinner table close to the President; George's wife was placed on the other side of the table, a few seats away. He looked around for Ernest Ramsey, his nemesis, but he didn't see him. George hoped he wasn't coming, it would make things a lot more comfortable.

Across from George sat Hollis Wakefield, the financier

116

from Texas, the only man left who was any competition in his quest for the job of chairman of the Federal Reserve. Hollis Wakefield, a born-again Christian, had been a pioneer in interstate banking; he was not wealthy, but had many wealthy supporters. He was thin, a former Olympian, smooth in his manners, and absolutely ruthless when he had to be. George knew he wanted to be chairman of the Fed more than anything in the world. George had no idea why, and so far his investigators had not been able to find out. It had something to do with his belief in money as a moral *force*. George never quite grasped what that meant. Money was a force, true. But it had no morality of its own, George figured. It took on the morality of the man whose jeans it was stuffed into.

The first thing the President did after making an apology for being late was to tell what George considered a totally tasteless joke:

"This man went to the doctor with a pain in his stomach. They did tests and X rays, and that kind of thing. Finally the results were in. The man sat down in the chair opposite the doctor. The doctor leaned forward and said, 'I have some bad news for you, young man, you have cancer and have only six months to live.' The man wailed and wept and got faint, and finally he said, 'Doctor, what am I going to do?' The doctor thought and thought. Finally he said, 'I have it! Go to Russia and tell them you want to become a citizen. Shout on the street corner that Premier Krukov is an idiot. They will take you to the Gulag. Your six months will seem like a lifetime.' "

Everyone within earshot laughed and laughed, including Linda, and especially Hollis Wakefield. George laughed, too, but it made him nauseous.

Senator Waxman, who had the million dollars of KGB money in his back pocket, was at George's elbow. He deferred to George every chance he got and generally let it be known by his demeanor that he thought George was one hell of a guy. He asked George what he thought about this stock or that debenture, what was silver going to do over the next six months, and so on. George, who had the answers ready, played the role of expert-at-everything well. He told a humorous anecdote about a naive farmer losing a million in the futures market and making it up on his price support; everyone laughed. George was pleased with how things were going. It was obvious that Hollis Wakefield didn't know beans about the stock market or precious metal, and Waxman kept the conversation on those subjects and off interest rates, bonds, and the foreign money markets, subjects more to Wakefield's liking.

The meal consisted of a thin eggplant soup, then a romaine salad with marinated artichoke hearts, and two entrees: one, duckling with orange sauce; the other, rack of lamb with plum sauce. Both were served with potatoes Anna and undercooked carrots and snow peas. The portions, served on ornate blue china, were small and the food was lightly seasoned; the wine, dry and excellent. The courses were put in front of George and he sampled them, but he was playing his role so intently he paid little attention to what he was eating.

The President suddenly switched the subject to football: how were the Redskins going to do, and his own Chicago Bears—who he called the team of destiny—and most everyone leapt in.

George said, "I think they will be fine if Hobbs, their new running back, can rush for a hundred yards or more in at least fifteen games. And of course, Mitch Cunningham, their quarterback, must stay healthy. I look for them to be in the playoffs as NFC Central Division champs. Only then, they must look out for Dallas!" George looked at Wakefield, his rival and a Texan, as he said it. The Texan was smiling and tried to say how he didn't follow football much, which was no way to endear himself to President Hustead.

"Right you are, Corbett," the President said to George. "Just what I've been saying. They've got to run Hobbs right up the middle, get those linebackers frozen in there, that'll take the pressure off Cunningham. Very astute, Corbett, very good."

George, of course, knew the President's opinions on nearly every subject. At least as far as was known in Moscow Central. Football was the President's private passion. George found the game a bore, but he knew the fundamentals and it didn't take his research staff long to find out all he needed to know about the Chicago Bears.

The dessert was a delicate apple flan, which George hardly touched. The dinner over, the President rose and excused himself. "Business to attend to," he said. Everyone else was led into the Lincoln Room for coffee and conversation. A young aide asked George to come with him. George excused himself and gave a knowing nod to his wife.

When George entered the third-floor study, the President was sitting in a large high-backed chair, part of a "conversation group" of four chairs and a couch. Five other men were in the room: Budget Director Ernest Ramsey, George's principal opponent; the secretary of the treasury, Timothy McAfee, George's ally; Chad Spense, the President's chief of staff, who had gone, George knew, for Damian Carter; Harold Waxman, the bought senator; and the Texan, Hollis Wakefield. The President's chief economist, James A. Preston (one of George's allies) was to be there, the President explained, but he was called away unexpectedly to settle a trade dispute with China.

In the middle was a coffee table, crowded with liquor bottles and glasses and a bucket of ice. George poured himself a thin bourbon and water. He knew the President preferred drinking men and drank only Kentucky sour-mash bourbon. George passed up some excellent cognac. Hollis Wakefield was having a soda and lime.

The first surprise of the evening came when the President

took off his homey mask and let everyone have a look at the hard-bitten face of the real man underneath. "Well then, we are here for one reason and one reason only. That is to see which of you will be the next chairman of the Federal Reserve System. As you both know, or may not know, I had decided to pick Damian Carter for the job, so the one who gets it is definitely second choice. I'm saying this right out because I don't want any pretense between us. The Federal Reserve must work with this administration if we're going to get this damn economy off the rocks and make it work again. Unemployment at ten percent and inflation running up there at fifteen, twenty percent, is unacceptable. Now then, I want each of you to tell me just what you would do as chairman to help bring about these two goals: significant improvement in the unemployment situation, and bringing the inflation rate down to where Ronald Reagan had it before the deficits got him. Okay now, which one of you wants to go first?"

Hollis Wakefield said, "I don't mind." His thin face was drawn. "I think there is no doubt that this nation is facing a crisis of confidence. It is time, I think, to announce an austerity program. If we don't face it now, in a year or two we're going to be looking at inflation around two hundred percent and unemployment of forty percent. I sincerely believe that. These figures come out of studies conducted by the office of the Budget and Management. I'm not an alarmist, I'm a realist. The role of the Fed, in taking corrective action, is to hold the money supply down, which will hold inflation down. Unemployment will rise, bankruptcies will rise—in the short run—but it is the only way to save the nation from disaster. We've got to face the realities of the perilous situation now and act decisively; hold the lid on interest rates, let some of the weaker banks fold if they must, and try to defuse the bomb before it goes off. Any other course of action will result in an unparalleled disaster. I mean that sincerely."

Ernest Ramsey, the director of the budget, adjusted his wire-rimmed glasses. He had a boyish look about him, which George hated. Ramsey said, "I think Mr. Wakefield is absolutely correct."

"That certainly is a point of view," Senator Waxman said with a smile and a shrug. He had a way of trivializing what someone said without ever disagreeing with them.

The President was sipping his bourbon and looking at Hollis Wakefield over the top of his glasses. His eyes were fixed and his head was moving up and down as if he were silently assenting, but George got the impression he was keeping his mind open.

George poured himself a little more bourbon. "You don't bring prosperity and enterprise to a free people by putting the economy in a straitjacket," he said indignantly, giving Wakefield a hard glance.

Hollis Wakefield reddened. "Call it what you want. I say if we don't take control and manage the economy in some rational way, it will become a monster that will devour us."

George smiled easily. "If you lack imagination, foresight, and faith in the resources of the American people, I suppose that is all you can do."

"What's your theory, George?" the President asked.

George drained his glass before answering. He put the glass down on the table and, with an almost theatrical flourish, said, "I believe that the way to recovery is to expand the money supply at this time, to give the economy a shot in the arm. Consumer spending is down. Faith in the future is at an all-time low. There is more psychology to the economy than is generally recognized. If the people see the dark cloud coming, they brace for it; this alone can make the dark cloud into a destructive storm. The Reagan prosperity came about because he virtually *wished* it into being. People believed him when he said things were rosy; they went out and bought things, and when they bought things, they created jobs. And that is what this administration has to be about: creating jobs, not creating straitjackets. When the Fed increases the money supply and thereby frees up some credit, the American people will be given a 'buy' signal. Now is the time to get a car, a house, an appliance. We must create not austerity, but the monetary and fiscal climate of prosperity. Austerity is a wet blanket on an economy and it chases investment capital underground. Mr. Wakefield's ideas have been practiced by the British since World War II, and where has it gotten them? A stagnated economy and a confused body-politic. No, sir, Mr. President, the economy needs a shot of enthusiasm, and if I'm chairman of the Fed it will get it."

The President was looking at George over his glass now, nodding. But he said nothing.

"A blueprint for disaster," Hollis Wakefield said.

"Pie in the sky," Ramsey, the budget director said. "We've got to rein things in, just as Mr. Wakefield says. Christ. It's just this kind of crap that got us in the mess we're in."

Ramsey, George thought, was young and hot-headed, and well known for saying exactly what was on his mind. A trait common to young fools and senile old men. He was trying to anger George, but George wasn't going to fall for it.

Senator Waxman said, "I think George Corbett can help the administration save this damn country, and I want to see him get the chance to do it."

George thought for a moment the President was about to appoint him to the job right then and there, but they were interrupted by an aide who said there was a crisis in Lebanon and the secretary of state was on the phone.

"Duty calls, gentlemen," the President said, putting his folksy, friendly mask back on. "Thank you for your time. I'm glad I've had the chance to meet you both. We'll be letting you know."

On the way down the hall, Ramsey asked to speak to

George in private for a moment. His face was gray. He held George by the lapels and said, "I don't know what hold you have on Waxman, but I'm telling you, even though you may have mesmerized the President tonight, you will never be Fed chairman so long as I'm in this administration. The economy is fragile and you know it. I don't know what your game is, but I intend to find out. I suggest you withdraw your name from consideration, Mr. Corbett, because if you don't I intend to fight your nomination so long as I have a voice to do so."

Ramsey started to walk away. George grabbed him by the sleeve.

"Wait a minute, Mr. Ramsey. Listen to me, please. The President is not an economist, and so tonight I had to speak in layman's terms. Perhaps if you and I got to specifics we would find we are not so far apart when it comes to approach, even though our philosophical orientation is different. We, after all, want the same things . . ."

"You might cloud the issues with the President," Ramsey said, interrupting, "but you aren't clouding them with me." He strode off down the hall.

As he watched him go, George felt a sudden terrible anger rising in him. He knew then that Ramsey was not a problem that would just go away. He had to be dealt with, and quickly.

NINE

Carson Black, in the fifteen years she had known George Corbett, had never seen him so agitated.

They had been having breakfast, alone, in the dining room of her condominium in Falls Church, Virginia, outside of Washington. Before becoming a news anchor on WCBD, Washington, Carson Black had been a world class figure skater from New Jersey, had done TV sports commentary, and had appeared in a few made-for-TV movies. Her reporting was hard hitting; she was a feared interviewer, an abrasive lecturer, a workaholic, and an uncompromising feminist. He'd recruited her for the cause while he was a guest professor for one summer at Washington College.

George, pacing back and forth in Carson's dining room, said, "I had the President of the United States in the palm of my hand! I was saying all the things I knew he would want to hear: revitalizing the economy, ending inflation without unemployment—all the magical words the politicians coo over. And then this—this—this . . ."

"Blockhead," Carson said with a smile.

"Yes! Yes! Ramsey, the colossal blockhead, backs Wakefield to the hilt. To the hilt! Then in the hall, he tells me if I don't withdraw my name he's going to see to it that

I never make it anyway. And he could, too! He'll be working on the President day and night to see that I don't get it."

"You do take these minor setbacks so hard, George," she said with a mock-serious tone. "You should try to take a longer view of things. From the prospect of the historical dialectic. It is only a matter of time anyway until America folds." He knew she was only joking.

George, pointing a finger skyward, said, "When I'm chairman of the Federal Reserve Board, my dear, we won't have to wait much longer . . . I had the chairmanship sewn up. When Damian Carter was eliminated—"

"I thought you might have had something to do with that."

"I meant, ah, eliminated by fate . . ."

"Sure you did, George. Go on. When Damian Carter was eliminated by fate . . ." She gave him a wry smile.

George sat down at the table again. "It was Ramsey who got Hollis Wakefield to take Damian Carter's place."

"So you get rid of Wakefield like you got rid of Carter, what's the difference?"

"It would never work. I already thought of that and rejected the notion. Too coincidental. People really would start to take notice. No, no, it can't be Wakefield. What I've got to do is knock the prop out from under him."

Carson took a sip of coffee. "Which brings us to the purpose of your visit, am I right?"

George nodded. "We have very little time, Carson. What can be done?"

"I don't know much about Ramsey. What's he like, what are his habits?"

George took a few sheets of paper out of his suit coat pocket. "This is all I have on him. Let's see . . . he's a strict fundamentalist Christian, married with two young children, his wife is Senator Rumford's daughter. He's a graduate of Yale and has a Harvard M.B.A., got his law

125

degree also from Harvard."

"Seems Mr. Ramsey went to the right schools, married the right woman, lives in the right neighborhood. Do you know his itinerary for the next couple of days?"

"No."

"Our news department may be able to get it. Any bad habits? Wine, women, song?"

"No."

"Dope?"

"Not as far as I can tell."

She looked over the few sketchy notes. "Doesn't seem to be any cracks in the fortress wall, does there?"

"Not many."

"He seems to be of somewhat rigidly moral character."

"I think so."

"We might be able to work with that. Sensitive to scandal."

"Where's the scandal?"

"We might be able to find something after we dig a little bit."

"We're talking just a few days on this, Carson. Once the Senate receives the nomination of the President on Wakefield, that's it. I think this guy's Mister Clean. We're not finding any scandal here."

"Maybe we can *create* a scandal, then."

He looked into her confident eyes. She nodded her assurance. George said, "I would forever be in your debt, Carson."

"You already are, Comrade."

He reached across the table and patted her hand. "I'll leave it in your capable hands."

Carson watched George get into his rented Cadillac and drive down the driveway, past the pool and tennis courts, and head back to Washington. She admired the man, even loved him. But she had never been to bed with him. She didn't want to change the nature of their relationship.

It wasn't just that he'd helped her enormously with her career; the importance of that paled next to the fact that he had taught her how to transform her revolutionary leanings into direct action—without living like an outlaw.

She went into the bathroom and stripped for her shower. She liked the water nearly scalding hot and let it run while steam filled the room.

She often wondered what she would do without her underground life. Be bored to death, she supposed. Like most people she knew, she'd have no meaning or purpose to her existence. What was it she really did? She'd made a profession out of smiling into a camera for an hour and a half each day, reading stupid, biased news reports to ignoramuses too lazy to read a newspaper. So she was famous. So every Harriet Housewife and Johnny Lunchbucket knew her face when she went to the supermarket. So what?

She stepped into the shower and felt the first blast of hot water on her back. A stinging sensation ran up her spine and her whole body started to tingle. It was going to be a special day. She knew it.

Once she was out of the shower, she put on her robe and went into the bedroom and picked up the phone. The first call she made was to her newsroom. She said she wanted to do a story on Budget Director Ramsey and was going to try to do an interview. She asked to have someone call to get his itinerary for the next couple days. Her second call was to a woman named Rita Montgomery.

"Have to see you, Rita. Noon, okay?"

"Same place?"

"Same place."

"Yippeee!"

Carson donned a bright red sleeveless dress and a white jacket. She was careful with her makeup, putting on just a little more eyeshadow and longer eyelashes than she normally did. And *Sincerely Yours* cologne. It wasn't exactly to her taste, but Rita liked it a lot.

She knew all about what Rita liked and what she didn't like.

At ten-thirty Carson drove her BMW to her office at the television studio. She chatted with her rather affable but dull-witted co-anchor about an upcoming charity fund-raiser they were doing together, got the file on Ramsey from the file room, and told her secretary she'd be back at four. By eleven-fifteen she was driving north on Arizona Avenue.

She loved it when she had a project. She was always vaguely frightened when doing work for the cause and wondered how she would hold up under interrogation by the FBI if she ever fell under suspicion. She imagined they would beat her and do unspeakable things to her, put electrodes on her nipples and the like, even though in her more rational moods she realized she would have lawyers and would be out on bail. Then she'd imagine herself going on *Phil Donohue*, telling him he knows how bad things are for women, minorities, homosexuals, and so on in this country, crying needs which demand not reform, but retribution! She'd tell him she was righting wrongs the way our forefathers would, the way he would if he had any balls—yes, she'd say that right to his face! She hated mealy-mouthed liberals like Donohue who said things like "This issue needs looking into," but, damn it, never looked very deep and never in his life committed an act of retribution. Time was long since past when inequities needed looking into. Revolution time was here.

She wouldn't be pretending to be anyone else then; she could be herself. She'd say words like "balls" on television. Why not? She'd say "fuck 'em all." She'd set them on their goddamn ears.

The safe house was located in the hills outside of Essex, Maryland. It was surrounded by sycamore trees and completely hidden from the road. Less than thirty minutes from downtown Washington, D.C., it had been used for secret

128

meetings and had twice been the staging areas for assassination attempts. One, an Iranian target, back in the days of the shah, had failed. The other, a cousin of Somosa, had gone down in a hail of bullets on the streets of Philadelphia and his picture had been on the front page of the paper. Carson had interviewed the man not twenty minutes before. What a celebration there was that night!

The caretaker was sweeping the large porch when she drove up the circular driveway. He was an old Marxist from Romania who had fought against Hitler and came to the United States after the war and had worked in petty State Department jobs, sending what little information he could back home. He was retired now, took care of the house, told small lies to the neighbors about who owned the mysterious house on their street, and kept to himself with his homemade wine.

The caretaker nodded to Carson, came down the steps, and asked how long she would be needing the place.

"Just a few hours. Is there plenty of food and drink in the house?"

"Yes, as always."

"Good. I'm expecting company, see to it I'm not disturbed."

The caretaker walked off to his cottage. Carson entered the main house and found it a little stuffy. She opened some windows and turned on a fan. The interior was masculine: a heavy leather couch and chairs to match, thick carpeting, heavy oak dining room. The paintings on the walls were all Depression-era street scenes. The kitchen was well stocked with plenty of food. Upstairs there were three large bedrooms with extra closets. In the attic were cots and blankets. Twenty people could be put up in the house for a month and no one would ever have to go outside. There were two hundred cartons of cigarettes and eighty cases of beer and twenty cases of liquor in the storeroom in back.

Carson went up to one of the bedrooms, the one room in

the house she had been responsible for decorating. There was a small vanity, a large ornate dresser, and a chest in the Louis XIV style. Carson opened some drawers and found a yellow silk nightie. The ceiling and three walls were mirrored. The bed, which rotated, tilted, and could give a massage, was round and had a red satin spread and pillows that matched the drapes. Built into the headboard were speakers and tapes to play almost any kind of music. Behind one mirror were a serving bar and a cache of cocaine and the latest in designer drugs. The switches for the lights were behind another mirror. The lights could be soft candlelight yellow or colored, and could change and swirl and create a kind of fantasy, coordinated to the music. Like being in a rock video, only more mellow.

She stripped and put on the silk nightie, then fluffed her hair over her head and tied it with a yellow ribbon. She heard the car in the driveway about ten minutes later. She'd opened some champagne and was sitting on the bed sipping it. A car door closed. The front doorbell rang. She pushed the intercom.

"Yes."

"It's me, Rita."

Carson pressed the button to let her in; she came bounding up the steps and stood in the doorway. Rita was a blonde now, with frizzy-permed hair, bright red lipstick, and thick dark eyeliner, which made her look wild and reckless. She had on a black shimmering jacket and a loose-fitting high-fashion kind of jumpsuit and sandals. She was staring at Carson. "Christ," she said, "you look absolutely delicious."

"Care for some champagne?"

"How long have we got?" Rita asked.

"A couple of hours," Carson said, pouring champagne into a second glass.

Rita's eyes closed momentarily. "Heaven." She kicked off her shoes and sat on the bed, running her hand along

Carson's leg.

"Have some champagne, get you in the mood." Carson handed her the glass.

"I'm already in the mood," Rita said breathlessly. "I'm always in the mood. Why haven't you called? Where have you been?"

"Business."

"Business, always business." Her mouth formed a small pout. "Do we have any business? If we do, let's settle it first."

"There is a little something I want you to do, yes."

"Will I have to do it with a man?" Her eyes shut for a moment.

"I'm afraid so."

"Damn."

Carson said, "I promise if you do this for me, I won't be neglecting you as I have been. We might even go to Jamaica again."

"Do you swear to God, Carson? I mean, when I don't see you for a few days I get the dark depressions something terrible."

"I promise." She raised her champagne glass. "To us."

"What do I have to do? I'll do it, but I want to know."

"All you have to do is meet a man at a party, take him to our favorite motel, and let him fuck you. We'll have people there to get some good footage of it, and say ta-ta."

Rita gulped the champagne. "Who is he?"

"Some government guy. There's five thousand in it for you."

"You know how I hate doing shit like this, Carson. I hate it, hate it, hate it!"

"Please," Carson cooed as she untied the drawstring of the nightie, exposing a breast. It seemed to glow in the soft light, the nipple large and inviting.

Rita considered for a moment, her gaze going from Carson's breast back to her face. "This is the last time, okay? The very last time."

"Sure," Carson said. "Come to me now, Rita, let's forget everything else but each other." She leaned forward and pressed her lips against Rita's, taking Rita's hand to her breast.

Rita murmured, "Love me, Carson, love me, love me, love me!"

Catlyn and B. B. Hanson spent Friday morning checking on Maximilian Franks. Lieutenant Somers ran the license number through the state computers for them and found it was a rental car belonging to Manhattan Economy Rentals on Thirty-eighth Street. A clerk at the agency, once he heard they were looking into a murder, gave them Franks's credit card number, which Catlyn turned over to her attorney, who had a client in the credit card business. By ten-fifteen they had Franks's address on Green Street in Boston. Catlyn contacted a private eye firm in Boston to check him out. The first thing she did when she got home was put a call through to the private eye and leave a message on his machine.

Catlyn and B. B. spent the rest of the day showing the sketch around to fences and street thieves all over Manhattan Island until B. B. felt he was ready to fall down from exhaustion. Where'd this woman get her energy, he wondered. Drugs or somethin'? They got back to her apartment at eleven o'clock that night without having a particle of luck. A couple of guys in a pool hall on West 131st showed something in their eyes when Catlyn showed them the picture, but they wouldn't say anything.

B. B. slumped into a chair. "Ah tole yo over an' over, there ain't no way this guy who done in poor Mr. Carter is a reg'lar working junkhead."

Catlyn said, "I told you that's what I thought in the beginning, but now I'm not so sure. How do you explain the fact that the man at that warehouse in Brooklyn definitely recognized the drawing of the man? My original idea that Damian's killer was disguised might be right. But still, I'm sure that man recognized the picture, now how do you explain that?"

"That's a great puzzlement. 'Cept how we know he did reconnize it?"

"I read it in his face. I've made a science of reading people's faces, Mr. Hanson."

Anybody else said that, he'd argue with it, but he believed her. He said, "Why doan yo call me B. B., everybody else do."

"That's fine. My friends call me 'Cat.' "

"Cat. Like a cat, too. Like ta nap."

"Are the men you've had watching that warehouse absolutely certain our man didn't show up today?"

"Yeah, they'd call, they find out anythin'. They good men."

"Okay, we've pretty much covered Manhattan, where do we go next?"

"Doan know." B. B.'s eyelids were drooping. She let him go to sleep. Catlyn made some coffee and took a seat by the window, watching the traffic and thinking. She was exhausted, too, but she knew how to push past the exhaustion, like a long distance runner pushing past his fatigue.

The traffic below was light for Friday night. If Damian hadn't been killed she'd be down there in one of those cabs, she thought, going to a symphony at Carnegie Hall, or to a theater. Instead she was hunting a killer. And tomorrow she'd be at a memorial service in his honor, which would take time away from her investigation, but she figured Damian's son would be needing her. But then she'd be right back at it. Somehow, encountering the man who called himself Maximilian Franks had encouraged her. She was feeling more confident that she had been right all along in assuming Damian's murder had not been a random

133

street crime.

The phone rang. She answered it in her study so she wouldn't wake B. B. It was the private eye from Boston returning her call.

"What have you found out?" Catlyn asked.

"Got a little lucky, Ms. Cavanaugh. The Green Street address of the subject turns out to be one of those private post office box places. I was able to get it out of the clerk that this Franks guy—he's supposed to be a legit writer who's on the road a lot—but after I greased her palm with a few Thomas Jeffersons she tells me he don't ever pick up his mail there."

"Where does he pick it up?"

"It's forwarded to another box in New York, New York, but she couldn't tell me where, 'cause the guy that owns this rent-a-box joint keeps where he sends the mail strictly to himself. So I had to give her a couple more Thomas J's and she tells me there's an emergency phone number in case certain kinds of letters come through, which she will give me. So I says, if that's all I can get, I'll take it. Here's the number: 556-9840."

"The area code?"

"Two-one-two. Okay, Ms. Cavanaugh? I got you down for one day plus ex'es. You'll be getting my bill Monday, please pay it promptly."

"I always do."

Catlyn hung up the phone and immediately dialed the number. The woman who answered said, "Good evening, Israeli Consulate."

"Mr. Maximilian Franks, please."

After a pause, the woman said, "There is no one here by that name." She hung up.

Catlyn went into the living room and shook B. B. He sat up and rubbed his face. "Ah dreamed Ah was still in the can. Man, that place sure do work on yo mind."

She said, "That man, Franks, he's not a reporter. He's

an Israeli agent. I'll bet you anything."

B. B. shook his head. "He look about as much like James Bond as my foot."

"I think, Mr. Hanson, you are a victim of media stereotypes. Think about it a minute. He's been trained to fight. He doesn't live anywhere. His mail goes to another box someplace. If certain mail comes in, the box rental place in Boston has instructions to call the Israeli Consulate in New York."

B. B. scratched his head. "Ah thinks this matter gettin' complicated. Yo mind if Ah have a little taste of somethin' from yo bar ta oil my imagination?"

"Of course not, Mr. Hanson. Help yourself."

"Here we go again. B. B. they calls me. B. B., like a BB gun."

"Why would an Israeli agent want to follow me around?"

B. B. poured himself some Russian vodka and drank it straight down. It rocked him back on his heels. "Oooooo, that set a cannon off in yo haid."

Catlyn took a long look at the portrait of Franks she'd sketched. "You're right, though, he doesn't have the look of a cold-blooded espionage agent. A spy should be steely-eyed, square-jawed."

B. B. laughed. "Guy Ah knows used to be robbin' banks down in Florida. He say every gun he ever knew any good looked like Woody Allen, somebody like that." He tried a swallow of brandy, then a little Scotch. "Nice place yo got here. Nice little bar, too. Have a real party here, invite a few hundred friends, everybody have a real good time."

"What do you say we head over to the Israeli Consulate and see if anybody knows this face?"

"It almost midnight, Cat!"

"Afraid you might turn into a pumpkin?"

"Ah ain't slep' but two hours since Ah took this job."

"You can sleep in the cab on the way over."

135

As they were going out the door, the telephone rang. Catlyn grabbed it.

"I hope I didn't wake you, Ms. Cavanaugh. This is Lieutenant Somers. You said to call you as soon as we found something out."

"Is it good news?"

"We've got the man who murdered Mr. Carter. We'd like to see if you could identify him."

"That's wonderful news! Where are you holding him?"

"The coroner has him, I'm afraid. Somebody went and cut his throat."

TEN

Lieutenant Somers ran his hand through his unruly hair. He had looked tired when Catlyn first met him, and now he looked even more so. His tie was loose and his collar unbuttoned, and a cigarette dangled from his mouth.

"I'm sorry to have to put you through this," he said to Catlyn. He'd been waiting for her when she came through the door of the old morgue building on First Avenue. She had expected the place to smell like chemicals and look like a dungeon. It looked more like a hospital and smelled of flowers.

Somers said, "I'm afraid I don't need you to see the body after all. Charles McMurty, the doorman from your apartment, was already here and gave us a positive ID."

"Please, Lieutenant. I'd like to see the body. I want to know it's the right man myself."

The detective took a drag on his cigarette, then nodded. "Who's this?" he asked, referring to B. B.

B. B. hadn't looked at the lieutenant at all. His distaste for cops was written all over his face.

"This is Mr. Hanson, Lieutenant. My bodyguard."

B. B. nodded. "No crime in bein' a bodyguard."

The lieutenant said, "Why do you feel you need a bodyguard, may I ask?"

137

"These are perilous times in which we live."

"Words have gotten back to me that you've been doing some digging on your own."

"Not afraid of the competition, are you, Lieutenant?"

He snorted. "Anybody wants this job can have it."

"I'd like to see the body now, Lieutenant."

"Okay, this way."

They went down the hall to a small room with some folding chairs set up near the elevator on the first floor. Somers's partner, a tall black man, was standing by the door with his hands in his pockets. He looked at B. B. and said, "I know you, man."

B. B. said, "Small planet, ain't it, tightass?"

"Watch with the mouth."

"Sorry. Ah means 'Sergeant Tightass.' Yo still takin' a little grease ta let the boys do a little dealin' by the 137th Street and Broadway subway station?"

The sergeant flared, but Somers told both of them to cool it.

The four of them went in to see the body, which was on a stretcher under a sheet. There were bright fluorescent lights over the stretcher. Somers gestured where he wanted Catlyn to stand, near the body's head. B. B. stood next to her. The lieutenant pulled back the sheet gingerly, leaving it folded over the dead man's throat.

"Just like you described him, Miss Cavanaugh," Somers said. "You said a hundred and forty pounds, and he's just a little over that. He even has the thin little scar down the side of his nose."

"Could you take the sheet down a little?"

"It isn't pretty, Miss Cavanaugh."

"I want to see his neck, Lieutenant."

"All right. Fine." Somers pulled the sheet down to the shoulders. The gash in the neck looked like something went into the side of the neck and cut outward, toward the front. The windpipe, veins, and arteries were sticking out through

138

the gash like hoses. The blood around the wound had dried to a dark brown.

B. B. and Catlyn both examined the neck closely. "That's the way they teach you to do it in the Army," he said. "When you take out a man from behind, you shove the knife in the side and push it out to the front."

"Were you in the Army, Mr. Hanson?" Catlyn asked.

"No. A partner'a mine, he tell me."

"The edges of the wound are clean, except for some tiny marks," the lieutenant said. "It was a clean, sharp knife, with a serrated edge. Could have been a kitchen knife."

"Could be a combat knife, too," B. B. said.

Catlyn put the sheet back over the man's head. "He looks very much like the man who killed Damian Carter, except this man is not as muscular."

Somers grunted and said, "That's because, in death, the muscles relax—until rigor mortis sets in, which usually occurs twenty-four to thirty-six hours after death."

"May I see the clothes he was wearing?"

"If you like."

He sent his partner, the tall sergeant, after them.

"He had the watch on him, too," Somers said. "Inscribed exactly as you reported. His name was Ambrose Poindexter; he was arrested as a juvenile for purse snatchings. No adult offenses—that's why we didn't have a mug shot of him."

"He stupid?" B. B. asked. He was looking at the dead man's arms and between his toes for needle marks. "Only a stupid man not gonna throw that watch in the river, he kill a man for it."

"You have made an excellent point there, Mr. Hanson," Catlyn said.

"Somethin' else," B. B. said. "This fella, he no junkie. He not even snortin'. No tracks. What he doin' workin' the streets?"

Somers lit a cigarette. "Not every young black in this

139

town working the streets is a junkie. This is the man, Miss Cavanaugh. I'm sure of it."

"Well, I'm *not* sure of it."

Somers made a face and stared up at the ceiling. His partner returned with a technician holding two brown bags, one large, one small. Somers opened the small bag and handed a watch to Catlyn. "Here, look at it. This is the watch which was taken from Mr. Carter the night he was killed, is it not?"

She looked at it, turned it over, and nodded. "Yes, it is."

"Thank you," Somers said with a nod of satisfaction. He handed the watch back to the technician, who returned it to the small bag.

"May I see the clothing?" Catlyn said.

The sergeant opened the large bag and spread its contents out on a table. Catlyn checked them over: a jacket, a shirt, a pair of jeans, a pair of brown shoes, socks with holes in them, underwear. The sergeant put the contents of the smaller bag on the table. In addition to Damian Carter's gold watch there was a wallet with a library card, a membership card to the Boys' Club, eight dollars in bills, fifty-five cents in change, a few subway tokens, and a gold cross on a gold chain.

"Look at this," Catlyn said to Somers. "This is a tight chain. When Damian was attacked, his attacker had his shirt open, and I would have noticed if he was wearing this."

Somers's hand went to his forehead as if he'd been suddenly struck with a headache. "Perhaps he didn't wear it all the time," he said. "And it might just be possible that in the thirty seconds or less that you had to look at the man you didn't see everything about him there was to see."

"If he'd been wearing this chain around his neck, I'd have seen it. And the man who killed Damian was more muscular. This man is definitely *not* the man who killed Damian Carter."

The tall sergeant said, "Sheeeeeeeeeeet."

"So," B. B. said, "the next question is, who kill this blood here, 'cause yo sure as hell know it weren't no dumb-ass mugger. A knife expert done that work."

"Good point, Mr. Hanson."

"Thank you, Cat." B. B. folded his arms across his chest and looked smugly at the sergeant, who glowered at him.

Lieutenant Somers said, "We have here the body of a man who perfectly matches the picture you yourself drew of him. We have checked with the man's mother and she says he was not home and his whereabouts were unknown at the time Damian Carter was killed—listen to me now, Miss Cavanaugh—and he had the very same watch in his pocket that had been taken from Mr. Carter at the time he was killed. You yourself have verified that."

Catlyn said, "Can I have a cigarette, Lieutenant?"

He shook a Camel out of his pack for her and lit it with his Zippo.

"Before you continue with your argument," she said, "listen to me. You are faced with a dilemma. I'm telling you this is not the man who killed Damian Carter. I am ready to swear to that in a court of law. This man was obviously killed by a professional hit man using combat techniques. Someone has gone to an awful lot of trouble to convince you to close your case, Lieutenant. I think you ought to start asking yourself, who could that be and why did he do it?"

"Miss Cavanaugh," Somers said evenly, "I hate to disillusion you, but Damian Carter was killed by a common street criminal in a random act of violence. By this man here. And that's the way I'll tell it to the coroner at the inquest."

"Then I guess we have nothing else to talk about," Catlyn said. "Except I would like the name and address of this man's next of kin, his employer—anything else you know about him."

Somers sighed and looked at his partner. "Give it to her," he said.

At nine-thirty the following morning, Catlyn's cab stopped in front of the brownstone on West 103rd. She put down the paper she was reading. There was an article on page 8 about the killing of Ambrose Poindexter, which included a statement from "a police spokesman" that definitely identified Poindexter as the killer of Damian Carter. Catlyn shook her head.

She pushed a fifty-dollar bill at the driver. "Wait for me, even if it's an hour."

"Okay, lady, hey, you bet." He kissed the bill and shoved it in his shirt pocket.

Catlyn was wearing a skirt and blouse and a short, tan leather car coat. Her hair was combed back and she had put on her reading glasses, which she almost never wore when someone could see her. She claimed she didn't look good in glasses. The truth was, she associated glasses with growing old, and she didn't like to think about that. She was wearing them now so she'd look "professional."

The front door of the apartment building was ajar and she could have gone in, but she didn't. She pushed the bell for Apartment #2 and waited. A man's voice said, "Yeah?"

"My name is Catlyn Cavanaugh. I'd like to speak to Mrs. Poindexter if I could, please."

"We've had a tragedy in the family lately and we don't wish to see nobody—especially reporters."

"I'm not a reporter, I have some information for Mrs. Poindexter that I'm sure she'll want to hear. I know her son didn't kill Damian Carter and I'm going to try to prove it."

A moment later a black woman came out and stood in the doorway. Her face was drawn; her eyes, puffy and red. She was wearing a black dress and had a gold cross on a chain around her neck. Catlyn guessed she was in her late

142

forties and had done a lot of living.

"You with the police?" she asked Catlyn.

"No. I was with Damian Carter the night he was killed. We were friends. I don't think your son had anything to do with Damian's murder. May I speak with you for a few minutes?"

She nodded and attempted a smile. But her eyes were full to the brim with suspicion.

"Come in," she said.

The apartment was tiny and cramped, and the ancient flowered wallpaper had faded to a pale yellow. The threadbare gray carpet was worn through in spots. But the place was clean. Mrs. Poindexter introduced her brother, Simon Liston.

"Simon came up last night from New Orleans. He's the only family I got now."

Simon was a bit younger than his sister, more suspicious. Catlyn noted a lot of bitterness and sadness in his eyes, and pride, too.

"I know this is a terrible time for you and your brother, Mrs. Poindexter, but the man who killed Damian and probably killed your son is at large and I want to see him brought to justice. May I sit down?"

Mrs. Poindexter glanced at her brother for a silent okay before she nodded. "Go ahead, we'll hear you out."

Catlyn told her about Damian Carter's death and what she saw and why she thought it couldn't have been her son. When she was finished, she saw relief flood into the woman's eyes. "I knowed that boy of mine was no killer, nobody be listening."

Simon gave her a hug. He smiled at Catlyn now. "Even if you don't never prove it, we grateful you coming here and telling us."

Mrs. Poindexter came suddenly to her feet. "I be forgetting my manners, I didn't offer our guest a little refreshment. What would you like? Coffee, tea?"

"Nothing, thanks. I do have a few questions, if you don't mind."

"Fire away," Mrs. Poindexter said.

"The police have been here, I'm sure. Did they ask you where your son was the night Damian Carter was killed? Tuesday evening, the day after Labor Day."

"My Ambrose would never say where he was going, and so I don't know. He weren't here, that's all I know. He got into trouble sometimes, I guess there ain't no hiding that fact. The Lord knows I tried the best I could with the boy. He was bad sometimes, I admit it. He talk to me terrible vulgar, too, sometimes. He had a lot of hate and anger in him. But he weren't no killerman. No ma'am, he didn't have the killer in his soul." She shook her head and the tears started coming.

"What did he do? How did he spend his time?"

"He play a pretty good game of pool," Simon Liston said.

"I tell him that game gonna be the death of him," Mrs. Poindexter said. Her voice cracked.

"You think he might have been playing pool last Tuesday?"

Mrs. Poindexter shook her head. "He left his stick right there in the corner."

"Where is his stick now?"

"He had it with him when he . . . when he got murdered." Her lip curled when she said it.

"The police didn't recover it?"

She shook her head. "We don't know where it is. It came in a case, you know, it would unscrew and you carried it in two pieces."

Catlyn nodded. "Could I see his things?"

"He didn't have nothin'."

Ambrose's bedroom was not much more than a large closet. In the nineteenth century, when the building had been a single-family house, the room might have been used

144

for storage.

Catlyn went through Ambrose Poindexter's drawers and found nothing but clothes, a few dollars, some jewelry, clippings of his days as a high school basketball player, a few crude poems he'd written to a girl, some pictures cut out of *Playboy* magazine, and a book: *The Complete Book of Billiards.* She looked behind the dresser, under the bed, and in the closet. No hidden compartments.

"Not much, is it?" Mrs. Poindexter said.

"Is this everything?"

"He didn't like to have many things. What you looking for?"

"I'm trying to convince the police to continue their investigation. I was hoping your son might have had a knife."

"What difference that make?"

"The doctor who did the autopsy on Damian Carter might be able to prove it wasn't your son's knife that killed him."

Mrs. Poindexter looked at her brother, who nodded. Then she said, "I found it hidden under the rug out in the hallway one day, a month ago. I know it be his. I'll get it."

The knife was a cheap switchblade with an imitation ivory handle. "Can I show it to the police?" Catlyn asked.

"Sure."

"I don't know if it'll mean anything to them. I just want to show them what kind of knife your son carried, because the one that killed Damian was twice as big." Catlyn put it in her jacket pocket. "I'll see you get it back," she said.

"I never want to see it again," Mrs. Poindexter said. "I don't even know why I kept it. Maybe I was hoping he'd grow more responsible and I'd use it to remind him of what he left behind." Then she said, "I'll pray for you, the Lord might keep you safe."

When Catlyn came out and got into the cab, Shirley Dills was watching from across the street. She watched the cab drive away and thought it over for a couple of minutes—should she mind her own business or maybe try and see if there wasn't a few bucks to be made? She decided it was possible. She went to the phone and called Robert Park at The Horned Toad.

B. B. was chatting with the doorman when Catlyn's cab pulled over to the curb. He waved at her excitedly and came running over. "That turkey Franks, we found him! Come on, hurry!"

He got into the cab and told the driver to head for Forty-second and Second and added, "Keep the pedal to the metal, friend."

"We spotted him goin' inta the Israeli Consulate 'bout an hour ago," he said to Catlyn. "Ah called and left a message on yo machine."

"I should have called in, sorry."

"How'd it go with Ambrose's mama?"

"He was an only child. She knew he was bad, loved him anyway."

"She got somebody with her?"

"Her brother."

"Tha's when family counts. When death makes his call at yo house."

The traffic was heavy and the cab had a lot of trouble making its way down Second. When they got within a few blocks, Catlyn paid the cabbie and they started off on foot. As they turned the corner onto Forty-second, B. B. spotted a young Puerto Rican leaning against a car.

"Tha's my man, Diego." He pushed some bills into the kid's shirt pocket. Diego beamed.

"He still in there," Diego said.

"Good," B. B. said. "This Miss Cavanaugh. She good

people."

Catlyn thanked him for his help. Diego beamed again, tipped his hat, and headed for the subway.

"Now then," B. B. said, "what's next?"

"Mrs. Poindexter said Ambrose was a pool player. He went out with his pool stick the night Damian was killed. Could you check around and maybe find out if Ambrose was playing pool that night, and with whom?"

"What yo be doin'?"

"I'm going to talk to Mr. Franks."

B. B.'s eyes went to the consulate and then back again to her. "Maybe this ain't such a good idea."

"You worry too much, Mr. Hanson."

"B. B., like a BB gun."

ELEVEN

The consulate had a high brick wall around it, topped by wrought-iron bars with pointed tips. Decorative, yet hard to scale. The heavy wooden gate was ajar, opening on a courtyard with thin-slatted wooden benches. No cover for anyone trying to storm the place. An Israeli Marine stood guard by the front door and told her they were not opened on Saturday. She told him she was waiting for a friend who worked there, and asked if she might wait in the courtyard.

She took a seat on a wooden bench with full view of the front door. She lit a cigarette. A man wearing a suit and walking a small dog on a leash came out and tethered the dog to a bench and went back inside. She finished her cigarette and started on a second. A woman in a housecoat was watching her idly from a second-floor window. Suddenly the front door opened and there was Maximilian Franks, shaking hands with a bald-headed man. Then Franks came out the door and started across the courtyard. He spotted her right away. He stood frozen for a moment, staring at her. Then a slow smile showed on his face. He walked over to her.

"Somehow the credit card got me, didn't it? At the rental place."

"Yes," she said.

He bowed and clicked his heels together. "I congratulate you on your resourcefulness."

"Can we go someplace and talk, Mr. Franks?"

"Do you like Chinese food, Miss Cavanaugh?"

"Anything but Cantonese."

148

The Hung Chow Restaurant was across the street and down the block. She ordered fried squid. He ordered Mongolian beef. They agreed to share some sizzling rice soup and fried won tons. The restaurant was small, with tiny red and black Chinese lanterns hung from the ceiling. The waitress was an old Chinese woman who mumbled English and didn't smile. Her steps were short and quick.

"Your name is not Franks, is it, Mr. Franks?"

He looked at her innocently, then his slow smile spread across his lips. "No," he said, "it isn't."

"And you aren't a newspaperman, are you?"

His eyebrows went up. "Yes, I am."

"No, you're not. You're a spy for the Israelis."

"No, I'm not. Really. I'm an economist working as a reporter."

"Are you an Israeli?"

"Yes and no."

"Would you mind explaining that?"

"I hold dual citizenship. I'm Israeli, but I'm also an American. Red, white, and blue. Baseball, Mom's apple pie. I was a Duncan yo-yo champ when I was nine, won a rhinestone-studded yo-yo. I grew up in Boston. Pittsford, actually. Right out of Boston. My parents still live there."

"Don't they hang spies these days in the good old U.S.A.?"

"I wouldn't know."

"Why were you spying on me?"

"I told you, I'm not a spy," he said firmly, exasperation creeping into his voice. "I'm an economist. Did my undergraduate work at Syracuse. I also have an advanced degree in economics and an M.B.A."

"What's your real name?"

He sighed. "You're not buying any of this, are you? I'm such a god-awful liar. Okay. My name is Cohen. Roger I."

"What's the *I* stand for?"

"Do I have to say?"

149

"It's not Irving, is it?"

"It is—God, I hate it." He puckered his lips.

"Okay, your name is Roger Irving Cohen and you're from Pittsford, Massachusetts."

"That's right—I wasn't kidding you about that."

"You have a degree from Syracuse University—"

"In international finance."

"And an M.B.A.?"

"Yes. *Hahvahd.*"

She watched his eyes closely.

"And you're a spy for the Israelis?"

"No, no, no, no." He waved his hands in front of him as if he were wiping away the accusation. "I'm just a reporter. The *Manhattan Business Times-Journal*—and occasionally I'm a stringer for the *Tel Aviv Times*, the Israeli English-language paper."

She said nothing. She waited. She didn't even blink.

He said, "It's not polite to stare."

"It's not polite to lie."

"Okay. You want the truth, unembellished, Boy Scout's honor?"

"From the very beginning."

He looked around, perhaps to stall, perhaps to see whether anyone was listening. He straightened his tie. He brushed his hair back on the sides, then said, "It's simple really. The Israelis are dependent on America, right?"

"Right."

"If America crashes, so does Israel. What happens here economically is very important to Israel."

"Let's not have a civics lesson. Give me the who, what, why, when, and where."

"All right. I went to Israel a few years back to work on a kibbutz. You know, get back to the earth, my ancestral roots, that kind of thing. Very idealistic. I had been working for Lehman Brothers Investment Bankers at the time. Right here in New York. When the Iraelis found out that I was a boy wonder economist I was referred to the *Tel Aviv Times*. I went to work for them but it wasn't a full-time salary, so they got me this job working with the *Manhattan Business Times-Journal* under another name—Henry Bledsoe. You call and ask if they have a Bledsoe, they'll tell you. I do write for them. And I write for the *Tel Aviv Times* under my own name. It isn't like working on a kibbutz, but I feel like I'm doing important things keeping the people informed."

"Why Maximilian Franks?"

"My American editor doesn't want me to do investigative reporting using my Bledsoe pen name. Hey—all these names even confuse me."

"Your story is getting weirder by the minute—what's your connection with the consulate?"

"They take messages for me. The Israelis know the importance of information, so the government helps out all the papers." He was smiling affably now.

"I saw you fight with Mr. Hanson. For a bookworm, you handle yourself pretty well."

"I have a black belt in judo—third degree. I learned it at the Jewish Community Center on O'Farrell Street in Pittsford. Honest. I'm not a spy. I wouldn't know the first thing about it."

The waitress arrived with the sizzling soup and ladled it into bowls. It was still early and the restaurant was nearly deserted.

"And why were you following me?"

He was relaxed now, tasting his soup. "I was on assignment to cover the appointment of a new chairman of the Fed. I figured it was going to be Damian Carter because Ernest Ramsey was behind him, so I was going to do a story on him. When he was killed, I thought that it was a strange coincidence. You seemed to believe the same thing, so I was following you around to see what you were up to. I had to satisfy myself that it was not some vast conspiracy. I'm satisfied."

151

"That there is no connection between Damian Carter's death and the fact that he was going to be named Fed chairman? How do you know that? Do you believe he was killed by Ambrose Poindexter?"

"Yes."

"He wasn't. I was there when Damian was killed and I have twenty-eight stitches to prove it. I saw the killer from as close as you and I are at this moment."

"And?"

"And it was not the same man I saw lying on the slab in the morgue."

He shook his head. "I spoke to Lieutenant Somers. He's satisfied this Poindexter was the killer. He told me how witnesses imagine things sometimes. When the killer is caught, eyewitnesses often can't identify him."

"I'm not your typical witness," she said coolly. "I know what I saw. The man who killed Damian had a more muscular neck and smelled of furniture stain."

He nodded agreement and his expression was thoughtful, but she could tell he didn't believe her. He had that look in his eyes men get when they don't want to argue with a "dumb" woman.

"Okay," she said. "Let me tell you some things about yourself, okay?"

"Sure."

"So far, Mr. Cohen, most everything you've told me is one hundred percent bullshit."

His eyes widened.

"Your name isn't Cohen, just like it isn't Franks or Bledsoe."

"It's Cohen, really. You want to see my ID?"

"Don't bother. You work for the Israeli Intelligence. I'm positive of that. You never learned martial arts in any community center."

He smiled at her and shook his head resolutely.

"Okay," she said. "When we first met you said you were

following me because you wanted to do a story of a murder victim's woman friend chasing down clues to his murder. It would make a good story, don't you think? Even if I'm just a nut, I have to be a printworthy nut. So how come you aren't following through on that?"

"I probably should. I would if I were a good reporter, but I'm not. Primarily I'm an economist."

"*Primarily*, you're a spy."

He cleared his throat and looked around. "Please don't say that so loudly."

She reached across the table and tapped his hand. "Listen to me, Mr. Double-O-Seven, I have to know what you know. Your people are onto something, aren't they? There's no reason to hold it back, we both want the same thing. Maybe I could help you."

"I can't tell you anything, I don't know anything."

"You know that Ambrose Poindexter didn't kill Damian, don't you?"

"I have to believe the police."

"But you don't."

"But I do."

"No, you don't. What did you find, Mr. Spy? Tell me! I happened to think a great deal of Damian Carter, and by God I'm going to see somebody pays for what they did to him—and you and anybody else better not stand in my way!"

"All right, relax, take it easy."

"Talk to me, Mister Franks-Cohen-Super Spy."

"All right. There was a little something I picked up—in my research as a reporter."

"And what was that little something?"

"At the time Damian Carter was murdered Ambrose Poindexter quite possibly was at a VD clinic in Brooklyn. I showed a picture of Ambrose around, they said it could have been him. They see a hundred patients a night, so they couldn't be sure. He checked in under the name of Andy

153

Washington."

"Now isn't that interesting? Now isn't that extraordinarily interesting?"

"We thought it was."

"We? Your outfit? The Israeli secret service?"

"I meant, we at the paper. Come on, I've told you who and what I am. I've been completely straight with you."

"Have you told the police what you've found?"

He shook his head.

Catlyn was quiet for a moment, thinking. The waitress brought the fried won tons. Catlyn was feeling a strange chill. She had never had a clear notion as to who had had Damian killed, but it had never occurred to her that his murder might be political.

Suddenly she looked at him and said, "Tell me your real first name, please."

"Sam . . ."

"Come on. Let's be friends. At least let's tell each other who we really are."

"Oscar. Oscar Feldman."

She smiled. "That's really it, isn't it?"

He nodded.

"I like it."

"I do too," he said.

"May I call you Oscar?"

"May I call you Catlyn?"

"Cat."

"All right—Cat." He smiled.

Catlyn said, "You have no hard evidence that Damian's murder was politically motivated?"

"None. But if you're right and Ambrose Poindexter did not kill him, it means someone else did. Someone clever enough to pin it on Poindexter. Someone who is a master of his craft, no doubt hired to do it, and he probably didn't come cheap."

"So all we have to do is figure out who would pay to have it done. Who would that be, do you think?"

He shrugged. "I'm baffled. A rival? Someone with a grudge?" He hushed his voice: "There are five people who I believe would gain a great deal from Damian Carter's death. I've done quite a bit of checking. One is Damian Carter's son, who stands to inherit somewhere in the neighborhood of fifty million dollars."

"I know Damian's son, you can cross him off your list."

"I'm painting by the numbers, that's all. I'm not saying any of these people necessarily had anything to do with it. If you don't like the son as a suspect, how about Herman Whiteside?"

"Who's he?"

"One of the stockholders of Carter Shipping who wanted to sell out to Bank of Canton and turn a tidy profit. Damian didn't want to sell. Whiteside is ruthless. Known to be involved in shady deals. He stands to make, oh, six or seven million dollars if, with Damian Carter now out of the way, he can persuade the directors to go along with the deal."

"He sounds like a likely prospect. Next?"

"Lisa Boatharbor."

"The playwright?"

"Yes. She applied for a large grant from the Huckleberry Foundation. It was going to be approved, but Damian Carter was a trustee and held it up for reasons no one is quite sure of. But it gives her a motive, that's all I'm saying."

"I've met her. She could do it. So far we've got Herman Whiteside and Lisa Boatharbor. Who else?"

"Stuart Daly. Damian Carter was contemplating suing him for stock fraud—something to do with a theater chain."

Damian talked about Stuart Daly often, she remembered. If Damian Carter hated anyone on earth it was Stuart Daly. "Who's number five?"

"The man who's likely to be nominated to the Fed chairmanship."

"His name?"

155

"George Corbett."

Robert Park paced around Shirley Dills's living room, stopping to pull back the curtain every few minutes.

"Tell me again," he said.

"I already told you four times."

"Tell me again, damn it!"

"It wasn't nothing. Like I told you, sugar, I seen this blond woman come up in a taxi cab and she went in the house. All the time she's in there, the taxi's waiting for her. Maybe half an hour. Then she comes out. What else is there to say?"

"How old was she?"

"Thirties. I didn't get a good look at her. Honest."

"How would you know to call me?"

" 'Cause of all the time you spent over here looking at that place across the way. And then I heard this boy was killed—"

He turned swiftly and grabbed her by the throat. "You don't know nothing about no boy being killed! Got that? Not one fucking thing!" He shoved her into a chair and took out a picture he had of Damian Carter with Catlyn. "Is this the bitch? This her?"

Shirley Dills looked at the picture, then nodded.

Park said, "Son of a bitch!" He picked up a pile of magazines and threw them against the wall. "Who does that fucking cunt think she is? She's gonna curse the fucking day she meddled into my business!"

He went back to the window breathing heavily through his nostrils.

"Would you like a beer or something, Robert?" Shirley Dills asked quietly.

"Yeah, and a sandwich. Come, hurry up." He ran his hand through his hair. "I got some serious thinking to do."

By the time the first sandwich came, he had already made one decision. His old sergeant had always said, never go into action 'less you reconnoiter first. Okay, that was what he was

156

gonna do. Get the lay of the land. Find out what this Catlyn Cavanaugh bitch was up to. Then he could take appropriate countermeasures.

It was three in the morning when he left Shirley Dills's place. He was sated with beer and had had a pretty good time with Shirley, tying her up with leather, and a piece of chain around her neck. Banged her good. She was old, he thought, but so what? She was tight as a mousetrap. And he liked those little yelping sounds she made when he was pounding away. Maybe it was play-acting, but he liked it. A good old broad, that Shirley. Twenty years ago she must have been the best pussy in New York. He gave her a hundred bucks for the evening and she was grateful as hell.

He slept till noon then watched a Road Runner cartoon on his VCR while he ate breakfast. He had a cheese omelette, toast, and a Canadian ale. Just one glass of ale; he wanted to keep a clear head. After breakfast he smoked a cigarette, sipped hot black coffee, and watched Wily Coyote blow himself up trying to catch Road Runner. He sat astride his chair, laughing and slapping his knee as he watched. When the last explosion was over, he shut off the TV, crushed out his cigarette, and did some stretching exercises, a few sit-ups and push-ups. His head felt a little sluggish and a light workout always perked him up.

Then it was time to get to work.

He unlocked the door and went into the cave. He sat looking at himself in the mirror for a while. He ran over in his mind what he knew of Ambrose Poindexter's family. No father. Lived alone with his mother. Originally from New Orleans. Catholic.

That was it. Catholic. That was the key. Ambrose's mama had a strong liking for the Church. Who better to come visit than a Holy Joe?

The first knock on the door was so soft she hardly heard it. When she went to the door and looked through the keyhole,

157

she was surprised to see a priest there. It wasn't Father Quinlan from the parish, or his new assistant, Father Dade, the nice young black priest. This priest was rather dark and a little stooped, moderately built. She opened the door thinking he probably had the wrong address.

"Mrs. Poindexter? Mrs. Charlesetta Poindexter?"

"Why, yes."

The priest's expression was somber behind a pair of thick-rimmed glasses. "I'm so very sorry, Mrs. Poindexter, to bother you in your time of grief. My name is Father Delgado, I'm not with your parish, I'm on the bishop's staff. May I come in?"

"Yes, of course."

"I understand your brother is visiting . . . perhaps I should talk to him as well . . ."

"He's not here at the moment, Father, he's—he's making the arrangements."

The priest touched her reassuringly. "I'm afraid I have a shocking thing to tell you."

"What is it, Father? What's the matter?"

The priest adjusted his glasses with both hands. "There is a reporter for one of the worst of those scandal tabloids doing a story on the neighborhood and on our schools. She passes herself off as a friend, but she is writing some very bad things—about boys who get into trouble. Boys like Ambrose, Mrs. Poindexter."

"I don't understand," Mrs. Poindexter said.

"She wishes the Church ill, that's all I'm allowed to say. All we ask, if she contacts you, is that you tell her if she has any questions to call the rectory at St. Mary Magdalene, or Father Devlin, the principal of the school. Will you do that for us?"

Charlesetta Poindexter nodded her head.

"We knew we could count on you. Now then, she's a white woman, blond, about thirty-five, very attractive, and seems very nice. She uses several names, hardly ever her own, and usually passes herself off as a friend of somebody or other."

"I thought she was a reporter when first she come here!"

"She's been here already?"

"Yes, Father. Said she was a friend of the man Ambrose killed."

The priest shook his head. "And the funeral Mass not even said yet."

"After she left, my brother say she was up to something funny."

"Can you tell me, how long was she here?"

"Twenty minutes, a half hour."

"Did she ask a lot of questions?"

"She sure did. Wanted to know all about Ambrose, what he did, where he went, who his friends were."

The priest nodded knowingly. "What did you tell her?"

"I told her he liked pool, that he hung around at a pool hall somewhere. I gave her a knife I found of his—least I thought it might be his—she took that along. She looked around in his room. She said she was trying to prove that someone else killed her friend Damian Carter because she don't think Ambrose did." Her eyes flooded with tears. "I wanted so much to believe her. I did believe her."

"Of course you would," the priest said, patting her on the arm.

Mrs. Poindexter continued. "She said she wanted to prove my boy innocent. That's what she told me. She gave me a business card." She took it off a table and handed it to him.

"Catlyn Cavanaugh," the priest read. "I'm sure that's not her real name." He put the card in his pocket. "Thank you, Mrs. Poindexter, you've been very helpful."

She bowed while he made the sign of the cross, blessing her and her home.

"Thank you, Father, thank you so much."

"May the Lord God give you strength in this your hour of need."

The priest went outside and down the hallway. She

watched him go. He waved to her from the bottom of the stairs and disappeared.

Ten minutes later he went into a rest room at a nearby bar carrying a briefcase. He emerged a few minutes later wearing a motorcycle jacket and dark glasses, his hair combed straight back. Nobody paid the least bit of attention. He was smiling because he was thinking how easy it was to soap a dumb nigger bitch like Poindexter. She saw the collar and right away she was yessiring all over the goddamn place. She wasn't any smarter than her dumb-ass son, who never paid any attention to what was coming up behind him until the blade was in his throat.

An hour afterward, nursing a beer in his apartment and watching an old Zorro movie, Robert Park thought about Catlyn Cavanaugh. So she was gonna try and prove Ambrose Poindexter was innocent, was she? Who the fuck she think she's playing with, a cretin minus? He chuckled to himself and looked at her picture. This might be some pretty good action here. He thought of her tied to the bed, squirming and turning all red in the face, struggling against the chains.

"We gonna have a time, lady, we gonna have a real good time!"

TWELVE

Rita Montgomery had good instincts about men. From the moment she met Ernest Ramsey, she knew her assignment would not be easy. She also knew that in the end he would be totally hers.

He had a certain schoolboy look behind his wire-rimmed glasses. His hair was thick and brown, with a cowlick that added to the schoolboy look. He had a thin face and a narrow chin and rounded shoulders. It was the eyes, though, that gave him away. Here she could detect the rigidity of his character and the uncertainty of his manhood. That was the key. She would reassure him and he would turn to putty to be molded any way she liked.

They met in the middle of a crowded cocktail party at the Peruvian Embassy. She had been stalking him, drifting around, waiting for him to turn her way so she could bump into him, making their meeting seem one of those random occurrences that happen at such parties.

In that first moment his eyes did not drift down to her cleavage, the way most men's did, but she knew he was intrigued nevertheless. He smiled at her, and for a moment she thought something flickered in his eyes, but then he settled back on his heels and spoke to her as if he were no more interested in her than a garage mechanic.

Still, she knew he would yield, knew because she knew men. She didn't like them, but they were like glass to her—she could see right through them. Ernest Ramsey was interested, but he had his deflector shields turned up high. Carson had told her that he was a fundamentalist Christian nut. They always had their deflector shields up. But once you put a crack in them, they shattered like cheap crystal. And Ramsey's would crack.

"And what do you do?" he asked, trying to make polite conversation.

"I'm a model."

"Here? In D.C.?"

"Yes."

"That must be interesting work, and I'll bet you're good at it." He looked away, as if someone had just caught his attention. "Will you excuse me, there's a man over there I just have to talk to."

He drifted off through the crowd. She waved at him.

That, of course, was only the first move. The mouse hadn't taken the cheese, but he'd had a sniff. He'd be back, Rita thought. In the meantime, she sipped some overly dry, overly flat Peruvian champagne and kept smiling. Carson Black had somehow gotten her invited to the party. Her escort, a minor network functionary, had already gone home.

Rita kept her eye on the mark, smiling to herself. She sipped more champagne and started circling the room. She noticed a couple of men she had known in the past. They had been sex-therapy clients. Neither could get hard-ons. She had helped one; the other just had a permanent limp dick, she thought wryly. Both avoided her gaze. She smiled to herself, thinking men were nothing but little boys with smelly armpits.

She never made love to one of them yet, she thought, that had Carson's fire.

A couple of men spoke to her; she nodded to whatever

162

inane thing they had to say and turned away. She was maneuvering closer to Ernest Ramsey. He kept glancing at her with a strange, worried look in his eyes. She kept smiling at him through the crowd.

A Peruvian string quartet in the corner played some quiet classical background music. There were examples of Peruvian trade goods on tables lining the walls: blankets, boat models, copper wire. An Indian-looking woman was drawing portraits of everyone who wanted one. Her hand darted across the paper like a firefly.

Ramsey kept talking. Rita kept her eyes on him.

At nine o'clock the Peruvian ambassador made a speech about economic cooperation. The speech was mercifully short and typically optimistic. Rita maneuvered herself next to Ernest Ramsey. When the speech was over, a magician was brought out to entertain.

Rita turned to Ramsey. "I hope that you don't think I'm following you around. We certainly seem to keep bumping into each other."

"Yes, we do."

"May I ask you a personal question? Isn't your wife Senator Rumford's daughter?"

"Why yes, she is."

"I went to high school with her in Freeport, Iowa."

"Really?" He seemed surprised.

Everyone applauded briefly. The magician had made a giant rabbit appear out of a baseball cap.

Rita said, "We were in the Christian Fellowship together at the United Methodist Church. I don't think Sonja would remember me. I was a very quiet girl then, hardly said a word. Wore my sister's hand-me-down dresses. Sonja traveled in higher circles."

Ernest Ramsey was grinning with genuine delight. "Why, I've never met anyone who knew Sonja in Freeport. How very interesting."

"Is she here tonight? I'd like to say hello."

"I'm sorry, but she rarely comes to these things. I had to come because the President has a special interest in Latin America."

"That's a shame. I hardly ever get a chance to meet anyone from the old home town." Rita hoped Ramsey didn't know much about Freeport. She'd never been there; she'd actually grown up in Detroit. All she knew about Freeport is what Carson had told her.

Ramsey said, "You look so much younger than my wife."

"She was a few years ahead of me."

"You've got to tell me what she was like as a girl."

"She and I were not exactly in the same social strata, Mr. Ramsey. My parents were poor as dirt."

"No disgrace in that. My father was a coal miner. But he was a man of pride and principle, a man who counted in this world."

"Sounds a lot like my daddy."

"You've got to tell me more about Sonja." He was smiling easily now. "Let's see, her father was a county prosecutor then, right?"

"I'm not real sure. He was an important man, that's all I know. Everybody was terribly afraid of him."

"The senator can be intimidating."

They were interrupted by a young man, apparently an associate of Ramsey's, who said Ramsey had to talk to somebody else before they left. Ramsey promised to be back in a moment.

An hour later he was still talking to a small group of gray-haired men in the corner. One was the ambassador who had made the speech. The crowd was thinning out. The magician had finished his act by sawing the ambassador's wife in half. The string quartet was playing again. Rita recognized the piece. Brahms. She hated it. Too sappy. She noticed that Ramsey kept looking at her as if he were worried she might leave.

Rita passed the time talking with two older women about

how damn hard it was to get a good maid in D.C., and Georgetown was even worse. She bragged about her maid and cook, even though she had neither. The women seemed envious.

When he was through talking, Ramsey walked over to Rita. He apologized for taking so long. "Why . . . why, Miss, ah, Montgomery, I'm sorry, I was deep into a discussion of tuna fishing."

She bent over, pretending to fix a problem with her hem, letting her fullness show over the top of her dress. "Think nothing of it, Mr. Ramsey, I became involved in a rather heated discussion myself. In fact, I'm afraid I've lost my escort." She straightened up. He'd gotten a shot of what was down her dress. He was looking a little flustered; his ears had taken on a deep red color. He cleared his throat and didn't say anything.

"I'd like a glass of champagne, Mr. Ramsey," she said. "How about you?"

"I think a Perrier."

"Aren't you a drinking man, Mr. Ramsey?"

"I tried it a few times in college, never went in for it much, though."

"I love champagne, even Peruvian. Try a glass, I promise to make you stop at one."

"All right, what the heck."

He kept looking around as if he were hoping no one would notice him with her. She accepted a glass from the waiter and passed one to Ramsey. She had a tiny ampule of a drug attached to a ring on a finger of her right hand. The drug was supposed to reduce a man's inhibitions, get him to relax. In the past, she'd found the drug was often unpredictable and sometimes caused headaches. But if she was going to use it, now was the time. She looked up into his eyes. He was still looking around nervously. She thought: I can have him, no need to risk the drug.

He took a sip of champagne and said, "That's really

good. You certainly have big brown eyes."

"Thank you." She looked at him over the top of her glass. He took another sip. "You certainly don't look like a girl from Freeport, Iowa. You don't look corn fed."

"I'm not."

He gulped his champagne. She summoned the waiter for another. He gulped that one, too. His shields, she thought, had cracks in them. He took another glass of champagne. The waiter went for more. Ramsey's face turned a little pink as the alcohol hit him. He pulled his rounded shoulders back.

"Shall we dance a little?" she said.

He looked around. "Better not." Then, as if he suddenly remembered something, he put the champagne down and said, "I'd better be going, really."

"I hate to ask you, but could you give me a lift?"

He hesitated.

"Please," she said. "I promise I won't molest you." She smiled pleasantly.

"I, ah . . ."

"I'll wait for you out in front," she said with a wink. "No one will see us leaving together. Okay?"

He seemed confused for a moment. Then he nodded tentatively. Rita went to the cloakroom for her wrap. She left the embassy and walked to the corner. It was raining lightly. She stood on the corner shivering for a few minutes. Two cars left the embassy and drove down the street. Was he going to pass? she wondered. Maybe she had not seen through him quite as clearly as she thought she had. Panic rose in her. Carson didn't like failure and this was a top-priority mission.

Suddenly one of the cars turned around, passed Rita on the opposite side of the street, then turned around again and came back. It was a maroon Cadillac Seville. The door opened. "Get in quickly," Ramsey said. They headed down Delaware Street. She turned on the radio, found some soft music, and slid over next to him.

After a moment he said, "I can't believe I'm doing this."

"I don't bite," she said.

He said nothing.

She turned in her seat and put her hand inside his coat and rubbed his chest. He seemed to freeze up, then he hit the brakes. The car slid to a halt. The street was deserted. No cars coming either way. He sat there for a long moment, looking at her in the gray light. The windshield wipers swished back and forth. Water ran down the edges of the windshield. Finally he said, "Who are you?"

"I told you."

"You never knew my wife in Freeport, did you?"

Rita sighed.

"You going to tell me, or do I call a cop?"

She sighed again, and slid over next to the door. "No," she said, "I've never even been to Iowa, and I don't plan to go."

"Then why did you hand me that line of bull?"

"I just wanted to meet you. I like you."

"You couldn't possibly have known I was going to be there tonight. No one did until the last moment."

"I knew."

"How?"

"I'm a Russian spy."

He laughed. "Come on now. The truth. What's your game?"

"Can't I just like you?"

"How did you know my wife is from Freeport?"

"I asked someone who knew you at the party, I was told he worked for you. Men tell me things when I ask."

She was trembling all the way down to her shoes, but wasn't letting it show. She'd never had so much trouble with the come-on before.

He said, "What do you want from me?"

She turned to him. "You're a very good-looking man,

and I like very good-looking men. You have that sort of intelligent look, and I like that. Isn't it obvious what I want? I want to go to bed with you, isn't that plain enough? Why do I want to go to bed with you? Who understands the chemistry of men and women? You turn me on, that's all there is to it."

He wiped his forehead. God, she thought, the jerk is actually sweating.

He started driving again. "Believe it or not," he said, "this has never happened to me before."

"I know a place where we can go. Very discreet. Let's have a little more champagne, talk, see if we like each other."

"Jesus, I don't know."

"It's very private. If you don't want to make love to me, that's okay, too."

He kept going, driving slowly, eyes straight ahead. Rita slid over next to him again. She ran her hand gently up and down his leg. "Just for a little while," she said. "We can relax, just have a little fun. I get the very definite impression you don't have any fun in your life."

"You're right, I don't."

"Don't you feel the electricity between us?"

He stepped on the gas; the car sped up. "Yes," he said, "I do."

Ten minutes later they turned off Rhode Island Avenue and pulled into the parking lot of the Coronet Motel. It wasn't much of a motel: a long, low fifties-style motor court with a sign in front that said, Economy Rooms. It was raining heavily now. There was an overhang above the driveway in front of the office door. He pulled up.

"Just sit tight," she told him, kissing him on the cheek.

"I don't know about this."

"Nobody's going to see you. Honest." She went inside and came hurrying back to the car a minute later with the key. She closed the door behind her. "There now," she said.

168

"Everything is going to be all right. Just drive around in back—watch out for potholes, okay?"

He drove slowly and cautiously. The motel was not a large one, and there weren't many cars in the driveway. She put her hand softly on his leg. His muscles were tense. She thought: Damn, he's scared right down to his socks.

"It's right over there," she said, pointing to a small cottage near the end of a hedgerow, secluded by trees. "There's a real nice stereo and lots of champagne on ice." There were no cars parked nearby, and no lights on in the other cottages. She noticed his breathing was quick and shallow.

He stopped the car in the space before the cottage but didn't open the door. "Look," he said, "it's getting late. I, ah, really don't think this is a very good idea."

She reached over and turned off the ignition. "You don't have to go in if you don't want to." She kissed him. "Let's just sit here and talk, okay?"

"No, I think we'd better go." He tried to push her away, gently, but she wouldn't budge. She pressed her lips against his and parted them with her tongue, making a humming sound. Her hand was inside his shirt. He tried to push her away again, but she moved his hand to her breast. For a moment he sat there frozen, then he gave a tentative squeeze . . .

And she knew she had him.

Nicolai met George Corbett at the Baltimore-Washington Airport at six-fifteen the following morning. It had stopped raining and the skies were clear. It was a cool and crisp September day. But Nicolai was not in a good mood. He had taken photographs until three-fifteen and then had had to develop them in his motel room immediately, so he had not gotten much sleep. His stomach was sour and he had a headache, and was probably coming down with a

169

cold from standing out in the rain and shooting in through the window. It was horrible! On top of all this, he had a feeling he was gong to have to be the one to approach the mark to see how far the hook had sunk in. Things at that point could go very wrong. The mark might scream for a cop, he might come out shooting, he might do anything. There was just no telling. If there was one thing Nicolai had learned both in the training school in Gorki and from his twenty years in the field it was not to leave things to chance, to control the situation at all times. This situation was definitely out of control.

He made his usual switch of cars on the way to pick up George. It was common practice. A pain in the neck, but it would lose any tail. He left his regular car, an old VW, parked on the street, walked through a building, and came out on the other side where the second car, a big old Dodge, was waiting. This time he chose an office building. Not that he had anybody on him, but George insisted on strict observance of the procedure. Nicolai pulled up in front of the United Airlines terminal and waited only a few minutes. George got in wearing a false beard and a hat pulled down over his ears. He looked ridiculous. Nicolai couldn't help but chuckle under his breath.

"Take it easy, Nicolai. It may be ludicrous, but it is a useful technique."

"Sorry, Colonel." He pulled the old Dodge into a travel lane and headed for the parkway going south. The traffic was stop and go.

"You have the photos?"

"In the glove box."

George took them out and looked at them. "These are excellent, Nicolai, you are to be congratulated."

Nicolai smiled at the compliment.

Nicolai said, "He seemed reluctant at first, but then he got drunk quickly and went after her like a hungry animal. She knows how to arouse a man, that is the truth."

George nodded. "That's why we used her. Now then, Nicolai, I suppose you have guessed it will be your job to make the contact with the mark. You should have contact in an open area with many means of escape."

"You should have Rita make the approach, not me! She could control him."

"Easy now, Comrade. We asked her to bring him to the motel so you could photograph him, and she did."

"Still, let her make the approach."

"Perhaps you do not know how important a man Mr. Ramsey is in our scheme of things. How could we trust such an important mission to so empty-headed a girl? Listen to me, Nicolai, let me tell you how important he is. He is the man who stands in the way of my becoming the next chairman of the Federal Reserve. Once he is out of the way, I'm in. Once I'm in, the days of America the Great Pig of the World are numbered."

"But he already knows who she is. If he doesn't buy in, she's compromised already."

"But if he sees her, he might become enraged. I have seen it happen before, Nicolai. You do it, I know it will be handled correctly. She works for us because we pay her and give her nice presents and we let her have sex with her true love. She is not one of us. She has no commitment, no philosophy. I have to give you the assignment, Nicolai, because I trust you. If things go bad, I will see to it that you get out on bail and then you can go home. The charge will be extortion or something like that, not espionage. If you pull it off, Nicolai, I will have you recommended for a medal. Order of Lenin, second class. And you know I do not make such promises lightly."

Nicolai rubbed his throbbing temples and drove onto the expressway. Their speed picked up. Such a high award, could it be possible? he wondered. He looked at George, who had a very determined look in his eyes. He knew George well enough to know that when he wanted something badly enough, he would get it. "I'm a lieutenant, you are my superior," he said. "I have to obey orders."

In Russian, George said, "I order you, Lieutenant."

Nicolai saluted crisply. An order of Lenin would look so good on his uniform, and wouldn't his family be proud, he thought.

THIRTEEN

That same morning Ernest Ramsey had awakened confused, angry, and worried.

He had always been a man who was sure of himself. But this morning he couldn't quite remember what he'd done the night before. This worried him. Images of a young woman, naked, flashed through his mind. His mouth was sour with the taste of champagne.

He broke out in a cold sweat. His hands trembled.

He looked at the clock. It was six A.M. He was in his pajamas, in his own bed with his own wife. Could it have been just a nightmare? His head felt as if it had been battered. He eased out of bed and put his bare feet on the cold floor. He looked out the window. In the gray light he could see his car was parked half on the driveway, half on the front lawn.

His wife, Sonja, stirred, but didn't wake up. She was a heavy sleeper, thank God. Clicking on the light, he could see his clothing thrown about the floor. He had no recollection whatever of coming home. The last thing he could remember was leaving work the night before . . . getting into his car . . .

A terrible thought suddenly struck him. Had he lost his mind? Had he had some kind of schizophrenic break? He knew of two such cases. Both hard-driving, ambitious young men like himself. Was it that? Or had he been drugged? Yes, that was possible. He could have taken something by mistake. Or someone gave him something.

But who? Why?

He picked his suit and shirt up off the floor. Vomit was encrusted on the front of the pants and shirt. Lord of mercy. He folded them up and stuck them in an athletic bag in the closet. He gathered up his underwear and socks and put them in the laundry hamper.

He looked at himself in the bathroom mirror. There was dried vomit on his chin and his eyes were yellowish pink. Once or twice in college he had gone overboard with the beer—before he had found Christ—and he knew what a hangover was like. He was having one. Those had been bad, but not as bad as this. He scrubbed his face.

A flash of something came into his mind. The ambassador's party. A young blond woman. He remembered a moment of wanting her. Just a moment. He didn't do anything, did he? He'd excused himself. That he remembered, that he *definitely* remembered. The ambassador made a speech. Then . . . what? It was raining. Yes, yes! He remembered the rain on the windshield. The wipers going. The woman beside him, touching him. Her eyes were large and brown and warm, and she was looking at him *that* way. He remembered thinking what nice breasts she had . . . then . . . then . . .

How queer not to remember.

He went downstairs to the kitchen and found some Pepto-Bismol in the cupboard. He poured some into a glass and drank it down. Then he took a couple of Extra Strength Tylenol.

She suggested they get to know each other. Yes, and she kissed him. Soft and warm, nice. Then what happened?

He sat down at the kitchen table. One of the kids was up, going to the bathroom upstairs. That would be Raymond, who was six. The toilet flushed. A door closed. He was going back to bed.

Ernest Ramsey asked himself, what if he'd done something really wrong. He worked for the White House. Chief

174

economist. His father-in-law was a senator, chairman of the Foreign Relations Committee. Ernest Ramsey had carefully built a career since the day he entered graduate school. No, since the summer before, when he'd met Sonja and her father and he'd realized that the chubby little wallflower was well connected. And her father liked him. Ramsey's father was a Presbyterian minister and he had been brought up right, the old senator had said. From that moment on, the doors were open.

The image of the naked woman flashed again in his mind. He had done something terribly wrong, he knew it now. His face burned with shame.

Behind him: "You're up early." It was Sonja, wearing a shocking pink bathrobe and bunny slippers. She wasn't wearing her glasses, so she had to feel her way along the counter to the refrigerator. An odd thought entered Ernest Ramsey's head. He'd married her because of her father. But he loved her now. Somehow between then and now, he'd become very attached to this dumpy, funny-looking woman. What would she do if she found out?

"You want me to make you something?" she asked.

"I have to get going, Sonja, just coffee."

"If they didn't invent the bean, you'd have no nourishment at all. They having another Big Meeting this morning?"

"No. Just the usual. We're way behind. The budget people are screaming for our revised estimates from HUD and the Treasury. Things are a little uncertain at the Fed."

"Okay, I'll have Mr. Coffee doing his thing soon as I let the cat in."

He went upstairs and took a shower; his hands were trembling. He'd never felt like this in his life. But then he'd never done anything wrong before. Not like this. More of it was coming back now. Tasting champagne. His stomach burned. The fire of guilt, his father had told him, could eat away a man's stomach lining. That's what he had all right,

175

the fire of guilt.

He dressed in his good blue suit. He knotted his tie, looking at his pasty face in the mirror. It was then that it occurred to him that he might be getting all upset over nothing. Maybe no one saw him leave with the woman. And even if they did, what would happen? Rumors. Rumors were to Washington what rain was to the monsoon season. Sonja hadn't awakened when he'd come in. He had been out four nights out of the last five at meetings, speaking, parties, receptions, Okay, so he slipped once. He'd say a prayer and ask God's forgiveness. Keep quiet about it. He'd never see the woman again. Ever.

He went back downstairs and drank some coffee, sitting at the kitchen counter on a long-legged stool. Sonja had found her glasses. Her long, smooth brown hair was combed straight down and covered nearly half her face. She looked all hair, glasses, and nose.

He kissed her, holding her face in his hands. "I love you," he said.

"Finish your coffee."

"Have to run."

The truth was, he wanted to get the car off the lawn before the neighbors noticed his new method of parking.

On the way into Washington on I-270 he recited the Lord's Prayer and asked God for forgiveness in Christ's name. There, it was done. It made him feel better. He had the athletic bag with his suit and shirt in it in the trunk; he'd have them cleaned. He told himself he was safe. If the blonde showed up, he'd tell her thanks for the nice time, but get the hell out of his life.

For having only a couple of hours sleep he felt fine when he got to the office. The Anacin had worked a miracle for his head, the Pepto-Bismol had done the job on his stomach, and the good Lord had healed his spirit. He was ready to go to work, ready to prepare his argument as to why Hollis Wakefield and not George Corbett ought to be the next Fed chairman. George Corbett was a manipulator and the tool of the Banking Establishment, an easy-money man who, Ramsey was certain, would pursue policies that would line the pockets of the bankers at the expense of the nation.

His office was on the third floor of the Executive Offices Building, across the street from the White House. As chief economist for the President, he had a secretary and seven staff members, who did mostly research and helped him draft proposals. Most of his days were taken up answering petty questions put to him by the President's other key advisers, mostly grassroots politicians and state functionaries the President had brought with him from Iowa. The Iowa Mafia, the press called them. Ramsey also had meetings to attend. Endless meetings of endless committees. At present he was chairman of thirteen committees with gaseous names like "Committee to End Federal Mismanagement" and "Executive Budget Priorities Task Force." He'd bury himself in his work. He'd forget about the blonde, the champagne, and the night that should not have happened and would never happen again.

The house of cards came down around his head at 10:45.

His secretary buzzed him on the intercom: "A call for you, Mr. Ramsey, line 2. He won't give his name, says it's a personal matter and that you'll be happy to talk to him. He wouldn't leave a message and is absolutely insistent he speak to you."

Ramsey was suddenly overcome by a terrible dread. His hand went to the phone. He lifted it. Strange, the receiver felt as if it weighed a hundred pounds.

"This is Ernest Ramsey. Who's calling?"

A man's voice said: "I have something to show you, Mr. Ramsey, of a personal nature. It involves a Miss Montgomery."

Ramsey thought: Yes! That was her name!

The man said, "Do you know the Benjamin Franklin

177

statue in Lafayette Square? Be there in fifteen minutes and don't call the cops." The line went dead.

Ramsey's first impulse was to call the police. But calling the police would accomplish nothing. If he went to the park with police the man would not show himself. There wasn't time to set anything up with the police. He was amazed at how lucid his mind was. Of course he could simply not go, just forget it. What could the man possibly have to show him? Pictures? Pictures of what?

Of the naked woman. And him. Naked. In bed together. The shame was back, burning through the skin on his face.

It seemed so preposterous. Could this be happening to him? He was set up. Sure. She'd come to him on purpose. What was it she had said? Something about knowing Sonja. Yes, the come-on. She had laid a trap. And he, like a fool, had fallen into it headfirst. His father had said over and over, never let your glands do your thinking for you. That's what he had done.

If nothing else, Ernest Ramsey was a logical man. He would have to investigate first, find out what the man wanted. Maybe the man had no sinister intent whatever. Maybe he was a reporter, something like that. Maybe an old friend . . .

Even as he went down in the elevator, he knew that the man was no reporter and certainly not a friend. He was feeling physically ill now.

The sun was bright. There were a lot of people in the streets, mostly tourists gawking at buildings and clicking away with cameras. Ernest Ramsey felt strangely disconnected, yet his whole body was trembling with fear. He had wanted the woman, he remembered that. He remembered thinking how nice it would be to fondle her breasts. He remembered her warm eyes. They seemed to say, let's do it, let's have fun. It'd been fun. She knew all the right buttons.

He who dances must pay the piper, his father had said to him ten million times.

178

Nicolai watched Ramsey cross the street and go into Lafayette Square, pigeons scattering in front of him. Nicolai followed him. He was wearing a red hunting jacket and a wool knit cap pulled down over his ears and large sunglasses that covered half his face. An expression of relief filled Nicolai when he saw how dazed Ramsey was; he knew instinctively that the mark had not called the cops. The mark had obeyed.

Nicolai caught up to him. There was no one else around. Nicolai said, "Hello, Mr. Ramsey."

Ramsey turned to him. "Are you the man who called me? I'm Ernest Ramsey."

"I know, Mr. Ramsey. I took this photo of you last night." Nicolai handed it to him.

Ramsey stepped back; his hand went to his forehead. The photograph fell to the ground. Ramsey shook and slowly dropped to his knees, covering his face with his hands. An anguished moan escaped his lips.

Nicolai had never seen a reaction quite like this before. It fascinated him. He said, "Can you hear me, Mr. Ramsey?"

Ramsey nodded, making a whining sound now.

"Get up, Mr. Ramsey, I have a proposition to make to you."

Ramsey looked at him, then turned around and stared at the White House across the street, as if he were surprised suddenly to see where he was. He got to his feet slowly, his face wet with tears. "I haven't much money," he said. He handed Nicolai the photograph.

"We don't want your money," Nicolai said.

"You don't?"

"No. We just want a little information."

The mark closed his eyes, then opened them again. "W-What kind of information?" He swallowed.

"You were in Berlin last month at the European Economic Ministers' Conference. We'd like a copy of the minutes, that's all. No big thing." This was a test, of course. Just to try the mark, see whether he's reliable. If he went for that, there'd be a little something else, then bring up George Corbett. Getting the hook into the guy, that was the important thing.

Ramsey just stared at him.

"We give you the film, all the prints, everything. All you got to do is give us the minutes of that meeting. You hear me all right, Ramsey? You don't look too well. Believe me, this is no big deal."

Ramsey nodded mechanically.

"Tell you what, Mr. Ramsey—listen to this now—I'll call you at four o'clock this afternoon. I'll say this is Mr. Clark, and ask you if the meeting is on. You say yes, I'll be here tomorrow same time to pick up the package. Okay?"

Ramsey nodded again, then turned and hurried away, taking short little steps like a kid that had to go to the bathroom. Strange man, Nicolai thought. But most Americans he found strange.

Ernest Ramsey didn't go back to his office. He wandered off toward 18th Street, stopped at a bar, and had a beer. It tasted harsh. He hadn't had a drink of beer in twenty years. He had another, but it didn't settle him down. He walked back to the executive office building, but didn't go to his office. He went down to the parking garage, got his car, and drove over the bridge to Maryland. He didn't know where he was going, he just felt himself swept along by the traffic. The blonde, the photo, the man with the sunglasses. It all seemed like scenes from a surreal movie.

He went north on I-95 and got off at Monroe Street in Baltimore. He drove up and down streets automatically until he found himself at his father's old church near Druid

Hill Park. He parked in front and sat in the car for a long time, looking at the church. It was boarded up now. Old, crumbling, like the neighborhood. His father was buried in the churchyard. His mother was in Florida, living in a rest home.

He got out of the car and took a look around. For a moment he could hear the old church choir his mother directed. He had been a soloist when he was nine. *Rock of Ages rest with thee . . .* This is where he grew up. The old neighborhood. It was mostly black now. A lot of bars on the windows. Old cars in the streets. But when he was a kid it was white, mostly Germans, Italians, some Scots and Irish. He played baseball in the empty lot down the street.

He went around the back of the church and looked at the gravestones. Some of them were knocked over. A couple had black spray paint on them. Weeds grew tall all around. His father's monument was in the far corner under a large elm. The headstone was rough, heavy. The inscription read: "In loving memory, Reverend Harold Ramsey, 1925-1983.

Ernest Ramsey stood over the gravestone for a few minutes, his head bowed as if he were praying. But he wasn't. He was thinking how much he had loved his father. And how much he'd let him down.

There was a knot in his throat the size of a lemon. He felt bone cold. Suddenly he started crying, openly. "Oh, God. . . . I'm so sorry."

He stood there for a while and then went back to his car and started driving again. He didn't know where he was going, he just kept driving. Tears streamed down his face. An hour and a half later he was back in Cedar Grove, pulling up in front of his house. He went inside. His wife had gone out. The cleaning lady was just finishing up.

"Why, Mr. Ramsey, are you all right?" the cleaning woman asked. "Strange to see you home this time of day."

"I'm fine, Mrs. Johnson," he mumbled. "Everything's

fine."

He went into his study and closed the door. He opened his file and took out his personal investment portfolio. There wasn't much. Eighteen thousand in tax-free municipals. Four hundred shares of IBM. Two seventy-five-thousand life insurance policies. That's what he wanted, to check the clauses. Double indemnity. Not that he had made any decision. He hadn't. He was just going over his options. He was a logical man.

The house wasn't paid for. In fact he owed ninety thousand. But there was maybe thirty thousand equity.

His father's voice came out of nowhere: *the wages of sin are death.*

The phone rang. It was his secretary. He was fine, he told her, he'd forgotten something at home. Could she cancel all his appointments? Domestic problems, he said. Not serious, but they needed immediate attention.

Ernest Ramsey was sitting in the living room watching the six o'clock news when his wife came home with the kids. Penelope had been to day care, Raymond was visiting his friends.

"You're home early!" Sonja said. "You haven't been home this early since your teaching days."

"I thought I'd take you and the kids out to dinner."

"What's come over you?"

"I need a break from the paperwork. I'm going snow blind."

Raymond came out of the kitchen. "Somebody cut the telephone cord," he said. "I didn't do it."

Sonja looked at her husband. "Who do you suppose would do a thing like that?"

"It wouldn't stop ringing. They're supposed to fix it tomorrow."

"Oh."

"Get ready. Let's go for pizza."

"Sure," Sonja said. "Why not? Long as we've flipped

out. Let's have one with marshmallows."

Sonja remembered later she had never seen her husband so relaxed and jovial. He sang along with the singer at the pizza parlor, played video games with the kids, ate pizza, and drank four glasses of root beer. They got home at nine o'clock, he read the kids stories until ten, then came downstairs, took his wife by the hand, and led her up to the bedroom. He had taken out some candles and, in the soft glow of the candlelight, he undressed her slowly, kissing her, running his hands slowly over her body. It was maybe one of only two or three times in her life she ever really liked making love. Not just sort of liked it, but *really* liked it.

About eleven-thirty, she was just drifting off to sleep when he got up and started dressing.

"Where are you going?" she asked him.

"I left some very important papers at the office. I have to have them in the morning." He was speaking strangely. Mechanically.

She said, "Get a messenger to pick them up."

"I'm the only one who can get these papers. Some things a man just has to do on his own. Good-bye, darling." He kissed her one more time.

The Montgomery County sheriff's deputy who saw the wreckage against the bridge abutment just couldn't figure it. No skids. The guy doing maybe a hundred. Clear night. It looked like the guy was just aiming for it. The car like turned into crinkled Kleenex. The guy wasn't wearing his seat belt. He didn't look too pretty splattered all over the dash.

But then again, who looks good dead?

George Corbett, in his suite at the Hilton, read about the tragedy in *The Washington Post*. Front-page stuff. There

183

were pictures of the car on page 3, lots of passersby standing around. George was delighted. The reporters hinted it might be suicide. But the article said there was no note, and that the dead man's wife and secretary said he was suffering no depressions, that nothing seemed amiss. He was apparently just in a hurry to get the papers he left at the office and get back home. His wife said he was an absentminded-college-professor type. Perhaps he just wasn't paying attention to his speed. She said she sometimes had to remind him to slow down when they went someplace on vacation.

That was just the right thing to say, George thought.

Now then, old business out of the way, down to new business. Wakefield was still being considered for the Fed job. With Ernest Ramsey, his chief advocate, dead, some of the others, for sentimental reasons, might take up his cause. George was going to make sure that didn't happen. That morning he was having a breakfast meeting with an old friend, Andrew R. Rolland, an assistant to the director of the Internal Revenue Service. They met at nine A.M. at the Golden Image Restaurant, which had private booths where businessmen and bureaucrats often met.

"You're still looking good, George, you old reprobate!" Andrew R. Rolland said. Rolland was forty-seven but looked sixty-seven. The pressures of his job were obviously grinding him into dust. His was thin, with a gray pallor and dark lines under his eyes.

"I work out," George said. "I eat right, I don't let my troubles bother me after four P.M. I drink only the best brandy and smoke only the finest cigars."

The waiter took their order. George wanted the poached salmon; Rolland ordered a soft-boiled egg, rye toast, and Darjeeling tea. Then lit a Camel filter. His dark eyes became even darker.

"You want to be Fed chairman badly, don't you, George?"

184

"Yes, I do."

"The rich and the powerful always want to be more powerful. I can't understand it, myself." He attempted a smile, but it was fleeting.

"How's the wife and kids?" George asked.

"My wife left me a month ago. She left me for a woman. A gym teacher."

"What a travesty!" George said. Of course he had known about it. It was his business to know such things. "How terrible for you and the children."

"The kids are away at school." Rolland inhaled deeply on his cigarette and blew the smoke away from George. "I'm riding it out. What else can I do?" He looked at the hot tip of his cigarette. "I've been reading about you in the paper, George. Now that Damian Carter is dead, you'll be the next Fed chairman."

"Me or Wakefield."

Rolland shook his head slowly. It was dawning on him what the purpose of their meeting might be. "Ernest Ramsey was Wakefield's number-one supporter, wasn't he, George?"

"That's right. But perhaps Wakefield will have converts, a sentimental vote since Ramsey's accident. I want to make sure that does not happen."

Rolland stared at him, his eyes narrow. "I hope," he said slowly, "this has nothing to do with Internal Revenue."

"As a matter of fact, it does," George said.

Rolland leaned back in his seat. "I can't," he said.

"How do you know you can't when I haven't even said what it is?"

"Whatever it is, I can't do it."

The waiter brought the tea for Rolland and coffee for George. George watched the waiter glide back down from the aisle. George said, "When we first met, my friend, let me remind you where you were and what you were doing. You were a field auditor, going nowhere fast."

"I admit you've helped me along."

"More than just helped you along. Let's not trivialize. I have a lot of time, money, and favors invested in you."

"You made my career. Okay. I owe you. And I've done things for you."

"You have passed along a little information, that's all I ever asked of you."

"I promised that, and I delivered."

"Now all I want is a little more. Could you please at least have an open mind about it?"

Rolland crushed out his cigarette. "I'm listening."

"Wakefield is a wheeler-dealer, we both know that."

"He's audited every year, same as everyone else in his bracket."

"All right, so a little discrepancy has been found."

"No."

"I'm telling you what is going to happen, Andrew, please listen. A newspaper friend of mine is going to print a small story in the paper. He's going to say there's a rumor that Wakefield is being investigated for income tax evasion. The editor will want to know his source. He will give your name. The editor will call you. You will say that you can say nothing about it on the record but, confidentially, it's true. That's all you have to do. Your tea is getting cold."

Rolland lit another cigarette. "The shit will hit the fan," he said.

"Of course it will."

"What I mean is, my superiors will want to know the confidential source. The editor will be questioned."

"I can guarantee you, they will not give your name."

"Everyone will be questioned. It will have had to be someone high up."

"True."

"Somehow they'll find out. They'll have us vetted."

"You've taken lie detector tests before."

"And they've always shown me up."

186

"Okay, then all you have to do is tell them right off the bat that you did say it—in error."

"No one will believe that."

"They will have to believe that. Tell them you called some department and they confirmed it. You don't remember who you talked to."

"It's against policy . . ."

George felt suddenly angry. "Look, I don't give a damn about policy. I'm asking you as a friend. A friend who has been one of your best supporters and allies over the years."

Rolland wasn't looking at him now. "No," he said, "I can't."

George glared at him. "Listen to me, Andrew Rolland. I made you. You wouldn't be there unless I stuck my neck out a few times. Unless I did a thing or two here and there that wasn't quite right."

"And I've helped you."

"The scales are not balanced. I've given you everything, you've given me crumbs."

"What you're asking, George, is morally reprehensible."

George reached across the table and grabbed Rolland's fist and squeezed it. Rolland looked at him in amazement, then in pain. George squeezed with all he had. Rolland tried to pull away, but couldn't; his fist was locked in a crusher.

"Hear this, my friend. That reporter is doing his story. His editor will be calling you at a few minutes to twelve. You'd better decide what you want between now and then. Do you want to continue your meteoric rise, or do you want to be out the door? I can do it. I swear to you, I can have you on the street by the end of the week."

George let him go.

Rolland rubbed his hand, looking at George as a frightened schoolboy looks at the playground bully. His eyes were watering. "You've actually lost your mind, Corbett. You need psychiatric help. Your lust for power has made you mad."

George sneered at him. "I'm merely impressing on you the importance of your mission. You have until noon to decide if you want to someday be the director of the Internal Revenue Service, or if you want to be ruined. Because ruin you, I will."

The waiter was approaching; George fell silent. The waiter put their breakfast in front of them and said, "Enjoy your meal."

George dug into his poached salmon. Rolland just sat there, staring at his plate.

"This is wonderful," George said. "You should have ordered it."

"I feel sick," Rolland said. He got up from the table and tossed his napkin on his plate. "You're contemptible," he said, and walked off. George watched him give some money to the waiter and leave through the front door.

George finished his breakfast, paid his check with cash, and went back to his hotel. He was worried now. He had perhaps pushed the man too far. With weaklings like Rolland gentle pressure worked better than brute force, because brute force often broke them. And then what would Rolland do? Go to the newspeople and tell them that George Corbett was pressuring him to expose Wakefield? It could be verified that they met. George could deny the charge. He could say he had heard the rumor and was just trying to find out whether it was true.

Still, his chances for the job would be jeopardized. He had overplayed his hand with Rolland and he knew it. Now what was there to do? He could call him and tell him to forget it. But his instincts told him that might not work either. With a weakling, you never back off. That makes you look weak and you never want to let the weakling think he's your equal.

He spent most of the rest of the day on the phone handling routine business matters, packed, and took a cab to the train station. He rode to New York, sitting in the club car and looking out the window. So many of his colleagues over the years had been tripped up over small things. Perhaps when he got home the FBI would be waiting to ask him some very embarrassing questions. Well, if they were he would have to handle it. Somehow he would handle it. Andrew R. Rolland would have to disappear or commit suicide, or go mad. Bribes would be paid. It could be handled.

It was best to wait and see. No sense worrying about it, what's done is done. Once a gambit is launched, don't look back. That was drilled into him in training. More agents had been compromised by their own failure of nerves than any other way.

In the meantime, he had promised Mr. Peabody he would be Fed chairman, and Mr. Peabody was a more formidable enemy than the FBI.

George got off the train at Pennsylvania Station. As he walked through the lobby he looked over at the newsstand. The afternoon edition of one of the big papers was on the rack; the headline read: Hollis Wakefield Caught in Tax Scam? George bought the paper and read the article. "IRS officials confirmed today that Hollis Wakefield, the Texas financier, is being investigated for impropriety . . ."

George walked with a skip in his step across the lobby and out the door. He took a cab home, and when he got in the door, Linda was standing by with a bottle of Dom Pérignon champagne.

"What is it?" he asked.

"The White House called. You've been nominated to be chairman of the Fed by the President of the United States."

FOURTEEN

Nicolai had never seen George so drunk before.

George had been celebrating nonstop for the two days since the announcement of his nomination.

Leaning back in a chair, a napkin stuck in his shirt, George was saying, "And you Nicolai, you have handled everything wonderfully. I will see to it you will get the Order of Lenin, too, just as I promised. And you, Esther, my darling." He gave his mistress a sloppy kiss on the neck, and patted her ample bottom. A smile spread across her round face.

They were at Esther's apartment. She had cooked a sumptuous beef stroganoff dinner with dumplings, served with coarse black bread, smoked salmon, caviar, a good Freneh red wine, interspersed with shots of good Russian vodka. George was glowing.

Nicolai was always careful not to drink too much, especially when around his superiors, but George had been filling his glass and now Nicolai, too, was a bit under the influence. His brain was sluggish and he had trouble pretending to pay attention to what George was saying. In truth, capitalist economics, banking, high finance, and the like bored him. It was devoid of Marx and, therefore, he thought, shallow and stupid.

"Listen to me, Nicolai, and you, too, Esther," George said in a more serious tone. "Of all the people I have known since leaving the motherland when I was yet but a boy, it is only you two I regard as family. I have another family, of course, whom I love dearly and from the bottom of my heart; however, when I am with them, I am another man. But that is the nature of the business. Each of us must be two people. Our surface selves we wear like a coat when we go into the street, and our real selves, which we can only be when we are together. That coat is a heavy one sometimes, is it not, Nicolai?"

"At times." His tongue seemed cut off at the roots. He hated the feeling.

George grinned. "Soon you will not have to wear it at all. Soon you will be reunited with the motherland." He got up from the table suddenly. "Come here, Nicolai." George took him by the arm and dragged him to the window and pulled open the drape. "Here, look, tell me what fills your eyes."

Nicolai said, "I see the city. A lot of lights, cars. I see what anyone would see."

He had no patience with drunkenness. He didn't like it in himself and he didn't like it in others, especially his superiors.

George waved his arm. "You see the greatest city in the capitalist world. The hub. There, look, the Empire State Building. There, down there, the World Trade Center. Bridges. Cars. Buses. People by the millions. Hustle and bustle. All humming. Why? Why does it hum? I will tell you. I have been a student of that hum all my life. Listen to it. Hummmmmmmmm. It hums because the capitalist economy is humming. *Money* makes it hum. But soon, very soon, great upheavals are going to happen. Let me tell you how capitalism works and how I am going to destroy it. Pay attention, Nicolai, I will tell you a great secret. Esther, you, too, listen: Money is an idea." He repeated it softly,

191

solemnly: "Money is an idea. Have you got that, Nicolai? That is all it is, nothing more."

"Money is an idea," Nicolai said, uncomprehending. *So what*.

George said, "Here, look in your wallet, what do you see? Green money. Paper. What makes that paper worth anything more than this newspaper?"

"I don't know," Nicolai said.

"Let's have a drink." George led him by the arm back to the dining room. "What do you want? Wine? Beer? Vodka? No? All right then, a little wine won't hurt you. Esther, pour my comrade some wine." They sat back down at the table which Esther had cleared of dishes.

"I see, Nicolai, your eyes are full of skepticism. Being skeptical is a virtue. Let me tell you about money, I have made a lifelong study of it. It is the most fascinating thing, when you get down to it. It is a study in greed and control. Here is how it began: In the old days, when men first started trading with one another, there was barter. I'm talking about long ago, when men, shivering and shaking, first came out of the cave and started to grow things. Barter is all they had. You give me a goatskin, I give you a basket of grain. Something like that. You understand that, don't you?"

"Of course," Nicolai said, irritated. "Like children."

"Yes! You have the idea! Trading things. Like children. And what do children like to trade? Things that sparkle and shine. Gems, gold, silver. Things you could make jewelry out of. Trinkets. So they made coins. They had value. You could always take a coin, melt it down, and make a bracelet."

Nicolai nodded absently. He didn't see what this had to do with anything.

George pointed upward, lecturing now like a professor. "Money. Yes. Coins. Valuable coins. The Romans built their empire on them. Let's see now. Then came the Middle

Ages, things broke down. Society. Law. Everything. This stupid Christianity took over. Every little town became like a country unto itself. Even the minting of coins became a problem. Gold and silver bars were used for barter. People with lots of gold or silver didn't like lugging it around so they left it with the goldsmith—pay attention to this, Nicolai, it is the most crucial thing: The goldsmith must have had guards. Big dogs. Perhaps a vault or something. The gold was safe there. The goldsmith gave people receipts for their gold. The key to the new system was the receipts. The receipts had no one's name on them. They simply said if you brought this piece of paper to the goldsmith you could cash it in for, say, an ounce of gold. Ah! The receipt was worth an ounce of gold! The piece of paper became the thing that everyone bartered with because it was so easy to carry and because everyone would accept the receipt instead of gold. That was the beginning of the monied economy." George chuckled. "And do you know what the crooked old goldsmith did?"

"What?" Nicolai asked.

"He started to give out more receipts than he had gold. A clever trick? And why not? Sometimes people came in and asked for their gold, but never everyone at once. It was a safe thing to do to write all the receipts you wanted. He found he could spend his own receipts just like gold—he could actually create wealth with a stroke of a pen!" George banged his hand on the table and lit up a cigar. "What a great and wonderful profession! The goldsmiths became bankers overnight. And rich. Ohhhhh, how they became rich with their corrupt and wicked cheating. The very first capitalists!"

"They should have been killed," Nicolai said.

George leaned forward on his elbows. "Open your ears, Nicolai, what I'm telling you is the key to smashing America into a billion pieces. You see, Nicolai, the very first receipt he cannot redeem, the goldsmith is exposed for the crook that he is, and is hanged or beaten to death by the angry mobs."

"You tell such a good story," Esther said.

"You have not heard the best part. Let me tell you the rest of the story. Thousands of goldsmiths all over Europe started getting in on the con game. Soon, princes and kings, the biggest crooks and swindlers in the land, wanted to be able to create their own money, so they became repositories of gold, and gave out phony receipts of their own. They, too, gave out four or five times more receipts than they had gold. These receipts were paper money. This is what is called 'marginal' banking, and starry-eyed capitalist economists have been defending the crooked practice for years."

Nicolai said, "It's good we will bring them down. On with the revolution. Marginal banking, what do I care about such things? We are revolutionaries on an international scale, are we not? We should worry about that. That is our proper business."

"I am trying to broaden your horizons, Nicolai." George was getting cross with him now. "I want you to pay strict attention to the next part. You will see what all this has to do with the revolution."

Esther poured them all some more wine. "This is fascinating, George," she said. "Really."

"Wait, my sweet, until you know the rest. You have never heard of a panic? Either of you? You must know about these things if you are ever to understand the human condition. In 1857 there was a panic in America. Angry mobs stormed the banks. The stock market was shut down. Thousands of businesses went bankrupt. Unemployment soared. Same thing happened in the 1890's. That's the reason the Americans started their central bank, which they called the 'Federal Reserve System.' If something starts to go wrong, the Federal Reserve System can move in and stop the problem with unlimited money. Fluctuations, that is the problem with the capitalist system, and why our system is so far superior. The capitalist system is vulnerable at times. Panics. I called them windows of vulnerability. When the window opens, when there is a panic, the Federal Reserve moves in and shuts the window. They did it in the 1970's when the commercial paper market collapsed. They did it when the Continental Bank failed. But they were a little late with the stock market crash in 1929 and what did they have? Chaos, beautiful chaos!"

"Chaos would be wonderful," Nicolai said.

"The bills in your wallet were once called silver certificates, and you could cash them for silver at one time, Nicolai. They were issued one for one. Then they were issued two for one, then ten to one. For every dollar in circulation there was ten cents' worth of gold or silver somewhere. That was 'marginal' money. Now dollars are only notes of the Federal Reserve and cannot be redeemed for anything. They are only paper. What makes them have any value at all? I'll tell you. Belief."

"But you pay for groceries with them," Nicolai said. "So what difference does it make?"

"What if one day the grocer doesn't any longer believe in them? I told you, Nicolai, money is an idea! What if the public finds out it has been fooled and hoodwinked by the crooked central banks who are not backing the money with gold or silver or anything? When the people of this country find out, it will be just like in the old days, when they hanged the goldsmith. They will want to hang the bankers. The traffic will stop. The hum will stop. America will stop. There will be looting. The ghettos will burn. Students will riot on campuses. Food stores will be empty. Farmers, fearing they will get nothing, will not ship food. All the guns Americans own will be used on each other. And we will have our people ready to give them bullets and throw gasoline on the fire. America will go up in flames!"

"You can do all that, George?" Esther asked.

George puffed on his cigar, smiling. Then he said, "I can . . . and I will."

To be a pro, you gotta be cool at all times.

Park had that written on the front part of his brain. He told himself all the time, be cool, be cool.

He had the instincts of a bird of prey, that's what he told himself. Sometimes it was best just to circle and keep an eye on things, see what was going down.

One of the first things Park had done after his priestly visit to Poindexter's mother was to look up a woman he knew who worked for the New York City Police Department in Records for Internal Affairs. Cops who watch cops. It cost him four hundred bucks, but he got a good look at Lieutenant Somers's file on the Damian Carter case. The case was closed. The coroner and the district attorney's office had both inspected the evidence and made the same presumption based on the evidence: Damian Carter was killed by Ambrose Poindexter, subsequently found murdered. Poindexter's murder was being investigated by two rookie detectives who had no clues and were already busy with 152 other cases.

Robert Park figured he got his four hundred dollars worth. He celebrated by getting himself an ounce of coke and having himself a time.

But the next day, watching a film at the Pussycat called *Flying High*, he started thinking about Catlyn Cavanaugh. Twelve beautiful girls naked on the screen in front of him, good crotch shots, everything, and all he could think about was that Cavanaugh bitch. Okay, she wasn't the law, and she probably wasn't very bright. Just some rich bitch stirring up some shit. Nothing to worry about. But a pro's gotta be cool all the time, and part of being cool is keeping an eye on what's going on.

He knew her address on Park Avenue. No problem there.

He took a walk past the place. Asked the doorman for the time. He noticed it was the same jerk doorman that was there the night he dumped Carter. The doorman looked right at him and said, "Ten after three." Park knew then for sure there was no way in hell the doorman could ever recognize him. How cool can you get, just walking up to the jerk like that? Truly cool.

He walked a couple blocks over to Lexington Avenue and had a doughnut and a cup of coffee at a small luncheonette run by an Iranian Mom and Pop. The cash register, Park noticed, was stuffed with bills. If he ever needed a quick fix, he might stop by sometime. Place would fall if you sneezed loud, he told himself.

He sat in a corner booth, alone, with just one question on his mind: what the hell was the Cavanaugh broad up to? Okay, she was a victim. Her boyfriend got himself iced. But she was still alive. Why the hell didn't she just go on about her business and forget about it? Get some psychotherapy if she was bothered. It was like an itch he couldn't get to. He had to know what her game was, that was all there was to it. So he might as well get on with it.

He walked back over to her apartment building and took a close look at the place. No first-floor windows, no fire escape. Lots of plate glass. A small sign on the facade said it was the Firestone Apartments, managed by Fredco Management Co. Out front there was the doorman; inside, a security guard. Lots of electronic shit. The damn place had more security than Fort Knox. He walked around the block and found an alley that ran behind the Firestone Apartments. He walked down the alley and found the service entrance. He lighted a cigarette and watched for a couple minutes while a rug company pulled up and two guys carried in a Persian carpet. When the guys came out, he could see inside. There was another security guard, a fat guy, sitting at a table. He had half a dozen TV monitors in front of him.

Okay, so who said life was supposed to be easy?

Park took a cab back to his place and watched some Bugs Bunny cartoons, smoked a little Thai stick and let his imagination run. Ideas started to percolate in his brain. After a while he turned off the cartoons and looked up Fredco Management in the phone book. He practiced his best highbrow British accent for a few minutes, then dialed the number and asked for the manager.

"My name is Smyth-Philby, sir," Park said, "and I've been considering purchasing a lease in your building belonging to a Miss Catlyn Cavanaugh, subject to your approval, of course. I did have some questions, though, about the cleaning staff. I have at the moment a very good woman who does that sort of thing for me, and I was wondering whether the lease arrangement includes cleaning staff . . . It doesn't? No, I didn't really suppose it would. Miss Cavanaugh is out of town at the moment, I don't suppose you could give me her cleaning person's name, could you? I'd love to know what arrangement has been made, so that I might deal with it equitably . . . You do? Thank you much. Is she a short colored woman? . . . No, tall? Caucasian . . . Yes, I have seen her, I do recall now."

The next morning as the cleaning staff were arriving Park walked up to one of the women. She was white and tall, with a long, sad face and stringy hair. Since she was the only white cleaning woman he'd seen, he figured she must be the one.

Park was wearing a suit with a vest, hanky in the pocket. He'd darkened his complexion and was wearing a wig and heavy framed glasses far too big for his face.

"Mrs. Velma Jasco?"

"Yes?"

Park put ten one-hundred-dollar bills in her hand.

Her eyes lit up. "Why . . . what?"

Park said all she had to do was meet him for lunch at noon and she might get five more of those little beauties.

He gave her the address of the Iranian Mom and-Pop coffee shop. "Tell no one," he said, and walked away.

He was waiting for her when she showed up at ten minutes to twelve.

Mrs. Jasco ordered a third-pound hamburger for lunch, which Park paid for. The place was crowded, so Park didn't talk business. He chatted with her about the weather, what it was like working for those rich bitches, what Catlyn Cavanaugh was really like. She wanted to know why he was interested. He said he was a reporter doing a story on Catlyn Cavanaugh.

"Why, is she famous?"

"An heiress. The famous Cavanaughs of Houston."

"My, my—how can I get the rest of my money?" It didn't seem to Park that she believed he was a reporter, but so what.

Park said, "Let's talk in private."

On the way back up the street Park said, "Is she home today?"

"No, she's down in Miami someplace. Left this morning."

"All right. Good. What time do you finish up?"

"Around three."

"I'll come by about two, I'll say I'm there to fix something. The garbage disposal. You tell the guard to buzz me in."

Her eyes narrowed. "You ain't gonna steal nothin'?"

"All I want to do is look around. That's it. Why the hell would I spend all this money if I wanted to steal?"

She shrugged. "You got a point there."

At 2:05, when Park showed up wearing overalls and carrying a tool box, the fat security guard hardly looked at him. Mrs. Jasco had already called him, saying the man to fix the garbage disposal would be coming. The guard asked to see his ID, which Park produced—showing him to be Pete Wilson, a member of the plumbers' union, local 3291.

He went up in the elevator. Mrs. Jasco let Park into Catlyn's apartment. He gave her twenty one-hundred-dollar bills. She sat down on the couch to fondle them. "It's going to be a merry, merry Christmas this year."

Park took a look around the bedroom first. Closet full of nice clothes. Nice furniture, everything neat. Two framed pictures of Damian Carter on the bureau. The little jewelry he found was nice. Not gaudy. A few strings of pearls, some small flawless diamond earrings. A ruby brooch that looked like an heirloom. Next to the bed were a few books: a couple of murder mysteries, a travel book on the Bahamas, a book on tennis, another on exercise and diet. In the bottom of the underwear drawer there was a gourmet sex manual and a couple of joints wrapped in tinfoil. They looked old. She sure wasn't any pothead. The cleaning lady was watching him from the doorway, not saying anything.

Next, Park checked the living room. There wasn't much. A small desk by the window had a checkbook and an appointment book, filled with places, but no names. After the day of Damian Carter's killing the appointments were scratched out.

"What do you make of this?" he asked the cleaning woman.

She shrugged. "This Cavanaugh woman ain't the talkative type. When she's here, she don't say boo to me. I don't know what she does. She comes and goes. Yesterday she said she was going to Miami, that's maybe the first time she ever said where she's going."

"She go away often?"

"Every couple of weeks she's gone for a few days. She comes back real tired. Sleeps all day sometimes."

"What's she do when she's gone?"

"I got no idea."

"There any other rooms?"

"The study."

As soon as the cleaning woman opened the door, he knew

he'd struck it. Here were stacks of police reports, autopsy reports, sketches of Ambrose Poindexter, newsclippings, notes of interviews of witnesses. He turned around and said, "How about you get back to work? You can search me when I leave, make sure I ain't stealing anything."

"I will, too," she said.

"Hey, it's okay," he assured her. He closed the door. He went carefully through the notes and newsclippings, private eye reports. He marveled at her thoroughness, but he knew she hadn't any idea who he was. And the way she was going about it, he didn't figure she would find out, either. She had B. B. Hanson trying to track down all the possible hit men in the New York area who were about the same size as Ambrose Poindexter and were known to use disguises. So far, Hanson had gotten nowhere. And he would continue to get nowhere, Park figured, because Park didn't have that many clients and he was very selective. A real pro. He also found out Catlyn was off someplace trying to figure out who might have paid to have the job done, checking out some guy named Whiteside.

When he came out of the study an hour later, Velma Jasco went through his pockets and patted him down. He had a big smile on his face.

"See, not so much as a scrap of paper."

"I still got to check, that was our deal."

"Give me your home phone," he said to her. "We maybe can do business again."

"That would be more than my pleasure."

Back on the street, Park was feeling good. Nothing to do now but keep an eye on things until everybody gets real tired of not finding out nothing, and forgets about it.

FIFTEEN

It was raining in Miami. Catlyn was dressed for it; she stepped out of the airport terminal wearing a good waterproof trench coat. She had arranged for a driver to pick her up at the airport in a limousine. They headed down the Dolphin Expressway toward downtown Miami.

She didn't like Florida much. Palm trees always meant retirement and relaxation, with sun, beaches, and nothing much to do but play golf and lie around growing old. She'd been to Palm Beach for a couple of high-stakes low-ball games, won some big money a couple of times, but still she didn't like it. Even the games were slow-paced, lacking the kind of passionate intensity found in New York, California, and Europe.

The driver deposited Catlyn at Biscayne Boulevard and 5th Street. The Panax Building was a modern mirror, glass, and stainless skyscraper. She took the elevator to the tenth floor and walked into Suite 1054. She told the bleached-blond, deep-fried tanned receptionist she wanted to see Mr. Herman Whiteside.

"Your name?"

"Catlyn Cavanaugh." She took off her trench coat and put it over the back of a chair in the reception area.

"Is Mr. Whiteside expecting you?"

"No. I spoke to him yesterday from New York and told him I would phone him this afternoon. He said he would be in. Instead of phoning, I decided to come in person."

The receptionist's eyebrows went up with mild surprise. "I'll tell Mr. Whiteside you're here," she said.

The receptionist disappeared into the inner office and came back a moment later. "Mr. Whiteside will see you."

Whiteside's office was huge, decorated in a modern tropical motif, the wallpaper suggesting coconut palms, the deep green rug in a fern-leaf pattern. The glass-topped desk was cluttered with papers and cigar ash. He had a view of the bay and the causeways over to Miami Beach. A leafy palm tree in the corner of the office looked, Catlyn thought, as if moths had been at it.

"I'm rather surprised to see you, since we only spoke on the phone yesterday," Whiteside said, offering a small, pudgy hand with a diamond pinkie ring. "Won't you have a seat?" He was plump, fiftyish, and bald, and was dressed in a pale blue leisure suit with a tie tack. If he were transformed into an animal, Catlyn thought, he'd no doubt be a toad.

As she slid onto the sculptured clear plastic seat, Catlyn looked Whiteside over carefully. All she really knew about him was that he was a partner in Carter Shipping and had tried to oust Damian Carter as Chairman of the Board a year before in a proxy fight. He and his associates had lost. In the process, Damian put the Securities and Exchange Commission onto him and some of his crooked manipulations. He was now under indictment by a Federal grand jury. Rumor had it Whiteside had friends in the Mafia and was laundering drug money through a bank he owned in Jamaica.

"Now then," Whiteside said, sitting back in his chair with his legs crossed. "You said you had a quarter of a million to invest and were thinking of Carter Shipping. You also said that I was recommended to you by the Crupiano family of Brooklyn."

"I'm acquainted with the son of the elder Crupiano."

His eyebrows went up. "Are you now? Junior's quite a poker player, I hear. Won the biggest pot in the history of the world, I'm told. Over a million dollars. One pot." Whiteside whistled.

Catlyn said, "I did not actually come here about an investment, Mr. Whiteside."

"Oh?"

"I'm here about Damian Carter."

Whiteside sat up. "I see." He straightened his tie. "And what about him?"

"On the night of September 4, he was murdered on Park Avenue in the city of New York by an alleged mugger named Ambrose Poindexter."

"I read about it, of course. Big piece in *The Wall Street Journal*. A terrible, terrible tragedy." His voice lowered to emphasize the magnitude of the tragedy.

"Three days later," Catlyn said evenly, "Ambrose Poindexter was found with his throat cut."

"Oh, really? I hadn't heard that." He was looking out the window where the rain was streaking down.

"At the time he was found, Ambrose Poindexter had on his person a very expensive wristwatch I had given Mr. Carter for his birthday last February. The watch had been taken by Mr. Carter's assailant the night he was killed."

"Why are you telling me this, Miss Cavanaugh?" He was looking at her now.

"I want to impress you with my command of the facts, Mr. Whiteside."

"Why should I—if you'll forgive the expression—give a good goddamn?"

Catlyn shifted her weight in her chair, but did not take her eyes off him. She smoothed the folds out of her skirt and said, "Damian Carter was the man responsible for your indictment on stock fraud charges, isn't it rather obvious? You wanted him dead, didn't you?"

"Damian Carter was not the man responsible for my current troubles. *I'm* the man responsible." He smiled a snide quirky smile and his cheeks glowed pink. "You think I might have had Damian killed. Very funny." He sputtered out a small laugh. "Not true, simply not true, what else can I tell you?"

She was watching his eyes closely; they were darting nervously. If he didn't do it, he'd been dreaming of it, she thought. She wasn't quite sure. He was looking directly at her, which usually meant a lie, but his pupils were large and open. She said, "I know a great deal about the man you hired. He's a master of disguise, a combat veteran. He's five nine or ten, one-forty, white, in very good physical condition. I don't know his name, but I soon will."

He swiveled in his chair toward the window shaking his head. His face was very red now, laced with blue veins. He took a deep breath and said, "I don't want to hear any more of this. Get out, Miss Cavanaugh. I don't have people killed, that's all there is to it." He faced her and said, "I had absolutely nothing to do with the death of Damian Carter and I have no idea who did."

Catlyn stood up. She was still staring at him and he was staring back. After a moment, she said, "You know what, Mr. Whiteside? I believe you."

Oscar had lied to Catlyn; he was a spy. Especially now, driving out to see Ernest Ramsey's widow in Cedar Grove, Maryland. It was a crisp autumn day, windy and clear, the kind he used to enjoy walking with his dog along the Nashua River, throwing pebbles. On a day like this, going on a mission like this, he longed to be just a professor of economics maybe. Or an investment banker. Something like that. Anything but a spy.

He didn't like to think of himself as a spy, but that was

what he was. He was working for the economic policy analysis section of the Mossad, and was a grade seven junior officer, equivalent to a second lieutenant in the Army, assigned to the North America desk. His boss, code-named Euripides, was an economist and a spy also. Euripides had not been out of Israel in twenty years, running everything through communications channels and dead drops, message runners, and other intermediaries.

Almost everything else Oscar had told Catlyn was the truth. He had grown up in Boston and earned degrees from Syracuse University and Harvard and had gone to Israel to work on a kibbutz. He had been hoeing onions when the man from the Mossad came to call. The proposal was simple. All they wanted him to do was read field reports and write papers explaining what was going on in the American economy. Easy enough. Necessary work. Since Israel was dependent on American arms, Israel had to be informed about America's economy.

Of course, they said, he would have to be trained as an agent "just in case." A formality. That was the way they seduced the unwary. He might have to go into the field on an emergency basis from time to time, they said. Euripides called him in on his first "emergency" the day he finished training.

Oscar had been in the field now for eighteen months because, they explained, there was a critical shortage of field agents. Old-timers told him there had been a critical shortage since Ben Gurion signed the order creating the Mossad in 1948. And there would continue to be a shortage until the last Arab put down his gun, which seemed like a very far time in the future.

He had filed a report about Damian Carter's death to Tel Aviv through his superior at the consulate, the military attaché. The report stated that, according to the available evidence, Damian Carter had been killed in an act of random violence by a petty street thief named Ambrose

Poindexter. Oscar had included copies of the police report, autopsy, and summaries of interviews with various witnesses, including Catlyn Cavanaugh. Two days later he received orders to check into the accidental death of Ernest Ramsey.

It had been fairly easy to convince Sonja Ramsey to see him. He told her he was a reporter for the Tel Aviv English language paper, and that he had interviewed her husband the year before. He told her he wanted to interview her not about the tragedy, but about the personal side of her husband's life. He said he had considered Ernest Ramsey, as chief economist of the Hustead administration, to be the one voice of sanity howling in a forest of lost souls. She said she would be free at noon. He parked on the street in front of the house in the elegant little suburb at five minutes to noon and walked up the driveway to the house. The lawn was trim, the bushes manicured. The house had a brick facade and pillars on the front porch. Sonja Ramsey opened the door and asked him in. She directed him to a comfortable couch in the living room where he sat with his back to the window.

Being in Sonja Ramsey's living room under false pretenses, having lied about why he had come and making up more lies as he went along, made Oscar feel very uncomfortable. Thoughts of telling Euripides to go jump in the Red Sea were flashing in his head. She sat in a rocker nearby, wearing a black dress, her plain brown hair combed straight down. She stared at him blankly, looking confused, as if she wanted to explain something and didn't want to speak out of turn.

Oscar said, "Now then, Mrs. Ramsey, I'm sure you are very tired of answering this question, but I know our readers would like to know . . ."

"I know he didn't kill himself, I know it was an accident."

Oscar hadn't even planned to ask that. He already knew,

from the physical evidence, that the man deliberately drove into the concrete bridge abutment. Even the rather dull-witted deputy sheriff at the scene had come to that conclusion.

"I know he didn't do it deliberately," Oscar said softly. The lie felt cold on his tongue. "He just wasn't that kind of man."

The woman smiled. Her face seemed made of putty. Maybe she was on Valium, Oscar thought. Maybe she was in shock. Her lips were trembling, as if she wanted desperately to say something and was fighting the urge. Oscar remained silent and kept looking at his notes, waiting for her to speak.

Finally, she said, "Ernest would never have done anything to hurt himself. Ever. He loved his family too much." A tear rolled down her cheek.

Oscar thought: God, I hate this job.

She inhaled deeply, rubbing her hands together as if they were cold. She said, "The FBI investigated. They think he killed himself. They didn't say so, but I could tell from the kinds of questions they asked. Was he depressed? Was he secure in his job? Was he getting along with his family? I told them exactly how it was. He wasn't depressed. He loved his family. He loved me. Everything was just fine, he loved his work . . ." She shook her head, uncomprehending.

Oscar said, "One theory is your husband just caved in to the pressure of work and was hiding it from everyone. The afternoon of the day he died he visited his father's grave."

"I know," she said. "He loved his father. He visited the grave often. He missed his father. Does that make him suicidal?"

"No, of course not. No." Oscar's mouth was dry. "Was there . . . was there another woman?"

She turned to him and said, "Would you like a cup of tea?"

Obviously, Oscar thought, she was turning off her mind to certain possibilities. He said, "I think I should be going. But could you tell me where he might have been the night before he was killed?"

"The Peruvian Embassy. At a party."

"I meant after the party."

She stiffened. "Whatever rumors you may have heard, they are not true."

The question, as it formed in the back of his throat, had a bitter taste. "What rumors are those, Mrs. Ramsey?"

"That he left with that blond woman."

She burst into tears. It was as if she was made of butter and suddenly melted, bringing her legs up and burying her head in her lap. He tried to comfort her, but she wouldn't stop crying. Her whole body shook. "Oh, Ernest, my beloved!" she wailed.

Oscar left her there and crept out the door. He felt like a thief.

It cost the Mossad $3,030 in bribes to find out who the blonde was. Most of it, $2,500, went to the assistant protocol officer at the Peruvian Embassy for an official list of invitees; the rest went to various butlers, clerks, and musicians to find out that her name was Rita Montgomery. And that she had been a sex surrogate. It also cost Oscar a week of his time.

None of the local phone books listed a Rita Montgomery. He called twenty-two other Montgomerys to see whether anyone knew a Rita Montgomery. None did. In a throw-away newspaper called *The New Age Washington* he found six sex surrogates listed. He called them and only found two of them in; the others had answering machines. The second one knew Rita—at least knew she had her office in an apartment building on Stevenson Avenue near Lincoln in Baltimore.

Oscar found the right building on the fifth try. The building manager was young, Latin, and greedy. "We can't give out no addresses, man," he said. "Company policy."

Oscar offered him a hundred dollars.

"I don't put my fucking job on the line for no hundred bucks."

Oscar offered him two hundred. "That's it, friend," Oscar said, " 'cause that's all I got."

Twenty minutes later Oscar was standing in the entryway of Rita Montgomery's apartment building in Roxbury Park. He hadn't quite figured out how to handle this one. He figured the best way was professionally. He pushed the button.

"Yes?" a finely tuned woman's voice answered.

"You don't know me, Miss Montgomery," he said hurriedly, "but my name is Roger Cohen. I'm in need—desperate need—of your services."

"Where'd you hear about me?"

"I, ah, was at an embassy party the other night. Someone pointed you out and said that you were good . . . he said you could, ah, cure my problem. Listen, if you're too busy, forget it. It was just, ah, a thought. But could you recommend somebody? I'm desperate. Money is no object. I'll pay anything . . ."

There was only silence for a long moment. Then she said, "Come on up," and buzzed him in.

She was waiting in the doorway across from the elevator wearing a long fur-lined robe open to her navel. Her hair was fluffy and she had big brown eyes that said, come on, let's play.

The apartment was done in blues and golds, the floor covered with a plush gold-colored carpet. The furniture was ultra-modern. The music was soothing, the lights were down low, the shades pulled tight.

"I'm pleased to meet you, Mr. Cohen. Why don't you take off your coat, make yourself comfortable."

210

"In a moment, perhaps."

She was trying to read his face. She smiled. "All right, in a moment then. We're a bit tense, are we?"

"I'm always tense," Oscar said.

"Maybe that's your problem. It's four o'clock. I was just about to have a splash of Scotch. Join me?"

"No."

Her smile faded.

"I'm not here for what you think," he said. "I'm here about Ernest Ramsey."

"Who's he?" She seemed genuinely not to know.

"He was the President's chief economic adviser until last week, and now he's dead. I'm trying to find out why."

"I assure you, I haven't the slightest idea. Sex is my business, I don't fool with the economy or the President. Unless, of course, he needs a little help in the bedroom arts." She drifted away from him, heading behind the bar.

Oscar put his hand in his coat. "Keep your hands where I can see them," he said.

She froze. "Who are you?"

"I'm just a guy who wants the truth and you're going to tell it to me. I know you were at the party at the Peruvian Embassy. I know you deliberately introduced yourself to Ernest Ramsey. I know you talked for over twenty minutes. I know you left alone and waited for him on the corner. I know he picked you up."

"No . . . I . . ."

"Where did you go?"

"I don't know what you're talking about."

"You goddamn do know what I'm talking about. Ernest Ramsey left that party with you. He came home very late, parked his car half on his lawn. The next day he went to the office. Nothing amiss, except maybe he had bloodshot eyes. Then he got a phone call. A few minutes later he left and never came back. He was seen visiting his father's grave. That night he took his family out to dinner. Later, he got up

211

out of bed, got in his car, and drove into a bridge abutment at one hundred and ten miles an hour. Now do you know what I'm talking about?" She stared at him.

He said, "Sit down, relax, I'm not going anywhere until you tell me the whole thing, so you might as well begin. Tell me what you told the FBI."

"I haven't talked to the FBI." Her face seemed to go blank with fear.

"You will talk to them," he said. "Tell me and I might be able to fix it so you won't have to." He didn't know why he said that, and he immediately regretted it. He didn't like making false promises. Spies were always having to make false promises.

"The FBI can be here in fifteen minutes," he said.

She stared at him rigidly for a long moment, then nodded. "All right, all right. I did leave with him. Somebody at the party told him what business I was in and he wanted to talk to me. We didn't *do* anything. We drove around for a while. Talked. That's all. Just talked. He told me how unhappy he was working for the President. How he hated his wife. How he hated being on his best behavior all the time. He wanted to bust loose. He asked me to go to Europe with him for a few days. I told him he better think about it before he threw his life away. We stopped at a motel. We were going to make love, but he got cold feet. I don't think he ever did it with anyone else but his old lady. He put me in a cab and went home. That's it, I swear to God."

"Give me the name of the motel."

"The Coronet, over on Rhode Island. Ask the desk clerk, Satch, his name is. He knows me. He'll remember."

"You got a phone book?"

"Right over there."

"Get it. Look up the number of the Coronet."

She made a face, but did what he told her. He told her to dial the number. She did.

A woman answered. "Coronet Motel."

"You have someone working there called Satch?"

"Our night man. Comes on at eleven."

"He going to be on tonight?"

"If he's sober."

"Thanks."

Oscar hung up.

"Told you," she said.

"Okay, you went there with Ramsey, but he got cold feet. What time was that?"

"I don't have a watch. Three, maybe."

"Had you been drinking?"

"Sure."

"Drugs?"

"A little weed is all."

"And you just talked."

"Yeah. That's what my job mostly is. Talk. Guys get hung up, I let them talk. Sometimes I let them touch me. I'm a surrogate. Psychologists send me clients. I got references."

"I'm sure you do. What's your theory?"

"What theory?"

"Why'd the guy kill himself?"

"I thought he was in an accident. Paper said he lost control of his car."

"So he didn't seem all that despondent to you?"

"No more or less than ninety-eight percent of the jerks I see in this business. You want anything else? I don't know anything more about Ramsey. Now if you want my services pull down your pants. If not, would you please get the hell out of here?"

"Good night," he said.

Oscar drove away from Rita Montgomery's place a bit confused. Was that all there was to it? Had Ramsey just gone off with this so-called sex surrogate and just gotten a little drunk and talked? Maybe she was making it all up,

213

maybe that wasn't the way it was at all. He wasn't going to beat the truth out of her. He wasn't going to drug her or use the new electroshock techniques. He wasn't that far gone yet. Too much civilian in him, not enough spy. Even thinking about such things gave him a cold shiver.

Lord, did he hate this job.

One of the first things the Mossad taught him in spy school was to follow up every lead. Believe nothing, double check, triple check. Find out the truth. He'd believed her. She was into sex, nothing more. Sexual hangups, job pressure, the pattern was there. Still, he had to nail things down, cross all the t's and dot all the i's.

Oscar had to wait until eleven to meet with Satch. In the meantime, he had dinner, saw a movie, and drank some coffee in the coffee shop at the Coronet Motel. All the while, he was asking himself how he ever let himself get talked into this racket. Make your mother proud, was one of the things they said. Of course, he couldn't tell his mother what he was doing. He couldn't tell anyone. The Mossad was strict about such things.

At eleven-fifteen he showed up at the Coronet. It was a little run-down, but clean. Satch was forty-five or so with a big beer gut and bushy eyebrows. He had a beat-up face, as if he might have once been a boxer or a football player. Oscar held a hundred dollars out in front of him.

"What's this for?" Satch asked.

"For a little truth."

"You came to the right guy."

"Rita Montgomery. Know her?"

"Fuzzy redhead—now she's a blonde. That's right. Yeah, I know her."

"She here on Monday the tenth?"

He nodded. "Yeah. With a guy in a suit. Nice-looking guy, real quiet. Looked like a government guy. You can smell 'em a mile away."

"Was he Ernest Ramsey?"

214

"Who's he?"

"It was on the news—the President's adviser who got killed in a car wreck."

"I don't pay any attention to that shit."

Oscar showed him five pictures. "Was he one of these men?" They were photos of five Israeli actors.

"Nope."

Oscar showed him another picture. It was Ramsey. "That him?"

"That's the guy."

"You win," Oscar said, dropping the hundred-dollar bill on the counter. "How long they stay?"

"Just a couple of minutes. Five, tops. He left in his car, Rita took a cab."

On the way back to his motel, Oscar Feldman was feeling old and tired-out for thirty-three years old. All that work and what did he have? Ernest Ramsey couldn't get it up, couldn't stand his wife, hated his job, and so he took a nosedive into a bridge. How the boys back in Tel Aviv were going to moan and groan over his expense account this month. And not a damn thing to show for it.

Carson Black, coming out of the studio where they were shooting the nightly news at eleven, was told by the assistant producer that a young woman was waiting for her in her office. Carson asked whether she gave a name. "Rita something" was the reply.

Carson burst into her office, slamming the door behind her.

"What the hell are you doing here," she screamed at Rita. "I told you never even to phone me here! Who the hell let you past security?"

"I have a way with men, remember? I showed him a picture of us together down in Jamaica."

"Christ. You idiot!"

215

Rita's eyes flooded with tears. "I wouldn't have come, but you haven't been home and there's been trouble!"

"Trouble?"

"A guy showed up at my place asking questions."

"What guy, who?"

"Said his name was Cohen. Tall. Brown hair. Sharp features."

"What was he, a cop? He show you an ID?"

"I thought he was a john, or I'd have never let him in. He said he had a problem. I thought he had a limp dick. Christ."

Carson took Rita by the shoulders and guided her to a chair. She poured her some Scotch from a bottle in her desk and handed her the glass. "Just slow down and tell me everything that happened. What you said, what he said, everything."

Rita told her everything, taking small sips of Scotch and big gulps of air between sentences. When she was finished, Carson said, "He was sure the FBI was in on it? Did he say why he was so sure?"

"No."

"Okay, we can find out. It might have been a bluff. Why the hell did you tell him you went to the Coronet?"

"I thought we might have been seen—he acted like he knew everything. He had me off balance. I figured that was the best way to cover. Just say we went there but nothing happened."

"Okay, then what?"

"I called Satch at home and told him if the guy showed what to tell him. I told him what Ramsey looked like, what he was wearing, everything."

"And did he show?"

"I don't know. Satch went on at eleven, I was on my way down here."

"Call him now."

Rita dialed the number and asked Satch whether the guy

216

had been in.

"Sure, baby."

"And what did you tell him?"

"I told him what you told me to tell him. He gave me a hundred dollars. Nice fella."

"Thank you Satch, old friend. I owe you a little something. I'll give it to you, too. Just the way you like it."

"You set my heart on fire."

Rita hung up the phone.

Carson smiled and said, "It's going to be okay. We're covered."

Rita got up from her chair and threw her arms around Carson. "Oh, Carson. I was soooooooo worried. I hate this business. Don't ask me to do this kind of thing again, okay? When he was giving me the third degree, my brain turned to a goddamn block of ice."

"It's all over now, sweetheart," Carson said. "Look, tell you what. Why don't you drive over to the safe house and wait for me there? I'll see, maybe I can get some time, we'll go on a vacation."

"You mean it, Carson? That would be wonderful!"

"I've got some time coming. Wait for me. Might take me a day or two to spring free. Go over there, help yourself to whatever you want. I'll call the caretaker and tell him you're coming."

"Oh, Carson, I knew you'd make me feel better. You always do."

Carson kissed her and gave her breast a squeeze. "Okay, Rita. Just get over there, relax, and stay beautiful. Okay? Get going, I've got things to do."

Rita was asleep in the big round bed when Nicolai got there at six-fifteen the following morning. He had let himself in with the key hidden behind the mailbox. He went upstairs and into the big bedroom. She was wearing a white lace nightgown and looked, he thought, beautiful.

He nudged her on the shoulder. She opened her eyes, smiled, then frowned. "Oh, it's you. What the fuck do you want?"

"Not a very nice way to say 'good morning,' is it? I'm sorry to wake you, but you have a job to do."

"What job?"

"I have orders to drive you to Durham, North Carolina, today. You have to get to know a business executive down there tomorrow."

"Ah, Jesus."

"Complaining about it isn't going to make it any easier. Your control is going to meet us there."

"You sure?"

"That's what they told me. I'm supposed to leave you off at the Holiday Inn, contact will be made. We have a long drive, so let's try to get along, how does that sound?"

"Okay."

Nicolai said, "Let me cook you some breakfast, what do you say?"

She reached for her cigarettes on the bedside table. "I told my control I was out of the business."

"After the Durham deal, you're supposed to go to some resort down in Georgia."

"Really?"

"That's what they said. I'm supposed to take you and your control to the plane."

"Okay!"

She rolled out of bed. "I'd like eggs over easy and whole wheat toast."

"Coming right up."

She headed for the shower.

Two hours later they were fifty miles south of Richmond on I-95 in rural Virginia in a rented Ford. He listened to the classical music station as he drove. It calmed him, and he needed to be calm. Rita said she didn't mind classical music, but she preferred rock. She loved Cindy Lauper, she said. And Madonna. New Wave. But this Bach and Beethoven stuff was okay in small doses.

Near Rockville, Nicolai pulled off the interstate and headed up a country road. The leaves were just beginning to turn. Rita took a look at a map and said, "Where're you going?"

"Left my camera junk up the road here a little ways at an equipment drop. We're supposed to get pictures of this businessman. Only take a few minutes."

"Okay." She looked out the window for a few minutes, then turned to him and said, "You ever think about getting out of this business, Nicolai?"

"Me? No."

"Where you from?"

"Here and there."

"Not supposed to say, are you? I forgot."

"You know the rules. It's best to live by them."

"Once they got you, they got you. Know what I mean? I got into this because I fell in love with the wrong person."

"Hey, you're not the only one that's happened to."

"Is that what happened to you?"

"I'm an idealist."

"You know, I think you are."

"My father was a soldier, then a spy. I was raised since I was little to do this kind of work. I'm good at it. I'm doing the most I can for international socialism, I really believe that. Espionage is a very effective weapon in the class struggle."

"I haven't got the stomach for it."

"Not everyone does, Rita. Don't be hard on yourself. I heard a rumor you were in a little trouble. What happened? Can you talk about it? You don't want to, you don't have to."

"I'll tell you. It's not that complicated. A man came to see me and I got scared. I went to my control."

219

"Your control got angry or what?"

"What is it you're not telling me, Nicolai? You know something, don't you?"

"I think some people are a little unhappy with you, that's all I know."

"Well, I'm a little unhappy with them, too. I should never have had a job in my own city. I was using my trade name, for chrissake. You know, I'm going to have to move permanently. I had friends in Washington. I liked it there."

"Well, we all have to make sacrifices—for the cause."

"The cause. What the fuck do I care about International Socialism?"

The road was narrow now, barely one lane wide. They came to the foot of a hill and turned into a driveway. Nicolai sounded his horn. A man came out of a shack and opened the gate. They drove in.

Rita said, "That man. He's the caretaker of the safe house."

"Is he? I guess you're right."

"What's going on, Nicolai? What are we doing here?"

"I told you, I have to pick up some equipment. Relax. You think I'm going to rape you or something?"

She smiled. "No, I guess not."

They drove up over a small hill. Nicolai followed some tire marks which led to a flat spot in a grove of trees. Here the tire marks ended and it looked as if there was some work going on. There was a back hoe. All she saw was the narrow slit dug into the earth and the pile of dirt alongside it.

"What's going on here?" she asked Nicolai. He'd taken a gun out of his jacket and was affixing a silencer to it. "It's a grave—for me . . ."

Nicolai said, "Don't run. I might not do it quick and clean if you run."

"If you'd let me talk to my control, Nicolai, I'm sure I could fix it."

220

"I have my orders, Rita. Please step out of the car."

"Don't do this, Nicolai," she said, her voice a whisper. "I'll make love to you. Let me make love to you like nobody else has ever made love to you. Please, Nicolai, I don't want to die."

Nicolai said, "Everybody's got to take their turn. This is yours, Rita." He reached across and pulled the door handle and pushed the door open. A rush of cold air swept in. Rita stepped out, holding the door to support herself.

"I did everything they asked," she said. She looked back up the hill. The old caretaker was waving his hands. "Look there!" she said. "He wants to tell you something. Maybe they've changed their minds!"

"He's only saying the coast is clear, Rita."

He took her by the arm and started walking her over to the hole dug in the ground. Her knees buckled under her and he had to hold her up. She was mumbling now, tears streaking down her cheeks. Then she straightened up and turned to Nicolai and said, "You tell Carson I love her even now. Tell her, Nicolai."

"I don't think she cares, Rita, one way or the other," Nicolai said, shoving the gun up under her sternum. He squeezed the trigger.

The sound in the cold morning air was no more than the snapping of a twig.

SIXTEEN

Of the five people Oscar Feldman had told Catlyn he thought had reason to murder Damian Carter, Catlyn had eliminated two: Christopher Carter, whom she had known since he was thirteen, and Herman Whiteside, whom she had visited in Florida. The next one on the list was Lisa Boatharbor, the playwright. Lisa Boatharbor was not quite as easy to get to see as Whiteside had been. When Catlyn called to make an appointment, a secretary said she was busy writing and was taking no calls. Send a letter, the secretary suggested. Catlyn protested, saying it was an emergency and a matter of utmost importance. "Sorry," the secretary said.

It was time, Catlyn thought, to be creative. She called a poker player she knew by the name of Thornhill, an editor of a national newspaper. He once owed her a gambling debt of twenty-five thousand dollars, which she was letting him pay off in installments of two hundred a month. She offered him his IOU in return for a favor. He was anxious to help.

Lisa Boatharbor was almost sixty, thin, a chain-smoker, and, as far as Catlyn could tell, totally wrapped up in herself. Just the kind of person who could pay to have someone killed, Catlyn surmised.

Thornhill arranged to have a reporter interview Lisa

Boatharbor about her latest play. Lisa Boatharbor couldn't pass up an interview in a newspaper with 2.5 million subscribers. Catlyn went along as the photographer. The reporter was Scott Byrne, a serious young man who had no idea of Catlyn's real identity and mission; but he knew she wasn't a photographer. He had to show her how to load the film in her new Pentax 35 millimeter camera and which button to push to snap the picture.

The interview took place in a backstage office of the theater where *A Matter of the Mating Instinct* was playing. The office was tiny, cluttered, and stuffy. Lisa Boatharbor sat on an old wooden chair in front of a roll-top desk. Scott Byrne was given a metal folding chair. Catlyn remained standing.

Scott Byrne asked Lisa Boatharbor all the usual questions: what did she think of the current state of Broadway, how did she feel when the critics called her previous play a complete bore, and so on. Catlyn just kept snapping pictures of one or the other of them, or both, as they talked. Lisa Boatharbor kept dragging on cigarette after cigarette, crushing them out in a big blue ceramic ashtray, as she went on griping about the critics, the unresponsive audiences, and her director, whom she called a "small fart, caught in a big wind." Scott Byrne got all this on a tape recorder.

When the interview seemed to be winding down, Catlyn said, "What I'd like to know about is Damian Carter."

Lisa Boatharbor looked up at her and said, "What did you say?" It was the first time she'd really looked at Catlyn.

"I said, what I would really like to know about is Damian Carter. He was murdered. Someone was paid to kill him. I heard you and he had some violent disagreement about a grant the week before the murder took place."

Scott Byrne blanched. He sat back in his chair as if he expected Lisa Boatharbor to detonate. But she didn't. She simply picked a piece of tobacco off her lower lip and looked dully at Catlyn. "I thought he was killed by a mugger. Some black kid."

"Ambrose Poindexter. He didn't kill Damian Carter. Damian Carter was killed by a paid assassin."

"I suppose it's possible." The playwright inserted another cigarette between her yellow fingers and lighted it with a butane lighter. "I don't see what this all has to do with me and the disagreement Damian and I had—but I'm sure you're about to make a connection, aren't you?"

Catlyn said, "It doesn't take too much to see the connection. The man who killed him is of muscular build, about five nine or ten. He's quite possibly a combat veteran—Vietnam, probably. He's a master of disguise, most likely had professional training in the theater. You're in the theater. You were having trouble with Damian Carter."

"More than just trouble." She laughed a throaty laugh and took a deep drag on a cigarette. She looked at Scott Byrne and said, "I loathed the son of a bitch. I had a Huckleberry Foundation Grant to do a string of workshops with the Young Actors' Studio. You know why Damian nixed it? I don't. Just plain wanted to be an asshole and I was handy." She looked back at Catlyn. "I get it. You think I went out and hired somebody and had the son of a bitch knocked off."

"Yes, I do."

Scott Byrne winced. Lisa Boatharbor smiled at him, then said to Catlyn, "You're right, I did it. Call the cops, get them down here! Call the networks, you've got the scoop of the century! But you're wrong about one thing, I didn't pay somebody to have him knocked off, I did it myself. Disguised as a man. Shoved a knife right through his gizzard." She made an awkward gesture of sticking someone with knife, then laughed, throwing her head back. "I enjoyed every moment of it." She laughed again, her

224

whole body shaking, then she flicked an ash into the ashtray. "Man, wouldn't that fill this place up! Lisa Boatharbor arrested for murder!"

"Let's get out of here," Catlyn said to Scott Byrne.

That afternoon she met B. B. Hanson for a late lunch at a small Hindu restaurant in the East Village. Catlyn loved the curries; B. B. had to wash the food down quickly with vast quantities of red wine, but he professed to like it. She told him that she took Lisa Boatharbor off her list.

B. B.'s report was not favorable, either. He'd talked to some uptown sports, he said, who supposedly had heard about some dude that would do a wet job for anybody, but he wasn't working for any of the gangs, so nobody knew him. B. B. was also still trying to find out where Ambrose Poindexter might have been at the time Damian Carter was killed, because he didn't believe the guys at the Brooklyn clinic. A Harlem kid wouldn't go to Brooklyn to clear up a dose.

"Have you been able to find out if Ambrose tried to sell Damian's watch?"

"Ah checked out every fence in this town and nobody seen the lad."

"We've got to keep looking for a hired killer who uses disguises."

"He might be an out-of-town hitter."

"Okay, we'll get some people on it in Chicago, Detroit, L.A., Miami."

"Ah got a new thing ta try. Ah'm gonna start askin' around, try ta hire a dude, say Ah needs somebody fogged and Ah needs a pro."

"Watch yourself, B. B."

"You watch yo'self, too. How's Mr. Getsong doin' on my case?"

"He told me he's waltzing the D.A., he'll let us know.

225

Stop worrying about that, it'll be handled."

Early that evening she telephoned Stuart Daly, the fourth name on Oscar Feldman's list. Stuart Daly was the largest stockholder in Carter Manufacturing and a member of the board. For thirty years, whatever Damian Carter wanted, Stuart Daly saw to it he didn't get easily. Catlyn was told by a butler with a dry voice that Mr. Daly was in the hospital with a mild stroke and was not expected to return to his normal activities for at least a month. She asked what hospital he was in so she could send a card.

At nine-fifteen she walked into Room 318 at St. Francis Hospital. Stuart Daly was lying in bed staring into space, an oxygen catheter in his nose. He appeared to be in his eighties, hollow-cheeked, toothless, a thin wisp of white hair sitting like smoke on the top of his head. He opened his eyes and looked at Catlyn. His eyes were yellow.

She hesitated for a moment, startled by how bad he looked, then she stiffened and walked directly over to him and said, "I'm Catlyn Cavanaugh, Mr. Daly, do you know who I am?"

He looked at her, puzzled for a moment, then nodded.

"You were stricken the day after Damian was knifed to death, I believe."

He nodded again. Spittle ran down from a corner of his mouth.

Catlyn felt cold in her throat. She shut her eyes for a moment. When she opened them, the old man was staring at her. He nodded, as if he wanted her to continue what she was saying.

"I'm trying to find out who had him killed."

He nodded again, and a trace of fear crossed his eyes.

"Your name came up on a list of possible suspects."

He just kept staring. Catlyn thought he understood her, but she wasn't sure. "I've got a good idea about the man who actually stabbed Damian . . . He's a Vietnam veteran, he's about . . ." She couldn't go on, that's all there was to

226

it. Even if this man did it, she did not want to add to his suffering at this moment. She backed away. "I'm sorry to have bothered you," she said, touching his hand.

She started to leave, but Stuart Daly made a noise, a gurgling sound. Catlyn turned back toward him. He crooked a spindly finger at her. She went back to his bedside. He pointed to himself and shook his head.

"Thank you," she said.

The last person on her list was George Corbett.

George Corbett heard the story from his friend at Columbia, Margo Yost-Konning, who had heard the story from a colleague in the drama department who knew Lisa Boatharbor. She phoned him at home to say he could be expecting a call from Catlyn Cavanaugh, Carter's flaky girlfriend, who was going around accusing people of killing Damian Carter. Lisa Boatharbor confessed! Wasn't that something? George laughed and said the world was crammed full of weirdos these days.

But after she hung up, George was worried. It was always small things that tripped agents up. Some overlooked detail. Some knucklehead on the sidelines jumping into the game at an unexpected moment. He was so close to being the chairman of the Federal Reserve that he could taste it! He wasn't about to ignore any potential problem.

Linda and Rudolf were watching *Dynasty* on television, one of the few things they enjoyed together. He thought it was stupid and melodramatic, but since they liked it he pretended to like it also. He'd been watching it with them when Margo Yost-Konning had called. He didn't go back to the family room; he had some thinking to do. He smoked a cigar as he paced in the study. What could she gain from going around accusing people of murder? Nothing. It was an act of desperation. If only he had told Park to take care of her at the same time he had taken care of Damian

Carter. Little things like that could finish you. He'd made a mistake. Park would have taken her out, too, at the same time. He still would, for what—twenty-five thousand? Why not, this was no time to be foolishly frugal.

He'd give Park a call in the morning. Problem solved.

But in the morning he changed his mind. He realized that if Catlyn Cavanaugh were murdered, or even disappeared, the people she was going around accusing of murder would be suspect. Some scandal sheet would get hold of it. A scandal would ruin his chances of getting control of the Fed. No, he'd have to deal with her straight on.

He was going through an exercise set that morning at his health club when he got an idea. How perfect. The carrot and the stick. Khrushchev had preached that. If you can't get what you want with the stick, try the carrot. He called Marla, his secretary, and told her to call Catlyn Cavanaugh and ask her to meet him in his office that afternoon.

George rubbed his hands together and went back to work with renewed vigor on the Nautilus machine.

When his secretary showed Catlyn into George's office, he was struck not only by her beauty and poise, but by her air of confidence which filled the room. She was wearing a gray tweed business suit and a red blouse with a large bow tie. The suit was designed to cover her shape, he thought, but it failed. She was a beauty, with a look of hard intelligence and determination in her eyes. Maybe greater than Carson Black's. He thought she would make a marvelous agent.

She introduced the mountainous black man she'd brought along as her associate, B. B. Hanson. B. B. nodded and didn't accept George's hand when he offered it. He merely glared. George ignored his glaring and said, "Have a seat, won't you, Mr. Hanson?"

"Rather stand, yo doan mind."

"Whatever you like."

Catlyn sat in one of the chairs opposite George. He said, "I've not had anyone refuse to shake my hand in this room in fifteen years."

"Mr. Hanson is particular, Mr. Corbett."

"Particularly rude, I'd say," George said, glancing in the big man's direction.

B. B. grunted.

Catlyn said, "Why have you asked me here?"

"A colleague of mine at Columbia said that you'd accused a woman by the name of Lisa Boatharbor of having something to do with killing Damian Carter."

"That's right, I did."

"Have you any evidence that she did?"

"I have a lot of evidence that *somebody* did."

George nodded. "I think you may have already figured out why I asked you here, Miss Cavanaugh. Pretty simple. Damian Carter was murdered. If it wasn't just an act of random street violence, then he was killed for a purpose. It might just have been because he was being considered for the Fed chairmanship. As you probably know, I am now being considered for the job. See what I'm thinking?"

"Whoever killed Damian might want to kill you?"

"Exactly."

Catlyn turned and looked at B. B. He shrugged. She looked back to George, who said, "If you have any evidence that he was killed because of the Fed chairman business, I'd like to know about it."

"I don't know why he was killed."

"But it might be possible it was because of his possible nomination?"

"It might."

George got up and walked to the window and looked out for a long moment. Then he turned to Catlyn and said, "If you would like, I would be glad to pay for the best investigators in the business to find out. They would report to you, of course, I don't really have the time to direct such an inquiry. You see, Miss Cavanaugh, it would be a shame to get killed over the chairmanship of the Fed, a job that I never really wanted. That would be truly ironic."

"Never really wanted?"

"Yes. I reluctantly agreed to accept the nomination at the request of the President after Damian's death, but I never wanted the job. I thought Damian should have it. If you don't believe that, check with *Barron's* last June, they interviewed me. I told them all the reasons why I *didn't* want the job."

"But you would take the job if offered, that it?"

"Yes. You see, I've had a lot of success in my life. I feel a moral obligation to serve if called, but I'd just as soon not be called. Now that it looks like I might be getting the job, I sure as hell would not like to be killed for it. Please, if you have any suspicions about who killed Damian or why, I'd like to know. I'll put an army of investigators on it right away."

Catlyn was studying his face. "I'd rather not have investigators muddying the waters, Mr. Corbett, but you probably figured that out already." She looked him squarely in the eyes and said, "I'm not buying it, Mr. Corbett."

"Buying what?"

"That you don't want to be chairman of the Fed. I happen to know differently." She said it with dead certainty, even though she had no way of knowing whether he wanted it or not. She was just trying to shake him up.

"Oh, you have inside information, do you, about what goes on inside my head?" He tapped a finger on his temple.

"I made a mistake accusing Lisa Boatharbor. I know now that you hired the assassin to kill Damian Carter and I mean to prove it."

A slow smile formed on George's lips, although his cheeks were orange. He continued to stare directly into her eyes. "I never had anyone killed in my life," he said, "certainly not Damian Carter. I'm sorry that his death has so upset you that you have to go around accusing innocent people." He paused and the smile on his lips grew larger. "I've never been accused of murdering anyone before. In a way, I guess it's a compliment. A man who would murder to get a big job, he's some kind of gutsy fellow. What do you say we have a cup of coffee?"

Catlyn stood up and leaned over the desk. "No thank you. We'll be meeting again, Mr. Corbett, I'm sure. Good day."

George said, "Wait a minute, I'm not finished. I *did not* kill Damian Carter. I *did not* pay to have it done and if you spread rumors to that effect, I'll sue your shoes off. I mean it."

Catlyn nodded, staring coolly into his eyes, then she turned and walked toward the door, Hanson following. George said, "Wait a minute, Ms. Cavanaugh. Did I pass the test?"

"The test?"

"I've got a feeling you've got lie detectors built into your retinas."

"You passed."

"Good. I want us to both be on the same side. You learn anything about who might have killed Damian Carter, I want to know."

"I'll keep you informed, if you'll do the same."

"It's a deal."

After she was gone, George sat back down in his chair and swiveled around so he could look out on the skyline. He held up a finger. It was trembling. At the moment she had looked deep inside him and accused him, his blood had run cold, but he hadn't let it show. For a moment, it had flashed into his mind just to throw her out, then start running, but he'd stared her down and she'd bought it. He was positive she'd bought it.

The intercom buzzed. George pressed the button. "Yes, Marla?"

"An aide of Senator Wilcox, Mr. Corbett."

George picked up the phone: "This is George Corbett."

"The Senate will be holding confirmation hearings on your nomination next Monday, October first, at ten A.M. They'll he held in Hearing Room 4 in the Senate office building. Can we expect you to make it, sir?"

"Yes, yes! Thank you!"

Catlyn was making a pot roast. She wasn't much of a cook, she said, but her butcher guaranteed that if she followed directions she couldn't miss.

Oscar sat in the living room feeling something like an embarrassed suitor, but he didn't quite know why.

Oscar was in a quandary about Catlyn. For one thing, he liked her. He wasn't supposed to like her. He was a spy. He was not supposed to like anyone. Not only did he like her, he was infatuated by her. He'd never met a woman with so much keen intelligence who wasn't constantly trying to prove how damn smart she was. She wasn't what he called a fisticuffer. That's what the Harvard women were like, and the professional analyst types he'd met in the ministry and the Mossad were even worse.

He didn't know quite what to call the quality Catlyn had that he found most attractive. In a man, he would call it guts. But it was more than guts. It was more kinetic than that. He'd call it *force*. It was almost psychic. Spiritual.

"Why are you staring at me, Oscar?"

"You're a marvel of nature . . . Did that come out as dumb as I think it did?"

Velma Jasco, the cleaning woman, was just finishing up. She'd started late that day and had spent a long time waxing the floors. "Will that be all, Miss Cavanaugh?"

"Yes, Velma. Good night."

"Good night." She left through the back way.

Catlyn said, "She's been acting very strange lately. I would suspect she was stealing, only I haven't found anything missing. . . . Would you like another drink?"

"I don't know what to think of you," he said.

"There's nothing to think."

"Are you now, or have you ever been, Jewish?"

"No."

"My mother will be so disappointed."

"Disappointed, why?"

"I was just thinking out loud."

"You didn't say if you wanted another drink."

"I'm light-headed already."

"The roast is almost done. I think. That's if the thermometer is right. And I'm reading it right. And the oven is set right. There are so many variables to cooking, it's amazing anyone ever gets a meal fixed right."

"Have you ever been to Israel?"

"Yes. Once. For three days. I didn't get to see very much of it. I was there on business."

"How would you like to live there?"

"Why are you asking?"

"I'm daydreaming awake."

"If what you're asking is whether or not our relationship has a future, I think it does, what do you think?"

"I'm hoping."

"We'll talk more about it, once we've found Damian's killer."

"That's what I like about you, Cat. Single-minded. Determined. Nose to the grindstone. Okay, let's talk business. Did you check out the five people whose names I gave you?"

"I did."

"And what did you find?"

"Nothing. They all deny it and I believe them."

Oscar said, "I think I will have another drink." Catlyn

got up to make them one. Oscar said, "Tell me something, Cat. Why are you doing all this?"

"Doing what?"

"You know, investigating? What are you trying to prove?"

"To tell you that, I'd have to tell you my whole life story."

"I'd like to hear that."

"Have your people done any investigations on me?"

"What do you mean, *my people*?"

"The Mossad." She smiled as he grumbled a denial. "Anyway, if you did, and you didn't dig too deeply, you'd find that I'm the daughter of a Houston oil tycoon by the name of Rowdy Cavanaugh, who left me oil wells when he died in 1975. I made that all up a long time ago to explain how it is that I live so comfortably. If you run a credit check on me, you'll be amazed at how solvent I am."

"Made it up?"

"You did check on me, didn't you? I knew you would. All that stuff was a lie. I'm not a Cavanaugh from Houston. My father's name was Tim O'Toole. He was from Cold River, West Virginia, poor as dirt. I was born Betty Lou O'Toole. Isn't that horrible? God, how I hated that name. My father was pretty much a worthless no-good bum. My mother was sickly. I don't know what she had. Ailments, the neighbors called it. Probably she was tubercular. She died of pneumonia when I was six. I loved her. She used to wrap her arms around me and hug me all the time. Baked cookies. She was never too sick to bake me cookies. Two years after she died, my father got hurt when his still blew up. He was a penny-ante bootlegger and card shark. While he was in the county hospital mending, I went to live with my aunt Sophie in New Mexico for a year and a half. She was wonderful. Taught me how to ride a horse, shoot rattlesnakes, curse, chew tobacco, drink tequila. Then she died of a bad liver, and I went back to my father. It just seemed to me that everything I ever loved was taken away from me. Dad wasn't in such good shape either and figured he didn't have much time left on God's good earth."

"Looking at the beautiful and elegant woman sitting in that chair, it is hard to believe any of this."

"It's all true. When I was fifteen my father sent me to a Catholic girls school in Cincinnati. Saint Mary's. They believed in teaching young ladies to be young ladies. My father died soon after. For a short while I went to New Hampshire Women's College on a scholarship, got bored out of my mind, then moved to New York because I wanted to live-live-live! You know, dreams of the fast lane. I married a guy. Joe, his name was. He was in the rackets. Big time. I didn't know it then. He was producing a Broadway play when I met him, I thought he was old money. Anyway, he got shot. Twelve times. It happened on our honeymoon."

"I'm sorry."

"He survived. The doctors called it a miracle. He requires constant care, which I can't give him. Nurses take care of him. It's some kind of curse. I love my husband. But you can love more than one person. I loved Damian Carter, too. I never told him about Joe. Damian didn't know I was married. It was a small deception, one which I'd never pull again. You shouldn't deceive people you love. Damian wanted to marry me, and I just wasn't free to marry. I'm sorry, Oscar, I'm not usually this sentimental."

There was no Mafioso husband, of course. But it was a good story, and he seemed to believe it.

"I'm sorry I was prying," he said.

"That's okay, Oscar, I wanted you to know. I wanted you to know, and now you know. I'll check on the roast." She went into the kitchen and came back a moment later. "Be another ten, fifteen minutes. Now then, how'd it go in Washington?"

"Okay, I guess. I was looking into the circumstances surrounding the death of Ernest Ramsey, the President's chief economic adviser."

"I read about it in the papers, of course."

"I think it was suicide. He was all alone on the road. Not too much alcohol in his blood—hardly any in fact. He just got up out of bed early in the morning, put on his clothes, went down to his car, and eight point three miles away he slammed into a bridge abutment. No skid marks. Nothing."

"Do you think that his death is somehow related to Damian's murder?"

"I don't see any connection. It looks like Ramsey met a 'sex surrogate' named Rita Montgomery at an embassy party, had a few drinks with her, took her to a motel, chickened out, went home, the next day he probably had a terrific fight with his wife, stormed out of the house, drove like a maniac, and lost his head for a moment and killed himself. He was one of those up-tight straitlaced church-goer types who strayed off one night, far as I could tell. The coroner down there told me he thought pretty much the same thing. I think I'll have another drink now."

Catlyn poured him a drink and put a Rachmaninoff concerto on the stereo.

Oscar said, "There was one thing that bothered me, though. When I questioned Rita Montgomery, she seemed scared to death. She gave me the right answers, but she was petrified. I checked out her story, and it held."

"Give me her address, will you? I'd like to talk to that lady."

SEVENTEEN

The Banking and Commerce committee, George knew, could ask him questions for two hours or two days. Or twenty days. It was up to them.

They could ask anything they wanted to ask, about *anything*, no matter how personal, private, irrelevant, or foolish. And a lot of the questions were apt to be just that. Foolish. They were human after all, and not experts in economics. They were seven politicians, with all the faults and foibles, George thought, of that strange breed.

There were no set rules for the committee. It could reject him for any reason. Four of seven made a majority; any four could nix his nomination. Any four could decide they didn't like the way he answered the questions, combed his hair, tied his tie; or they could perceive that he would be too tight with the money supply, or too expansive, or too anything.

They'd rejected good men before. They'd approved bad ones. Storkweather, the previous chairman, answered questions for six days and was nominated five to two. The Senate approved unanimously.

George arrived in the hearing room five minutes late without apology. The members of the committee were waiting for him, sitting behind a table on a raised platform, each with a nameplate. Six men, one woman. George was directed to a table facing them. He strode down the center aisle, shaking hands with a few people in the audience whom he knew, one a *Wall Street Journal* reporter.

George wore a conservative blue suit and a wide, slightly out of fashion, tie. He didn't want to look flashy. He had on a banker's vest and a gold pocket watch with chain. Staid. With his hair combed straight back and wire-rimmed reading glasses, he looked like a sober, somber expert in finance. Like all spies and politicians, George was an actor trained to play a life role, and he was confident as any great actor, and always able, even when inwardly terrified as he was at the moment, to exude confidence. The audience was sparse. He found that strange in view of the fact that the second most powerful man in the country was being picked; he had assumed there would be more interest.

George took his place at the table facing the committee. The only member of the committee he was certain he could rely on was Senator Waxman, to whom he had paid the one million dollars of Mr. Peabody's money. Waxman was sitting on the end, to George's right, with a quiet smile on his face, his glasses on the end of his nose.

Everyone had a glass wrapped in a small paper covering, a pitcher of water, a large blue file folder prepared by the committee staff, and blank pad of notepaper. George was given the glass with the paper cover, the pitcher of water, and the notepad.

The committee chairman, Bennett Dixon, opened the proceedings with a banging of his gavel. A stenographer started punching the keys on her machine. The chairman said, "Good morning, Mr. Corbett. I think we need not go into a long dissertation about what we're here for. We're here to perform a constitutional duty. The President has nominated you for the position of chairman of the Federal Reserve Board. We are going to ask you some questions, hoping to determine your qualifications for the job. You are entitled to have legal counsel present during this questioning. Were you so informed by our staff?"

"I waive the right to counsel," George said calmly. He looked over the committee. They seemed relaxed. He wasn't sure what to expect, but none of his contacts had heard anything to indicate that he would not get swift, perfunctory approval. The Fed chairmanship had been open too long and it needed to be filled; besides, the Senate was due to recess and there was a colossal backlog of business to be taken care of.

Bennett Dixon, the committee chairman, began:

"You were born in Hamilton, New Hampshire, is that right?"

"Yes, sir."

"Your father owned the Chevy dealership at the time you were born."

"Yes, sir, that is correct."

"Your mother was a schoolteacher."

"Third grade, yes, sir."

"When you were eight years old, your father's business went bankrupt and a few years later he moved the family to Australia, is that right?"

"My mother thought my father had lost his mind. Maybe he did. He took the bankruptcy very hard. My father thought Australia was a land of milk and honey. It didn't turn out that way. Both my parents were killed in an accident," George said softly, as if the memories were still painful.

"They were prospecting for gold, is that right?"

"That is correct, sir."

"That was July, 1950. You were thirteen years old."

"I was."

"At first you were reported lost and probably dead as well."

"People thought I was with my parents, but I hadn't gone with them on their last fateful trip. Measles. I was

239

staying with family friends in the little town of Penn, near Shippingdale, I think it was called. Too small even to have a school. It was more of a mining camp, really. I don't even think it exists anymore."

"Shortly thereafter you went back to the United States."

"I remained in Australia until I went to college."

"You went to a small community college in New Bedford, New York."

"I did, sir. Albert's."

"Which has since been closed due to financial problems."

"It was closed the year after I graduated. I worked for a year selling shoes, then went to graduate school at Columbia." The truth was, he had just entered the country. But he couldn't think of that. He had to think of the answers he had rehearsed over and over again when still a boy in the Soviet Union.

Bennett Dixon said, "The FBI had problems getting your records from Albert's."

"I wasn't that good of a student, anyway," George said with a smile. "I majored in chasing blondes . . . Sorry, Senator Stahl." Senator Stahl was the female member of the committee.

Everyone on the committee laughed, including Senator Stahl. She said, "In college I chased a few male blonds myself." Laughter again. It was going well, George thought. Nice camaraderie here.

Dixon continued. "The records were turned over to the state college so former students could get transcripts."

"I was so notified."

"Your transcripts have been destroyed in a fire, did you know that?"

"Yes. I believe I still have a copy . . ."

Senator Stahl interrupted. "Sir, must we go through all this? There are substantive issues here to discuss. Do we have to get bogged down in all this trivia?"

240

The chairman flared. "I was trying to nail down the man's background, for the record."

"The FBI has gathered an immense amount of material "for the record." I hardly think we need to waste a lot of time with a waltz down memory lane."

"I could provide a copy of my college record if the committee wishes to see it," George said quickly. Of course it was a forgery, but it was the best forgery by the best forgers in the world.

"That won't be necessary," Dixon said, scowling.

George inwardly sighed with relief. Even the best forgery can be detected by an expert.

Senator Waxman said, "Mr. Chairman, I, too, would like to proceed with more substantive questions. The FBI's thorough investigation and our staff reports—and the reports of the President's Council of Economic Advisers—have certainly persuaded me that this man has the maturity and qualifications for the position for which he is being considered. I believe we should move forward now. I, for one, have some questions about how he might view the role of Federal Reserve as it faces the challenges of the present and in the future."

The other committee members nodded their approval. All but Wendell Pickering. "Mr. Chairman," he said, "as you know, I represent the state of New Hampshire. Since Mr. Corbett comes from my home state, I had some of my people look into his background."

George's heart raced in his chest while he folded his hands on the table in front of him and tried to look relaxed and affable.

"Yes, Mr. Pickering," Dixon said. "And what did you find?"

Pickering opened a file in front of him and cleared his throat. Being appropriately theatrical, George thought. Pickering was thin and dressed a little too nattily. And he had the eyes of a jackal. Here it comes, George thought, the

241

bomb of the day.

Pickering said, "Mr. Corbett's father was a Nazi sympathizer."

George felt a jolt of electricity go through him.

Pickering, after a dramatic pause, continued. "I have in my hand documents which show that from 1933 to 1938 he was a member of the German-American Bundt, a group of rabid antisemitic Nazi sympathizers. And, we are certain, he took his family—including his son George—to rallies, picnics, and other outings." He passed the contents of the file to Dixon, who seemed momentarily befuddled.

George's mind was feverish. How could the KGB have made such a blunder? They gave him the cover ID for the child of a Fascist! This was the first he had ever heard of it, but he didn't make any indication to that effect. A Nazi! He remained calm, saying nothing. Finally Dixon said, "Would you like to comment on this for the record, Mr. Corbett?"

George smiled and said, "If I had it to do over again, I would have chosen my parents more wisely." This elicited mild laughter from the audience. "If you're asking me if I am a Nazi or do I have Nazi sympathies, the answer is I don't even like knockwurst." There was scattered laughter again. George sat up straighter in his chair. "All right, I will tell you the truth, gentlemen—and lady. Perhaps it is good you should know this. My father was a hopeless dreamer. He dreamed of a better world and he didn't know how to get it. He had gone bankrupt in his Chevrolet dealership, which was bought, I think, by a Jew. He resented it. He joined the Bundt. He became disillusioned later, not because he stopped wanting to make a better world, but because he could see that the anti-Jewish thing was misguided and clearly wrong, and he told me that many times. Today I am in business with many Jews. There are four Jews on the board of directors of my bank. Clearly I could not have taken to heart any of that nonsense and do business the way I do business today. I hope that satisfies you."

He thought: Every damn Jew-hater on earth says *some of my best friends are Jews*. He hoped they didn't take what he'd just said that way. But by the sour expressions on most of their faces, it looked as if they had.

"I am more than satisfied," Waxman said. Waxman was worth the million, George thought, no doubt about it. Waxman added, "Now let us get on with it."

Dixon glanced at Pickering, who had nothing more to add. "All right," he said, "then there's no reason why we shouldn't proceed. We shall begin the questioning with a general review of your knowledge, Mr. Corbett, of the Federal Reserve and its functioning . . ."

The tone of the hearing had changed. They were suspicious of him now; it would be an uphill fight. No more joking around.

George was sitting as straight as he could now, making eye contact with the committee members one at a time, trying to project as much sincerity as he could. "As to the Federal Reserve and its functioning," he began, launching into his well-rehearsed answer, "a few years ago, *Newsweek* magazine said that the Federal Reserve Board was the economic equivalent of the Kremlin, and this is true . . ."

He recited, by the book, his understanding of how the Fed functions, how and why it began in 1913 in response to the Greenback Party's call for "free silver." He mentioned William Jennings Bryan's famous "cross of gold" speech which helped him capture the hearts and minds of the Democrats at their 1896 convention.

Then he gave a brief outline of the Fed's history, how it was brought into being with the mission of providing monetary stability in the face of farm credit demands which varied sharply from season to season and year to year. Then he outlined the failure of the Fed to cope with the 1929 crash. George called it not only a failure of policy but a failure of "moral courage" as well.

He was not reciting the history of the Fed merely to show off his knowledge; by subtly criticizing the policies of the past, he was implying that his stewardship would be superior. He also wanted to control the direction of the committee's inquiry to keep them away from anything controversial. He managed after half an hour of almost constant talking to lull them a bit. They were listening.

He went on to explain how the New Dealers had brought the modern Federal Reserve into being. Finally, in a quick summary, he demonstrated a remarkable memory for facts and figures, as he traced the growth in the money supply (M-l, currency, and bank deposits) over the decades since and explained how it affected inflation and the cost of living.

George lavished copious praise on Stockweather, the outgoing chairman, and many of his predecessors, including Paul Volker, who George called a wizard. He knew that most of the committee members were admirers of Volker. The committee interrupted him often with questions, which he always considered for a moment, then answered with unswerving directness. His answers had all been sure and swift, showing a rare mastery of the subject. George was feeling better now, but he still didn't think he had it solidly in his grasp.

Bennett Dixon, the chairman, called for a two-hour recess at noon.

Oscar Feldman was waiting for George as he made his way up the aisle. George was shaking hands and accepting greetings from well-wishers. The place was quickly emptying out. Oscar smiled and said, "One moment, sir."

George looked him over. By the keen look in his eyes, he appeared to be both intelligent and personable.

Oscar said, "Maximilian Franks, sir, *Manhattan Busi-*

George said, "Always happy to know members of the Fourth Estate." He shook the younger man's hand. "Well, what do you think? How am I doing? What do you think of the process?"

"Fascinating," Oscar said. "I think they're very impressed with you, sir, if you don't mind me saying so."

"Why thank you, Mr. Franks, I'm very glad to hear that. I didn't look too nervous, did I? My father being a Nazi, that set them on their ear, didn't it? Well, you choose your friends but not your relatives."

Oscar said, "Would you mind answering a few questions? My readers of course are very interested in your views of the money supply. The last round of inflation was generally regarded as disastrous. And interest rates, too. What do you see in the next two or three years . . ."

"Whoa there, I'll be happy to discuss these fascinating and grotesque and mysterious things with you, but I only have two hours. Why don't you have lunch with me? I'm going to walk across the street to this little Italian place."

"Wouldn't you rather relax? I mean . . ."

"What's this? A reporter turning down a chance for an interview?"

"I'm an economist actually, sir. As a reporter, I'm afraid, I sometimes just don't seem to have the knack of it. Handling people is not my forte."

"People is what economics is about, isn't it? Come along. If I eat alone, I'll think about the committee and come down with a case of nerves."

They both ordered pasta with clam sauce and shared a bottle of red Chianti. George ate four thick slices of bread spread generously with butter. He explained that he thought no matter what, the country would see a prime of twelve percent before the end of the year and an increase in the consumer price index. The picture he painted was mildly optimistic and completely agreed with the way Oscar saw things going. George also said he saw an end at last to the civil war in Lebanon; the Syrians were tired of fighting and it was a terrific drain on the Arab economies, oil prices being depressed. If Russia stays out of it, there will be peace, he predicted. He said he saw Russia as finally getting the idea that it couldn't have its way everywhere in the world. Afghanistan taught them a valuable lesson.

He kept talking with a checkered napkin tucked under his chin and his mouth bulging with Italian bread. He chewed and spoke rapidly, nervously, somewhat distractedly, losing his train of thought from time to time, then going off on another subject.

Oscar liked him. He liked his quick mind and his encyclopedic recall. Although George had a way of talking down to him, he did it with a little humor, and Oscar didn't find it offensive. After all, George Corbett was a brilliant man, a self-made multimillionaire who was about to become the chairman of the Federal Reserve. Of this, Oscar was certain.

They finished their meal off with a small dish of creamy spumoni, which George talked Oscar into. Oscar took one bite and said it was too rich. George laughed and said he was a Florentine banker at heart and nothing was too rich, for him.

On the way back to the Senate Office Building, George suggested they go for a walk around the block. "I love the hum of a big city," he said. "And New York is the biggest, and so I love it the most. But Washington is good, too. You can just feel the energy, the pulse. Keeping the finger on the pulse, that is what an economist does. That is all. We are the diagnosticians of the economic health. If we apply our balms and salves with skill, the economy will be healthy, and our people, happy."

They crossed the street and strolled through Capitol Plaza. It was a pleasant day: clear skies, mild temperatures, soft breeze off the Potomac. Office workers were eating their lunch on benches. Some old people were feeding the pigeons.

Oscar said, "I have a horrible confession to make to you, Mr. Corbett."

"Oh?"

"Last month I was doing a story on Damian Carter and I met the woman who was with him the night he died."

"Catlyn Cavanaugh—a singularly remarkable woman. Yes, we met. A meeting I will be unlikely to ever forget."

"Your meeting her was, well, my fault."

George turned to him. "How's that?"

"Well, first, we've become friends. Good friends really. She wanted to know who would benefit from Damian Carter's death. I gave her a few names. People who I knew through my reporting. I had no idea she was going to go around accusing each of them of murder."

George tore the cellophane from a cigar and laughed. "Don't worry about it. Had I gone through what she went through, I might do something just as crazy. In fact, I have some of my people right now trying to find other suspects for her. After all, if Damian Carter was murdered because he was about to be chairman of the Fed, then I may be next, right? I should, I suppose, be more careful, get bodyguards, stay indoors. But then, I have never believed in hiding. Men in bulletproof cars get blown up every day. I'd rather walk in the sunshine and take my chances."

The afternoon session of the Banking and Commerce Committee began promptly at 2:00 P.M.

"Now then," said Bennett Dixon, the chairman, "let us move on to more specific questions regarding the national and world economy . . ." This field was far broader and the possibilities endless.

Senator C. Henry Davis from Arizona came first. Davis was a rock-hard, broad-shouldered cattleman. He wanted to know what George thought of the Eurodollar "float" and the ramifications of the pullout of Arab investment in the farm belt.

George was ready. He had had Moscow Central do a detailed analysis for the questions most likely to be asked by each committee member. George had returned from his walk with Oscar in the park with one thought in mind: he was going to overpower them with the vastness of his knowledge. He would not hedge, but would be forthright and direct.

"I think, sir," George said to C. Henry Davis, "that the fate of the farmer is the fate of America. The Fed should do everything in its power to see that the price of the dollar is stabilized, and that the value of the dollar be generally lower over the next few years so that our agricultural products are lower in price for the Japanese and European buyer, and that European products are more expensive for the American buyer. I think the day of the inflated dollar, which may be good for the urban foreign car buyer, should come to an end. I would not, however, wish to jolt the dollar downward. The transition needs to be gradual and planned . . ."

He had their rapt attention now, because many of the questions were political, not just economic. The political end of things they understood. He fielded several additional questions with equal ease. Then came the question of extending credit to the Communist bloc; he answered that the Fed should support whatever policy the President, the State Department, and Congress thought prudent. His personal opinion, however, was that all dealings with the Communist bloc, including the Soviet Union, ought to be strictly cash and carry from now on.

That jarred them. George heard the rustling of the reporters behind him. His remark would make headlines; in the past the Fed had always supported ever-expanding trade credits to increase the flow of goods and support the world economy. Bankers had a tendency to see the world in terms of cash flow, not politics. George, in announcing that he was ready to play hardball with the Soviets, knew it would greatly please the three conservatives on the committee.

Marian Stahl smiled. George knew he had just captured her vote. She was anti-Communist down to the bottom of her pantyhose.

Marcus Honeywell, junior senator from South Carolina, had the next question. Of all the committee members, he was the most conservative, and the most treacherous. He reread his notes at length, then jerked his glasses off and said, "Far West Oil of California has a very extensive oil refining operation in the Marxist State of Angola. Although it is not strictly within the authority of the chairman of the Fed to do anything about it, I'm very interested in knowing if you favor the extension of trade credits to that country, and what you think America might do to keep its own companies from aiding and abetting the international Communist conspiracy."

George sat back in his chair and rubbed his chin. After a moment he said, "It is my firm belief, Senator, that a strong America is the first necessity in countering international communism. The strength of this country is tied to the strength of the dollar, and the dollar is strongest when our oil supplies are firm. If the American economy is sound, and the dollar strong, I believe that it is not only good policy, but our moral duty to use economic pressure both on our own companies and on foreign governments to see that, as an example, human rights within those countries are not violated."

Senator Richard Gruver of Ohio said, "Mr. Corbett, I want to know what your feeling is about interest rates and do you think that an expansion of the money supply beyond the current four percent rate of growth will bring inflationary pressures?"

George gave a long-winded theoretical explanation of his stance on interest rates and money supply and how the American economy was tied to the European and Asian banking communities. He was wearing them down. Waxman asked a few tame questions, then Marian Stahl asked about consumer prices, to which George gave an elusive answer that seemed to satisfy her. Wendell Pickering had retreated, having caused the sensation over his Nazi question that morning. He'd gotten his headline back home; apparently that was all he was interested in. His constituents knew he was on the job.

At four-thirty the committee members sequestered themselves to decide whether they wanted George to return for another day of testimony. When they came back fifteen minutes later Bennett Dixon said, "Mr. Corbett, I have been hearing testimony in this room for almost twenty years, and rarely have we seen a man so confident, qualified, and knowledgeable as yourself. We have taken a vote. We have decided unanimously that we will recommend to the full Senate tomorrow that your nomination be confirmed." Since there was not even the remotest chance of a floor fight in opposition, he should expect confirmation within a few days.

On the way out of the hearing room, Oscar Feldman was standing in line to congratulate George. He said he'd never seen anyone with such a profound understanding of the global economy. He meant it, too.

That night he reported to Euripides that in his opinion George Corbett was going to make a splendid Fed chairman, and the American economy should improve and stabilize during George Corbett's tenure. He said he'd never been more certain of anything in his life.

EIGHTEEN

Catlyn Cavanaugh was also in Washington that afternoon. She had flown down from New York in the morning and checked in at the Biltmore, but she had no desire to sit through any lengthy and boring confirmation hearing. At two in the afternoon, the moment the Senate Banking Subcommittee was starting the afternoon session, she was in a cab on her way to Chevy Chase, hoping to have a talk with Rita Montgomery.

Though she would never let it show, Catlyn was beginning to get discouraged. She felt she was no closer to finding out who had hired Damian Carter's killer than she was the day she began her investigation. B. B. Hanson was having no more luck finding who the hired killer might be. None of the people who had profited from Damian Carter's death seemed to be likely suspects and her accusing them face to face had turned out to be a waste of time. The police thought she was crazy. She had a sneaking suspicion that Oscar was just going along with her because he liked her.

Any sane person, she thought, would just hang it up. Forget about tracking down the killer. Maybe she wasn't sane. When a friend got killed, sane people got out of the way and let the police handle it.

But whenever she thought of quitting, she'd think about

the faceless and nameless men who had decided, coolly and rationally, that Damian Carter should die. Whoever they were, they were now cashing in on his death, smugly gloating, perhaps, certain they'd gotten away with murder. Well, she had news for them. They weren't going to get away with it.

You keep anteing up, eventually you get dealt aces.

The cab pulled up in front of Rita Montgomery's apartment house and parked. Catlyn went to the front door and pushed the button under Rita's name. No answer. She rang the manager, who buzzed her in.

Catlyn was wearing casual pants and a pullover sweater, her glasses, and just a little makeup. She told the manager that Rita was her sister, and she was supposed to be home. The manager, a stone-faced woman, said, "Hasn't been here for days."

"You don't think something might have happened to her?"

"Wouldn't know about that."

"Would you let me have a peek into her apartment?"

The manager's gaze rolled over Catlyn, and she started to shake her head no. Catlyn pulled a hundred-dollar bill out of her pocket and handed it to the woman.

"For your trouble. I sure would like a look around."

"Can't see why not."

The apartment was slightly messy. She took a look in the bedroom first. The closet was packed with clothing. Six pieces of empty luggage sat on the top shelf. The two chests of drawers were also filled with clothes. In one of the drawers, under some negligees, she found a book: *The Joy of Lesbian Sex*. On the bed was a six-day-old newspaper. That might mean that Rita hadn't been there since the day Oscar came to see her.

Catlyn took a quick look in Rita's appointment book. A lot of first names and initials, with dates and times. No last names. The milk in the refrigerator was sour, the lettuce

252

wilted. The bread in the breadbox felt like cardboard.

"Been getting a lot of calls wanting to know where she's hiding," the manager said. "Mostly from men."

Catlyn said, "My sister's always been popular."

"Hmmmm," said the manager, her hands on her hips.

In the living room Catlyn checked out the bar, then the bookshelf, which was full of leatherbound books, all apparently unread. There were a few glamour magazines under the coffee table. On the walls were rows of video tapes, all dated. Catlyn put one in the VCR and turned on the TV. It was the Nightly News with Carson Black. Catlyn used the fast forward. That's all there was, different editions of the same news program.

She checked two other tapes. Same thing. All the Nightly News.

The manager said, "Must be your sister's got an interest in what's going on in the world."

"Must be," Catlyn said. "Anybody see if she left with anyone?"

"Nope. People in this building mind their own business mostly."

"Looks like she's been gone for almost a week. She do this often?"

"Don't you know? She's your sister."

"I suppose she is a bit unpredictable," Catlyn said with a smile.

On the way back to Washington Catlyn was excited. There was some link between Oscar's visit and Rita Montgomery's being gone. Oscar had been there because Rita had been out with Ernest Ramsey the night before he was killed in an automobile crash. Ernest Ramsey was the President's chief economist. Damian Carter had been about to be nominated by the President to be chairman of the Federal Reserve. Somehow she knew this was all connected. Maybe she was close to a misplaced wild card.

* * *

That night Catlyn checked with the night man, Satch, at the Coronet Motel.

She was sitting at the bar just off the lobby when he came on at eleven. The bartender pointed him out to her. He was just as Oscar had described: a beer gut, a boxer's face, big, bushy eyebrows.

He looked up from what he was doing and smiled at her. She smiled at him and said, "I'm Rita Montgomery's sister."

"Who?"

"Rita Montgomery. She's a working girl. Calls herself a sex surrogate. Comes in here sometimes with her clients."

He shook his head. "Don't think I know her."

"It's possible she's been murdered."

His eyebrows went up. He looked around the lobby, perhaps checking for the police. Then he said, "What's this got to do with me?"

"About a week ago a man came in here asking about her. You told him she was here with Ernest Ramsey. She may have paid you to say it. You see, Ramsey was murdered, too. And when people came around asking questions, Rita got nervous. Then the people who'd hired her probably got nervous about her, and now she's disappeared."

Satch reached in his shirt pocket and plucked out a cigarette. "You ain't a cop?"

"Furthest thing from it."

"What you want me from me?"

"The truth."

He lit the cigarette. "I remember her now. And I remember the night she came here with the guy. That's all I know. What the hell you staring at me for?"

"How would you like to save your life, Satch?"

"You're the weirdest lady I've ever met." He took a couple of quick puffs on his cigarette.

Catlyn said, "No, I mean it. All I have to do is let it be

254

known that you're getting nervous and some very bad people will start to think maybe you're dangerous to them."

"I told you the truth."

"How long were they here?"

He shrugged. "Five minutes, he finked out on her. Yeah, I remember that part real good. I told that guy who was here askin' the same thing."

She smiled at him. "I'll give you this one chance to save your life. Just tell me if she told you to tell the story of her being here with Ramsey, or someone else told you."

He ran his hand through his hair. "Nobody told me. She was here with the guy. They went up to the room and came back in five minutes. She got in a cab. He got in a car. Vavuuuuum, they drove off. End of story."

"Thank you," she said. She started to leave, but turned back to him. "One more thing. Take my advice. Never play poker."

On the plane back to New York, she wondered just what went on in the room that was so important that Rita Montgomery should have bothered to lie about it. Satch had clearly lied about two things: one, they were in the room for far more than five minutes, and two, they didn't leave by separate vehicles. Now then, Catlyn thought, what happened, why did he lie about it, and where's Rita Montgomery? And the big question: What's it got to do with Damian's death?

"Being President," the President said, "is like having your cock caught in a revolving door. At first it feels pretty good, but before you know it, you've fucked yourself."

George laughed, and puffed on his cigar. The President laughed, too, his round face turning crimson. Then he stopped laughing and took a sip of hundred-proof bourbon.

"You know what, George my boy, I liked you from the minute I met you, when I heard what you had to say about the Redskins. Seriously, I think a good understanding of football shows a man with a strategic mind, a man who can think. And I like a man who can think."

"Thank you, Mr. President."

"Only reason I went for that—what's his name—Damian Carter? Was because of Ramsey—God rest his soul."

"Damian Carter was a good man, though. Ramsey wasn't too off base there."

"Ah, Ramsey. A goody-goody. Brilliant young man, but too, too goody-goody. I have my own theories about such men. Does something to their mind after a while. I like a man who likes to live a little, you know, let loose once in a while. Loosen the belt."

George drank to that. He knew the President was playing the cornball down-home farmboy he was famous for. He knew, too, that the President was a shrewd manipulator and that the cornball stuff was put on so George would loosen up and say what was really on his mind. George used a similar tactic with his own underlings, Carson and Nicolai, and his mistress Esther.

The President poured them both another drink. They were in the President's study, sitting in leather recliners by a roaring fire. Rain beat against the windows. It was ten-thirty in the evening. The President leaned back and said, "Have you settled in over there at the Fed?"

"Yes, I have. I met my secretary—a very comely woman indeed by the name of Mrs. Farrow. Let's see, what else? The board of governors meets next Monday at noon. I think everything's under control. At least I hope so."

"You'll do just fine, I know you will. I thank you for coming tonight, I know you have a lot of work to do. And I also know once you get into your duties over there, it won't be quite so easy to get a few minutes just to let our shirttails hang out and talk to each other."

"I'm glad you asked me, Mr. President. Jens O. Parssons, an economist I much admire, said once that the

Federal Reserve must accommodate itself to the government in power, and I agree. He said there cannot be two captains of a ship."

"Well said."

"I'm hoping to be able to make a contribution to administration policy, but I have no inclination of making any on my own. My job is to help you keep the economy in balance."

The President, grinning, loosened his tie and unbuttoned the top button of his shirt. "Say, George, they tell me that you gave the most brilliant answers to the Grand Inquisitors over there at the Senate that they ever heard. You even impressed that witch from Iowa—"

"Senator Stahl."

"That's the broom jockey. My God, man, if you get a good word out of her, you've got witchcraft working for you yourself!" He burst out laughing. Suddenly he stopped, took a deep drink, and bent over and tossed another piece of wood on the fire. Then he said, "Do you know why your predecessor had to retire?" He was leaning forward in his chair; his eyes were serious now.

"Ill health, the papers said," George said.

"You know better."

"I think I know."

"I'll tell you my side of it. We've got an election next year. The primaries are starting soon. Unemployment is now at 12.9 percent, which is a heavy load to bring into an election year. Inflation is running 4.5 percent at an annual rate."

"Not ideal, but acceptable."

"Exactly. In fact, I think we can suffer through six to eight percent for the year."

"Which would drop unemployment down to maybe nine percent," George said, "all things being equal."

"That's right. This is just between us now, George," he said in a conspiratorial whisper.

"Of course, I understand. If the Fed eases the money restrictions between now and next November, lets the economy heat up a little . . ."

"I think it would be good for the country."

"I do, too," George said. And, he thought, the lowering of unemployment would give the President's reelection bid a tremendous boost.

The President smiled broadly and toasted George with a big drink of bourbon. "I knew you were a man I could count on."

On the way down in the elevator, escorted by a White House aide, George thought: Poor man, worried about an election. By Thanksgiving, George estimated, he wouldn't even have a country. George rode back to New York City that night with Nicolai. Because of the heavy rain, traffic was slow and visibility poor. Nicolai was driving George's black Mercedes, keeping to the right and staying under forty-five.

"You know something, Nicolai," George said, "I have known few men in high offices I didn't think were complete *duraki*. The President, he is a great man when it comes to getting elected. That is the main job of American politicians. The main job of our politicians, on the other hand, is obtaining results, or they are gone to Siberia. If you come right down to it, that is why their system is about to be eclipsed by ours. They have leaders who think only of themselves and care nothing for the people. They let the corporations steal everything from the people because the corporations give the politicians money to get reelected. It is such an inane system. Few will mourn its passing. And to ensure that passing, we have much to do. And the first thing I have to do is to take a trip."

"A trip?" Nicolai said.

"To Europe for a series of meetings. We are going to decide the fate of the earth for the next several thousand years. In the meantime, Nicolai, my friend, there is much

258

for you to do."

Nicolai looked at George suspiciously. "What have you in mind?"

"You still have all your contacts? The revolutionary parties? All those weird little underground groups we've been romancing all these years?"

"Yes, of course."

"Tomorrow I want you to recontact these groups, make sure they understand what they're to do. Get them ready."

"Now? So soon?"

"I see no reason to wait, Comrade. When the system begins to collapse, we must be ready to take advantage of it. You worry these groups will have informers in them. Some will. By the time the FBI decides to act upon the information the informers provide, it will be too late— What is the matter, Nicolai, you look perplexed."

"I just never thought it would really happen. I mean, I've been working for it, but I just never really expected to see it happen."

In the light of an oncoming car, George thought he saw a tear of joy in Nicolai's eye.

BOOK II

NINETEEN

The Federal Reserve Board met the following Monday morning. George shook hands with the other board members and asked them each what they thought were the major problems facing the Fed, both long range and short range, and whether they had suggestions about how the Fed should move. The topics addressed included where the discount rate should be by spring, what the impact of the new administration farm policy should be, whether falling oil reserves would drive the price back up over twenty dollars a barrel, and so on. The members were all trained economists or bankers, and the meeting took on the air of a graduate school seminar, with a lot of good-natured ribbing.

George knew half of the board at least casually and, of course, he had detailed reports in his files on each member. Most of them seemed to like George and listened to him with rapt attention. Only two would give him any trouble: Dean Bergen, the vice chairman, who was his own man, and Vance Lapsley, a young ambitious upstart from Harvard. The rest were government careerists who would follow like sheep until the collapse had progressed to the point where nothing and no one could stop it.

The two troublemakers would be taken care of when the

time came. If they became too troublesome, Nicolai could always make them disappear.

The meeting broke up at twelve-thirty.

So far George was comfortable at the Fed headquarters. The staff was cordial and anxious to please, and his office was spacious but lacking the personal touches he liked around him. He decided to bring in the Monets from his New York office to give the place more class.

Arrangements were made for a meeting the following week with the heads of the central banks of England, West Germany, Italy, and Switzerland for informal talks. George had his secretary work in six days of uninterrupted rest and relaxation at a secluded Swiss chateau, where he would be incommunicado.

He returned to New York from Washington at nine that evening. Rudolf was staying at a friend's and Mattie had the night off. Linda was in one of her moods, George discovered, as soon as he came through the door.

She said, "What's this I see on TV, George? You're going to Europe?"

"May I at least get my coat off?"

He removed his coat and hung it up. She stood by with her arms crossed. "May I fix myself a drink?" he said.

"I had my bridge club today," she said. "Penelope Fisk asked me if I was going to Italy when I was over there. I said, why I'm not planning to be in Europe. I must have seemed like a boob to her. She of course didn't press the issue. And then on the six o'clock news I see where you're going to Europe and Penelope Fisk must have heard about it and just assumed I was going."

George poured himself some brandy and sat down at the dining room table. Linda stood over him, hands on her hips.

"Will you sit down, please," George said. He was tired. It had been a long day and a dull trip back from Washington. He'd been looking forward to coming home; now he wished he'd stayed in Washington. He hated domestic disputes.

She sat down, crossing her arms again.

George said, "I've had a lot on my mind lately."

"You just forgot to tell me, is that what you're saying? I'm your wife, George, and you *forgot* to tell me?"

"I was going to tell you, of course. I haven't hardly seen you for a month."

"When are you leaving?"

"Day after tomorrow."

"Are you taking me?"

"No."

"Most men take their wives. These kinds of trips are mostly social."

"That's true, in most cases."

"What about this case?"

"I just can't take you, that's all there is to it."

"I'm still waiting to hear why not."

Her eyes were cold. He'd never seen them so cold, or her features so hard. "What's really bothering you?" he asked. "You've been to Europe before, what's the big deal?"

"The big deal is this: you are now the chairman of the Fed, and I am your wife. You are no longer an anonymous banker. You are in the public eye, and I am in the public eye. How do you think it feels to have practically a perfect stranger tell me what is going on in my husband's life? I was mortified!"

"A failure of communication. I'm deeply sorry." He sipped the brandy. He wanted a cigar, but he only smoked them in his study because Linda didn't like the smell. He knew whatever he said wasn't going to mollify her. When she was in one of her angry moods nothing could mollify her, so he said nothing and simply sat and waited for her to speak. For a few minutes she glared at him, lips tight against her teeth. Finally she said, "Do you want me to continue being your wife?" She said this in a softer tone, but by the look in her eyes George knew she was serious.

"What do you mean by that?" He poured himself some more brandy.

"What I mean, George, is that if you are going to treat me like a dog, I'm not going to stay married to you, and that's that."

"I don't know how you are able to make such a huge Cecil B. DeMille production out of a simple lapse of communication."

Linda got up from the couch. "Decide, George. Right now. We're either going to be partners in life or we're not. I don't want any halfway stuff."

"I think I would prefer to continue this discussion when you are in a slightly better mood."

She went into the bedroom and slammed the door behind her. George spent the night, fitfully, on the leather couch in his study. Why was it women had a way of mixing into things at the wrong time and getting them all fouled up? But it was far more complicated than that. He was two men. She was part of his cover life, not a part of the real Gyorgi Vlahovich's life. She didn't even know of the real man that lived inside the skin of the pretender. And she could never know. What did he owe her? Nothing. Then why was this so upsetting, he wondered. It bothered him that he could not "objectify" his cover identity.

The next day George turned his entire investment portfolio into a trust, to be administered by his good friend Charlie Van Nuys. George's instructions surprised Charlie. He wanted everything liquidated within thirty days and put into Swiss gold certificates. At his New York office, George said his farewells to his staff and put a trusted ally in charge of closing things down. The only research assistant he retained was the one working on the Damian Carter affair, so he would have more information to give Catlyn Cavanaugh to keep her off his back. He stopped by his spa for a workout, then took a cab home, hoping to find Linda in a better frame of mind.

Linda was out.

He checked the mail. There was a copy of Margo Yost-Konning's book manuscript he'd promised to write a jacket blurb for. He packed for his trip. Linda came home at six, in time for dinner.

He knew she'd been at her tennis club by the glow in her cheeks. By the guilty look in her eyes, he suspected she'd been flirting with some young stud. Maybe she'd even gone to bed with him. For a moment, thinking about the possibility, George burned with rage. But he quickly decided he was too deeply involved with his mission to get enmeshed in a domestic World War III. He had to objectify his emotions. He was a spy, and that's what a spy had to do; it was the most important thing they'd taught him in school.

George and Linda said nothing to each other. Mattie, humming to herself in the kitchen, seemed amused by the chilliness. They went through the entire four-course roast lamb dinner without saying a single word. Rudolf came late to the table. To George he looked half stoned, grinning and chuckling to himself. He barely touched his food, then excused himself before dessert.

George had already made arrangements to spend the night with Esther before leaving for Europe. He said good-bye to Rudolf and hugged him, said farewell to Mattie, and carried his suitcase to the front door. He interrupted Linda, who was watching television.

"I thought you weren't leaving until tomorrow."

"I decided to go to a hotel. I have to get my thoughts in order. There are many things I have to think about and I don't want any distractions."

"We have to talk, George."

"It can wait until I get back."

"No, George. Now."

George shrugged his shoulders resignedly. "Okay, if we

267

must talk, let's talk."

They closed the door from the kitchen, then went into the bedroom and closed that door. Linda sat on the bed. George went to the window and closed the blinds.

"All right," he said. "You wanted to talk. Talk."

"You've changed, George."

"I have? How?"

"I don't know. You aren't the same man you were a year ago. Two years ago. You no longer pay any attention to the house, to Rudolf, to me."

"It hasn't been easy, getting this business with the Fed taken care of."

"What do you want, George?"

"What do you mean, what do I want?"

"I mean, what do you want in our relationship?"

He looked at her now. Large tears were rolling down both cheeks. He suddenly felt a heaviness inside, and for a moment he saw her again as he had when they first met and he had felt an intense fire for her. He sat down on the bed next to her and kissed her on the cheek.

"I feel—I feel left out of your life," she said. "I feel like we came to a crossroads someplace and we went off in different directions without even waving good-bye to each other."

"If we did, I did not notice it."

She took hold of his hand. "Such strong hands. You know, George, you're still a very handsome man."

"And you are still beautiful," he said, pushing her hair back away from her face.

"Can you tell me why you aren't taking me to Europe?"

"I have a secret mission to go on. That's all I can tell you. It's for the President of the United States and I am not supposed to talk about it."

"Not even with your wife?"

"With no one. The world economy is in a mess. The whole structure is dangerously weak. Third World debt.

Rising oil prices. Inflationary pressures on the British pound. Certain things must be done to avert catastrophe and only I can do them. It is something that I must do alone, because there are certain forces in the world that might try to interfere, and they might get the idea they can get to me through you. I should have explained it to you before. I'm sorry I didn't."

"I still don't understand, but I'll accept it."

"Listen to me," he said. "When I get back we'll take a weekend up at the cabin. Get snowed in. Just the two of us. Not even Rudolf. What do you say? I won't even take a briefcase."

She smiled now. "It sounds cold."

"We'll bundle up."

He kissed her. She dried her eyes with some Kleenex.

"Now, I must get to work," he said. "When I get back, it will be just the two of us."

He kissed her on the cheek. She smiled now and started unbuttoning her dress. "I want you to take me, George, like you used to."

"Right now?"

"Now, come on." She kicked off her shoes. "I'm not waiting until you get back."

"I, ah . . ." He started to say something, but she was unbuckling his belt with an impish smile.

He turned suddenly and scooped her up and tossed her, as if she weighed no more than a pillow, onto the center of the bed. "This is crazy," he said.

"Just hurry it up," she said, slipping her panties off, "crazy is good."

Middle-aged women have the hormone thing. It disturbs their minds. That is what George attributed his wife's strange behavior to—hormones. She wanted him twice that night, and once more in the morning before he left for the

269

plane. But then, as he thought it over, he decided that perhaps it was not the hormone thing. After all, she was not having hot flashes and headaches and the bitchiness women were supposed to have during the change. Perhaps she was worried that with his newfound authority he would be losing interest in his old wife. Whatever it was, it was a great mystery to him.

He traveled TWA, first class, to Frankfurt that morning. The breakfast served him on the plane was remarkably good. Scrambled eggs, rye toast with a delicious peach marmalade, French roast coffee, and fresh-squeezed orange juice.

None of it mattered about his wife, he kept telling himself. It would not be long until he was back in Russia. When it was time for him to make his exit from America, he would give her fifteen minutes at most for her to make up her mind whether she wanted to go with him. She would no doubt decide to stay. He would not have time to tell her that the country was about to fall apart. Strange, but he was feeling some remorse about Linda. Especially after last night. She had enjoyed herself. Or seemed to. That was the first time in maybe a decade she'd liked it. She had been almost as good as Esther. Esther, of course, was a pro. She had a natural talent for pleasing men. But Linda had been good when she wanted to be. He'd give her that.

The next three days were a whirlwind; they went by in a blur. He met the chancellor of Germany and the British prime minister, ministers of trade, international financiers, economic ministers, Common Market ministers, trade envoys. They were all angry about the strength of the dollar against every currency in the world, and what they called the artificially high interest rates in America that were drawing foreign capital like a magnet.

And what was America doing to stop its terrible ballooning national debt?

George promised everyone that he would take their

concerns back home to the President and the Council of Economic Advisers. He stayed away from the press, granting no interviews. The Fed officials who accompanied him found their new boss knowledgeable, good-natured, friendly. They liked him.

He saw the last ministers and assistant ministers and directors of the Banco d'Italia at four in the afternoon at the Hilton Hotel in Luxembourg. He was tired and somewhat dazed. He said good-bye to his staff and took a cab to the airport where a chartered plane flew him to Geneva for his holiday. By the time he got off the plane he'd feasted on roast pheasant and had drunk half a magnum of Dom Pérignon champagne and was feeling refreshed. He was excited, and anxious. He had no intention of taking six days off for a vacation. For the first time since leaving for America thirty-one years ago, he was about to return to the Eastern bloc.

It was a homecoming. Yet, it was more. It was a strategy session, and he knew that, unlike the U.S. senators, these men could not be bluffed or fooled. He would have to be prepared for every question and reply with no hesitation if he expected them to support him. He had a detailed plan and he knew he would have to answer for any and all mistakes. If all went well, America would be in ruins quickly.

A Mercedes limousine was waiting for George at the airport in Geneva. Customs officials, knowing he was coming, whisked him through the formalities. An hour later the Mercedes was twisting its way up a mountainside to a chateau. When he arrived, a servant showed George to the library where a tall, aristocratic German Swiss by the name of Baron von Klieve was waiting for him.

"I trust you had an enjoyable trip?" Baron von Klieve said in guttural English.

"I did indeed."

"I had the cold roast pheasant sent along. I supposed

you'd be hungry. Care for a drink?"

"A Scotch, please, splash of seltzer."

The baron's servant made them both a drink. They sat on a couch in the massive living room.

The baron was looking at George over the top of his glasses. When George had first come to the West and found bluebloods working for the cause, he'd wondered what possible motivation they could have for seeing the destruction of their class. Perhaps it assuaged their guilt. Perhaps it gave an otherwise totally worthless life a particle of meaning. Then again they might just have been coerced or blackmailed or bought. You could never tell about these things, George mused. Maybe the baron was insane. Carson Black had a touch of madness in her. He'd known that for a long time.

The baron said, "I've seen you on the television these past few nights. Quite a tour you've been getting."

"Yes. I haven't been to the Continent often. Every time I come, though, I feel somehow broadened by the experience."

"Yes, quite," the baron said dully. He wiped his nose with a handkerchief he took from the pocket of his smoking jacket. He shook his foot as if trying to wake it up.

George said, "Wonderful place you have here, Baron."

"Too cold in the winter."

"I suppose."

The baron went back to shaking his foot. He had no doubt been instructed not to ask any questions, George thought.

The baron said, "You'll be going behind the curtain tonight. Won't get much sleep I'm afraid. If you have any emergency calls, we'll route them through by short wave. If anyone comes for you, I'm to say you met a friend and left. If they press the point, we're to make a veiled suggestion the friend was a woman. We don't suppose anyone will come. Your offices in Washington and New York have been told you are not available, period. Is that correct?"

"Correct."

"Good. Perhaps you'd like to freshen up. Your transportation arrives at eleven-thirty."

The chateau was magnificent, with high, gilded arches, Louis XIV furniture, rich tapestries. A servant showed George to a large bedroom on the second floor with a four-poster bed and a private bath. George sipped his drink, lying on the bed, and let his mind wander over the landscape of a ruined America. He dozed off and was awakened at eleven by a servant and taken to a black Fiat sedan at the back of the chateau.

"Have you got my luggage?" he asked the driver.

"All's been taken care of, sir," the driver, a dark burly man in a black uniform and a chauffeur's cap, said.

They drove down narrow, icy mountain roads, ever descending, through thick pine forests, snow-covered mountain meadows, and small sleepy villages. George dozed on and off in the backseat, but he was too excited to sleep fully. They crossed a river on an ancient stone bridge, then crossed a large rolling plain with farms and a railroad running parallel to the road. The driver had the radio tuned to a German radio station which was playing American music. He sang along with the tunes, tapping his fingers on the steering wheel.

They pulled off the road next to a farmhouse and followed what looked to be little more than a cow path over fields and through a small wooded area to a clearing where a small two-seater plane waited. It was painted with dark paint and had no markings. George was seated in the back. The pilot said nothing to him, but "strap yourself in." He said it in English, but with a heavy accent.

The engine sputtered, then caught. The pilot gunned the engine, the plane lurched forward, bumped along the ground, and took off. The pilot flew low over the trees, keeping an eye on some sort of radar device on the panel in front of him.

George felt his heart pounding in his chest and his palms were wet with sweat. Not because he had a fear of flying. It was the idea of going home. What reception awaited him, he wondered. They could not have a parade, but they might have a reception with dignitaries. Perhaps he would be given some medals. He was, after all, probably the most successful deep-penetration agent in history. Surely he was overdue for some recognition.

In view of the fact that he was about to bring America to its knees, they should make him at least a brigadier. George let himself bask in the glow of such thoughts as they made their way east.

They landed an hour and a half later on a small landing strip, lit by rows of red lights. There was no one around. A hundred yards or so from the landing strip were a couple of darkened buildings.

George stepped out of the plane. The wind howled through the trees. The pilot gestured toward one of the darkened buildings. George gestured for him to go first. The pilot grinned and started off at a rapid pace George could barely keep up with. They went in the back door of the building. The pilot switched on a light. They were in a long narrow corridor. It smelled musty and there were holes in the plaster.

"Are you quite certain you've brought me to the right place? Where is everyone?" George asked in Russian. He was amazed at how easily he spoke the language, despite the years of disuse.

"My orders were to bring you here, and here is where I brought you. If you don't like it, bring it up with General Kosnoff."

"I was questioning you, not the general."

The pilot showed George to a room. It was tiny, musty, and cold, lit by a single bulb hanging by a frayed cord from a crumbling plaster ceiling. There was a bureau, a chair, and a small writing table.

"What is this?" George asked.

"This is where you are to wait. You will find a uniform in the closet, Colonel. An aide will come for you in the morning, a little after sunrise."

George checked his watch and guessed sunrise was no more than an hour and a half away. "I'll be ready," he said. He returned the pilot's stiff salute.

George watched the pilot walk down the hall and go out the door at the other end of the building. He heard the plane start up and fly away. George was alone. He went into the room, closed the door, and locked it. He took out the uniform. It was new, and fit surprisingly well. He felt good in it. His Hero of the Soviet Union medal was pinned to the front. There was also a pair of black gleaming boots. What efficiency! So what if he had to spend a few hours in a horrible little room? They were trying to humble him a little, remind him he was first of all a member of the KGB, a soldier on the front lines in the war against capitalism. It was probably a good idea. He would do the same, he thought, if he were running this show. As long as they didn't take it too far he wouldn't complain.

He turned off the light and lit a cigar. Across the parking lot he could see another building in outline against the gray sky. No lights on anywhere. No cars in the parking lot. There was some movement along a fence, guards perhaps. Sentries. But there was no one else about.

His heart was racing and he was sweating. He had to stop that nonsense. Espionage was theater. He was about to play the most important part of his career. He had to be in total control.

The thing to do, he decided, was to spend this time thinking through exactly how to present his plan in the morning. He went over the salient points in his mind, trying to think of every possible objection. He could not bring America down alone; he needed help, and a lot of it.

He would have to get a commitment and a timetable from his superiors. Every day wasted was one more day he might be uncovered, and if he were to be uncovered the greatest opportunity in the history of their glorious movement would be lost.

The sun had been up for a full hour when George heard a car driving up. He looked at himself in the bureau mirror, his chest puffed out, his hat slightly tilted to the side. A little touch of cockiness, not overdone, he thought.

He waited for the footsteps to come down the hall before he opened the door. It was a young man in a military uniform. He saluted George and asked him to come; General Kosnoff was waiting to see him.

TWENTY

The driver opened the rear door of the black sedan for George, then got in behind the wheel, started the car, and drove down a country road. George looked back at the compound they had just left. It was a small cluster of ramshackle wooden buildings surrounded by a wire fence. It might have been a military barracks at one time; he couldn't be sure. One of the buildings was leaning over. It was not quite the royal reception he had been anticipating.

He did not mention the fact that there was no offer of breakfast.

It was a brilliant day, but cool. They drove through a pine forest for a few miles, then through some farm country. George strained to look for some signs of farmers, but didn't see any. He wanted to see some happy Eastern European peasants. He often imagined that these were the people he was devoting his life to. He saw a tractor and a hay wagon in a field, but no smiling peasants.

Soon they were driving through forest again, speeding over rolling hills. They stopped at a police checkpoint where they were waved on through. The police wore insignias in Czech and Russian-style caps and carried AK-47 assault rifles. At a second checkpoint the car was searched, but George was not asked to step out. The driver spoke in

Russian to the officer in charge and bummed a cigarette from him. No one paid George the least attention. They were allowed to leave after the driver's papers were examined.

The driver turned right at a fork in the road. After a few miles he turned off on what was little more than a dirt path, hardly wide enough for the car. The car bounced around a curve and came to stop in a small area where half a dozen cars were parked. Some guards saluted George and apologized in Russian, saying they had to search everyone who went further. George said he understood completely the necessity of such precautions.

They patted him down, then told him to follow a lanky corporal who would show him where to go.

They walked along a small frozen creek on a narrow wooden ramp. It was obvious that the compound—or whatever it was—was still under construction. They went up a small wooden staircase to a square, windowless concrete-block building. It looked as if it might be some sort of barn or workshed, built a year or two ago, that no one had gotten around to painting. It had a small metal door covered with rust. The corporal knocked on the door and waited. He looked back at George with a small enigmatic smile. The door opened. An armed guard stepped out, saluted, and patted George down again, this time without apology. "Enter," he said in Russian.

Inside it was brightly lit and freshly painted; the exterior neglect was no doubt to fool outsiders. George was led down a flight of stairs which opened on a wide hallway. Many uniformed officers and soldiers were scurrying around carrying files and pushing carts stacked with paperwork. George realized he was in some kind of bunker. He was shown to an elevator; the guard did not step aboard with him, but saluted as the doors closed.

The elevator descended two or three levels, then the door opened. George thought: Be military and show no fear.

A young KGB lieutenant was waiting for him. He saluted crisply and said, "Welcome, Colonel, the others are waiting." George followed the lieutenant through a pair of doors and into a meeting room. There were six men around the table, five of them in uniform. George saluted and was told to have a seat. He scanned the men at the table quickly as he sat down at the end. General Kosnoff, his superior, was at the opposite end of the table. They had met in Montreal years ago during the planning stages for the Arab oil embargo. And he recognized the man next to the general: Mr. Peabody! George smiled at him. How different he looked wearing general's stripes on his shoulder pads, George thought. His face was gray and, as usual, humorless.

Kosnoff puffed on a long brown cigarette. He rested his weight on his arms, which were folded in front of him. He had a wolfish face, disheveled gray hair, and a steely stare. The last time George had seen him, Kosnoff was a nobody, running errands for Andropov, who was then the head of the KGB. His rise in the apparatus was meteoric. But George was never one to denigrate a man's accomplishments. There were many ways to play the game.

"I believe you might not know everyone, Colonel Vlahovich," Kosnoff said. "Of course you know General Davydov." Peabody nodded at him. So that was his name, George thought. Kosnoff introduced KGB Major Raevsky to Peabody's left; on the other side of the table, Brigadier General Melnikoff and Vladimir Batyushkin, a civilian. George felt a shot go through his brain. Batyushkin was acting head of the KGB. "I'm honored," George said. Batyushkin nodded.

The other man at the table was a stenographer, an Army private.

George said, "I am pleased to meet all of you, and very glad to be here. I expect to accomplish much in the coming months and I hope I can count on your cooperation."

They looked at him and nodded, but no one said anything. They were there, apparently, to listen to him. Kosnoff nodded to the stenographer, who began writing in a brown notebook.

Kosnoff said, "We have given you a great deal of money, Colonel, and so far have been given very little in return. Now, in your latest proposal, you are saying we should give you, quote, 'All the financial resources of the great Soviet State.' "

"I know I am asking for much, but I will deliver much in return," George said, flexing his fingers. "We have committed ourselves to the destruction of the American capitalist system. The means to do that are now at hand," he said, with a note of high drama in his voice.

"We gave you one million dollars, so that you could become head of this . . . this bank. Now you are the head of it, you want us to give you even more money."

George said calmly, "I am the head of the Federal Reserve, General. I am now, in fact, the most powerful man in America, with the exception of the President himself."

Peabody scowled. None of the others reacted at all. Batyushkin's bushy eyebrows, George thought, might have raised a particle of an inch. George figured he was a man who understood power and what it was about.

Kosnoff leaned back in his seat and flicked some ashes on the floor. "Your idea is to start the biggest run on a bank in the history of the world, that is what you said. These things are strange to us. A run, that is what you said."

"Exactly. The plan calls for a global currency crisis, the magnitude of which has never before been witnessed. The results will be catastrophic. We will strangle the Americans with their own greed."

"Explain to us exactly how you plan to do that."

"I spelled it out in my proposal, General."

"I want to hear it from your own lips."

"All right, General, here is how it works: The Soviet Union has tremendous gold supplies. We use these gold supplies to buy dollars. No one will suspect anything. We will simply announce to the world that we need hard currency. The world will see this as a hopeful sign, believing we are about to go into the world marketplace and buy a lot of goods. At the same time we convert all our foreign hard currencies into dollars. The effect of this will be an upward pressure on the value of the dollar. As the dollar rises, other investors will join the bandwagon—private bankers, institutional bankers, individuals of great wealth. Capitalists can always be counted on to get in on an upward spiral. This will make the dollar rise even faster. In one month's time, the dollar should rise perhaps one hundred and fifty percent. If we're able to convince our Arab friends to do likewise—and with enough military armament promised I'm sure we can—we may effect a two hundred percent increase."

"I don't see how this will hurt the Americans," Peabody said. "They will be able to buy up the world cheaply. It is what they've been doing with the overvalued dollar for years—we will only be making fat pigs fatter."

"We will be stretching the dollar out, General," George said. "Like a rubber band. I call it the 'slingshot effect.' " He made a motion, imitating a slingshot. No one seemed impressed. He let it go, tracing the trajectory of the imaginary stone with the flat of his hand.

General Kosnoff said, "Phase two, I believe your theory states, would be the selling off of dollars on a grand scale. Upward of forty billion dollars."

"I've since recalculated. I now believe it may take as much as sixty-eight billion. Sixty-eight billion is the ceiling."

This got a reaction from the sober-faced men around the table, but not quite the one George had anticipated. They were staring at him as if he were a lunatic.

281

"Listen, gentlemen, please," George said. He knew his tone was a little too condescending, but he felt he could risk it. "I will explain why and how it can work, and will work, without fail. For the last twelve years or so, America has had a policy of bleeding off capital investment from her trading partners. The way it works is this: America pays high interest rates. Two to four percentage points higher than Europe or her Asian allies. Money flows in the direction of higher rates like water flows downhill. At the same time, America is having huge trade deficits, so there is a lot of American dollars overseas not being spent on American goods. When we bid the dollar up, more dollars will flow into American banks, until they are stuffed. American bankers must get the money loaned out quickly because of the high rates they are paying, so they put it into shaky loans. Believe me, gentlemen, the American banking system is a shambles. Most of its loans to Brazil and Mexico have been in default for a decade, propped up only by the American government, which is paying the interest. Huge loans made to companies to buy supertankers are in default. The bottom has fallen out of the condominium business, and high rise mortgages . . ."

"Please do not lecture us on the workings of the world capitalist system," Kosnoff said with irritation.

"Let him speak," Batyushkin said.

Kosnoff reddened and told George to get on with it.

"When we let the slingshot go," George said with renewed confidence, "and start selling off this enormous stash of dollars—and pressure our Arab friends to do the same—the dollar will fall like a rock. European and Asian depositors will pull their vast sums out of American banks. In the past, America bailed England out of a similar problem. The dollar was rescued twice by its trading partners in similar situations during the eighties. Japan has been reinvesting her dollars and could commit perhaps ten or twelve billion to shore up the dollar; she will not be able to commit more without crippling herself. Japan always looks out for herself first. England cannot at this time commit more than a few billion. Five at the most. It will be too little and too late. West Germany—that is your problem. If we pressure West Germany, she will do nothing."

Batyushkin smiled now. "Go on, Colonel, tell us more."

"Comrade Batyushkin, what you will have then is beautiful chaos. Student political action groups will be encouraged, supplied with small printing presses, bull horns, training, even weapons. Revolutionary cadres are at this moment being readied. As industrial plants close, the working classes will flock to the only groups around who seem to know what they're doing. Spontaneously, armies of workers and the mass unemployed will spring up, just as Lenin predicted. These armies will take a few radio stations, surround the White House—it will be over before they realize what's happened to them."

"And what is your role in this?" Batyushkin asked.

"The Americans long ago feared a currency crisis; that is why the Federal Reserve was created. The function of the Federal Reserve is to step in to save the country when any segment of the economy is going to collapse. It is my job to see that it steps in with too little, too late."

Peabody banged his fist on the table. The army private jumped with a start, but the others didn't even blink.

Peabody said, "What are we going to get for our billions? I'll tell you. We're going to get the Americans to declare martial law. Then what will we have? A truly fascist state, with all those missiles. No. This whole scheme is folly. Colonel Vlahovich can get us much good intelligence in the position he now holds. He has private meetings with the President, they have drinks together in the President's private rooms. He can give us good intelligence about where America will be spending her resources. I say, no. I say this scheme is too grandiose, too full of risks. America will fall. Marx has shown it to be inevitable. We do not need to risk all of our wealth."

Now it was George who banged his fist on the table. "And Lenin has shown it doesn't pay to wait! Where would our glorious revolution have been, had the great Lenin taken your advice? The window of opportunity is open. Now! I say we strike!"

"Agh!" Peabody said. "Fool." He turned away from George, looking off into a dark corner of the room.

No one spoke for a moment, then Kosnoff said, "I agree with the general."

KGB Major Raevsky nodded in agreement. Brigadier General Melnikoff nodded also. Batyushkin said, "We should perhaps talk it over. We will have some more questions for you later. Thank you, Colonel."

George stood up and saluted with a little flourish. Then he said, "Gentlemen, if I do not get approval, I am going to the premier himself."

"I will forgive you that remark," Batyushkin said coolly. "You have been out of the country a long time and have forgotten some of our customs."

The young lieutenant was waiting in the hall. He saluted with a clicking of his heels, then told George there was some refreshment waiting for him. The refreshment turned out to be a few slices of black bread, a slab of cheese, and hot tea, served in a glass with a saucer. Not what he was used to, but he didn't complain. Already he was thinking how nice it was going to be to get back to New York and have a vigorous workout, a hot steam bath, a good meal, and a pleasant evening with Esther.

But he stopped himself from thinking that way. He felt a sharp pang of guilt. His country was not rich and decadent. It was growing and changing, bringing the wonders of socialism to the world, bringing into being a new kind of man: unselfish, strong, decisive, not looking to any god to solve his problems for him. He had to be prepared for some inconveniences when so many had given even their lives for the cause.

The bread was good and the cheese was good and he liked drinking his tea from a saucer according to the Russian custom. It cooled the tea so he didn't burn his mouth, he told himself.

He waited almost an hour in a small room with a few wooden chairs, chatting with the lieutenant. George wanted to know where he went to school, how he liked working for the Committee for State Security, how hard promotions were these days, whether the dormitories were as much fun as they used to be. The lieutenant assured him they were.

The lieutenant was open, obviously bright, personable. He told George a joke about a shipment of potatoes that went to the wrong place in the central transit depot and was made into shoes; George did not get the joke, but he laughed right along with the lieutenant. The telephone rang. It was a loud, coarse bell, coming out of a crude-looking black box on the wall. The lieutenant picked up the phone, gave his name, then listened. He said only one more word before he hung up:

"*Da.*"

George said, "What is it?"

The lieutenant's face clouded. "Colonel Vlahovich, you are as of this moment under arrest."

TWENTY-ONE

The young lieutenant opened the door. Two armed guards, a sergeant and a corporal, rushed in and each took hold of one of George's arms and spun him around. George shook them off with a shrug of his powerful shoulders.

"Just a minute here!" George yelled.

The corporal answered by throwing a punch in George's face, knocking him backward. George staggered around in a small circle, trying to regain his balance. Blood ran from his nose. His face felt numb for a moment, then began to throb. He was confused and angry. "Don't you know who I am?" he yelled. "There's been a terrible mistake!"

"Are you going to continue resisting?" the sergeant asked. The corporal held a rifle butt in front of George, ready to hit him with it.

"You best go quietly, Colonel," the young lieutenant said with genuine sadness in his voice.

George put a handkerchief to his nose. "Tell General Kosnoff," he said to the lieutenant.

"The general knows," the lieutenant said.

The sergeant and the corporal marched George down the hall. The clerks and soldiers who were in the hallway going about their duties turned their heads away; no one wanted to make eye contact with someone under suspicion. George was taken down a dimly lit stairway into the lowest level. Water ran down the walls and there was a foul, oily odor coming from the ventilator. There were heavy doors on both sides of the hallway, which was lit with two naked bulbs, spaced far apart, giving it a feeling of gloom. George thought: right out of a Bela Lugosi movie. The corporal opened one of the doors, revealing a small windowless room.

The room had no ventilation. There was only a chair facing a table with two chairs behind it. Two powerful lights were mounted in the ceiling behind the table, facing in the direction of the single chair. The sergeant stood by the door. He was tall and broad-shouldered, with a linebacker's meanness in his eyes, George thought.

"You ever play ball?" George said. It was obvious the man didn't have the slightest idea what he was talking about.

The corporal positioned the chair on a spot painted on the floor. The corporal was, George judged, meaner. He was lean and raw-boned, with a bovine peasant's face. He put down his rifle and said, "Take off your clothes. All of them."

George looked at the linebacker sergeant by the door. He had a grin on his face and was holding his rifle across his chest. It was an old bolt-action job with a gleaming walnut stock, no doubt more ceremonial than anything, a prop used for guard duty around civilians. George figured it wasn't loaded, but it would work well as a club.

George tensed his muscles. There were few men his age in his condition. Once, he'd been trained to fight. These two were in their late twenties or early thirties, but he might be able to surprise them. He looked at the sergeant, who was grinning broadly now, as if he knew this was the moment of truth and wanted nothing more than to bash in someone's head.

George said, "If the two of you help me out in any way, I

will see that you are graciously rewarded. I have friends very high up in the Party."

"You had better hurry," the sergeant said. "We have a schedule, and if we don't keep to it, we don't get any vodka ration tonight." The corporal chuckled.

"If you prefer," the sergeant said, "we will knock you cold and then strip you naked."

"That won't be necessary," George said.

He put his uniform in a neat pile on the table and stood naked before them. He had often been naked with other men around in the steam room at his health club, so he would show no shame. He knew they wanted to shame him. He'd studied these techniques when he was in training and he knew how they worked. They would not work on him, he told himself. But it was such an overpowering insult that he felt degraded. It was the first thing the Nazis did to the Jews at the camps. Strip them naked, and with their clothes went their human dignity.

One day, the man who was responsible for this indignity would pay for it with his life, or at least a few years of his life in the Gulag. He swore an oath to himself under his breath.

George sat on the cold chair and crossed his arms, keeping his massive chest expanded. He made no effort to stop the blood running from his nose. He glared at his guards, first the sergeant, then the corporal. They were standing casually by the door. The corporal was smirking now; the sergeant merely looked bored. The room was cool and there were bloodstains on the cement floor. There was a drain. A shiver of fear rose in him; he clenched his teeth. He had heard of agents getting this kind of treatment to teach them humility and to make them fear their masters. He wondered how far they would go. He had to be back in six days or the FBI would be looking for him and his cover might be blown. For six days he could withstand anything.

"Nice legs," the corporal said with a whistle.

The sergeant chuckled. George ignored them. They both chuckled.

A moment later the door opened. The sergeant and the corporal came to attention. Two men entered. One was Vladimir Batyushkin, the KGB chief. The other was a big man in a white coat with a businesslike expression on his deeply lined, dark-complected face. He looked vaguely Oriental, Siberian perhaps. He had cruel black eyes with a strange look in them. Insanity, perhaps. He took up a position behind George, his arms folded, no doubt waiting for instructions. If they were going to torture him, this would be the man to do the job, George thought.

"Why are you doing this to me, Comrade Batyushkin?" George asked.

Batyushkin ignored the question. He sat behind the table and reached around him and turned on a switch; the lights were dazzlingly bright. George pretended not to notice, keeping his eyes fixed on Batyushkin, although all he could see through the intense glare was a vague outline. When George had used light to hide his identity from Robert Park, he had not realized the effect it could have on a man, how insignificant it could make him feel.

George was vaguely aware that the sergeant and the corporal had left. "You are responsible for this abuse?" he asked.

Batyushkin said, "I will ask the questions, you will answer them."

"I wish to put my clothes on."

"You will answer questions and make no more demands, understood?"

George said nothing; he just kept staring into the light at Batyushkin's outline. After a moment Batyushkin said, "What we want to know is who you are."

"I am Colonel Gyorgi Andreyevitch Vlahovich of the KGB, North American department, deep penetration finance sector. My cover is that of George Henry Corbett. I have been thirty-one years under cover."

"A long time," Batyushkin said. "Time enough for you to become quite another man."

George shivered. It seemed as if the room was getting colder. "I demand to see General Kosnoff. I demand that you get in touch with the premier. Perhaps you do not understand, Comrade, the importance of my mission or my importance to our historic cause."

"You cannot make any demands here, Colonel." Batyushkin's tone was even, almost matter-of-fact. It gave George a curious feeling of dread. Batyushkin said, "Your wife's name is Linda, is it not?"

"You know that it is."

"Have you confided in her—your situation?"

"I refuse to answer any questions until I've been given my clothes and I've spoken to the premier."

The man in the white coat moved swiftly: he hit George on the shoulder with something hard, a rod wrapped in leather. It stung maddeningly on George's cold skin. George came out of his chair and took a swing at him, but the man in the white coat was faster. He hit George in the groin, dropping him to the floor.

George weaved in and out of consciousness for a moment. Hold on, he told himself. Don't let them see your pain.

The pain gradually subsided.

"Get back in your chair, Comrade Vlahovich," Batyushkin said in a dull monotone. "Now that you understand the ground rules, let us have no more of your telling us what you will and will not do. Just answer the questions. If you lie, you will be punished. Are you understanding that, Comrade Vlahovich?"

George nodded and sat back down. He no longer tried to look through the glare at Batyushkin. He sat with his head down, his thoughts in a muddle. How could this happen to him? He was the most successful agent, perhaps, in the

290

history of the KGB. Had they gone mad? He was finally in position to strike a tremendous blow against the hated enemy and now, at this moment, they chose to move against him.

"Now then," Batyushkin said. "What have you told your wife?"

He wiped the blood from his nose. "What have I told my wife? Nothing. She has no idea even that I'm Russian. When she finds out, she'll probably jump out a window."

"How much rent do you pay for your apartment?"

"I have a condominium. It cost, as you know, seven hundred and forty thousand dollars."

"How much is it worth today?"

George shrugged. "A million and a half, maybe a little more."

"You are a rich man," Batyushkin said.

"I am an officer in the KGB, I make eleven hundred rubles a month."

"How much did you earn last year in your cover identity?"

"Eight hundred and three thousand dollars. It was not a particularly good year."

"You have a servant."

"Yes."

"She's black?"

"Yes."

"Has she ever been a member of the Party?"

"No, of course not."

"Do you trust her?"

"I trust no one, that is how I was trained. I have stuck to my training."

"Did you know your servant has a brother who is a member of the New York City Police Department?"

"Yes."

"Don't you think you are taking a great risk having such a person around?"

"Obviously I don't."

"Please watch your tone with me."

"Sorry, Comrade. Her brother, as far as I know, works traffic in the Bronx."

"It shows remarkably poor judgment that you would hire the sister of a policeman to work in your home."

"How could I have known when I hired her? I did not ask her who her brother was."

George detected his voice rising in pitch, becoming almost plaintive. He would not allow that. He sat up straight and crossed his legs. He would keep the appearance of dignity no matter what; he would keep the same command authority in his voice he used in his business dealings and with his agents.

He said, "I have gone undetected for thirty-one years. I have made contacts in government, I have associated with the most important men in America, including the President of the United States. I believe such a record proves my competency and good judgment. I want to know what you think you are doing by this ridiculous arrest."

Batyushkin lit a cigarette; the tobacco burned sweet, perfumed. Not the regular cheap Russian tobacco, George noticed. "Ridiculous? Not so ridiculous. You see, Colonel Vlahovich, I have come here to question you on a matter of high treason for which you have been accused. I am to decide whether you are to live or die."

"Die? High treason? What the hell are you talking about?"

"All in good time . . . first, there are things we have to know. Pieces to be fit together."

"What pieces?"

"We must have a full accounting of what you've done. Your control has asked you on many occasions to attempt to recruit more agents from the computer industry and the defense industry. With a few small exceptions you have not been able—or willing—to do so."

"I have not been able. Originally, I was to get into the banking industry, those were my orders. I have obeyed those orders."

"Unfailingly, Comrade?"

"Yes."

"You were required, were you not, to report all income and expenses?"

"Yes, of course."

"And any accumulation of wealth while in your cover identity naturally belongs to the Soviet State."

"Of course it does! When have I ever violated my trust? Never! Has someone accused me of failure to give a complete accounting?"

"Has someone cause to accuse you, Comrade?"

"No, of course not. On my honor as an officer of the Committee of State Security."

George had been staring into the light again. His eyes were burning, but still he would not look away.

"You have a son, do you not?" Batyushkin said.

"Rudolf."

"You are very fond of him."

"I have one child. He is never going to amount to much, but I like him."

"Like most fathers you have taken care that his future is assured, have you not?"

"I wish he would get an education. I wish he would take better care of his health."

"But what of his financial health?"

"What are you getting at, Comrade?"

"I am speaking of the millions you put away for the boy in Swiss banks."

George said, "I don't know what you're talking about."

"You deny it then?"

"Of course I deny it."

"It will do you no good to deny it, we will get the truth out of you. The whole truth. You will tell us all about the

293

money you have stolen from the State before we are through with you."

"I have nothing in Swiss banks."

George saw Batyushkin give some kind of signal.

The man behind George hit him on the shoulder again, knocking him once again to the floor. George lay there, blood running down his back. He was looking at Batyushkin's legs in boots under the table. They were crossed casually, like those of a man watching television with nothing whatever on his mind and all the time in the world. It didn't matter; George would never tell him. That money had been carefully siphoned off over the years, carefully nurtured and nourished, and it belonged to Rudolf. They had no right to it. Rudolf could not live in Russia. It would be like the moon to him. It was not his fault that his father happened to be a spy.

George knew that they could not know for sure there were Swiss accounts. The Swiss banks were absolutely safe, since the money was kept by account number only and there was no way to find out to whom the money belonged. George had told absolutely no one except Linda, and how would they have gotten the information out of her? So they were guessing.

"Get back into the chair, Comrade, and let us have no more lying. Tell me now, how much and which bank and number?"

The man in the white coat helped George into the chair. George feigned weakness as the man slid his hands under his arms and lifted him. When George was nearly upright, he spun around suddenly and wrapped his strong right arm around the mans' head and ran him forward into the wall with a crunching thud. The man's knees buckled and he sank to the floor. George turned to the figure behind the lights. He had no way to know whether Batyushkin was armed; he was feeling too much rage at the moment to make those kinds of calculations. He was going on animal instinct now and his quarry was on the move, heading for the door.

George leapt for him, feeling a surprising vitality. Before Batyushkin could make it to the door, George was on him, pummeling him with his fist.

"You leave Rudolf out of this, you hear me? He has nothing to do with any of this business! He is not a Russian, he is something that just happened and nothing that will happen is his fault!"

Batyushkin covered his head and yelled for the guards, but George quickly rendered him unconscious and moved the heavy table in front of the door. Then he pulled Batyushkin up off the floor and put him in his chair, slapping him.

"It wasn't your idea alone to do this to me, was it? You're not big enough!" George said. "It had to be somebody far up, in the Politburo, maybe even higher up than that!"

The guards banged on the door.

"Tell them everything's fine— Go on, tell them!"

"Go away!" Batyushkin yelled. "There's an interrogation going on in here!"

The pounding stopped.

Batyushkin looked at George as a sane man looks at a crazy one, full of fear and incomprehension. George slowly took hold of Batyushkin's throat and pushed him into a corner. "You know what, asshole? You could have blown about the biggest espionage deal in the history of the world. What if I escaped from this room and got to a radio and said I'd been kidnapped and was behind the Iron Curtain? Sure, I don't even know where I am, but it doesn't matter, all I have to do is get my voice out of here and you'll be up to your neck in the biggest goddamn crisis since Berlin, is that what you want?" George banged the man's head against the wall. "You listening?"

Batyushkin nodded. He was white with fear. George

could tell what he was thinking. What kind of fool would do something like this with a hallway full of guards outside?

"Take your clothes off," George said, releasing his grip on the man's throat.

Batyushkin said, "Listen to me, Gyorgi Andreyevitch. You have only one chance to stay alive, and that is to cooperate with me fully from this moment on. There is a terrible split in the consensus of the Politburo over what to do. You are to be interrogated so that they know you can be trusted. You have been very foolish. Submit, and take what's coming, it's your only chance. The premier himself has ordered the interrogation."

"But why? Why, damn it?"

"You are too much of an American. Even your control does not trust you. We have to know what is in you, we have to be sure you are one of us!"

The door suddenly flew open, smashed in with a bench propelled by three burly guards. George turned to put his hands up, but it made no difference. They clubbed him into unconsciousness.

When he came to he was in the chair again. He managed to straighten up. Everything was blurred now; voices were hollow echoes. A bucket of ice water was thrown in his face, making him more alert.

"The Swiss account," Batyushkin said. He was again behind the table, smoking the sweet-scented cigarette, as if nothing at all had happened. "You were about to tell me the number—the amount . . ."

"There is no account, no money," George said weakly.

"We know about the Barrett deal, Comrade."

George could hardly remember it himself. It had been twenty years ago; he was barely starting out. He took some cash in a gun deal from a starry-eyed idealist named

Barrett who was going to start a revolution in the South Bronx, and used it to buy some soybean futures through a small phony company he owned on the side. But no one knew about it. He'd never told anyone, and yet they knew.

"Tell us about Barrett, Comrade Vlahovich. One thousand war surplus Thompson submachine guns. He gave you twenty-six thousand in cash. You reported only six thousand. The other twenty thousand turned a profit of almost thirty thousand, which you reinvested, didn't you?"

"I don't know any Barrett."

Someone hit him from behind; he heard the sound of it, then winced, feeling the sting on his bare shoulders.

"Hit me all you want, I can't tell you anything."

"You took two hundred thousand when you laundered some money for a Mr. Munson."

"I know no Munson."

There had been a Marciano. How could they have made a mistake like that? Just where the hell were they getting their information?

"We want the name of the Swiss bank and the account numbers, Comrade."

"No, there are none."

They hit him again. And again.

He couldn't bear to look into the lights now. His whole body felt raw with pain. The questions kept coming:

"Where did you get the twelve thousand to buy your mistress a sable coat? It didn't come out of your personal account."

Did they have access to his accounts? How much could they know? How many networks did they have? Were their agents in every little corner of every little bank and brokerage? How he had underestimated their knowledge and their power!

The blows now seemed to come at random, each more stinging than the last. He was groggy now, and when his head drooped they hit him again. For a moment, the image of himself looking in the mirror that morning with his hat at a lightly jaunty angle poked through the cloud of his memory. How he'd been on top of the world!

They poured more water on him. He sat up straight. His body was going numb now. How much time had gone by, he wondered. A day? An hour?

"We are asking you about your mistress, Comrade Vlahovich. When did you first meet her . . ."

They seemed to want to know everything, every detail. Every whispered nothing. Then suddenly, as if another part of him had come awake, he said, "We have great work to do, great things to accomplish. Don't you understand that all this petty business is irrelevant? We can, if we work together, crash the American economy!"

"That will come later, after you have told us what you must tell us."

"The slingshot effect," George said. "We'll make the biggest run on banks in the history of the world." His words came out like babble. The blows continued. The hours passed.

How many hours passed, he didn't know. He denied knowing anything. He kept returning to the plan, the slingshot effect, the run on the banks, the revolutionary armies. His body felt as if it was sinking into the floor while his mind was floating above the room. He began to hear voices. He could smell the blood now. It seemed to invigorate him, filling him with a peculiar euphoria.

Batyushkin's voice droned on. Or had they changed interrogators? George could no longer tell. He no longer cared.

"You are going to tell us everything eventually," the interrogator said. "We are in no hurry. We always get a full confession."

Full confession. He knew now what they wanted. Once a man began to confess, he confessed all and, once he confessed all, they owned his mind. Stalin had perfected the technique for the show trials of the fifties.

They would get no confession out of him. He could hold out. He would hold out. He would never tell them anything.

"The plan will work, you must believe me. I have it worked out."

"We know about the plan. It is the Swiss accounts, Comrade . . ." They hit him on the back again and again. The euphoria passed now, and the sensation of pain that was on the surface of the skin was filtering into him. The pain was pervasive now; each blow seemed to go through him like electricity. He stopped talking altogether. He didn't speak for what seemed like hours and hours.

The light was burning in his brain. The leather went whap, whap, whap against his skin. His mind tilted toward insanity. He was alive in the middle of a nightmare. Through the center of the agony a thought entered his head: Rudolf, you will have to fend for yourself, I can't stand it anymore.

He started his confession at 8 A.M. on the second day. He finished telling them everything they wanted to know at 9:15 P.M.

TWENTY-TWO

Charlesetta Poindexter was a simple woman, but not a stupid one. She had survived a brutal childhood in the Louisiana bayous. Her father was a tubercular farmworker, alcoholic and violent. Her mother, a religious zealot, was superstitious, illiterate, and rigid. To escape her family, Charlesetta married an itinerant evangelist preacher, even though she was Catholic, and traveled all over the South with him for fourteen years, living in the back of an old Ford truck. He died of liver trouble in the late sixties when their son, Ambrose, was yet a baby.

She moved to New York because she'd hoped to find more opportunity there for herself and the boy. She found work as a domestic, took in laundry, accepted some food stamps, lived in subsidized housing. Got by. She devoted herself to her son. When he was murdered, accused of murder himself, she was devastated. It was only her simple faith in God's justice that sustained her.

Catlyn Cavanaugh's visit had given her some hope. Then the strange appearance of the dark-skinned priest had dashed those hopes—but only momentarily. She checked with the bishop's office and found out there was no Father Delgado working in the diocese. And then she knew. She knew for sure that her boy was not a murderer.

At first she didn't do anything about the bogus priest. She knew if she told the police they weren't likely to believe her. She was suspicious of police anyway. It was clear to her that Ambrose was killed to prevent him from proving that he didn't kill Damian Carter. Whoever did it was able to make himself look like Ambrose, so he would have to have been the same size. He must have known what Ambrose did, where he went, everything. Therefore, she figured, it must be somebody who spent some time in the neighborhood.

All she had to do was find out who had been interested in Ambrose. Somebody was bound to know something.

She could have simply reported this to Catlyn Cavanaugh, but she wanted to do something herself. It filled her hours, made her feel that she wasn't just standing around doing nothing while her son lay cold in his grave, an accused murderer.

She started by asking local merchants whether anyone had been asking about Ambrose. Nobody remembered anything. Then she asked Ambrose's friends. One, Flower Slater, said Ambrose had mentioned a couple of times that he thought he was being followed, but he always figured it was the cops.

That, Charlesetta Poindexter found extremely interesting. Things were starting to fall into place. The guy following Ambrose, Flower thought, was white, about Ambrose's height and weight. So he might be the one who killed this Damian Carter, she thought. And he might be the one who killed Ambrose.

He might even have been the one who dressed up as a priest and came to see her. Was it possible she had been in the same room with her son's murderer? Her hands trembled at the thought.

It was Abdul Hussein who owned the liquor store on the corner down the block from her place who told Charlesetta about Shirley Dills and the man who hung around her apartment all the time. She was in his store buying liquor one time with the guy. He'd asked Abdul whether he knew Ambrose, "the nigger kid" up the block, and what kind of booze he drank. Abdul remembered denying that he knew him, even though Ambrose used to come in Saturdays and clean up the back room for a couple of bucks. He didn't know the man's name, but he sure remembered how cold were his eyes . . .

Catlyn had just gotten home from Washington when she got the call from Charlesetta Poindexter, asking whether she could come over and see her. Catlyn told her to take a cab; she'd have the doorman pay for it and send her up.

An hour later, sitting in Catlyn's living room, Charlesetta was excited to the point of jubilation. On the way over she'd been afraid Catlyn wouldn't believe her, that she would think this was the fancy daydream of a grieving mother, but Catlyn was listening with rapt attention.

". . . so that's all I know," she said, finishing her story. "What do you think? Should we go to the police?"

Catlyn smiled and said, "Let me have a talk with this Shirley Dills. The police haven't believed anything I've told them so far, no reason to think they'll start now." She offered to pay Charlesetta for the information, but she refused.

"I'm doing this for Ambrose," she said.

Shirley Dills was expecting a john when she opened the door. She found herself face to face with a blond white woman and a giant black man.

"Name's B. B.," the giant said. "We gots ta talk." He shoved Shirley back into her living room.

The blonde closed the door and said, "I'm Catlyn Cavanaugh, Miss Dills. Do you know me?"

She shook her head. She couldn't take her eyes off B. B.; he had a terribly angry look on his face that made her tremble down to her toes.

B. B. said, "Yo seen Miss Cavanaugh goin' inta the brownstone across the street. Yo try hard, yo gonna remember." He stepped closer, looking down at her as if she might be a bug he was deciding whether to mash.

Catlyn looked out the front window. There was a clear view of the Poindexters' across the street. "We've come to the right place," she said.

Shirley Dills said, "I've never seen you before in my life, honest. What do you want with me? I'm nobody, really."

"You're an accessory to murder," Catlyn said.

"That mean the cops can fry yo ass," B. B. said.

Shirley Dills swallowed hard. She'd been dreading this moment since the day she'd met Park. She'd had an intuition about him, that he was evil and would get her involved in his evil someway. She sat down on the couch, trying to smile, trying to look unconcerned. Trying to look as if she had no idea what they were talking about. She said, "I'm not an accessory to anything. Certainly not to murder."

B. B. said, "We believes yo. The cops, they don't believe they got sand on beaches."

"You don't need to tell me about cops, they've been making my life miserable since I was twelve."

"We want the man's name," Catlyn said.

"And where we can find him," B. B. said. "Then we be leavin' yo alone."

Shirley Dills stared at him. "I don't know what man you're talking about. What man?"

"The man who disguised himself as Ambrose Poindexter and killed a friend of mine named Damian Carter," Catlyn said. "The man who killed Ambrose because he was afraid Ambrose was going to prove he was someplace else at the time. That man. The man who sat by your window that looks right out there on Ambrose Poindexter's place."

"I don't know anyone who's killed anyone."

Catlyn said, "Miss Dills, listen to me, please. We know the killer's spent a lot of time here. You've been seen with him in the neighborhood. He's Caucasian, about five nine or ten, one hundred-forty pounds, and he's got a cold stare. He used to be in the military, probably has some connection with the theater world. We're going to find him, sooner or later. You better pray we find him before he figures out that we know you're connected with him. Because if he finds out. . . ."

"Yo gonna be a statistic in the morgue." B. B. grinned, leaning down close to her face.

Catlyn said, "If you agree to help us, I'll be happy to give you money to relocate in another city."

"How much money?"

"How about five thousand dollars? Where would you like to go?"

"Florida someplace. North Florida, up around Tallahassee. Ain't so hot in the summer. Take at least ten thousand dollars, anyway."

"Done," Catlyn said.

Shirley Dills closed her eyes for a moment, then opened them. She took a deep breath. "You are very foolish people," she said. "You don't know how mean he can be."

"Yes, we do," Catlyn said. "We won't let him hurt you. Just tell us his name and where we can find him."

She shut her eyes again. "His name is Robert Park. That's all I know. I don't know if it's his real name or a made-up name or what. I don't know where he lives. I don't know his phone number. He always calls me."

She knew if she told them about the Horned Toad, he'd know she had given out the number. He'd kill her before she could get to Florida.

"Does he ever talk about people he lives with? Places he goes?"

"He likes the horse races. He loves to watch cartoons on television. He's not right in the head completely. There's pieces missing, know what I mean?" She was speaking with a kind of hushed awe in her voice.

"Yo ain't givin' us nothin' gonna help us find the sucker," B. B. said.

"Just relax, Miss Dills," Catlyn said. "Anything you know about him might help. What he likes and what he doesn't like."

"He drinks beer. He loves to drink beer, almost any kind. So long as it's cold. He goes to adult movies. He's got some very strange ideas of what makes good sex. That's about all I really know. What else? He hates animals. Loathes cats."

"Yo gots ta know more than that," B. B. said. "Jez think a minute here, it gonna come ta yo. What else he be likin'?"

She blinked. "Fighting. Never runs from trouble. He eats junk food. And he loves the smell of pizza. He says he lives over a pizza parlor and can tell how busy they are by how strong the smell is!"

"Yo wouldn't happen ta know the name of this here pizza parlor?" B. B. said.

"He never did say."

Catlyn looked at Hanson. "How many pizza parlors you think there are in New York?"

Nicolai Stepanovitch Pogorny saw his control, George Corbett, two days after his return from Europe and found him a changed man. They met on a Saturday morning at Esther's while she was away at the beauty parlor.

There were some bruises on George's face and his shoulders stooped. He seemed to have aged ten years.

"Can you tell me what has happened, sir?" Nicolai asked.

"A minor accident involving a motor vehicle. Nothing serious. Come, Nicolai, sit. We have business to discuss."

They sat at the dining room table. George didn't offer

Nicolai coffee or a drink, which was highly unusual. He was sullen and gloomy and there were dark circles under his eyes. He seemed almost timid. There was no boasting, effusive talk, or grandiose plans.

Nicolai said, "Did you get to go behind the Curtain?" George looked at him as if he did not understand.

"On the trip, did you go behind the Curtain?"

"No," he said. "I met with Western economic ministers, then took a small vacation. I was on vacation when this happened." He indicated the bruises on his face.

"I see," Nicolai said, but what he saw was the truth. George had gone behind the Curtain. And Nicolai knew they broke him. He had seen it before, a major in North Africa who had gotten a little too uppity. This major was gambling and drinking and running foolish risks. They took him home and beat him until he whimpered. Now they had done the same to George Corbett, and Nicolai had a pretty good idea why. They broke him because they were going along with the plan, and they wanted to be absolutely certain George would not be taking any independent action. Nicolai suppressed a grin, thinking how his foolish superior had been so puffed up with his own importance.

"Here, I have some keys for you," George said. "I have written down, in code of course, the location of the storage bins these keys unlock. In them, you will find the ordnance to distribute to all key groups and leaders. Instruct them on the proper use—even if they insist they already know. They don't. You are to caution them not to start activities until the code words are broadcast."

"Some of them will not wait."

"It cannot be helped," George said with a shrug.

"What is our timetable, Colonel? Can you give me a frame?"

"You must do your work quickly. The dollar should start to rise on the foreign money markets over the next few weeks. When it hits record highs against all major currencies, you will know we are about to begin. Go now, and good luck."

Nicolai rented a car using a phony name and headed first to New Jersey where he met with Ann Rutherford, a member of the Radical Student Brigade which had been underground for fifteen years. He gave her one of the keys, which was to a rental bin in Virginia Beach, Virginia, where two hundred pounds of plastique and fifty detonators and timers were stored. Ann Rutherford gave Nicolai the shivers. Her parents were rich and had put her through Yale University. She was working as a reporter for a TV station in New York when she did an interview with Samuel Glaston, a dedicated Marxist who had robbed a Brinks truck. She helped bust him out of jail by smuggling in a gun in a camera case. Glaston had since given up the cause and turned state's evidence, but she had continued the fight. She was smart, beautiful, and totally insane. Nicolai could see the insanity in her eyes; it would bubble up between sentences, forcing her eyeballs back up under her heavy eyelids. He was glad she declined his invitation to demonstrate how to work the detonators and he did not insist as George had instructed. Nicolai wanted only to get away from her as quickly as he could. As he started his car, he said. "Remember, your mission is to attack the power lines going into New York."

"Consider it done."

"You will wait for your coded signal."

"Relax, Nicolai, we're on your side." Her eyes rolled back into her head.

Next, Nicolai stopped at a farm in Pennsylvania. He arrived late at night, and when he pulled into the driveway he came face to face with a scruffy young man pointing a sawed-off shotgun at him.

"Put that away, Comrade," Nicolai said. "I'm a

307

friend."

The leader of this group, the September Tenth Brigade, was a black man, unshaven, slovenly, drunk. He had learned his Marxism in Attica, and was far more committed to murdering cops than to overthrowing the government, Nicolai thought. He was known by his revolutionary name: Brooklyn Red.

They lived in what Nicolai called "undisciplined squalor." Six women, eight men, two young kids, and a bunch of dogs. The dishes were piled high in the sink, the floors were filthy. Nicolai wondered what the hell they were going to do with such people after the revolution. They would end up being shot. No Marxist state could tolerate having such people running loose.

"I have many gifts," Nicolai said, handing him a key to the rented locker. "Ten Weatherby automatic shotguns with fifty boxes of shells. Four hundred hand grenades."

Brooklyn Red nodded. "We gonna kill a lot of pigs."

"Can you wait for your code word?"

"Ain't gonna be easy."

Nicolai headed north, figuring to drive most of the night. A cold shiver ran up and down his spine. He was beginning to realize that the world as he knew it would never be the same. Some part of him, at least, was a little sad at the passing of the old U.S. of A. He was enjoying himself. He liked the bars and taverns, the films, the wide variety of TV programs, the looseness of the women, the wide variety of music. What he did not like was the crime and the filth and the poverty. The anti-Soviet prejudice he heard everywhere. And the greed and the gluttony of the capitalist class. No, he would be happy to see all that wiped from the face of the earth.

He had twenty-eight groups to contact. That was his entire network, which he and George had been building up over the years. He wondered how many other networks there were. Dozens. Perhaps hundreds. He thought: So many fanatics with guns and bombs all hitting an organized society at the right time is going to create a firestorm. The idea made his whole body tingle.

Izzy's Pizza Supremo said the sign over the door. B. B. had walked four blocks from the previous joint, Milton's Jewish Pizzeria, which promised a matzoh-ball crust. He thought: nothin' ain't sacred no more.

Izzy's was a dump on the corner with streaked windows. Inside the front door was a hallway that led to the pizza place and a stairway that went up to the second floor where there were two flats. At least there were two mailboxes. An iron gate across the bottom of the stairs barred the way.

B. B. went through the door and into Izzy's. The rock music was loud even at four in the afternoon. A bunch of high school kids, blacks and whites, were playing a hot game of Space Invaders on a machine, yelling and whooping and cheering. B. B. ordered a small pizza and a draft beer. The cashier, a chubby black woman in her early twenties, gave him a little smile. He asked to speak with her privately. She said she wasn't that kind of girl, but she'd have a beer with him when she got off work at five.

Her name was Rose-Ann Jaffer, she said. B. B. had to listen to half her life story: how she came up from Georgia with her mother when she was eight, how she got pregnant when she was thirteen because it was what all the kids were doing, how she got hooked on H, then got off junk when she was born again as a Christian . . .

He finally got her on the subject of the guy who lived upstairs over the pizza joint. Which one, she wanted to know. He showed her a picture Catlyn had sketched from Shirley Dills's description.

"Oh, him," she said. "He's very weird. We bring him

pizzas all the time. He don't let us in, but sometimes you get a glimpse of the place before he closes the door. He's got cartoons on his walls, and pictures of Nazis and those camps. He's a weird guy."

"He have a name?"

"Dan Johnson."

B. B. said he had to make a phone call. He could hardly believe they'd finally found him. His heart was pounding. Now they had to take care not to lose him. He left a message on Catlyn's answering machine, then called some friends to take turns keeping an eye on the place. Then he went back to the table and finished his beer, moving his seat around so he had a view of the front door and the stairway leading to the apartments above.

"Guess what, Rose-Ann? I just called in and asked if this Dan Johnson could be the turkey we be lookin' for. Ain't the same guy. Guy we be lookin' for got his ass shot off in a fracas over in Queens last night. Must be twins. So I got a lot of time."

"So why don't you tell me about your large self?" she said.

"My favorite subject, but why don't you run along home now, fix us a little dinner, and I get us a nice bottle of wine and we can have us a good time."

She thought that was a great idea.

Catlyn and Oscar arrived at seven o'clock. By that time B. B. had three of his friends standing by, one across the street, one at a table by the door, and another on the roof of the building behind the pizza joint, with a good view of the alley. Oscar handed out some walkie-talkies to B. B., who passed them out to his men.

When B. B. returned, Catlyn said, "Is he home?"

"No lights on."

Oscar said, "Why don't we have a look around? Maybe wait for him."

"Where do we get a key?"

"No problem," Oscar said. He picked the lock on the gate going up the stairs.

B. B. said, "A newsman that can pick a lock, now ain't that somethin'?"

"Even a reporter can have a hobby," Oscar said. "Wish you'd wait in the car, Cat. The subject may be dangerous."

B. B. said, "Ah'd feel better if yo did."

"Not a chance, guys. I want to see the look in his eye when he sees we got him."

The gate swung open. Oscar closed it and locked it again. The three of them went up the stairs. It took ten minutes for Oscar to pick the dead bolt to the apartment. They shined penlights into the room. The place gave Catlyn a strange feeling. With its cartoons, American Marine recruiting posters, and blown-up photos of Nazi atrocities, the apartment had the air of a madhouse.

They looked around. Weight-lifting equipment, a rolled-up mattress, punching bags. Oscar went to work on the lock to the other room with the small sign on the door that said, "The Cave." After ten minutes he was ready to give up when B. B. said, "Let the old master give it a try." He inserted a lock pick, gave it a few twists, and the door popped open.

"No substitute for ability," B. B. said with a grin.

Oscar said, "I told you it was just a hobby of mine."

Inside was Park's dressing room, full of wigs and make-up and costumes. He could be anything from a cop on the beat to a country gentleman, a priest to a pimp.

"What have you to say about my theory now, Oscar?" Catlyn said. "Still think I just have an overactive imagination?"

He bowed to her. "Only a fool ever doubts female intuition." He started looking through the gun cabinet, whistling to himself.

Park's diary was open on the desk. Inside were the rantings of a racist maniac. She turned to the date Damian was killed. There it was, in a bold, maniacal scrawl: "Done a number on an uptown guy/made his beautiful Blondie cry . . ."

She dropped the book onto the floor. B. B. shined his light on her. "What the matter?"

She wiped a tear from her cheek and left the room.

B. B.'s two-way radio buzzed. "Yeah?" he said into it. "Turkey's comin' home."

Oscar pulled out a gun.

"Holy shit!" B. B. said. "What you gonna do with that?"

"It's a stun gun. Just knock the guy out."

B. B. grinned. "Yo sho do come equipped."

They took up their positions and waited. After a moment, they heard the iron gate below swinging open and then closed. Footsteps on the stairs. Whistling. Then the key in the lock, and the door swung open.

TWENTY-THREE

Park clicked on the light and froze. B. B. was standing in the doorway to the kitchen with his arms folded and a smile on his lips.

Park whistled and said, "Lookie here, I got me a fucking nigger burglar!" and reached in his jacket. Oscar, standing in the doorway to the bathroom, shot him with the stun gun. Fifty thousand volts surged through Park's musculature, dropping him to the floor like a tire suddenly gone flat.

Catlyn bent over Park, turning his face to her. She pulled back from him as if she'd been touching something revolting, like a lizard.

Oscar jerked Park's gun from him and handcuffed his wrists behind his back. Then B. B. lifted him up and put him in a chair and Oscar started tying him down tightly with some strong nylon cord.

"Now how we gonna make the dude talk?" B. B. asked. "We work him over, we gonna attract a crowd, he take to screamin'."

Oscar said, "Beating a man is hopelessly out of date, Mr. Hanson. It's only done to intimidate and humiliate. The Russians still use it, but it's not considered quite civilized. Besides, for extracting information it's too time-consuming.

No, I think we can use more sophisticated means than beating." He finished tying Park down.

"What means be that?"

"A drug. I have one that ought to do the trick." He reached into his coat pocket and took out a small carrying case with a hypodermic needle, a syringe, and a couple of medication ampules.

"Tell me again how you're just a reporter," Catlyn said.

"Friend of mine loaned me this."

"Nice to have friends."

B. B. said, "Yo two gettin' on just fine, ain't yo?"

They waited a few minutes for Park to come around. Oscar kept rubbing his face with a cold washcloth and Catlyn rubbed his hands to stimulate his circulation. His palms were moist.

B. B. said, "What we gonna do with him after he talk? Ah ain't never killed nobody on purpose. Ah mean, Ah only killed one guy and he juz went flyin' out the window before Ah had time to even think about it. Yo don' mind, if yo gonna do him in, Ah'll jez take a walk."

"You have me pegged for a cold-blooded killer?" Catlyn asked him.

B. B. said, "Yo ain't spent all this time and money jez to pass the time of day with the dude."

"Killing him would be putting him out of his misery."

Park moaned. Oscar rubbed his face harder with the washcloth. Finally Park opened his eyes. His eyeballs seemed loose in a sea of white, then they settled on Catlyn.

"Fuuuuuuck," he said.

"He knows me," she said.

Park turned his face away from the washcloth and spit at Oscar.

B. B. kicked him in the shins, "Yo best behave yo'self, hear?"

Park glared at him with hateful eyes. "You're dead, nigger."

B. B. kicked him again, harder. Park squirmed in his bindings and hissed, his mouth shut tight.

Catlyn said, "I don't think it would be wise of you to continue making racial slurs, Mr. Park."

"That fo sure," B. B. said.

Park just stared with hateful eyes. Oscar filled the syringe with the drug.

"What you gonna do?" Park asked with surprising timidity.

"You're going on a trip," Oscar said. "A very pleasant one."

"I don't want to go on a trip—I can't stand needles! Why don't you just ask me what you want to know? Hey, I know when it's time to cut a deal. I didn't want that Carter guy dead, it was a paid job. Hell, if it hadn't been me, it would have been somebody else."

Oscar held the needle at the ready. Catlyn looked at him, then at B. B., who said, "He wanna sing, we oughtta listen."

"All right," Catlyn said to Park. "Let's start with the beginning. How much were you paid?"

"Forty thousand dollars."

"In cash?"

"You think in my business we deal in checks? Small bills, lady, I deal in small, old, untraceable bills."

Catlyn felt a chill run down her spine. It was strange to hear it said so calmly. Damian's life gone in exchange for forty thousand dollars. She'd known it, but it had been an abstract, intellectual knowledge, without really feeling the coldness of it.

She said, "Who paid you? Give us a name."

"Timberwolf, that's all I know. He likes codes, that kind of stuff. Strange guy."

"What's he look like?"

Park shrugged.

"Give him the needle," Catlyn said.

"No—wait!" His eyes fixed on the needle. He licked his lips. "Listen. I never seen the guy, not so I'd recognize him. I did a couple of jobs for him before. Same thing. He calls me at this bar I go to . . ."

"Name the bar," Catlyn said.

"The Horned Toad. Call them, they know me. Go ahead. The bartender's name is Harry. Ask Harry if I ain't in there all the time."

"Okay," Catlyn said, "you get called at the bar, then what?"

"He calls. He says meet me at three and he gives a number. Two hundred fifteen. It's sort of a code, see—man, you got those ropes tight—he's giving me the room number of this hotel over at Twenty-third and Lexington."

"Name the hotel."

"I don't know what they call it, it's right there on the corner. Full of whores. Go on over, you can't miss it. See, he says 'two hundred-fifteen,' that means four-thirty. Timberwolf, he goes in for shit like that. Comic book stuff, but I go along, you know. Whatever the customer wants, the customer gets—Man that thing you hit me with, still's got my brain swimming. Stun gun, right? Gonna have to get me one of those babies."

Catlyn said, "Tell us about Timberwolf."

"He sits behind a light pointing right at me so I never seen his face."

"What did you see?"

"He's got kind of a thick body, you know, not fat, but thick. Not tall, not short. Voice not heavy or light. Just regular. No kinda accent. Real sort of thick body, know what I mean? Wait—I seen his hands, too, they look strong. He talks like real polite. *Please be seated*, that kind of shit. He don't like it when you say 'hit' and things like that. I got the feeling he don't go in much for killing, and only has it done when he has to. I seen his pantleg, too, and he wears real nice shoes, lots of polish. The guy must have a lot of dough. I tell him for a rush job it's ten grand more, he kicks it right in. He wanted me to call the hit the 'subject.' Funny, huh? The subject."

Catlyn paced back and forth for a moment, then she lighted a cigarette. Thick body. Polite. Wears fine clothes. That could add up to George Corbett. But it couldn't have been Corbett, she had been so sure of him. So damn sure. She remembered how she'd thought at the time she had interviewed him, *he's either telling the truth or he's the greatest liar of all times.*

Oscar said, "I know what you're thinking, Cat, and it just isn't possible. It must be someone else. There are a million people in New York who'd fit that description."

B. B. said, "Yo doan think this here turkey be tellin' the truth?"

"I do," Catlyn said. "Only question is, is it the *whole* truth?"

"It's the whole damn truth," Park said. "I was a Marine, we got pride."

Catlyn said, "You mentioned you did a couple of other killings for Timberwolf. Who were they?"

"The first one was some fucking Jew owned a supermarket chain. Kaiser, his name was, over in Brooklyn. Old fart. Four or five years ago, this was. He had an accident, fell down the stairs. The other was a young broad, a clerk—I don't remember her name. She worked for a bank. Timberwolf wanted her to suffer, so I made her suffer—whatever the customer wants, right?"

"What bank?"

"First Atlantic and Pacific."

Oscar froze and looked at Catlyn. She nodded. First Atlantic and Pacific. George Corbett's bank.

Park said, "Yeah, she had a note she'd left for her sister in case something happened to her and Timberwolf wanted it. I got it for him. Something about she knew her boss was a crook. Some fucking thing like that. I never did get all the

317

details."

Catlyn stared at him for a long moment. She had to be sure. "Give him the truth serum," she said to Oscar. "Let's make sure he's telling it all."

Park strained against the nylon cords. "You bitch! I told you what you wanted to know! I'm gonna kill your ass! All of you, you're dead. D-e-a-d, dead."

"Hold still," Oscar said, "or you'll break the needle off." He wiped Park's arm with alcohol, then shoved the needle in. Park watched him, his face turning red, every muscle in his body straining, the veins in his highly muscled neck sticking out. Then Oscar withdrew the needle and Park looked at Catlyn, making a hissing sound. A moment later his eyes glazed over and his head drooped lower.

Oscar said, "Now then, Mr. Park, how are you feeling? My name is Fred, and I'm your very best friend in the world . . ."

The ringing was intense. Park opened his eyes. What the fuck is this?

He was on a linoleum floor, broken glass all around him. He lifted his head. People running. Somebody shouting.

"Hey man," he screamed, "turn off the fucking noise."

He knew what the noise was—a burglar alarm.

A voice: "Police, freeze!"

"I ain't goin' nowhere."

He covered his ears with his hands. He wondered what happened to his apartment. The blonde. The nigger. The guy with the needle. He looked around. Jewelry display cases, some smashed open. He looked above him. A skylight with a big hole in it. A rope hanging down. *What the fuck?*

Two cops had hold of him now, dragging him to his feet, throwing him against the wall. The noise suddenly stopped. The cops emptied his pockets: a gun he'd never seen before, plastic bags of white powder, jewelry . . .

"You ain't going to believe this," Park said, "but I've been set up by a broad."

"Let me guess," one of the cops said, "The queen of England."

The paddy wagon and the blue and white patrol cars with their sirens screaming tore off down the street and disappeared around the corner of Fifty-seventh Street. The small crowd that had gathered quickly dispersed, leaving a couple of security guards to watch things.

Catlyn, Oscar, and B. B. Hanson sat in Oscar's rented car at the corner and listened to the sounds of the sirens recede into the night.

Oscar said, "Okay, so much for Park."

B. B. said, "Ah gots friends in the can, gonna let all the brothers know what a racist pig he be. Mr. Park, he gonna curse his momma for lettin' him be born, yo see."

Oscar said, "If he weren't a Fascist, murderer, and torturer, I might even feel sorry for him. I guess now the thing to do is go after George Corbett and whoever has aided and abetted him."

"What that mean?" B. B. asked.

"We're going to get him and his gang. Right, Cat?"

"I suppose," Catlyn said with a strange listlessness. She was still staring at the point where the paddy wagon had disappeared.

Oscar said, "We're going to need your friends again, Mr. Hanson. Maybe get a round-the-clock watch on George Corbett's apartment. And his office. We'll have to know who comes and goes, who his friends are. Everything. Where they live, where they work, who they associate with. He probably has servants, assistants. We'll have to check them out. Perhaps try to get to know one or two. He must be in it with others, probably big financiers who are going

319

to make a fortune off this."

B. B. said, "Why doan we jez snatch this George Corbett and give him a little shot, same as we did for Park?"

"We might have to," Oscar said. "But first we'll want to know his connections. There may be big people behind this even our Mr. Corbett doesn't know about. First we find out who he's associated with, then who his associates are associated with. What do you think, Cat?"

"I'm sure you're right."

Oscar said, "We'll need eavesdropping equipment, cameras, things like that. I can take care of it."

"Yo reporter guys sho do have connections," B. B. said with a chuckle.

"I have friends in the industrial counterspying business, just so happens." Oscar looked at Catlyn. He'd expected a little ribbing from her, but she said nothing.

B. B. said, "Anythin' else? Okay, Ah'll get my men set up. Ah'll need the address where this guy Corbett live."

"I just happen to have it," Oscar said.

B. B. chuckled again.

Oscar wrote down George Corbett's address and handed it to him. B. B. said, "Ah'm gonna get started tonight," he said. "This Corbett, he find Park in the can, he might decide ta spring him." He got out of the car. "Yo two take it easy on each other, okay? Ah'll get some fellas to keep an eye on Corbett, then Ah got to see this pizza gal, tell her how sorry Ah am ta be so late."

He hailed a cab and headed for Harlem.

Catlyn let out a long breath. "That man is such an angel."

"Funny, he doesn't look the part." Oscar started the car and headed for Catlyn's place. It was nearly midnight and the traffic was light. There was a fine mist in the air; Manhattan sparkled like a jewel around them. As they drove through the streets, Catlyn leaned her head against the window and stared out.

"You don't seem very happy, Cat," Oscar said.

She continued to stare out the window.

"Did you hear me?" Oscar said.

"What?—I'm sorry."

"You don't seem too happy."

"I feel kind of numb, if you want the truth."

"You got what you wanted. Park will be in prison for the rest of his life. That gun B. B. left on him was used in a robbery in which a man was killed. Park will never get out of prison."

"Vengeance is supposed to be sweet, isn't it?" Catlyn said. "It isn't. It just isn't, that's all. I don't feel clean about it. I feel like I've gone into the sewers and settled things on Park's level."

"We can forget about him now. Corbett's our man now. I wonder what his game is. Look at what's happened since he took over the Fed. The dollar has been mysteriously rising against all foreign currencies on the world money markets. Gold is down. Frankly, I don't get it. If he were helping the speculators, I'd suspect they'd drive the dollar down, buy dollars when they're low, then let the dollar shoot up."

"He's no ordinary man, I'll tell you that," Catlyn said. "I looked him right in the eye while he handed me a pack of lies on a platter and I gobbled them up."

"Haven't you ever been wrong before?"

"I've made a lifetime science of studying people's faces. I've often risked an awful lot of money on what I can see in people."

"Haven't we all."

"I guess we have at that." She turned to him suddenly and said, "Would you mind spending the night with me, Oscar? I want you to make love to me."

He looked at her.

"You can say no if you want to," she said. "No hard feelings."

"I wasn't going to say no."

Oscar phoned in a coded report on Park to the Israeli consulate that evening. In the morning when he called in for his messages he was told to report to Tel Aviv immediately.

"I hate to leave you," he told Catlyn, "but I've got a boss who won't take no for an answer."

"I'm feeling much better," she said. "I thought I was made of iron. I'm not, that's all. Perhaps we can finish things up quickly and be done with Mr. Corbett."

After he'd left her apartment, Catlyn called the Fed in Washington and arranged to meet George Corbett for a late lunch. He would hear about Park's arrest, she figured, and he'd know Park wasn't fool enough to get himself caught in a jewelry store burglary. George Corbett would have to figure Park was framed, and George Corbett was certainly bright enough to guess who framed him. Catlyn knew if she didn't convince him Park had told her nothing, she would be in great danger.

Catlyn took the train to Washington. It was Halloween and the club car was decorated with black and white crepe paper and a couple of train attendants wore vampire teeth. Catlyn was not in a festive mood. She was scared, a state of being she had rarely experienced in the past. She met George for lunch in a small restaurant on Constitution Avenue near the Fed headquarters.

She thought George seemed changed from the last time they'd met. And there were bruises on his head and neck. His eyes didn't look quite as intense and his voice held less authority. Her fear left her.

"How have things been going with you, Miss Cavanaugh?" George asked her. He sipped a Scotch and water and fingered the menu.

322

"I'm very well," she said. "I found out who killed Damian Carter. His name is Robert Park."

George's face was impassive. She kept watching his dark eyes. He gave no indication that he recognized the name at all. "Have you called the police?" he asked, as if he were really concerned. Not a flutter of fear. He was good, she thought, very good.

"Yes, I did call the police. They have him in custody."

George looked at her curiously. "I congratulate you. Was Damian killed because of his connection to the Fed?"

"That's why I wanted to see you, to let you know you can put your mind at rest."

"I appreciate your thoughtfulness."

"Apparently Park took Damian for someone else. Isn't that something? A tragic mistake."

"I'm always fascinated by the randomness of things," George said. He caught the waiter's eye and signaled him; the waiter gestured that he'd be there in a moment. "Order the prime rib," he said to Catlyn. "They have a prime rib that melts in your mouth." He took a breath and said, "Speaking of the randomness of things, you see these bumps and lumps? I was in an accident in Europe."

"How awful."

"It was a hit and run. I was worried that perhaps someone was trying to get me because of the Fed thing. Your coming here today has removed a terrific burden from my mind."

Catlyn marveled at how calm she felt sitting and having lunch with the man who had Damian killed.

"Ah," George said, "here's our waiter now."

George put Catlyn in a cab and waved good-bye, standing on the sidewalk in front of the restaurant. He watched the cab go down the street and turn the corner. There was a wet snow falling. He started walking back toward his office.

His brain was in a turmoil. He'd definitely underestimated the woman. Women were always a mystery to him. Especially brainy, high-class, headstrong ones like Catlyn Cavanaugh. She had actually found Park! Amazing, amazing.

He had known about Park's arrest, of course, and had already dispatched Nicolai to find out from sources in the police department what he had told the police. He had not heard from Nicolai yet, but he knew he had to have Park killed, either get to him in jail or help him escape and then get him. And he'd have to deal with Catlyn Cavanaugh, too. She was definitely a loose end. She could get in the way of the biggest espionage gambit in the history of the world and she had to be stopped.

She was on to him, he could feel it.

He went into an office building and found a pay phone. He called Nicolai in New York.

"Yes?" Nicolai said.

George gave him a code which could be easily translated into the number of the pay phone. "I'm sorry," Nicolai said, "I don't know what you're talking about." Nicolai hung up.

George sat in the phone booth with his hand on the phone cradle and the phone to his ear so it would look as if he was talking. It took Nicolai five minutes to get to a pay phone and call him.

"I think we can relax about Mr. Park," Nicolai said. "The police caught him in a jewelry store and they have no idea he's tied to the Damian Carter killing."

"See to it he is bailed out."

"It might cost fifty, sixty thousand for the bail bond and twice that for bribes. They're holding him on a murder warrant, felony possession of narcotics, and burglary."

"Whatever it costs, I want it done."

"All right."

"Then tell him he is to see to it that Catlyn Cavanaugh is sent to the cemetery as soon as possible. Her journalist friend and the black, too."

George figured to use Park to get rid of Catlyn, then have Nicolai get rid of Park. Very neat and tidy. "One more thing, Nicolai, I do not wish Mr. Peabody to know of this."

"I understand completely, sir."

"After our business is concluded I will reward you for your personal loyalty."

"Thank you, sir."

George walked back out into the street. His hands were shaking.

When Catlyn got back to New York that evening she found B. B. waiting for her. She had long ago given him a key and instructed the security people to let him in anytime. She'd never seen B. B. acting so nervous.

"They let him out."

"Who? Let who out?"

"Park. Somebody came up with the bail money, and there musta been some grease. A scum lawyer name'a D'Augustino got him out. Ah spoke ta him, he doan know who put up the money, it been done by phone. But it sure as hell gots ta be Corbett."

She took off her coat and hung it in the closet, then poured herself a double Old Granddad. "Have a drink, Mr. Hanson."

"Ah never drinks when Ah should be thinkin' clear."

"When you think about it, Corbett couldn't do anything else, could he?"

"That Park man, he gonna come and chew yo and me up inta tiny pieces and spit us out."

"George Corbett must be frightened, that's good. Frightened people do stupid things."

"Yo best be thinkin' of Park. Ah got five good men tryin' ta find where he at right now. He knew who yo is, and he be comin'. Look what Ah got." He opened his jacket to show a shoulder holster on each side. He lifted up his shirt; underneath it he was wearing quilted underwear. "This be Armorwear, make yo bulletproof. Ah got some for yo, too."

"Wouldn't I look silly."

"Yo look silly in a coffin, too, Cat."

"You have a point there, Mr. Hanson."

B. B. took out a small suitcase he had sitting next to the couch and opened it. He took out a gun and handed it to Catlyn.

"It a short barrel, but it shoot a .38. Here all yo do: push this here safety lever forward, point it, and pull the trigger."

"Where do I put it, in my brassiere?"

"Yo best jus' hold it in yo hand. Look, this man Park, he not gonna be foolin' around with yo."

The gun felt cold and strange in Catlyn's hand. "I've never held one before. Wouldn't it be just as well to have you stay close, be my protection?"

"He gonna get me first. Ah doan get him before he get me, yo goin' ta need this."

She put it on the table. "I'd feel a little strange toting this thing around. Aren't you supposed to have a permit or something?"

"This be no time ta be worryin' 'bout little things. Park a bad, bad dude. Yo got ta get this through yo head, Cat. He kill yo dead if yo not ready. First thing, we gotta get yo outta here, get yo someplace he can't find yo no matter how hard he be lookin'."

"I take it you don't have much faith in this hi-tech security building."

"Ah knows guys too dumb ta tie their shoes, be in here in six minutes."

"Okay then, we supplement the security with some of your men. But I don't think we could really hide from Robert Park. He'd find us one way or the other."

B. B. made a face. Catlyn started for the bedroom. "Here, Cat, Ah got somethin' else." He strapped a small cylinder that looked like a lipstick case on her wrist.

"See this ridge here by the cap? Yo push that off with yo thumb while yo got it pointed at his face. In case he try ta grab yo, yo can't get yo gun."

"What's inside it?"

"Some kinda stuff make a little explosion and throw this liquid in his face."

"What liquid?" "Acid, somethin' like that."

She touched it with her other hand. "I think I better have another drink."

B. B. said, "When yo started this, yo didn't think it was gonna be a piece of cake, did yo?"

That evening one of B. B.'s men called to say that the phone tap was in at George Corbett's apartment, where there had been a lot of excitement that day. It appeared that Rudolph Corbett had run away from home.

George put a call through to Nicolai from a pay phone in Washington as soon as Linda had phoned him and told him.

George told Nicolai his son was missing and to find him and bring him home. Nicolai protested that he didn't think it was a good idea, but George said he didn't trust anyone else to do the job, and would he do it as a "personal favor." Nicolai agreed.

Then George took a commuter plane to New York and a cab to his apartment. He got there at eleven o'clock at night and found Linda waiting for him. She seemed unusually cool, and at first he thought she might be a little drunk.

"Have you heard anything?" he asked.

"Not a thing. Who is this Nicolai person you've got out looking for him?"

"A very efficient fellow, never mind who he is. Where's the note Rudolf left?"

She had it on a table. It was hastily penned in Rudolf's immature scribble. It said simply, *I hate it here and I'm never coming back*.

"You see?" George said. "He hates it here. Ask yourself, why does he hate it? It's because you are always after him, always picking on him."

"I wouldn't have to be always picking on him if he would learn to meet his responsibilities and take care of himself."

"He is only a boy."

"He is sixteen."

"How can he even think straight with your nagging?"

She scowled. "You spoiled him, George, and I stood by and let you do it. Now it's too late. Maybe this is a good thing. Let him get out in the world, it might teach him something."

"How can you say that, your own son?"

"I want him to learn to be a man." She went into the bedroom and slammed the door.

George went into his study and smoked a cigar, sitting in his thick leather chair and feeling miserable. Where had he gone wrong with the boy? Had he indeed spoiled him? Yes, yes! That was true. He put the cigar out and started pacing. He had not been to the gym since he got back from Europe and he could feel his muscles getting flabby. He did some half-knee bends and his knees creaked. He tried a few push-ups and tired quickly.

He sat back down in the chair.

He would have to do something with the boy. Something to help him. Send him to some school, someplace where they might teach him a little discipline.

But then he remembered that soon he might be behind the curtain. And then what? Since the KGB had taken the stash he'd put away for the boy, he would have to do something quickly to get some money to help Rudolf. That's if Nicolai could find him. George knew that thousands of American kids ran away every year and were never

328

heard from again. When he thought of that, chills ran up and down his spine.

He went to the bedroom and knocked softly on the door. Linda said to come in. She was sitting at her vanity brushing her hair. George sat on the bed. "You are right," he said. "I have spoiled the boy."

She turned to him. "Do you mean that?"

"Yes. I have given him everything and demanded nothing in return. The result? He is shiftless and lazy. I take the blame."

She went over and sat down on the bed next to him. She kissed him on the cheek.

"I loved the boy too much," he said.

"Yes. You smothered him with it."

"We might save him yet."

"We can give it all we've got," Linda said.

Nicolai called at two-thirty in the morning. He had found Rudolf at a friend's apartment, somewhat drunk, and was bringing him home. George hugged Linda, and they opened a bottle of Dom Pérignon and toasted each other.

"He is not such a bad boy," George said. "Let's not be too hard on him when he gets home."

"He should have his ass kicked, but good."

"Linda, Linda, Linda. . . ."

Vicious Jack, one of B. B.'s men, was watching from across the street when Nicolai brought Rudolf home. He saw Nicolai leave a few minutes later in a cab. The next day B. B. went to the cab company and, for a fifty-dollar inducement paid to a clerk, found out who the driver of the cab was. Then, for a quart of liquor valued at twenty-four dollars, he found out from the cabbie where Nicolai was dropped off in the Bronx. Vicious Jack went out there the next day and walked around the neighborhood, but he couldn't find anyone who seemed to know him. One young man said he might have seen somebody who looked like that park his car in the neighborhood, but he wasn't sure.

That afternoon B. B. reported to Catlyn that they'd lost one of George Corbett's gang, but they'd keep looking. A Brooklyn hood type, keeping out of sight. B. B., of course, had known all along that it was some kind of massive money-laundering scheme. Why else would someone want to be head of the Federal Reserve Bank? Whatever the hell that was.

TWENTY-FOUR

Robert Park never went back to his apartment. He figured it was probably being watched. He tried to get hold of Shirley Dills, but discovered she'd disappeared. Right then he knew he'd have to kill her. Christ, how could he have been so stupid as to trust that stupid bitch? He'd fix her, he thought. He'd cut off her tits and shove them down her throat.

But first, he swore to himself, he'd take care of Catlyn Cavanaugh, her boyfriend with the needles, and her nigger. The lawyer who got him out of jail gave him a twenty-thousand dollar advance from Timberwolf to get rid of her as fast as possible. He'd have done it for nothing. Not only was she going to die, she was going to suffer the agonies of hell before she went.

Park took a walk past her place wearing a security guard uniform he borrowed from a guy he knew at The Horned Toad. He disguised his face with a pair of thick-rimmed dark glasses and huge mutton-chop sideburns. The place was well guarded front and back by two security guards and there were a couple of suspicious characters hanging around he thought might be lookouts keeping an eye out for him. He just kept on walking.

He spent the day in a bar in the East Village sitting in a

cool back booth just sipping a few beers, eating pretzels, and thinking. Being in jail had been bad for him. In the rec room two black guys from Brooklyn tried to find out how tough he was. He beat them both into a coma. One had a broken jaw; the other a ruptured spleen. Afterward he worried they might have friends who'd take revenge by sticking him while he slept, so he didn't sleep much.

Park was seething with anger now and, as an experienced professional, he knew what trouble he could get into if he went off half cocked. He wasn't about to do that.

He had to focus his attention on how to get the job done. The cunt was smart and well protected. She'd probably be armed. He would have to have a plan; he'd work it out carefully and pull it off with precision. He went through two dozen plans, rejecting them as fast as he could come up with them. Finally he remembered Velma Jasco. She was the key. At six that evening he had it figured out. Catlyn Cavanaugh would be dead in forty-eight hours, and not even God could save her.

Velma Jasco was the best and quickest way to get close enough to Catlyn to kill her. But he also knew it was highly likely Velma would blab if he made contact with her. She had probably been told by now that Catlyn's life was in danger and would be scared shitless. So he had to play it cool. He'd use her all right, but he wouldn't give her a chance to squeal. He'd control the situation. That's what a pro did. Control every factor.

That night he slept in a small hotel in the East Village. It wasn't much of a place, the bed was lumpy and the wallpaper ripped, but he figured the desk clerk would keep his mouth shut about his being there—just in case the Cavanaugh broad and her nigger were looking for him. The clerk knew what would happen to him if he didn't. The next day Park spent running around to Goodwill and St. Vincent de Paul stores getting the clothes he needed, buying a wig, a theatrical makeup kit, a couple of guns, ammunition, and a knife, and having a fake ID made by an old dago he knew in Queens. The old guy used to be an engraver, but arthritis had ruined his career. Now he made fake ID's of the highest quality. Cost a few bucks, but Park figured what the hell.

Robert Park slept very well that night. He always slept well when he had a project under way. He was already thinking about what he would do once this task was over with. He'd be looking for Shirley Dills, but he didn't figure that would take too long. He'd bet fifty bucks she'd be in Florida, and he'd bet another fifty that a friend of hers who ran a massage parlor up in the East Fifties would know exactly where. After he fixed Shirley, he'd have to be cool, he figured. Go someplace. Maybe join the French Foreign Legion, something like that. Lay low, look for something big like an armored car to hit, get enough maybe to live on for a long, long time.

The next day he got up at four in the morning and, carrying a small suitcase, took a bus to Velma Jasco's place. She lived in a run-down brownstone on the edge of Harlem. There was a lot of litter in the streets, and the houses had broken windows with cardboard stuck in them. Patches of brown snow were left over from a storm a few days before. A leaking sewer made a hell of a stink. A Hispanic kid, the only person on the street, was delivering newspapers door to door. Park was wearing a heavy coat with a hood, glasses, and the mutton chops. He had a knit cap pulled tight down around his ears.

The hallway in Velma Jasco's place was cold. An old bum with a heavy beard was sleeping in the hallway. Park looked him over carefully. Could be he was a plant. Could be Velma Jasco spilled it about him checking out the Cavanaugh bitch's apartment and the Cavanaugh broad had hired a guy dressed as a bum to keep an eye out.

But the bum stank so much he had to be a bum. And there were fleas all over him. But, Park thought, the pro covers all possibilities. He turned on the light switch at the bottom of the stairs, pulled out his .38 revolver and affixed the silencer, and crept up the stairs slowly. Nobody waiting. He found the door to Velma's apartment on the third floor and put a stethoscope to it. No sounds at all. He then checked the apartment across the hall. No sounds there except somebody snoring. Next he checked the landings on the stairways two floors up. Nobody around. He went back to Velma's apartment, picked the lock, and let himself in, a flashlight in one hand and a gun in the other.

Nobody in the living room. He pulled his suitcase in behind him and closed the door.

The living room was tiny. A couch with a few pillows, a couple of overstuffed chairs, an old TV with a stack of *TV Guide*'s on top. He eased out of his shoes and checked out the kitchen. Dishes stacked in the sink, a newspaper and a coffee cup on the small table. One chair at the table. Must live alone, Park figured. Good, good.

The bathroom was tiny. Just a john, a sink, a small shower. He pushed open the door of the bedroom and there she was, sound asleep. He clicked on the light; a blue-veined breast stuck out above the sheets. Velma Jasco opened her eyes and looked at Park. He smothered her scream with his hand, pushed the gun against her temple.

"You want to live, you do what I tell you."

She nodded. He took his hand away and smiled. "Remember me?"

She nodded again, pulling the sheet up over her chest.

"Catlyn Cavanaugh tell you about me?"

"Yes, yes."

"You tell her I was over to her place?"

"What kind of fool you think I am?"

"Good, good. I think we're going to be able to do business."

Her eyes narrowed. "What kind of business?"

"Time I made another visit."

"Don't see how you can do that. There's the house security people, then there's this black guy, Hanson. He's got a lot of men staking out the place. No way in hell you're going to get in there. What do you want to do once you get in, anyway?"

"Didn't she tell you?"

"Not exactly."

"I'm going to kill her dead."

"I ain't a-helping you do that."

He pushed the gun up under her eye. "Then I'll kill you. Choice is yours."

She stared at the barrel of the gun. "Tell me what I got to do."

"Call the Firestone Apartments, tell them you're sick. Tell them you're sending another lady in your place."

"Who?"

Park opened his suitcase and took out a wig. In a high-pitched falsetto he said, "Molly Amsterdam is the name, cleaning's my game."

A miserable sleeting November rain fell all that day.

Catlyn and B. B. spent the day collecting two full briefcases of records from two credit agencies and half a dozen banks on the finances of George Corbett. Such things were not, of course, in the public domain, but Catlyn knew people, and she was generous to clerks and functionaries who cooperated. She was trying to put together the life story of the man.

That morning she'd hired a private detective to find out all he could about George since he returned from Australia until he went to work at First Atlantic and Pacific Bank, and another detective to try to locate Park. B. B. had two of his men looking for Park as well, and two more staking out his apartment over Izzy's Pizza Supremo.

B. B. took hold of the briefcases when they stepped out

335

of the cab. "Ah shore hope yo doan plan for me ta be readin' all this tonight. Ah get a headache gettin' through the sports page of the *News*."

"Why don't you take the night off? Go have a little fun. I'm well armed."

"No thank yo, Cat. Ah won't be leavin' till Mr. Park back in the can, or in a hole in the ground."

"I don't see how a man your size can get comfortable on my couch."

"My mama used ta tell me, a man who do no sinnin' jus' need ta close his eyes ta sleep. A sinner, he can't get a mattress thick enough. Ah been leadin' a righteous life, so Ah can do my sleepin' anywhere," he chuckled.

They went through the front doors, nodding to the security men. One of them said, "The cleaning lady is still in your apartment, Ms. Cavanaugh."

"She's running a bit behind. It's nearly five."

"She's been in there since, let's see. Ten-oh-seven."

"Mus' be her day ta clean the toilet," B. B. said.

On the way up in the elevator, B. B. looked at Catlyn, her intense, serious eyes darting back and forth. Always thinking. He still hadn't quite figured her out. He'd known some high-class white women before. He had even made love to one who was high on coke and wanted a big black stud to do her. But he'd never known a white woman like this before. He once knew a black woman named Ruby LeRoy who ran a brothel down in New Orleans that came close. She, too, was strong, sure of herself, smart. Independent as hell. Bull-headed almost. But Catlyn had something else, something that even Ruby LeRoy didn't have. She really gave a damn about people. Including him. She'd never said it directly, but he sensed it. She liked him. He liked her. She was becoming like a little sister in a way. A damn smart little sister, but one that needed watching out for. Her damn bull-headedness could get her into a lot of trouble. In fact, it already had. This Robert Park was a crazy man.

They got off the elevator on the seventh floor, crossed the hall, and went on into Catlyn's apartment. The vacuum cleaner was going in the study. B. B. put down the briefcases and walked over and opened the door. He noticed it wasn't the regular cleaning woman, but she was running the vacuum back and forth like a maniac. She had blond hair and was wearing a print dress and gaudy red lipstick. She glanced at him, frowned, and kept right on vacuuming.

B. B. went back into the living room and took off his jacket and the two shoulder holsters with the .45's. He put the jacket over the chair and put the guns in a drawer in the bookshelf. Catlyn didn't like looking at them.

"Make yourself a drink," Catlyn said from the bedroom.

B. B. said, "Yo gonna have one?"

"Granddad on the rocks."

"Macho drink," he said. "Maybe Ah'll try one."

He went into the kitchen and took out the ice and put it into two glasses. The vacuum was still going. He poured some bourbon. Catlyn came out of the bedroom wearing a housecoat. He noticed she wasn't wearing the defense bracelet he'd given her. What the hell, she was home, he wouldn't give her an argument.

B. B. handed Catlyn her drink, then sat down on the couch with his, kicked off his shoes, and put his feet up on the coffee table. Catlyn dropped into a chair. There were dark spots under her eyes and she was pale. How long had it been now? Two months. She hardly ever slowed down, slept only a few minutes at a time. Women like that were one in a million.

The vacuum stopped. B. B. heard a small noise from the study. The cleaning lady must have tipped something over. He started to get up but thought, the hell with it.

Catlyn took down about half her Granddad in one swallow. B. B. tried to do the same, but coughed. "Went down the Sunday pipe," he said.

Catlyn smiled at him, then laughed mildly.

"We ain't havin' no drinkin' contest," he said.

"I know we aren't," she said. "What would you like for dinner? I could thaw some steaks, make a salad. I think I've got some frozen french fries."

"Sounds real good ta me."

On the way to the kitchen, she couldn't resist. She tickled the bottom of his feet.

"Ohhhhhhh, cruelty!" he cried. They both laughed. Catlyn went through the swinging door into the kitchen. B. B. put on some records. Real cool jazz. He preferred his music a little more bluesy than Catlyn, but he'd listen to Coltrane, Miles Davis, Dizzy Gillespie. He decided to see what was with the cleaning lady. The vacuum wasn't making any noise and she hadn't come out.

He opened the door to the study. "What the problem?" he asked.

"New place always takes some time."

"What happen ta what's-her-name?"

"Velma's sick. Call me Molly. I'm almost done here."

"Take yo time, no hurry."

B. B. went back into the living room. He didn't move fast, he just drifted over toward the bookcase, humming to himself. He had noticed something peculiar, something strange in her eyes. Something real crazy. His heart was going now, he thought, like a rock concert. He could feel sweat forming on his forehead.

"Gonna have me another Granddad," he called to Catlyn.

"Help thyself," Catlyn answered from the kitchen.

B. B. was by the bookcase now, sliding out the drawer where he'd put his .45's. He reached in and jerked one out, swinging around and cocking it with one motion. There was Park, standing in his silly wig and flowered dress in front of the windows with his hand raised. B. B. was fast, but he wasn't fast enough. B. B. saw Park fire: *Pffffft* was all the sound it made. The bullet hit B. B. high on the forehead. B. B. heard the sound and felt the bullet hitting his head like a hammer, then his body seemed to evaporate into the air, his mind fall into darkness.

B. B.'s body fell backward into the bookshelf and, as he hit the floor, the bookshelf came down on top of him with a thunderous crash. Catlyn flew out of the kitchen, a salad bowl in her hand. She saw B. B.'s legs sticking out from under the bookshelf and the strange cleaning woman with the gun in her hand. Catlyn flung the salad bowl at her and dashed for the bedroom.

Pffffft, Park's gun sounded again, the bullet striking Catlyn in the shoulder and slamming her forward into the wall at the end of the hall. She rolled sideways onto the floor in front of the bedroom door.

Park didn't hurry. He crossed the room and went down the short hall and stood over her, taking off his wig.

"Thought you was smart, didn't you, bitch?" He rolled her over with his foot. Catlyn moaned and her eyes came open. The bullet had made an exit hole above her left breast, just below the collarbone. Blood ran down her face from the gash where she'd hit the wall.

Park chuckled. He ran his hands slowly over her body to make sure she wasn't armed, squeezing her breasts. She glared at him now, taking short, quick breaths between clenched teeth.

"Nice little boobies," Park said. "That's what I said first time I seen your picture." He grinned at her. "You had your chance to kill me, you should have taken it. That's the difference between an amateur and a pro. I'd have ground you up and fed you to the dogs."

The phone rang.

Park said, "Now I wonder who that could be?" He went to the phone and picked it up. "Yeah," he said, trying to make his voice sound as husky as B. B.'s, "Miss Catlyn

Cavanaugh's residence, who be speakin'?"

The voice on the other end said, "Security here. We have a report of a loud noise coming from your unit."

"We be movin' the bookshelf. It fell over. Miss Cavanaugh thank yo for bein' so on the alert."

"Tell her she's welcome."

Park hung up, smiling. They bought it. You keep cool, you can pull off anything.

Catlyn didn't try to move. She felt weak, but clear-headed. There was no pain, no more than a soreness radiating over her body. The blood felt warm against her skin. She looked up at Park, who appeared strange standing there in the dress and makeup, holding a gun with a long silencer in his hand. It was a nightmare come true. Fear swept over her and she was momentarily paralyzed, but then she pushed the fear back. If she was going to get out of this alive, she would have to keep her wits about her. She was ten feet away from the automatic in the drawer by the bedside table. She had to think of that. Keep her mind focused. She had to get to that gun.

"You sure do look like you're in a bad way, Miss Cavanaugh," Park said. "Whatever got into you, you thinking you could fool around with me? You sure have messed things up now, haven't you? Your nigger is dead. You've been shot. Now you've got to ask yourself how you came to this grief. You tried playing a man's game and you're only a broad. A smart broad, granted. A good-looking broad, granted. Lots of moxy. But a broad nevertheless."

Catlyn said, "I'm ready to repent my sins."

"Are you now? Well, well. I'm afraid it's too late for that." He leaned against the wall, relaxed. "Know what I'm going to do now? I'm going to enjoy the victory. Did you ever see what happens after a sporting match? The winning team goes into the locker room and celebrates. That's what I'm going to do. Celebrate. And I'm even going to let you join me."

Catlyn inhaled deeply a couple of times. "I've been shot," she said. "In case you didn't notice."

Park said, "One of the penalties for making a misstep." He took a look around the bedroom, snooping in the closets and drawers. Then he opened the drawer in the bedside table. "What's this? My, my, a little automatic pistol. How cute. And one of those nasty chemical spraying bracelets. So that's what you had in mind for me. Well then, whatever happens to you, you can't complain now, can you? . . . You seem to be losing a lot of blood. Can't have you bleeding to death. I don't intend to do it with a corpse—although I tried it a couple of times in Nam and it ain't bad." He chuckled and gave his body a little shake, anticipating a thrill. He was enjoying this.

"Am I to be raped, Mr. Park?"

Park threw Catlyn's gun, the clip, and the bullets across the living room. He shoved the chemical bracelet into his pocket. Then he stood over her again, smiling. "You and me, sweetheart, we're going to make love. Rape is when one party doesn't want to do it, usually the female. Lovemaking is when both parties want to do it. You'll want to. You'll insist on it, knowing the alternatives. And if you do everything exactly right, maybe I'll let you live. Maybe I'll just cut off your nose, something like that. Cool, huh?"

"Do you know who I am, Mr. Park?"

"You're Catlyn Cavanaugh. You were running around with this Damian Carter who I fogged a couple of months ago."

"Cavanaugh isn't my real name. I'm not even Irish. I'm half Italian, half Swedish. My father is Sal Crupiano, the don. Brooklyn."

"What the fuck shit you trying to hand me?"

She pulled herself up on her elbow. "Sal Crupiano is my father. Sal Junior is my brother, two years younger. I took the name Cavanaugh after I left home and went to college.

If you kill me, my father is going to find you and he'll do very bad things to you. You help me now, I'll see to it my father doesn't come after you."

Park scoffed. "If the old don had a fucking daughter, I'd know about it."

"Call him," Catlyn said, still straining. "Really, go ahead, if you don't believe me."

Park rubbed his temples. He knew it was a game. The fucking cunt would try anything. Besides, if her old man was a don, it was already too late. You put a bullet into a Mafia princess, you might as well saw off your head.

Catlyn said, "Mr. Park, how would you like to be a rich man?"

"Doesn't everyone?"

"I'll give you one hundred thousand dollars if you'll let Mr. Hanson and me get medical attention and you forget your vendetta."

"Your nigger is beyond medical attention, he's been croaked. I ventilated his head." He sat down on the bed. "A hundred thousand. Now that is a fair amount of money." He crossed his legs, toying with the gun in his hand. "Not a bad place for the bidding to start. I've been thinking of going on an extended vacation. A hundred thousand for a man on the run is not very much money. You ought to be able to do better than that."

"A hundred and fifty is about all I could lay my hands on quickly."

Park cocked and uncocked his gun. "Well, why don't you let me think about it? Here, come sit with me."

She coughed, spitting up blood. Catlyn knew what that meant—the lung must be hit. Catlyn realized she didn't have long before she'd drown in her own blood. "I'm too weak to move," she said.

Park walked over and ripped away part of her housecoat to look at the wound. "Hmmmmm," he said. "You do seem to be leaking. We better get on with it." He stuck his

342

gun in his belt and paced around a little. Then he took out a jackknife and cut the cords off the drapes.

"Ah, these will do nicely," he said. "Something about a tied-up woman that makes my dick hard, never could figure out what it is."

"I'm dying," she said. "If I don't get to a hospital soon, I'll be dead. You won't get any money."

"You trying to cheat me out of my victory celebration, are you?"

He took hold of her and dragged her across the floor and pulled her up on the bed. It felt like she was coming apart. She didn't scream; she clenched her teeth and didn't make a sound.

"There now," Park said, positioning her in the middle of the bed. "Just how do you expect to get the money with the banks closed?"

"My attorney—Martin Getsong. He could get it. He's done it for me before."

Park wrapped a cord around one of Catlyn's ankles, tied it, then tied the other end to the bed. "Let me think about it." He tied the other ankle. She didn't resist him; she knew it wouldn't do any good. Besides, she thought it was better to save her strength, let him think she was even worse off than she was.

He took hold of her left wrist and tied it down. "Come on, let me call him," she said. "Let me live. A hundred and fifty thousand dollars can get you a long way from here."

"I'm thinking about it," Park said. "A pro always thinks things through." He grabbed her right arm savagely and twisted the cord around the wrist.

Catlyn thought she heard something in the other room. B. B.? *God, let it be B. B.* But it couldn't be. Maybe Security hadn't been fooled by Park's imitation of B. B. Hanson. Or was her mind playing tricks?

Her head had begun throbbing. Loss of blood, she thought. Soon she'd pass out. Panic welled up in her.

She said, "Please, Mr. Park, listen. Dial 767-9840, ask for Mr. Getsong." Park had her spread-eagled on the bed. Suddenly he rammed his knife into the bedside table. "Okay, Mizzzzzz Cavanaugh, let's see if we can do business. You want to live, I want money. Okay, so both parties can get something out of this deal." He wiped his lips. "But I happen to know what's going on in your mind. You'd like to kill me. How can we work it so I get the money and I don't get killed getting it?"

"Easy," she said, coughing up more blood. "I'll speak to Mr. Getsong to bring it here and leave it with Security downstairs. The moment Mr. Hanson and I are in the hospital . . ."

"Hanson, the nigger out there? He's dead, I already told you that. I don't miss what I'm shooting at and I aimed at his brain." He handed her the phone. "You tell him to put it in a package, leave it downstairs, you'll come for it."

"Okay. As soon as I'm at the hospital, you get the money."

"I don't like it. We'll go downstairs together. I get the money, I just walk out the door. You trick me, I kill everybody in the lobby."

Catlyn nodded. "No tricks."

"Give me that number again."

She gave him the number, he dialed it. He put the gun barrel against her temple, cut the cord holding her right wrist, and handed her the phone. He stuck the knife into the bedside table again.

"Okay, play it straight," he said.

"Martin? Catlyn. Got a cash flow problem. Need a hundred fifty thousand right away. Leave it downstairs with the building security. How soon can you have it over here? An hour? Fine."

She handed the phone back to Park. "I've got to have water," she said. "I'm losing fluid. I'm going to black out. She twisted her head on the pillow. "I'm starting to see

344

flashes of light."

"You'll hang in there, don't you worry none." He seemed to have a sudden fascination with the zipper on her housecoat, pulling it down and up. "You ain't going to die. It's only a flesh wound. Remember when they used to say that in all the old movies? What the hell is a flesh wound?"

She looked into his eyes and could see something besides the madness. Something alongside it: the child.

He pulled her zipper down again and ran his finger under the soft fold of her breast, streaking the blood. He held his finger up and looked at it as a kid would look at a half-squashed bug. He licked his finger.

"Sweet. You're sweet, Mizzzzzz Cavanaugh."

A grayness had invaded the room, she noticed; deep shadows crawled up the wall. Her vision was going. She could sense her heart beating rapidly in her chest. He was going to let her die and then he'd get the money from the security people. He was going to play with her like a child might play with a dying bird. She looked at the knife stuck in the table. How to get hold of it? Would she have the strength to use it? She'd have to hit him in a soft spot. An eye, maybe. She closed her eyes and gathered her strength.

"I'll bet you can really turn a woman on," Catlyn said in a whisper. She looked at him. His eyes were wide now as he was inspecting her wound.

He smiled. "You know I always did have the knack." He shoved a finger into the mat of her pubic hair, sliding it down between her labia. He folded over the open housecoat and fixed his eyes on her breast and the blood flowing down over it.

To Catlyn, the room was almost dark now. Her life was fading. Her breathing was shallow. Her left wrist was tied, both legs were tied. Her only hope was to grab that knife. She lay back and gathered her strength for a moment, trying to breathe as deeply as she could. He was busy running his hands over her, his eyes half closed. Suddenly she reached for the knife he'd stuck in the bedside table jerking it free.

It was slippery in her hand. She arched it over her head and brought it down toward his eye.

Park, as if he'd been waiting for it, blocked the thrust, grabbed her wrist, and twisted it. "There, there, naughty, naughty," Park said. She had no power left to resist him. He shook her arm as if it were a twig; the knife flew out of her hand and hit the floor. "But I like 'em with spunk and, baby, you are the spunkiest." He started to tie her wrist again.

She fell back onto the bed, closing her eyes. When she opened them again, the room had faded almost into darkness.

"Now comes the fun part," he said. "I got a dick like a brick." He started slowly ripping the housecoat off her.

"Don't you want the money, Mr. Park?"

"All in good time, my princess."

Catlyn could see something moving behind Park. A shadow? A man? A hallucination?

It was B. B. Hanson. His face was covered with blood and he was stumbling around like a blind man, but he was there, standing upright.

Park yelled, "You're dead, nigger!" For a second Park didn't move, like a rabbit caught in a hunter's flashlight beam.

Then B. B. grabbed his neck and lifted him straight up into the air, shaking him like a rag doll in the flower print dress, then swung him back against the sharp edge of the dressing table, raising him up and smashing him down over and over until his head was little more than pulp. Then he dropped him on the floor.

Catlyn said, "Thank God, Mr. Hanson, thank God you're all right."

B. B. came and sat down on the bed. He started to say something that sounded like "Name's B. B.," then his eyes turned milky and he slumped to the floor.

It was quiet and dark now in the room. She whispered, "Thank you, B. B."

As the darkness closed in around her, she heard the phone ring, and she knew it would be Security wanting to know what all the noise was about.

TWENTY-FIVE

Not only did Oscar Feldman not like *being* a spy, he didn't *feel* like a spy either.

If anything, he felt like a scholar *pretending* to be a spy.

Sure, he had been been taught tradecraft, from tapping telephones to rigging tripwire bombs. But he was not that good at it. He knew how to kill with a dagger, a garrote, poison, a gun, a bomb, and his bare hands—although he had never actually done any of these things. He never even imagined himself doing any of these things. He thought of himself as another kind of spy. He was a numbers man; his job was to monitor the American economy, which he didn't consider spying at all. Spying he thought of as something covert, dirty, and dishonorable, except in the most extreme cases.

Oscar Feldman was, after all, an American; in his own way, a patriotic one. He held dual citizenship: American and Israeli. He had a deep affection for America, the land of his birth. He regarded it as perhaps a little too brawny and not brainy enough, something like a teenager with too much muscle and not much sense. But the American people were basically optimistic and open, and loved the *idea* of America, where it was okay to be just about anything you wanted to be. America was chaotic sometimes, loud and ill-mannered, but he was proud to be an American. And he was proud to be a Jew.

He regarded Israel not so much as a country, but as family. Whenever he returned he felt as if he was among his aunts and uncles and cousins. He felt a warmth, a kinship he had never felt anywhere else. But he also felt he didn't quite know them.

He spoke Hebrew poorly, and even though most everyone he came in contact with spoke English, it was a formal, stiff British English, which seemed like a foreign tongue. And he had never been religious. The sight of so many black-dressed, bearded religious men in the streets always made him feel vaguely uneasy.

Then there was the problem of politics. Israeli politics baffled him. The two major parties, the Lukid and the Social Democrats, had joined forces and formed a grand alliance. Could anyone imagine the Democrats and the Republicans doing such a thing? Never. Yet the Israelis did it with very little problem. And then there were the religious parties, tiny minorities that wielded great power because of their ability to form coalitions—which meant that their programs got priority attention.

It was all a great mystery to him.

Still, when El Al Flight 1702 touched down at Lod Airport, Oscar was glad to be with them. With the crazy aunts and uncles and cousins clinging to a bit of rock at the edge of the Mediterranean, surrounded by enemies.

As he came down the ramp he was surprised to find two men in black suits waiting for him. He had been summoned back to Israel for briefings half a dozen times before and had never had a reception party.

"You are Feldman?" one of them asked. Like many Israelis, he had a thick Eastern-European accent.

"I'm Oscar Feldman, yes."

"Come."

He followed the men to a waiting Peugeot sedan and got

in the backseat with one of them. The other slid behind the wheel and they drove off.

"What's the deal?" Oscar asked the man sitting next to him.

"You will be told finally," the man said. Oscar had no idea what the hell that meant.

They headed north out of the airport, making a wide arc around Tel Aviv, the sprawling commercial and industrial hub of Israel. They passed warehouses and factories, and boxy apartment buildings laid out in rows. The man at the wheel drove fast, but expertly, cursing under his breath at the trucks and busses packed with tourists that were constantly getting in his way. To the west were the desolate hills of ancient Samaria baking in the sun.

Once on the Haifa Road, they picked up speed through Hadera, Binyamina, and Zichon Ya'ak. Occasionally Oscar caught a glimpse of the Mediterranean, silver blue and glistening. Here there were farms and small villages, and ordinary people going about their everyday lives, and Oscar was glad to see them. Aunts and uncles and cousins. As they entered the suburbs of Haifa, they turned off the main road and headed inland, up winding hills past suburban neighborhoods of apartment buildings, a hospital, a school. They were now on what Oscar guessed to be the foothills of Mount Carmel.

Finally, the Peugeot pulled into the driveway of a great house at the top of a small hill. It was surrounded by a high cinderblock wall and the lawn was peppered with palm trees. As they approached the garage, the door opened and the Peugeot drove in. The door closed behind them. The two men in black suits got out and pointed to a stairway leading up into the house.

"Thanks for the lift," Oscar said, brushing some dust off his jacket. He headed up the stairs. On the first landing was a Marine standing guard, who frisked Oscar for weapons. "You wouldn't want to tell me what's going on here, would you, sport?" Oscar asked.

The Marine shook his head. Like most Israelis in uniform, he did his duty quickly and professionally. No joking around.

"You may pass," he said in Hebrew.

Oscar expected to find a well-furnished modern home. It was nothing of the sort. The living room was being set up by a half dozen young men and women as sort of a large classroom, with a podium, a long blackboard, a projector with screen, and maybe fifty folding chairs.

A voice from behind Oscar said, "Ah, Feldman! There you are."

Oscar swung around and found his boss, Euripides, waving him into a small office.

Euripides closed the door and the two men sat down opposite each other across a Formica-topped metal table. Euripides was a dark-complected round little man with intense black eyes. He had hairy arms and a perpetual five-o'clock shadow. As usual, he seemed worried.

Oscar said, "Hello, Chief." Euripides liked to be called "Chief." Oscar figured it was because it had a military ring to it. Euripides was a disciplined, orderly man. He loved the Army and its ways.

"Feldman, tell me about the Cavanaugh woman."

"What would you like to know?—She's bright, determined, shrewd . . ."

Euripides shook his head. "Your relationship with her, tell me about that."

"We're good friends. What's this all about?"

"Are you sexually intimate with her?"

"Excuse me, sir, but if you don't mind me saying so, it's none of your goddamn business."

Euripides' face reddened, but he said nothing. He picked up a pencil from the table and bit on it. He stood up and walked to the window, drew back the curtain, and looked out for a moment, then returned to his seat.

"You are still ninety-nine percent American," he said.

Oscar slid his chair back and crossed his legs. "And proud of it," he said. "Now tell me why you want to know about my sex life."

"You changed your mind about the Damian Carter murder."

"That's right, I did."

"You now believe it was a professional hit."

"I know it was."

"Just what the Cavanaugh woman has been saying all along."

"Her name is Catlyn Cavanaugh, not 'the Cavanaugh woman.' Yes. I'm now convinced George Corbett hired Robert Park to kill Damian Carter."

Euripides rubbed his hairy arms. His face had a curious expression of bewilderment. "You must level with us, Feldman, it's essential we know exactly what is going on."

Oscar said, "I have slept with her—but that's not what changed my mind. Park told us everything."

"You had Park under Pentothal."

"Yes."

"Why is it the police aren't pressing this?"

"They believe it was a street killing because it is in their interest to think so. George Corbett and his friends are in very high positions of power. If a lowly police lieutenant goes sticking his nose where it doesn't belong, he could get it snipped off. Park cleverly made it look like it was a street crime, so the police can close the case without being accused of having failed in their duty. We cannot give them the information we extracted from Park because we did not follow legal procedures. But you can be assured Park was paid handsomely, and he killed Damian Carter at the behest of George Corbett."

Euripides bit on his pencil again. "You've noticed of course that the dollar has been rising."

"Yes."

"Which makes Israeli purchases from America most expensive."

"I know."

"The dollar has risen eighty-three percent against the West German mark in two weeks. Sixty-two percent against the yen. There hasn't been that much variance in six years, up or down. Why now? Where are the upward pressures coming from?"

"I can't account for it," Oscar said. "The question I've been asking is why hasn't the Federal Reserve started selling dollars to drive the price down?"

"What is George Corbett's public position?"

"He made a speech about the evils of currency speculation, but he's done nothing."

"Why?"

"I can't imagine. I can only guess."

"Go ahead—guess."

"He's either in the pocket of some very, very rich men who are into international currency speculation, or . . ."

"Or?"

"Or he's an agent."

"Which is it?"

"I don't know."

Euripides said, "Must be speculators. The Soviets wouldn't put a mole in a bank. They'd put him in the CIA or the FBI, but not a bank. Have you ever known them to do anything like that?"

"No."

"Sit there, wait a minute, there's someone I want you to meet."

He left the room for a few minutes and returned with a thin young man in a garish striped sport coat; his complexion was as yellow as goat's milk cheese.

"Hiram Ben Abbe, Oscar Feldman," Euripides said. "Sit down, Hiram. We've got some thinking to do, the three of us."

Ben Abbe's handshake was limp.

"Hiram has the German economics desk at Operations Central," Euripides said.

Ben Abbe straightened his tie. The tie was the only thing neat about him. His clothes were baggy and there was a coffee stain on his rumpled shirt.

Euripides said, "Feldman has just been telling me he suspects the head of the American Federal Reserve is in the pocket of some wealthy currency speculators—or he is an agent."

Ben Abbe flexed his thin fingers. "That would explain a lot."

"Explain what?" Oscar asked.

"As you know, the dollar has been rising like a hot air balloon on fire." He paused and smiled at the aptness of the metaphor. "The upward pressure on the dollar has been coming from three sources. The most important is an Arab connection working through intermediaries—we suspect South Yemen and Libya are heavily involved, and perhaps Syria, Iraq, and Saudi Arabia."

"Some Soviet clients, some American," Oscar said. The fluorescent light above him was flickering. He found it irritating. Neither Ben Abbe nor Euripides seemed to notice.

"And we think," Ben Abbe said with a dramatic pause, "American oil interests may be involved as well."

Oscar thought: that makes sense. George Corbett would fit right in with that crowd.

Ben Abbe continued in a monotone. "As you are no doubt aware, per capita the Arabs have the largest gold reserves in the world, some two million ounces. At the moment, through cleverly concealed dummy corporations set up in West Germany and Belgium, they are selling off tons of it—for dollars. Fourteen—maybe fifteen—thousand millions so far."

Oscar shook his head in disbelief.

Euripides said, "What do they know that we don't?"

"They may be strapped for cash," Ben Abbe said. "Could be they just need foreign exchange, what with the price of oil down."

"It isn't like the Arabs to buy in a seller's market," Oscar said.

"Exactly!" Euripides said, biting on a fresh pencil.

"Perhaps," Ben Abbe said thoughtfully, "they foresee a doubling or tripling of the dollar and they hope to cash in. It's simply a business deal. They can be sharp traders."

"Doubtful," Euripides said. "You ever know the Arabs to gamble with gold?"

"No," Oscar said.

"Not ordinarily," Ben Abbe said.

Euripides said, "If George Corbett is an agent, who is he an agent for?"

"I imagine he'd be Russian," Oscar said. "Bulgarian, East German possibly. It wouldn't matter a whole lot."

"He's not one of ours?" Ben Abbe asked.

"Not as far as I know," Euripides said with a smile. "But the way things are in the Cabinet these days, you can't be sure."

"You have Corbett's apartment wired?" Euripides asked.

"Yes, but we suspect he has his place swept regularly so we can't count on it yielding much. But we do have it under surveillance. We haven't tried to wire his office. It's under pretty tight security and we wouldn't want to tip anyone off."

Ben Abbe suddenly sat upright as if hit with a sudden realization. "I've got it!" he said. "I think I know why the Arabs are bidding the dollar up to the highest levels since World War II! The credit flow! The West Europeans are hurting with the dollar so high, credit-wise. It's the West European countries that are feeling the crunch . . . meaning the Arabs can leverage their European hard currency reserves."

"That's too Byzantine for me," Euripides said. "But if Corbett is acting in their interests you might be onto something. Our files on him indicate he's a greedy bastard."

Ben Abbe looked amused at the very idea. "The oil men have their man in as chairman of the American Central Bank. Hmmmmmmm."

Oscar said to him, "What you just said, the dollar being at the highest level . . ."

"Yes," Ben Abbe said. "Taken in terms of postwar noninflationary values."

Oscar said, "In 1929, the day before the crash, the stock market had hit an all-time high. What if someone is bidding the dollar up in order to knock the legs out from under it and let it crash?"

Euripides looked at him with a puzzled expression, then he suddenly burst out laughing. "Not even in my wildest dreams has anything of the like ever occurred to me. You mean somebody's engineering a currency collapse? Preposterous! How could they possibly hope to succeed? There are all kinds of mechanisms in place to see that such a thing cannot happen."

"And what is the single most important mechanism? The Federal Reserve Board."

Euripides glared at him. Ben Abbe looked at Euripides, then at Oscar, shaking his head.

"Not possible," Euripides said. "Nobody's got enough resources—nobody except the Soviets." He considered it for a moment, then shook his head. "The Soviets are neither that imaginative nor that bold."

Oscar thought: But George Corbett is.

Someone knocked, and Euripides leaned back in his seat and opened the door. A young woman put her head in. "The meeting is about to get under way," she said.

"Enough of this fanciful speculation," Euripides said,

"what we need is some good old-fashioned intelligence."

"Or a crystal ball," Oscar said.

The purpose of the meeting, Euripides said, was to map out Israel's response to the rising dollar. Oscar took his seat in the back row. The room was already crowded with somber-looking men in suits and ties. Like most Israeli clothing, the suits were a little baggy and not too stylish. Oscar recognized some of the men in the front: the minister of finance, the deputy prime minister, and Klein-Edan, head of the Mossad's economic division.

The meeting turned out to be long and dreary. No one seemed to know what the effect of the rising dollar would be on the Israeli economy, how it would affect Israel's already disastrous inflation rate of 135 percent, or whether the Americans would consider increasing Israel's aid package.

Throughout the discussions Oscar could think of but one thing: the collapse of the dollar. Ben Abbe was right, the value of the dollar was rising like a balloon on fire. And like any balloon on fire, it would rise into the stratosphere. And then it would crash to earth.

Three hours into the meeting a young female aide tapped Oscar on the shoulder. "A message for you, sir."

He opened the envelope from the Israeli Consulate in New York. The message was that Catlyn Cavanaugh had been shot and her bodyguard killed. According to news reports, Miss Cavanaugh was in stable condition and under guard.

Oscar called Euripides out of the meeting, showed him the note, and said he'd be returning to the States immediately. After studying the note for a long moment, Euripides told an aide to go ahead and make arrangements. Then he took Oscar into his office and said, "As you know, we have few assets in the United States. Every time we have been caught spying in the past, it has cost us dearly in support money and has even soured a few good friends in the

Congress. The Cabinet and the prime minister have thought it wise to reduce our networks, which we have done. We have a few analysts, like yourself, and a few longtime moles still in place, but it is a wholly inadequate setup." His small mouth made an expression of disgust. He took hold of Oscar by the shoulders. "You are an important agent doing important work. Don't let us down."

Oscar never knew what to say to things like that. He just shook his head and muttered, "You can count on me," which is what he thought he was expected to say.

Euripides slapped Oscar on the shoulder, as the military men did in British World War II films.

Oscar's El Al flight back to the United States stopped over in London for two hours. Oscar got off the plane and bought a *London Times*. On page 1 was an article whose headline read: Dollar Drops Twelve Percent Against the Pound, Largest One-day Slide in History.

Oscar thought: It's begun. A chill ran up his spine.

Now that it had begun, George Corbett, for the first time in his life, was scared to the bone.

For the last couple of weeks he had busied himself with tightening his control over the Fed, putting his own people into key positions, moving staff around, making himself look like a take-charge professional. Meanwhile, he had to convince his detractors that his policy of letting the value of the dollar float upwards was in the best interest of the economy. He told the President personally that the phenomenal rise in the dollar was a technical adjustment and any attempt by the Fed to drive down the price of the dollar would be playing into the hands of currency speculators. Besides, billions of European and Japanese investment dollars were flooding into American banks, which could be used to service the national debt and keep interest rates in check.

The President, only partially placated, grumbled and said, "Okay, George, but if you're wrong, I'll have your ass *flambéed*."

The other members of the board were not as easy to convince, but they went along grudgingly. George canceled the regularly scheduled monthly meeting so there would be no vote on it. The chairman did have his prerogatives.

Now that the dollar had fallen on all the currency exchanges around the world, taking the biggest one-day plunge in history, George called the President to assure him that such a dip was to be expected and indicated that the "technical adjustments" were in a self-correcting phase. The President seemed pleased when George told him they were beating the currency speculators at their own game.

Now George could turn his attention at least momentarily to his main problem: Catlyn Cavanaugh.

Park had missed. It was the first time that any covert action George had ever been involved in had gone completely wrong. Now Catlyn Cavanaugh would be even harder to get to. And maybe she'd be gunning for *him*.

George found himself looking over his shoulder wherever he went. He stayed in his office during the day, drove to his security apartment in the evening, and stayed home. She had nothing that could legally tie him to the murder of Damian Carter, or to the attempt on her life, but the expectation that any day she would make a public accusation hung heavily over him. George felt thrown off balance. She had to be dealt with, and soon.

He knew of several professional assassins. Each seemed competent and reliable, but none really impressed him. None was as good as Park had been, and Park had missed. George could have gone to Peabody, of course, and told him of his predicament. But ever since his trip behind the Curtain George was not so certain his superiors could be trusted. His request for assistance might be interpreted as a sign of stupidity, that he had assigned Park a task that proved too much for him. George decided, finally, that the only one he could trust was Nicolai. Using him was risky, however, because he knew the whole operation, which could be catastrophic if he were caught. But Nicolai was well trained at the best KGB schools and was no doubt one of the most able and clever assassins in the world.

George met Nicolai on the second morning of the dollar's downward plunge, Tuesday, November sixth, in the cluttered back office of a doughnut shop in suburban Washington, D.C.; the owner was one of George's old friends from his college days. It was a brisk fall day, and the maple trees along the street were showing a spectacular array of colors. George sat behind the desk sipping milk-white coffee and eating a chocolate cruller. He was feeling tired and old, but he managed to put on a buoyant and optimistic act for Nicolai.

Nicolai, in a black turtleneck and a new herringbone sportcoat, was looking quite dashing. He straddled a straightback chair and, with a smile on his lips, waited for George to explain why he sent for him.

"Nicolai, you didn't get any coffee. It is very good here, and old Henry makes a superb doughnut. Try the lemon jellyball."

"I'm watching my weight. What's the matter, Colonel? I can see it in your eyes, you're worried."

"I have a dangerous job for you, Nicolai."

"Catlyn Cavanaugh?"

"Yes. How did you know?"

"I read the papers."

George finished his doughnut and licked his fingers. "I don't like giving you such an assignment, but it must be done, and done quickly. I have no one else I can trust to do the task, old friend. It won't be easy. She'll be fully on the alert. Please, Nicolai, do it quickly. Do it any way you can."

Nicolai stood up and put his foot on the chair, leaning

360

with his arm on his thigh. "It would be better to use domestic help."

"Park was the best, and he failed."

Nicolai thought it over for a moment, then said, "It is no time for us to take such risks. If I'm caught, I would have to kill myself. Otherwise, who knows, they could drug me, torture me, make me talk. Then the whole game would be blown." He said it in an offhanded, casual way, with no fear in his voice.

"I have to have it done and you have to do it," George said. "Please, Nicolai, please. For me. For our friendship."

Nicolai smiled enigmatically. "I'll do it, Colonel, relax."

On his way out the door, Nicolai stopped and turned to George. "It must have been bad over there, when you were in Europe, wasn't it?"

"Why do you think so, Nicolai?"

"You haven't been yourself since you got back."

"I'm just tired. It's been a long hard struggle to get here."

"I think it is more than just tired. You've lost something. The edge of the blade is dull."

"Don't worry about me, Nicolai, just do your job!"

Nicolai saluted with a smile.

As the door closed behind Nicolai, George felt a wave of despair sweep over him. Nicolai was right of course. He had lost his edge. And there didn't seem to be a damn thing he could do about it.

When George arrived at his office at the Federal Reserve Building there were several messages waiting for him. Reporters from the *Post* wanted an interview. *Sixty Minutes* was doing a feature on the wild fluctuations of the dollar. Tim McAfee, the secretary of the treasury, had called twice about T-Bill rates. But the message that interested him most was from Lydia Wickham. It said that a book he'd been looking for entitled *The History of a Primitive Economy* was available at the Book Fare, 1794 E Street, open until six. The message was really from Peabody. George was being summoned to 7149 I Street that night at nine.

The rest of the afternoon George went about his duties like a robot, as if he were there but his mind had gone to the Arctic. He thought about what Nicolai had said about him. It was plaguing him. He *had* lost something. He'd lost his sense of power. They had wanted to make him crawl, to belittle him, to make him feel like only the smallest cog in a vast machinery. And they had done it. Ever since returning from Europe he'd found himself less decisive, less confident. He was now a fretful man where he'd never been fretful before. If he was to bring down America he would have to regain his purpose and sense of mission. And his arrogance. He had always been a supremely arrogant man; it was this which had enabled him to conceive his supremely arrogant plan.

But how could he be arrogant when he felt the great presence standing behind him? The Russian Bear. Huge, savage, cunning. The bear had one end of a leash in its monstrous paw; the other end was tied around George's throat.

And there wasn't a damn thing he could do about it.

TWENTY-SIX

George ate supper at Gino's, his favorite Washington Italian restaurant. Of course, he thought, it was usually not as good as the restaurants in Little Italy, but it didn't matter. It was a quiet little place where he could sit in the back and not be disturbed. He paid little attention to the food he was shoveling in his mouth anyway. It was spaghetti with clam sauce and a fresh green salad. He read *The Wall Street Journal* as he ate, taking a perverse pleasure in the bewilderment of the writers as to what was going on in the world money markets. George had not given the signal to begin the fall, and that miffed him a little. Some bureaucrat at Moscow Central had made the decision prematurely, he thought, but he never even registered a protest. It was falling now, falling fast, and that was all that really mattered.

There was an editorial on the fate of the dollar, which predicted that the price of the dollar would stabilize soon, then resume its steady increase. That was what the Treasury was predicting anyway. George chuckled over that one. American journalists, he thought, what naive fools!

He ordered half a carafe of Chianti. He couldn't keep his mind on whatever he was reading. What did the old general want with him? Whatever it was, it wasn't good. He was their lackey now. He would have to go along with whatever it was.

His dream of a dacha on the Black Sea and an honored place in children's textbooks was slipping away from him. Already he had lost the nest egg he had put away for his son. Poor, poor Rudolf, George thought glumly. Pampered and spoiled, facing the world penniless. He would have to learn to either beg or steal, or he would starve.

George could, of course, liquidate part of his fortune and turn it over to Rudolf, but Moscow Central, no doubt, would find out immediately and he would be killed in some dreadful way. George couldn't quite face thinking about that. He left it open as an option, but he knew he didn't have the courage it would take.

He ordered more Chianti.

His only other choice was to go to the FBI, confess everything, and get into their witness protection program. His stomach churned at the very idea. That would betray everything his life had stood for. Besides, the KGB would spend every resource to track him down and he would spend the rest of his life wondering when they would get him. Because they *would* get him. And Linda and Rudolf, too.

George finished his meal with a double order of spumoni, served with a chocolate cookie. He left the restaurant at a quarter to nine feeling slightly drunk. He sat behind the wheel of his Mercedes and ran his hand over the fine leather seat. Then he looked at his face in the mirror. He didn't like what he saw.

Okay, so they had beaten him, and he had, in his mind, turned on Rudolf. He thought: It is at the moment that you turn on a loved one that they know they have you. But here he was, alive, and in control. And Rudolf was untouched. They thought they had beaten George, but he was not beaten. In the end his plan would work, America would fall, and he would return to the Soviet Union and take care of his enemies. Batyushkin would be the first!

He started his car. He felt better. Even if it was all bravado—and deep down he knew that it was—he felt better.

He drove over to I Street, found the number, and parked down the block. It was in an industrial district with few streetlights and many potholes. As usual, he crossed the street and circled back to make sure he wasn't being followed. The address turned out to be an old warehouse with no lights on inside. A sign over the door said, "Smyth and Hallcroft, Ltd., Export-Import." What a terrible place for a meeting, George thought. He knocked at the door and it opened almost instantly. A young woman stood before him.

"Come in, Comrade," she said.

George stepped inside. She closed the door behind him, then turned on the light. He found he was standing in a hallway leading straight back into the building past dozens of small, dark, vacant offices. He looked at the woman who had greeted him. She was a rather pretty young brunette with bright eyes and a pleasant smile. He'd never seen her before. She put out her hand to him. "Svetlana Popov. I'm the cultural attaché at our embassy here in Washington," she said in flawless English.

"Pleased to meet you," he said. "I was expecting Mr. Peabody—General Davydov."

"He is here, come this way."

George followed her down the hallway and into a small room, a storeroom of some kind. Here, folded neatly on a chair, was a KGB uniform, without insignias, and, on the floor beside the chair, a pair of highly polished riding boots.

"A formal occasion?" he said.

She nodded with a smile. "A surprise," she said.

She left him alone to change his clothes. A surprise, George mused. What kind of surprise this time? Why didn't the uniform have his colonel's bars? Perhaps they had a demotion in mind. Perhaps they were planning a quick trial and an even quicker execution—for some real or imagined crimes. They didn't need proof of anything. He knew that. They made up their own reality to serve their purposes. He felt a cold chill at the base of his spine. He did not know what to expect because, after thirty years in the field, he no longer knew nor understood his own countrymen. His own comrades.

The uniform was tight in the shoulders and waist, and the boots were too wide at the instep. He felt like a clown at a costume party. Well, if this was what they wanted, so be it. *Espionage is theater*. One of his trainers had said that long ago. He didn't know what it meant at the time, but he understood it now.

Whatever they had in mind for him, he decided, he would accept it with dignity. Even if he no longer understood his countrymen, he still understood his mission.

Svetlana Popov saluted when he stepped into the hall. She, too, was now wearing a uniform, with lieutenant's bars on the shoulder. "This way, Colonel," she said.

"I'm looking forward to the surprise," he said with forced cheerfulness.

He followed her down a stairway into the basement. He could already hear talking as they started down the stairs. The voices were mostly male, and the language was Russian. When the lieutenant opened the door for him, George was astonished to see two or three dozen people in uniform, including General Kosnoff—and who was he talking to? Nicolai! Nicolai in uniform?

The room was pine-paneled, with a plush red carpet, draped in red and white banners, with rows of metal folding chairs. At one end of the room was a small serving bar crammed with liquor bottles.

Svetlana closed the door behind them. "Surprised?" she asked.

"What is the occasion?"

"I've been sworn to secrecy," she said with a smile.

Then George spotted Peabody, and it was suddenly exceedingly clear what was going on. Peabody was standing next to the wall wearing a hopelessly out-of-fashion suit and a flowered tie. Peabody seemed bewildered and his face was gray and drawn. George thought: Peabody's finished!

Everyone came to attention and saluted when George stepped into the room. Then they all clapped.

"Ah, my dear Colonel Vlahovich, welcome, welcome!" General Kosnoff said in Russian, walking toward George with his hand outstretched. "You are confused, no doubt. Well, perfectly understandable. I'm sorry we could not have forewarned you, but the use of codes . . . I'm sure you understand. Our purposes soon will become clear to you . . . Please, everyone, sit down, won't you? I have a speech to make—a short one, I promise you."

Svetlana Popov insisted that George sit next to her in the front row. George's heart began to race. Peabody looked as gloomy as a new arrival in the Gulag. George waved to him; Peabody did not wave back.

Kosnoff held up his hands for everyone to be quiet. He lit a long, brown cigarette. George had never seen him look so amiable. His wolfish face looked almost friendly.

"I have two very pleasant announcements to make today," Kosnoff said. "This is the end of an era. First, I would like to announce the retirement of a man who has had a most distinguished career spanning nearly fifty years. It is my very great honor and privilege to tell you that General Davydov—who many of you have known as Mr. Peabody—has taken his retirement and will be returning to the Soviet Union."

There was polite applause.

"And, with the blessings of the Central Committee, it is my very great honor to announce the promotion of Colonel Vlahovich to brigadier general!"

There was more applause. George was urged to his feet. He saluted General Kosnoff, who pinned the stars on his shoulders and vigorously shook his hand, then kissed him on both cheeks.

George was dumbfounded. Now everyone was congratulating him and shaking his hand. Lieutenant Popov opened bottles of champagne, and trays with smoked salmon on Russian black bread, red caviar on rye rounds, and herring and sliced hardboiled eggs were passed around. Toasts were made. Cuban cigars appeared. The national anthem was sung . . .

Tears filled George's eyes. He had to turn away and be alone for a moment. He was feeling great relief, all at once. Peabody gone. Now his promotion. General in the KGB! The dream of a lifetime.

General Kosnoff asked to have a few words with him. They went upstairs into a plush office. They were both puffing on cigars. Kosnoff sat down behind a desk, crushed out his cigar, and put on a pair of gold wire-rimmed glasses.

"Comrade Vlahovich, you are a man of genius."

"I thank you, General."

"The premier himself has asked me to give you his best wishes—and a personal apology for the way you were treated in Czechoslovakia. The man responsible for that outrage, Vladimir Batyushkin, is in a very shaky position and may lose his post."

"I found him a most unlikable fellow," George said, even though he didn't quite believe Batyushkin was in any trouble. He knew everything was run by committee and no one acted on his own. "I hope," George said, "they send him to Siberia."

Kosnoff smiled. "Perhaps they will—but that's out of our control. Now then, we feel we have put you to the test and you have passed admirably. We are overlooking your secret bank account and have returned the funds. We realized you did it out of a very human feeling for your son. The reprimand has been removed from your service record as if it never happened. You no longer have to worry about your son's future no matter what happens."

George's heart bloomed with joy. "Thank you, General! You don't know what a relief it is to me!"

"How terrible it must have been for you to watch him grow up in this deplorable capitalistic society."

George said, "Why all the generosity all of a sudden, General? Don't lie to me. What has happened? Peabody's retirement, my promotion, forgiving the secret account for Rudolf. Something monumental has happened."

Kosnoff thought for a moment, then said, "I will tell you. Why not? A professor of economics at the Foreign Service Institute has made a computer model of a currency collapse within the American capitalist system, and he has verified your projections. Your method."

"Yes, and?"

"The professor is a most distinguished fellow whom the premier has relied upon in the past for some very discriminating analyses."

George puffed on his cigar. It was the best cigar he had ever tasted. "Go on, General."

"This distinguished professor—one of the greatest economists in the world—has declared that what you are proposing has an extremely high probability of success."

George nodded. He had used Columbia University's computer, with Margo Yost-Konning's model, so he knew his predictions were accurate.

General Kosnoff continued. "Now everyone in the Central Committee is behind you one hundred percent." He paused for a moment and said, "Moscow Central has personal charge of Davydov's network and full control of his assets. Lieutenant Popov will be your link to us. If you need anything you can contact her. Use the same telephone and codes. We have instructed her to give you whatever assistance you require."

"Thank you. Now tell me, has there been any indication in the Western services that the recent currency manipulations are ours?"

"There has been a report made by a Mossad agent claiming you are either working with currency speculators, oil interests, or you are an agent. He is a very junior agent and not well regarded, but I'm warning you to try to bring matters to a head as soon as possible."

"This agent, who is he?"

"We only know his code name, but he claimed to be working with an American woman named Catlyn Cavanaugh."

"Ah, yes. Now I have the whole picture. I have told Nicolai to dispose of her—and the Israeli agent. I am very aware of the situation, General, and have it under control."

"Good. You have my full confidence. It looks to me that those two are the only possible obstacles standing between us and a very great victory for Marxist-Leninism."

George shook Kosnoff's hand. He was feeling his old self again and he knew the general could see it. "You tell them back in Moscow to keep the pressure on the dollar, sir, and I shall see in America that chaos and collapse follows."

George returned to the party and took Nicolai aside and said, "Nicolai, there is no time to waste, that Cavanaugh woman must be dealt with immediately."

"She has vanished, sir. We are doing everything we can to find her."

"Perhaps you didn't hear me, Lieutenant, because cement in your brain is clogging your ears! I want her dealt with immediately!"

Nicolai's cheeks colored. He snapped to attention, saluted, and hurriedly left the room.

George poured himself a tall glass of vodka.

* * *

After she'd gotten out of the hospital, Catlyn moved in with Oscar in a small apartment on the West Side, on Ninety-ninth and Broadway, which he called a "safe house." Oscar had stopped pretending he wasn't working for the Mossad, which pleased Catlyn.

Catlyn didn't think much of Oscar's safe house. It was cluttered and cramped, and she wasn't used to being cramped. The walls were painted a horrible rose color, the furniture was mismatched and utilitarian. There was no view, and the elevator next door made a god-awful noise. And there was no cleaning woman and Oscar made a mess of everything he tried to clean up. Despite the fact that she was still recovering from her wounds, Catlyn did the dishes and picked up around the place.

Oscar spent his time reading and summarizing financial accounts, drafting reports to his superiors, and asking for permission to present what he knew to the FBI. So far, permission had been categorically denied. He was told that the Mossad had independently investigated Robert Park and could find no connection to George Corbett, but they did find evidence that whoever Park was working for was trying to frame George Corbett. Furthermore, no connection could be made between George Corbett and the currency speculators who were putting the downward pressure on the dollar.

Oscar realized at once the climate in which this analysis was being made. The dollar was falling. Cheap dollars would relieve the enormous pressure on Israel's debt burden. Therefore, no dire warnings of a collapse would be listened to. Oscar knew this was a common problem of intelligence gathering organizations, often called the "wishful-thinking syndrome." High officials in any government have a tendency to hear only what they wish to hear. The wishful-thinking syndrome was one of the primary reasons the United States lost the Vietnamese War.

The wishful-thinking syndrome was only one possibility.

The other possibility was much scarier. Oscar thought: what if George Corbett was Moscow's man, and what if the upper ranks of the Mossad had some of Moscow's men of their own? It wasn't totally out of the question. Captured KGB agents often made boasts that they had moles in every intelligence service in the world. Oscar mentioned this sort of speculation to no one, not even Catlyn.

Then came Black Tuesday, November 15: The New York Stock Exchange opened at 2221, down 88 points from the high of the year. It was down four more points after the first hour of trading, ten more points after the second hour.

At eleven-fifteen, EST, the Concord-Belmont Bank of California, the fourteenth largest bank in the country, declared itself bankrupt. Rumors began to spread that more banks were about to go under. The Bank of the Pacific, the tenth largest, closed its doors. Panic spread throughout the financial community; the result was the biggest selling binge in the history of the stock exchange. "It's bargain day in Macy's basement!" one analyst cried.

By noon the Dow stood at 1843; at 12:25, 1789. By two it had dropped below 1700.

On the Tokyo currency exchange, the dollar stood at 367 yen at the morning fixing and 352 at noon. It had fallen forty-six percent in three weeks.

Oscar went down to the Stock Exchange to witness the turmoil and came back deeply troubled. He sat on the couch and Catlyn poured him a drink. "I can't understand it," he said. "Israel won't allow me to go to the FBI with what I know about George Corbett. I just don't believe Park was trying to frame George Corbett. And isn't Corbett's lack of decisive action in the face of the monetary crisis prima facie evidence he's up to something?"

"You don't have to convince me," Catlyn said.

"The only way I can figure it is that the sinking dollar is such a bonanza for them that they're willing to just let it sink. It can't be that they're afraid of being accused of spying. Then again, maybe it's me they don't trust. Maybe they think I'm a double agent or some damn thing—your typical spy master sees a conspiracy in his chicken soup."

Catlyn lit a cigarette and sat down on the couch next to him. "If you can't do it, and they won't do it, I guess that leaves it all up to us."

"As in you-are-now-under-arrest?"

"You mean for wiretapping and that kind of stuff? I've thought it all over. This is way too big for me. My quarrel with George Corbett is nothing compared to all this. I'm going to tell the FBI everything. I'll deal with Mr. Corbett later, should he escape punishment."

"I hope you realize it's a serious crime to break into an apartment, shoot a man, drug him into talking, then frame him for a robbery."

"So I'll be in trouble. It's nothing compared to what's happening. Besides, my attorney, Martin Getsong, is a magician."

"Let's hope so."

She took a deep drag on her cigarette. "I want you to go along with me."

"Not necessary. You know everything I know."

"But you're an Israeli agent. If you tell them that George Corbett is a suspected espionage agent they might believe you. Sorry, Oscar, but you haven't got a choice. This is ten thousand times bigger than your career."

Oscar got up and started munching on a croissant, pacing up and down in the living room. "Damn," he said.

Catlyn said, "It's a question of divided loyalty with you, isn't it, Oscar?"

He nodded.

"Israel versus America. You can't stay on the fence much longer."

"If I go with you to the FBI, the only way I could do you any good is to tell them who I am. If I tell them who I am, I've just wrecked my career, and even though I don't think much of it, I don't want to be kicked out. I might even be tried as a traitor. The Mossad doesn't screw around. Israel is in a constant state of war and I'm in effect a soldier. They might even have me shot."

She put out her cigarette. "I'm going to get dressed. I think the gray suit. You wear your blue one. You look good in blue."

He thought for a moment, then said, "I just hope they believe us. I wouldn't want to be sent to a firing squad for nothing."

Catlyn called and made an appointment, then they took a cab to the Federal Building. It was a cold, snowy day, but the streets were crowded with people, all seeming in a hurry. There was a sense of fear in the air. A lot of stores appeared closed.

The special agent who took their report was in his mid-thirties, with a tanned, square face and deep blue eyes. His name was Christian Able. He let Catlyn and Oscar tell their stories without interruption while a young woman took notes on a steno pad. When they were done, he said, "What exactly is it that you want us to do?"

Catlyn looked at him and said, "I suppose we want you to arrest Mr. Corbett before he ruins the country."

Special Agent Christian Able folded his hands on his desk. "Let me get this straight. You are Oscar Feldman, and you claim to be an agent of the Israeli Intelligence Service."

"That's right. Economic Surveillance and Analysis Section—North America."

"And you are Catlyn Cavanaugh, and you were a friend of Damian Carter, who you claim was killed at the orders of the chairman of the Federal Reserve Board. And the man who told you this later attacked you and a Mr. Hanson in your apartment?"

"That's right. They killed each other."

"But subsequent to that, you had this man Park put in

jail."

"That's right."

"And you'd given him truth serum?"

"Yes."

Special Agent Able rubbed his chin. "And you, Mr. Feldman, you claim that the Mossad has uncovered a possible plot by unknown nations—or currency speculators—to sell off the dollar, causing a currency collapse?"

"Exactly right, sir."

"But you say for some unknown reason the government of Israel is keeping this information to themselves?"

"Yes."

"Is there any way you can prove to us that you are an agent of the Mossad?"

"No."

"If we contact the Israeli Consulate, will they know you?"

"No, of course not. I receive messages there under the name of Maximilian Franks. By coming here I have violated orders."

"You know," Christian Able said in measured tones, "you have told me the zaniest story I've ever heard, but I believe you. I should hold you in protective custody, if George Corbett is as dangerous as you say."

"We're in a safe house," Oscar said. "Besides, you now know what we know. If you want to get in touch with us, call the Israeli Consulate and leave a message for Maximilian Franks."

Catlyn and Oscar took a cab from the Federal Building uptown and across Central Park. Two blocks before Oscar's apartment something was happening in the street. A mob had gathered in front of a bank and the police were trying to disperse them. Bottles and bricks flew as the police used their clubs.

"We gotta go around it," the cabbie said. "Been happening all over town today. This morning some Arabs take their money out of Manhattan First National and now every-body thinks they're going belly up. A run they call it. What the hell's wrong with people, don't they know their money's insured?"

Christian Able had the stenographer type up a report of what Catlyn and Oscar had told him and took it down the hall to Section C and showed it to Group Supervisor Laurence Zobell, who headed up the New York Action Committee which investigated political corruption. Zobell had made his reputation as one of the creators of Abscam back in the late seventies.

Zobell, silver-haired, with a ruddy, outdoor complexion, sat on the edge of his desk and looked at the report, nodding.

"I'm glad you've brought this to my attention—I'll get on it immediately. The director should be appraised at once. Good work, Able." He picked up the phone and dialed. "Thanks again, Able—I'll keep you informed."

Zobell put the phone down as soon as Able was out of the office. Then he put on his overcoat, took the elevator to the first floor, went outside, and walked three blocks to the Sullivan Building, being careful he wasn't followed. He got on the elevator alone, found a key under the fire extin-guisher, put it into a slot on the control panel, turned it, and the elevator descended into the basement. The door opened and he stepped out of the elevator and a young man appeared from a workroom.

"You can get a message to Peabody's replacement?" Zobell asked.

"Yes, of course."

"We've got a problem."

TWENTY-SEVEN

The Securities and Exchange Commission closed the New York and American Stock Exchanges after an hour's trading the following morning. The New York Exchange had dropped a whopping 108 points and the American, 106. George received a frantic call from the President shortly thereafter.

"The ship is sinking, George. What the hell are we doing to plug the holes?"

"It's not sinking, it's merely hit a sandbar, Jerome. Rest assured the Fed is taking the necessary corrective action. I'm preparing an emergency strategy that we're putting into effect immediately."

"The Treasury people are screaming that nothing's being done, that the lines of communication between them and the Fed have completely broken down. The F.D.I.C. people were in here this morning telling my people you won't even return their phone calls."

"This is an emergency situation, Jerome, and I admit I have to be a bit arbitrary, step on a few toes, but that's the only way I know to get the job done."

377

"I told them I had complete faith in you, George. When can we get together? I've got to get a handle on this thing in my own mind."

"This evening, we ought to have things in hand by then."

"I'm relying on you, George."

"You won't be disappointed."

"We'll expect you tonight then."

The meeting was set up for eight o'clock. George hung up the phone and leaned back in his swivel chair. Everything was going perfectly. The administration was in a state of confusion, and things were bound to get more confusing by the minute.

The President, he knew, had one great flaw. He ruled by his instincts, which were good but not infallible. By instinct he had picked very competent people for his Cabinet, and he showed his trust in them by virtually giving them a free hand. Jerome Hustead's theory of the presidency was that the President was an executive who delegated. He didn't have to be an expert in anything except in his ability to choose the right person for the right job.

And he believed in George Corbett. He trusted George Corbett. Since taking office, George had been carefully building a close personal relationship with the President. He was now almost an extension of the President himself.

There was one more thing about Jerome Hustead which made him the ideal President from George's point of view. He backed his appointees to the hilt. He demanded loyalty from his underlings and he gave them loyalty in return. Two of his senior staff members had been accused of impropriety during the past year. Hustead did not ask either to resign. He rode out the storm of criticism.

George would now use the President's unswerving loyalty to bring the nation down. It would take only a few more days.

He had met with various committees at the Fed, told everyone he wanted detailed analyses of the crisis and not to do anything hasty or rash, that he had spoken to the President and the President wanted it that way. George explained that his hands were tied, that they had to work with the Treasury people. This was all said with a pained expression on his face.

"Just do the best you can. I'm meeting with the President tonight, we'll get it straightened out."

Already there was talk about declaring a bank holiday—closing every bank in the country. George pretended to resist the idea. He'd hold off and wait until the public panic really got ugly. Then there'd be more than panic. There'd be revolution.

That afternoon he made a call to Nicolai in New York from a pay phone near his office. He left a coded message on the recording device for the underground groups to go into action. The time had come.

George met the President in the Oval Office that evening at eight o'clock. The President's eyes were rimmed in red. He looked old, George thought. Old and weary. Sitting behind his desk, he waved George into the room with a choppy motion of his hand. James A. Preston, the President's chief economist, was with him. Preston had been one of the Council of Economic Advisers who had backed George's nomination; he was part of the New York banking community, and his associates and supporters backed George. Preston was short, stocky, dark, and looked damn angry. He was pacing around with his arms folded, like a losing football coach prowling the sidelines.

"Hello, Corbett," Preston said, making it sound like a curse. "I don't know what the hell you think you're doing over there, but you couldn't be screwing it up any worse if you were trying to."

George remained standing. He said, "I'm sure that's what I'd think if I were on the outside and didn't know what was really going on."

The President said, "Just what *is* the inside situation? You know what's going on in the country, there's no sense rehashing it. Banks are folding, there's panic in the streets. The stock market's closed. Credit card companies have ceased operations. I keep hearing all kinds of conflicting reports. No one seems to know who's behind it, what's really going on, when it will stop, what measures can and should be taken."

"I'm not sure," George said, "that I can give a full answer. One thing is sure, there has been an unprecedented and unforeseen sellout of American dollars in every money market in the world."

Preston said, "We *know* that, Corbett, what we want to know is what the hell you're doing about it?"

"I spend all day every day on the phone with economic ministers from all over the world trying to get them to buy dollars. I've been talking to Baxter at the International Monetary Fund to get them to do more, to pressure West Germany and Switzerland. They've done some, but they haven't done enough."

Preston said, "Why isn't the Fed buying dollars with its foreign currency reserves?"

George shook his head. "That's the temptation, but therein leads the path to true disaster."

"There isn't a qualified economist in the country who believes that," Preston said.

George said, "Mr. President, I don't mean to be an alarmist, but I believe there's an international conspiracy on a very large scale aimed at destroying this country economically. It isn't just currency speculators as, I believe, Mr. Preston assumes. We're seeing here an economic gambit of truly epic proportions. The largest such gambit since the Arab oil embargo of 1974."

"Speculators or international conspiracy, what's the difference?" Preston said. "And the way to counter it is to buy dollars with our foreign currency reserves. You take Econ. 101 in college, they tell you that."

"Listen to me, Preston, I'll tell you something they don't teach you in Econ. 101. We're not facing an ordinary economic upheaval here. We're facing a planned, well-orchestrated economic attack. I believe it's the Soviet Union with the possible cooperation of Japan, but I have no proof. They are the only countries in the world with enough resources to pull it off. If that is true, we're going to need our foreign currency reserves to play the last hand in this game."

"Ridiculous!" Preston snapped. "What possible reason would Japan have for bankrupting us? We're their largest market."

"They don't want to bankrupt us. They want to bring us to the brink. Perhaps tomorrow or the day after, if the pressure keeps up, they'll come to us with a bailout offer that will include our rolling back all of the trade restrictions we've placed on them over the past dozen years. They'll save us if we agree, in effect, to make this country a Japanese economic fiefdom."

Preston wiped his forehead. "I don't believe it. I see no evidence of it."

"I have evidence of it. I will present it tomorrow. My staff is at this moment preparing a report."

The President was shaking his head. "If this is true . . ."

"It's true. That's where the Soviets come in. They will ask for other concessions and that's why I'm holding back the foreign currency reserves. I'll explain. We have approximately 16.1 billion in outstanding notes pledged in foreign currencies, mostly Swiss francs. If even half of them were called and we didn't have the foreign currency on hand to pay on demand, we would have to go into the foreign money markets on our own, with dollars, and buy francs at an extremely unfavorable rate. We would then be creating the pressure to drive the dollar down even further. It would be the death blow to the dollar."

The President sat staring at George, rubbing the back of his hand across his mouth for a long moment. Then he looked at Preston and said, "I'd like to speak to George alone. We'll be in touch tomorrow, Preston, okay?"

Preston nodded, but it was clear he would prefer to stay. He said, "All right, Mr. President, in the meanwhile I'll have my people looking into a Japanese connection."

After Preston left, the President seemed to relax. He sat thinking for a moment, then said, "What evidence do you have that there's a conspiracy going on?"

"There's a definite reluctance to come to our aid shown by our supposed allies. There must be counterforces acting on them to prevent their helping us. It is truly baffling, because a disaster for us would ultimately be a disaster for them. Here's what I think, and admittedly it's speculative: The price of gold and silver is rising. I suspect some of our best friends who have a lot of gold and silver are going to leverage what they have in the hopes of getting some of ours. That's the corner they hope to put us in, force us to sell off our precious metals."

"That would make sense," the President said, nodding.

The President, George thought, was a man who liked to be reassured. George said, "The most important thing to remember about economics, Mr. President, is that money is a *legal fiction*, but a *psychological reality*. What's been happening is pretty simple. Somebody—the Japanese, almost certainly—during the last few months have been bidding the dollar up on the money markets. We'd been experiencing a little inflationary relief of late, and the rise in the dollar might have been expected. But it rose far more than expected. Economists were puzzled. I was puzzled. A too strong dollar is just as bad as one that isn't strong enough. It means that our companies can't sell their products overseas. It means that foreign goods become cheap, and American markets are ruined."

"Yes, yes, of course."

"Naturally, the International Monetary Fund, and we at the Fed, began to take corrective action—along with our allies and trading partners—to sell off dollars in order to bring the value of the dollar down. That is our legitimate function."

"I remember discussing this with you, yes."

"We started selling hundreds of millions of dollars an hour. Suddenly, money brokers all over the world stopped buying and started selling. They've kept selling. What we intended as an adjustment has gotten out of hand. The forces who had bid the dollar up are now forcing it lower."

"I'll say."

"But like I said, money is a *legal fiction*, but a *psychological reality*. Remember when the dollar started its rise? If you compare the dollar's value today with the value then, it has only slipped maybe twenty-three percent, which is a considerable amount but wouldn't normally be causing panic. It is only if you count the decline in value since its artificial high a week ago that things seem catastrophic. That's the *psychological* reality, of course, and that's what we have to go to work on. Changing the public's perception of the psychological reality."

"How do we do that?"

"The first thing we have to do is give the public assurances of trust. I suggest that you, sir, go on television and tell the public that the control mechanisms in place are adequate for dealing with disruptions in the value of the dollar, and that the temporary decline can be seen as nothing out of the ordinary when you look at the long view of the ups and downs. Meanwhile, my staff is working on a paper which I intend to deliver tomorrow evening at a convention of financial planners in New York. The press will be there, and I think they'll come away with a clear idea that the crisis is in hand, and that the value of the dollar will level off and begin to rise."

"I don't know, George . . . I think we ought to take some action. I don't know what, exactly, but we've got to *do* something."

"One thing you have to know about economists, Jerome, is that half of them are balmy pie-in-the-sky optimists, and the other half are gloom-and-doom pessimists. The rarity is the realist like me. Remember this: In 1978 the commercial paper market in the United States collapsed overnight, which was certainly a much more serious economic disruption than the stock market crash of 1929, yet few Americans were even aware that it had happened. Why? Because the Fed moved in quickly and backed a few teetering commercial paper houses and kept them afloat. We will now do that with the banks. People will see that there is no reason to fear their money isn't safe in the banks, and there will be no flight of capital. The pressure will soon ease on the dollar."

The President let some air out between his teeth. "I like what you're saying, George, but everyone else I talk to is pushing the panic button."

"I know, but a week from now everything will be back to normal—or almost normal."

"How sure are you, George, that you can really pull it off?"

"One hundred percent. Give me one week—till Thanksgiving."

"All right, George. You've got it!"

"There is one thing we could do, sir," George said. "As you know, you have emergency powers to turn over all credit control to the Fed under Public Law 91-151. I think it would be good for the public confidence if you were to sign an executive order to that effect. I think it would demonstrate that decisive action has been taken."

The President thought about it for a moment while George sat there waiting and hoping. Then the President said, "Yes, I think it would reassure the public. I'll announce it at my news conference tomorrow morning."

George smiled and said, "Now you wouldn't happen to have any of that good sour mash sippin' whiskey around, would you, Jerome?"

"Just so happens I do," the President said.

George was staying in a furnished apartment in a high-tech security building in Washington, not far from the Fed headquarters. Lt. Svetlana Popov of the Soviet Embassy lived in the same building, down the hall. She was waiting for George in his apartment when he returned from the White House at one-fifteen in the morning. George and the President had had more than just a sip.

"Svetlana, what is it?" George asked as he came in the door.

"Trouble, sir," she said, "but we think we've got it handled. It seems there's been a report made to the FBI that you're an agent or you're conspiring with currency speculators. Our old friends, Cavanaugh and her Israeli boyfriend."

"Any proof?"

"Whatever Park told them, but Park is dead."

"I have had one of my men looking for this troublesome Catlyn Cavanaugh for several days and he reports no success."

"She has been staying at a safe house with this Israeli— whereabouts unknown."

George said, "Come and sit in the kitchen, I have to have an Alka-Seltzer. The President just got through drinking me under the table. . . . How is it we know this report was made? What is the FBI doing about it?"

"We have assets in that area, that is all I'm allowed to say," she said with a sly smile. Her hair was done and she was wearing a pink robe deeply open at the collar. He could see the top of her cleavage. He wondered whether she might

385

be coming on to him. He wouldn't chance finding out, though. It might be a test. The KGB was always testing.

George said, "You said the problem was being handled. I would like to know how."

"It seems that whenever charges are made against a high-ranking member of the Federal government—and that would include you as chairman of the Fed—the case goes to a special group called the Action Committee. It is assigned to a special investigator, sometimes working with a special prosecutor. Such cases are always kept from the press because of the political sensitivity. We have long been interested in the Action Committee, of course, and have penetrated it at a high level."

"Good." He tore open the Alka-Seltzer envelope and dropped the contents into a glass of water.

"So the threat is not immediate, but Moscow Central advises that you should be prepared to make an escape at any moment."

"Yes, yes, certainly."

George watched the Alka-Seltzer fizz, then drank it down slowly. Though he always knew that his assignment would eventually terminate, the thought that the time was imminent gave him a strange feeling in the pit of his stomach. But then he thought of his dacha on the Black Sea and the book he would write, and the feeling quickly passed.

George waited for the relieving burp, which made him feel much better. Then he sat down, folded his hands in front of him, and said, "I have some good news. Tomorrow morning the President will sign an executive order making me, in effect, dictator of the economy."

"He can do that?"

"He can and he will. Once he signs the order, America is finished."

She beamed. "You are such a remarkable person, Comrade General, no one else could have done this."

George shrugged off the compliment. "I want you to

contact Moscow Central and tell them to increase the pressure on the dollar. The banking system is teetering, but we need more pressure. This is no time to be thrifty."

"I'll tell them."

George covered his mouth while he burped again. The mixed taste of the bourbon and the Alka-Seltzer was sour in his throat. He said, "Tomorrow I'm beginning the next phase. How to explain it? All right. Banks are required to hold a certain percentage of their deposits in cash in their vaults. We, the Fed, tell them what that percentage must be. Say, four percent. The banks, realizing that the demand for cash fluctuates, will keep, say, five or six percent on hand, in order not to fall below the minimum if the demand for cash is unexpectedly high—and with the jitteriness of the public, it is often unexpectedly high. When a bank falls below their percentage they will be in technical violation of banking regulations. If a bank falls to zero percent—as happens even in the best of times—they are technically bankrupt. Now it so happens—perhaps a dozen times a week in normal times—that a bank goes technically bankrupt. They are out of cash and should close their doors. But the Fed bails them out by granting them a loan. It's automatic. The bank telexes in a request and the computer automatically deposits the money electronically in their account. During the present crisis the number of banks falling to zero percent—or near zero percent—has gone from a dozen to a few hundred. It is no problem, because the Fed has unlimited funds to bail them out. In effect, the Fed is a juggler of money. Panic cannot spread because no bank ever has to close its doors unless it is in such bad shape that it cannot continue to do business. Starting tomorrow, the Fed in at least six of the twelve districts, will begin to have trouble with their computers. Many banks will simply run out of cash because the computer will not credit them when they make a request. When that happens, they will have to shut their doors. Not

387

just a few, but dozens. Maybe hundreds."

Svetlana Popov beamed at him. "There will be blood in the streets."

"Yes. And credit card companies are ceasing operations, which will make the demand for cash even greater. Stores will not want to extend credit. You are going to see some wonderful things. In the next few days—so long as Moscow keeps the pressure up."

"This is so wonderful for you. For all of us. A lifetime dream come true!"

George smiled. "If only we have enough time. Keep Moscow Central informed of everything you see or hear on the news."

"I will, Comrade General. They are sending a submarine to be stationed just off the coast in case you need to leave quickly."

"Let me know when they are in position."

"I will, Comrade General."

George smiled at her. "I think, when there are no other people around, you could call me George."

"George," she said with a smile. "And my friends call me Froggie."

George laughed. "You look nothing whatever like a frog."

"I used to hop around when I was a baby. My mother called me that."

"Well, Froggie. Since we have a busy day tomorrow destroying capitalism, perhaps we should get some sleep."

"I was hoping," she said, "we could first have some recreation. Or are you a strong believer in Directive 47?"

Directive 47 prohibited sexual encounters between officers of any rank. She undid three more buttons of her robe and pulled it down from her shoulders, exposing her breasts. They were smaller than he liked, but they looked firm and the nipples were large and red. She slid her hand over a breast and looked at him with filmy eyes.

388

George had a lump in his throat that felt about the size of an orange. He said, "I think, Lieutenant Popov, we best obey the rules."

A faint blush appeared on her cheeks. "Of course, Comrade General," she said, covering herself quickly. "May I go now?"

"Good night, Lieutenant."

As he was getting ready for bed, he wondered what Moscow Central would think when they read her report. They would think he was too old, perhaps. They would have a chuckle over it. Then again, maybe she just had a strong attraction to him. Maybe he stimulated her. He was, after all, a robust man, still in his prime.

No. She was under orders. She must have been told to come on to him, to test him. He had resisted, and now he was glad. It would look good in his file. And so close to retirement he would need all the good things in his file he could get.

On Saturday, November 17, Oscar was summoned by his case officer to report to the Israeli Consulate at once. He got the message from his answering service. Decoded, the message read: You are hereby ordered to report . . . He had never gotten such a strong summons before. Obviously someone was very angry.

He told them he'd be in as soon as he could get there. He sat back down at the table and said, "I've been summoned."

"By whom?"

"My superiors."

Catlyn said, "What do they want you for?"

"They've found out I went to the FBI, that's my guess. They want to put me on the hot seat and cook my pants off me." He tried to smile at his own joke, but couldn't.

He looked at the newspaper in front of him on the table.

The headline read: Hustead Takes Action On Money Crisis. The action taken was to give full emergency powers to George Corbett. Oscar felt ill. The press and government officials kept assuring the public that the Treasury, the Federal Deposit Insurance Corporation, and the Federal Reserve were guaranteeing every dollar of deposit in the United States and there was no need to give it a second thought. If a bank failed, it meant nothing. Every nickel would be refunded to the account holder. The article speculated that through government support of shaky financial institutions, the current crisis would soon pass. It was not possible to have 1929 all over again; solid mechanisms were in place to ensure that it couldn't happen and all the mechanisms were functioning perfectly.

Yet there were runs and riots all over the country, and at least three fire bombings of banks and savings and loans overnight. A gang, armed with automatic weapons, had assaulted a police station in Chicago.

"What will they do to you?" Catlyn asked. "I mean, your bosses."

"I wish I knew."

"Do they know about this apartment?"

"No. They're afraid that if the agents give out their home addresses and the consulate gets overrun or there's a mole, the agents will be compromised. You see, you never give out your real name, your real address, your real occupation, your real anything."

"You mean your name isn't Oscar Feldman?"

"Only temporarily."

"And you aren't really from Boston?"

"I've only been there twice."

"But the accent?"

"Part of the put-on Cat."

"I'm amazed."

"We're taught to lie even to a polygraph. The trick is to think two thoughts at once."

"It's like being in a maze of mirrors. No telling what's real and what isn't."

"After a while, you just accept illusion, deception, and fraud as the natural order of things. You begin to think of it as normal."

Catlyn poured him some more coffee. He had made the breakfast. The soft-boiled eggs were overcooked, the toast underdone, the orange juice watery, and the coffee too strong. He apologized; he had other things on his mind, he said, and he wasn't such a great cook anyway.

She looked at his face. He looked pale. His angular features were drawn, his eyes dull. He looked frightened.

"Will they kick you out?"

"They probably will."

"I'm sorry," Catlyn said. "I know how much it meant to you."

"That's funny. I didn't. I kept telling myself I wasn't really into it, just doing my bit. But now that they'll probably have me turn in my decoder ring and disappearing ink, I'm feeling really strange. I guess I'm one of them now, whether I like it or not."

He closed the newspaper and looked at his watch. "I'm going to check with Christian Able and see what they're doing about George Corbett." He called the FBI office and was told that Special Agent Able was on assignment on the West Coast and would not be back for six weeks. He asked the operator who was handling his case and was told it had been turned over to Group Supervisor Laurence Zobell, who was at the moment in Washington.

Oscar hung up the phone, staring into space.

"What is it?" Catlyn asked.

"The case has been turned over to someone else. I wonder if it's just possible that Mr. Corbett's tentacles are longer than we imagined."

Catlyn said, "I can·sense when a deck's been stacked. This one's stacked."

Oscar said, "What are we going to do about it?"

"By the time you get back from getting chewed out, I'll have something figured out."

"I have a feeling this is going to be one of those days I'll wish I'd stayed on the kibbutz."

TWENTY-EIGHT

Milo Agrippa was an Italian Jew who had not taken an Israeli name when he emigrated there as a young man in 1963, a fact that may have impeded his career. He was the least senior Mossad staff man at the New York consulate, though he was now in his late fifties. He was well built and balding, and Oscar often found him ill-tempered and sometimes stupid.

Agrippa spoke, surprisingly, with a faintly British accent, though he had never been to Britain. He'd learned English at the Army language school in Haifa. He was dark as an Arab and gestured with his hands like a Sicilian. He told Oscar they knew he'd been to the FBI an hour after he left. They knew who he went with, who he talked to, and how long he stayed. What they didn't know—yet—was what he'd said.

"I said what I said to Euripides two weeks ago in Tel Aviv."

"You told them you were with us?"

Oscar nodded. "Yes—otherwise they wouldn't have had any reason to believe me."

Agrippa's eyes went toward the ceiling. He gestured futilely with his hands. "By now Moscow Central is trying to locate our agent to find out how we know what we know. You may have just ruined a hell of a good deep penetration network. And you might have sent a few dozen or even a few hundred Jews or friends of Jews to the Gulag!"

"I was trying to save Israel's greatest ally from ruin!"

Agrippa clapped his hands and stood up, shoving them into his suit coat pockets. "You have sworn an oath to serve Israel and only Israel," he said with another elaborate gesture of disgust. "Americans," he fumed. "May the Lord save us."

"What are you going to do to me?" Oscar said, trying not to seem too meek.

"We have a room for you upstairs, Mr. Feldman. I have to contact Tel Aviv and file a full report. I want you to stay here where we know you won't get into any mischief. We'll see what Euripides wants to do with you. If it was up to me, you'd spend the next ten years shoveling sand at Muchad Prison."

Agrippa marched out of the little room. Oscar followed him into the hall. A curly-haired Marine was waiting for him.

"I'm to escort you upstairs, sir," the Marine said in Hebrew.

"Am I under arrest?" Oscar asked in English.

"I am to escort you," the Marine answered in Hebrew. "Call it what you will. This way, please."

The Marine took Oscar upstairs and down a long corridor. He was armed with a side arm, but it was in his holster. He walked just ahead of Oscar, with a brisk, military gait, his shoes squeaking on the tile floor. Outwardly Oscar didn't show a trace of how distressed he was, but his brain was in a fever. He was an American, and a Jew. He loved America. He loved Israel. For his entire life those loyalties were in concert; now they were in opposition.

He was ready to endure hardships, torture, even death for the state of Israel. But he was also prepared to endure hardships, torture, even death for America—if it ever came to that. He'd never thought of himself as a patriotic American. But then, America never seemed vulnerable before. It had always been strong and formidable. It certainly had never needed him as it did now.

Besides, patriotic Americans had tattoos and waved flags at parades, something he'd never done in his entire life.

He had already decided to ignore his orders from the Mossad when he went to the FBI in the first place. But in the back of his mind he had the idea that somehow he would talk his way out of that one. He'd blame it on bad judgment. An impulsive act. Euripides would have reprimanded him and given him a desk someplace, which would have been better than field work anyway.

For what he had a sudden impulse to do now, there would be no reprimand and no desk job. There would be a court-martial and maybe a prison cell.

The Marine stopped and opened a door with a set of keys. "Would you, ah, mind," Oscar said in clumsy, halting Hebrew, "would you, ah, mind, ah, stepping inside? I-I want to write a note for Mr. Agrippa."

"Please be brief, sir," the Marine said.

Oscar entered the room and held the door open for the Marine. When the Marine walked past him, Oscar shut the door with his right hand and reached out with his left arm, snaking it around the Marine's neck. The Marine dropped to his knees and pushed up against Oscar's elbow, the expected counter, but Oscar already had his other hand around the Marine's throat, closing off his carotid artery. In five seconds, the Marine's blood-starved brain called a halt to the proceedings and shut off. The Marine passed out.

Oscar checked him to make sure he was breathing. He'd come around in less than a minute. By that time Oscar planned to be back on the street.

Nicolai, in a cabbie's uniform and mirrored glasses, was sitting behind the wheel of a cab across the street when Oscar came dashing through the wooden front gate of the Israeli Consulate. He had seen him going in, but wasn't able to make a positive identification. Now he was certain.

Nicolai had been hanging around most of the night and all of the morning, even though it was a Saturday and the consulate was closed. His patience had paid off. He swung around hoping Oscar would summon his cab, but another cab rounded the corner at that moment and Oscar hailed it instead. Nicolai followed them down Forty-second Street. No big deal, just as easy to follow along.

Nicolai had gotten a dossier on Oscar through a contact in Peabody's old network and had picked up a not half-bad picture of him from a drop at Grand Central Station. It had been taken, he figured, at a training base in Israel. The mark was a bit thinner in the picture, and his hair was shorter, but it was him all right. Oscar Feldman, aka Roger Cohen, aka Maximilian Franks. Economics specialist. Nine months training in tradecraft. That made him a "daisy." In the trade, a daisy was a man with little training, so called because he wouldn't last long in the field. He'd be in a grave, pushing up daisies.

The mark, according to the dossier, was considered a genius in economic matters, but rated below the norm in field operations by his own supervisors. He was something of a loner. Given a class B clearance, he did not have access to anything remotely considered a state secret.

Like going fishing in a bathtub, Nicolai thought. Oscar Feldman, Jew economist, daisy, would soon be taken care of. And the woman. This troublesome Catlyn Cavanaugh. Then Nicolai could get back home and look at the news. The goddamn American system was coming apart and he wanted to watch every minute of it.

Nicolai kept his battered Checker cab a couple of car lengths back from the one Oscar was riding in. Lead me to Catlyn Cavanaugh, daisy, take me right to her door, Nicolai thought, and I'll be a Hero of the Soviet Union.

Nicolai wondered what the daisy's problem was. He'd seemed in a hell of a hurry when he'd come out of the consulate. Now he was sitting in the back of the cab looking around as if he was searching for a tail, but not just any tail. He wasn't paying any attention to Nicolai at all. He seemed to be expecting pursuit from the consulate, but there wasn't any. Probably in trouble with his own people. Maybe the daisy was a little paranoid. A hazard of the business. Nicolai had seen agents so jumpy they'd look under their beds before retiring for the night, afraid somebody might have planted a bomb.

The daisy settled down a bit as the cab headed up Broadway. Nicolai followed. What the hell, the guy was a daisy. All he had to do, he told himself, was relax and be patient. Opportunities would present themselves. The difference between a daisy and a pro was vast.

There were mobs of people in the street, angry mobs, clashing with police. Store windows were smashed out. People were running around with their arms full of loot. Nicolai felt his heart take a leap.

The daisy's cab pulled up in front of an old apartment building on Ninety-ninth and Riverside Drive. Nicolai drove down the block and parked in a no-parking zone next to a fire hydrant. The daisy paid the driver and went inside. Nicolai had a good view of the front of the place.

Now he figured all he had to do was wait for the daisy to come out and hail a cab; Nicolai would be right there to pick him up. Maybe he'd have Mark No. 2, the Cavanaugh woman, with him. Nicolai would pull up to the curb, they'd open the back door, and he'd say, "Where to, sir?" They'd tell him and he'd drive on. He'd wait until they'd settled into a conversation, then he'd head up some alley that didn't have anyone around and he'd stop and say the trunk was open. He'd get out, go to the rear of the cab, fiddle around, and when he got back to the driver's seat he'd let them have it.

He had a .38 Smith and Wesson snub nose with a silencer. Most guys in the trade, East and West, went for automatics. That was pretty much standard. He didn't like an automatic. They were faster, true, but he didn't trust them. Too many moving parts, too many things to go wrong. He preferred a revolver. Nice and reliable. And he liked the Smith and Wesson. Good craftsmanship. He loaded the .38 with hot loads and Teflon-coated bullets. Even if the targets were wearing bullet-protective shields under their clothing, Teflon would go right through. He figured he'd pump one each into their chests, then a couple insurance rounds into their heads.

Nobody would hear anything. If somebody popped out of a doorway at the wrong moment, they'd get a bullet, too.

It was bold, sure. But he was wearing mirrored glasses, and had his collar up, so nobody would recognize him. He figured he'd do the job someplace near a subway station and he'd pop in there and be gone in the crowd. The .38, which was absolutely untraceable, would be dropped into a trashcan. He was wearing skintight driving gloves, so there'd be no fingerprints, no powder on his skin. Once he was away from the scene, he'd be safe.

One hour went by. Then two. The daisy didn't come back out. Nicolai saw swarms of people carrying bags of groceries and stuff home—hoarders. The news on the radio was that supermarkets were selling out their shelves as fast as they could stock them. There were shortages of bread, milk, and toilet paper. Most markets were limiting the latter to two rolls per customer.

Every little while somebody would bang on his window and ask to use his cab. He just waved them away. If they persisted, he gave them the finger. He didn't like the gesture, but it was effective.

In mid-afternoon there was some kind of commotion at a bank up the block. Hordes of people were trying to force their way in all at the same time. Cops showed up and tried to push them back, but couldn't. Nicolai loved watching it. The people started hurtling rocks and bottles. Nicolai thought about the President's speech. So the deposits were insured. So what? People wanted to hold onto the crisp green bills themselves.

It was happening just as General Vlahovich had predicted! What a genius!

On the radio, a bulletin: A group calling itself the Manhattan Liberation Army had attacked a police station and released rioters being held there. The police suffered sixteen casualties in the attack; two of them had died, and a third was not expected to live. Nicolai was jubilant.

He got out of the cab to stretch his legs. He walked to the park across Riverside Drive. In New Jersey there were half a dozen fires burning, and he could hear police sirens in every direction and shots being fired—sporadic bursts. Automatic weapons? Could be. Toward Harlem, a huge black cloud was rising into the air. Ten, fifteen blocks, he figured, were on fire. He could smell the smoke now, actually smell America's funeral pyre!

Maybe it was all going to happen. Maybe a revolution would follow, just as George had predicted.

Nicolai went back to his cab. It was starting to snow, but he left his window down so he could listen to the sound of the sirens. What a wonderful sound, what music.

What did George—Brigadier Vlahovich—call it? U.S.S.A.—Socialist America! Nicolai wiped a tear from his eye.

A couple of minutes later an old blue Buick pulled up in front of the daisy's apartment building, let off a woman and a young pencil-thin Puerto Rican, and drove away. The woman's hair was dark brown and Nicolai could see she was built even with a trenchcoat on. Nicolai took the picture of Catlyn out of his pocket and studied it. He couldn't be sure, but he had a hunch it was her. He got out of the cab to get a closer look.

The woman and the Puerto Rican stood on the sidewalk for a couple of minutes arguing. The Puerto Rican was pointing as if he wanted to go into the building and she was shaking her head. Finally the Puerto Rican gave up and started off down the street. The woman stood there watching him before she headed up the stairs and into the building. She let herself in with a key.

Nicolai was right behind her, catching the door before she let it close. She turned to look at him. "You Mrs. Kline?" he asked.

"No."

"I got a cab for Mrs. Kline. Okay if I wait for her here? All this crap happening on the streets, you can't feel safe."

"I'm sure it'd be okay."

The apartment lobby was surfaced with small octagonal-shaped tiles with gold inlay, which gave it a sort of men's room feel. It was old now, and grimy. There were two elevators and a stairway at the other end of the lobby. A desk had a sign that said, "All visitors must sign in," but there was no place to sign. Nicolai figured the black surveillance camera above the desk was a fake.

The woman was waiting for the elevator, watching Nicolai with a neutral expression on her face. He was certain it was Catlyn Cavanaugh now and he considered for a moment just doing the job on her on the spot. But then he wouldn't get the Jew economist, and he had orders to get them both. He wanted them both at once.

He stood there relaxed, chewing gum, his hands in his jacket, looking stupid like all New York cabbies, he thought. The woman got into the elevator and went up. Nicolai noticed just before the door closed that she was keeping both hands in her coat pockets and he wondered whether she was carrying a gun. If she was, he figured he couldn't take the safe way and go for the chest; he'd have to take the risk and go for a head shot instead. That was okay; he wouldn't miss up to fifty feet. He was very good with weapons.

He watched the indicator above the elevator door. It went to the fourteenth floor. He smiled. He'd found the daisy's hideout.

Nicolai stuffed paper in the front door lock so it wouldn't close and went outside to check the residents on the fourteenth floor: Turner, Cohen, Smith-Hampton, Mitsumoto, Juzuski. Could be any of them. Cohen was one of the daisy's trade names. Maybe, just maybe, he was using it here.

Okay, now what? He considered returning to the cab for an M-16 he had in the trunk. He figured he could go down to the basement and clip the phone junction box and knock out all the phones in the building. Then he'd go up and kill everyone on the floor. But he didn't like that plan. Too messy. Besides, somebody might cry out and alert the Jew economist and the woman. Even a daisy was dangerous with a gun.

Instead he'd go up to apartment 4-A where the directory said the manager lived. The manager ought to know which apartment the daisy lived in. The easy way was always to ask.

Nicolai pressed the button to summon the elevator, keeping his hand on the grip of his .38. Nicolai was a cautious man. His heart was doing a regular polka in his chest and he could feel his pulse in his neck. His whole body tingled with excitement. It was a peculiar high, better than any damn drug, drink, woman, anything.

He was becoming giddy on it. That and the fear. The fear put an edge on the high. The elevator came down and he stepped in and pushed the button for the fourth floor.

401

He remembered the last time. Rita Montgomery. Nice-looking woman. Nice body. Big brown eyes, pleading. He remembered sticking the gun between her breasts—just beneath them—feeling the barrel slip into the little crevice below the heart. He'd pointed it upward and remembered pulling the trigger with her looking right in his eyes and he saw the flash go through her head the instant death entered her. She had been scared. Scared and awed at the same time.

And he'd felt a tremendous jolt of feeling go through him. A feeling of godlike power. Seeing her on the ground. Not moving. Not breathing. Eyes as blank as pieces of quartz.

He hadn't stuck around to see the old man shovel the lime on top of her and push the dirt in the hole. She was a beautiful woman and that part of it was a shame. If only she'd done what she was told. Didn't she know that's what the whole thing was all about? Everybody had a job to do and everyone had to do it without squawking about it.

He got out on the fourth floor, went down the hall, and knocked at the door of 4-A. A moment later a little eyeball appeared through the hole.

"Yeah?" a man asked.

"Need some help," Nicolai said. "A guy left something in my cab. I went after him, but I couldn't catch up with him. He got off the elevator on the fourteenth floor."

The door opened. Nicolai found himself face to face with a white-haired man with suspenders and a cigar stuck in his mouth.

"What this guy look like?" the manager asked.

"Tall, kind of on the thin side, bony features. A woman was with him."

"Cohen, his name is. How'd you get in the building?"

"Somebody was coming out just as I was coming in."

The old man's eyes narrowed. He looked Nicolai over, up and down. "How about showing me some ID?"

Nicolai shrugged. "I got my license down in the hack. What's the fucking deal, you think I'm gonna rob you? When I'm gonna rob a place I don't go knocking on the manager's door."

"We're into the neighborhood crime watch program, anybody comes in the building we want to know who they are. Now let's see some ID or I'm calling a cop."

The man's face had turned pink, with blue lines of webbing all over it.

"Okay," Nicolai said, smiling affably. "I think I got something here that'll identify me." He jerked the .38 out of his hidden holster. The old man's red face suddenly turned as white as typing paper. He staggered back and started to speak, but only a few syllables came out: "Ah-ah-ah-ah . . ."

Nicolai pulled the trigger. *Puttt.* The man's cigar came flying out of his mouth. A splotch of blood appeared on the man's shirt a few inches above his belt buckle. He dropped to his knees, holding his hand over the spot where the bullet had entered. Blood ran between his fingers. He looked down with a dazed expression on his face. Then he looked at Nicolai for a moment before he fell over onto his side.

Nicolai looked up and down the hallway. No one in sight. He stepped into the manager's apartment and closed the door. The apartment was tiny. Living room, bedroom, bath. He took a quick look around. Nobody else there. He checked the manager's pulse at the carotid artery. There was none. He examined the bullet hole. He'd been aiming a little higher. If he had hit the heart, the man would have been dead before he met the floor. Sloppy work. He looked at the exit hole in the man's back. Hardly bigger than the entry hole. The bullet had carried on through and gone into the windowsill.

He opened the barrel on the .38, picked out the spent cartridge, dropped it into his pocket, and reloaded the gun. Then he removed the manager's keys from his belt. There was so many, he figured there would have to be one to Cohen's place.

"You should have minded your own business," he said to the manager's corpse.

Nicolai went back down the hall to the elevator. He noticed how relaxed he felt, completely at ease. His hand was steady. No cold sweat. The time he did a wet job in Philly—his very first—he remembered how he wanted to throw up. He'd fought it, and managed to keep his dinner down.

He noticed that the elevator he'd seen go to the fourteenth floor was still up there. That was odd. But in an old building like this one, the elevators were always getting stuck. Sometimes tenants would push the stop button and hold the elevator on their floor if they were going right back down. He pushed the button to summon the other elevator.

He put the manager's keys in his pocket and kept his hand on the grip of his .38. The elevator door opened. He stepped aboard and pushed the button for fourteen. A woman reading a thick paperback novel rode with him as far as ten. He wondered whether she'd heard there was a financial panic going on. She just kept her nose in the book as if she wasn't aware of it. Then again, New Yorkers were always facing some kind of crisis or other. Garbage strikes, subway strikes, muggers. It was like living a nightmare.

He pushed the button for fourteen again. The door closed and he continued up alone.

Soon, he thought warmly, the revolution would cure all that.

The ancient elevator creaked and groaned as it made its way up with jerks and starts. Then suddenly he heard a noise above him. He looked up. The trapdoor was open a crack.

The light flickered. The elevator stopped. Trapped! He threw himself back against the wall and pulled his gun, firing six quick shots through the ceiling: pfffftttttttttttttttt.

404

Silence. The smell of spent powder was strong in the darkness of the elevator. Nicolai reached into his pocket for more bullets, but then he heard movement above and saw the muzzle of a dart gun and felt the sting on his neck.

Feverishly, he shoved a bullet into the cylinder of his gun, snapped it shut, and pulled the hammer back. Already his vision was blurring. They had him. They'd make him talk. They'd squeeze everything out of him. Torture . . . Duty said never talk, never give up, never be taken. Never.

He put the gun in his mouth and felt the cold steel against his teeth. The strength was going out of him quickly. He squeezed the trigger and thought: done in by a damn daisy, isn't that a bitch?

TWENTY-NINE

The only thing bothering George was that he had not heard from Nicolai. Other than that, things were going exceptionally well. Even Catlyn Cavanaugh and her boyfriend seemed to have stopped making trouble and just disappeared. Maybe Nicolai had gotten rid of them and had not yet reported in. George was beginning to think that all the worrying he had done about her was for nothing. Soon the complete collapse would come and he'd be safely away and then it wouldn't matter anymore.

The only other thing he was worried about was his family. When the trouble began, Linda had refused to leave the United States. She was an American and would stick it out. But she did agree to take Rudolf to the cottage. At George's insistence, she took along two armed guards. George knew the cottage wasn't absolutely safe, because once civil disturbances got started there was no way to know how far they would spread. But it was remote enough, he hoped, to offer safe refuge. At least Linda and Rudolf were out of New York City, which very well might be burned to the ground.

Svetlana Popov came over to George's apartment at six o'clock Sunday morning. Zobell had squelched the FBI probe completely, she said. From here on out, there should be nothing in his way. Her eyes shone with admiration for George.

George kept his businesslike composure. There was still much to do and he didn't want to be whistling tunes of glory before the job was done.

He dictated a report to her which he wanted forwarded to Moscow Central. He told her he wanted the dollar to continue to fall and the pressure kept up any way possible on the Western and Japanese bankers so they would not buy dollars.

Lieutenant Popov said, "Our people all over the world are exerting utmost pressure, by any means they can, to ensure that no one supports the dollar. That includes the bankers, the ministers, everyone. We're using all means of persuasion possible. Priority orders."

George knew that meant coercion, blackmail, physical force, drugs, anything and everything.

Svetlana Popov continued. "Only the West Germans and the British are making a token effort to support the dollar. We are also using our Directors of Information to see to it that the media is flooded with the direst predictions of a world economic collapse—being careful of course to blame everyone except the Federal Reserve."

"Good." George poured them both a tall glass of orange juice.

"We've also been putting pressure on the governments more directly, including threatening to cut off the natural gas supplies on which most of Western Europe depends. They are beginning to sense that the Soviet Union is about to become the most dominant nation in the history of the world—the new Rome—and they want to do nothing to upset their relations with it."

"Very good—very *very* good. The bandwagon effect."

"We've sent signals to the Japanese Red Brigades operating there to begin bombings. We hope it will focus Japan's attention on their troubles and away from the international monetary crisis."

"No one will care if America's boat is sinking if their own is on fire. Can I fix you some eggs?" She nodded. George shut his eyes. "It's going exactly as planned! Exactly!"

"So far," Lieutenant Popov said, "America's allies have been even less inclined to help than we thought they would. It's almost as if they are rejoicing in America's difficulties. At the moment of crisis it is common for nation-states to think of their own self-interest, even though in the long run, if they analyzed it, they would know that if America goes down, the whole capitalist world goes down with her. By the time they wake up . . ."

"They will have a new master—us!" George interrupted. "What kind of toast would you like? Never mind, I don't have any bread. My dear Lieutenant Popov, things could not be going better! Everything is going our way. The few at the Fed who suspect me, I've managed to cower. Preston is suspicious, but he knows I'm tight with the President and won't go any further than he has. But by next Thursday—Thanksgiving—it won't matter, what we've started will be irreversible. I have arranged for the computers to stop functioning. That will mean banks in most of the country will be unable to get emergency funds. Already their cash reserves are depleted; this will finish them off. The President's call to be calm has not worked. The civil disorders can do nothing but grow and grow. The Army will be called out, but will not be able to stop it."

Lieutenant Popov toasted George with her glass of orange juice. "By the weekend we shall both be back in our homeland, I shall be a colonel and you shall be a major general, at the very least!"

He cracked some eggs onto a hot Teflon pan. Going home. Home to that strange and wonderful country. The prospect gave him a sudden chill. Free of all the subterfuge at last. But then what? Would Linda go with him? And what about Rudolf? Poor, poor, misunderstood American-as-apple-pie Rudolf. How would Rudolf think of his father? As a hero? Not likely. No, he'd think of him as a traitor. That thought gave George a shiver.

"You're burning the eggs, George!"

George turned the heat down quickly. "So many things on my mind . . . They're not ruined, just a little crispy around the edge."

He put the eggs on the plate and cut up an orange. He put water on for coffee. Then they sat down to eat.

"What is your next step?" she asked.

"Today should be glorious. The President, his chief economic adviser, the treasury secretary, and I are going to be on television to reassure everyone that the crisis has peaked and order in the financial world has been restored and that peace and harmony are returning. The President and his advisers think this is the thing to do. They think I'm a great communicator. But I will be so nervous and tongue-tied that everyone will be able to tell there *is* something to worry about. I will say one thing, but my gestures and mannerisms will betray me."

"Good, Comrade General, good."

"And then, right after, I will play perhaps the biggest trump card of them all! Wait and see, you will be amazed at the power of human speech. This afternoon, one of the most trusted people on this planet will in effect stand up in a crowded theater and yell 'fire'!"

"I do not understand, Comrade General."

"I am rolling out my secret weapon. What is more powerful, a hydrogen bomb or a television set? Then pen, they say, is mightier than the sword. Hah! A television is mightier than missiles! This afternoon you will see!"

* * *

At ten after nine that Sunday morning, November 18, the telephone on Carson Black's bedside table rang. Carson was still asleep, the drapes pulled tight against the morning sunlight. She'd been drinking heavily the night before and hadn't slept well.

She had been assigned the financial crisis segments at the end of the show, which meant doing a lot of taped interviews with international bankers, financiers, government economists, and politicians. She'd never worked so hard in her life. Every day, all day. The Nielsen people had said that ninety-five million people were relying on her for the straight facts about the current crisis, the highest ratings for a nightly news show in history. They wanted her to do a special Sunday edition of her show that night, right after the President and his people went on. She figured the ringing phone had something to do with that.

She rolled over and picked the phone up. "Carson Black speaking."

"Good morning," a woman's voice said. "This is Lydia Wickham."

"Yes, Lydia?" Carson felt her heart flutter.

The woman on the other end of the line said, "We're having a party tonight, can you come?"

Carson sat upright, feeling a surge of anticipation. "Say again, please."

"This is Lydia Wickham. We're having a party tonight, would you like to come?"

This was it, Carson thought. This was what she'd been waiting for. "I'll be there!" she said.

There was, of course, not going to be any party. This was a message from George Corbett. "Thanks, Lydia, thanks ever so much!" Carson hung up the phone.

She went to her mirror and looked at herself. Bags under her eyes, eyeliner smudged, hair a tangle. She made a face, sticking out her tongue. "The real fucking you, babe," she said to the image in the mirror, "is about to be let out of the cage."

She broke out in laughter, leapt up, and did a few twirling dance steps around the room. Then she headed for the shower.

Twenty minutes later she was on her way to the studio in her Porsche. She was wearing a bright red dress, which she had never worn to the studio before, but what better color to wear on such a day! The producer would want her to change it, but she could convince him easily that a bright red dress would be different. It would get people's attention, and maybe help to lift their spirits. The producer believed in advocacy news—that they weren't there only to entertain and inform, but to help create a just society as well. He'd never actually come out and said it, but she knew that's what he felt. He was a crusader.

Well, so was she.

There were police and units of the Maryland National Guard in the streets everywhere. Carson was stopped twice and asked for identification. All unnecessary travel had been banned for the duration of the "state of emergency." America was now a police state. And a police state was the easiest kind to overthrow.

Most businesses were closed. Carson could see vast columns of black smoke rising into the sky. It looked as if most of Baltimore and half of Washington were on fire. She drove over the bridge and into Washington. Debris clogged the streets, and crowds of people were challenging the police. Protesters gathered at almost every intersection with placards calling for President Hustead to resign.

As she drove up Rhode Island Avenue, Carson saw hundreds of store windows boarded up. Police on foot and horseback patroled every block. On every radio station there were news programs, reports, and official pleas for calm. The price of gold on the London gold exchange reached five thousand dollars that morning. Gold was rising against the dollar by hundreds of dollars per *hour*. Experts were predicting the dollar would be nearly valueless within a few days. Carson was bubbling with joy. The rate of exchange with the mark was once four marks to one dollar. It was now sixty dollars to the mark! She pulled into the parking lot of her station and parked in her spot near the door. There were two dozen security guards on duty. They were armed now; they hadn't been before.

She went in looking as grim as possible.

Her producer came flying into her office a few moments after she arrived. Malcolm Kremm had once been a presidential speech writer, later a press secretary, then he'd walked in the back door of the TV news business, starting near the top. He was a big man with curly black hair and a long face, which was showing signs of fatigue. He'd been sleeping in his office and hadn't changed his clothes in days.

"I'm glad you're in early, Carson. The President and some of his people are going on in two hours. We'll want you on directly afterward to explain things to the viewers, they trust you more than they trust them. Okay, how's that sound?"

"Fine, Malcolm. Has there been any *good* news? On the way over here I was listening to the radio—all that was on was more gloom and doom."

"Nothing. Rioting, looting, burning. The country's gripped in panic. The National Guard is fighting pitched battles in the black ghettos. I just can't believe this is happening."

"I can't either," she said, trying to seem bewildered.

"You'll be ready to go on as soon as the President is finished?"

"I'll be ready."

"The dress is a little loud."

"It's right for the occasion."

412

He wasn't going to argue about it.

After her producer left, she sat at her makeup table trying to restrain herself from laughing. Surrounded by fools, she thought. Well, wasn't she going to wake them up now?

Carson Black spent the next couple of hours in her office on the phone and reading telex messages and wire service reports, trying to look busy. It was beginning to dawn on her what a monumental thing she was about to do. She was the most trusted news voice in America since Walter Cronkite. Upwards of ninety million people would be watching her and listening to every word she said. And, boy, was she ever going to give them an earful!

President Hustead came on at noon. Carson went back to her dressing room to watch. He was with George Corbett, James A. Preston, the chief economist, and Tim McAfee, the secretary of the treasury. The President looked worn out, Carson thought. George looked as if he didn't quite know what he was doing there. Preston looked mad. And McAfee looked scared.

This, Carson thought, is going to be good.

The President did his best to put on a happy face. He was the first to speak. He stated that strong action was now being taken. He said looting would not be tolerated. Order was being restored in those areas where strife had broken out. He said there was no reason to hoard, that hoarded goods were subject to confiscation . . .

Carson thought: Good. He's giving them the hard line.

The next speaker was Tim McAfee, who talked about how it was not possible that the dollar would ever be valueless. He said that wild rumors and dishonest newspeople were making self-fulfilling predictions, that if people would only stop trying to draw their money out of banks, every bank in this country would be safe . . .

Carson thought: No one's buying it. It sounded too simplistic, and the American people had long been suspi-

413

cious of simplistic answers.

Now it was James A. Preston's turn. His message was that there had been panics in the past and there would be panics in the future; it was the nature of a free economy. The economy would soon right itself, so all Americans had every reason to see a stable and prosperous future ahead . . .

Carson thought: He's saying it with his mouth, but in his eyes there's a lot of doubt. Platitudes and bromides won't do it.

At last it was George's turn. He stepped up to the microphone, smiling feebly. He began by saying that the world's monetary system had taken a jolt, and that it wasn't only happening in America. He said it appeared at the moment that things were beginning to stabilize and promised an end to the current crisis by the end of the week . . .

Carson thought: Short, sweet, and stupid. Just right.

George was a genius at saying one thing and conveying an opposite message with his manner and tone. Anyone listening to him would lose all confidence, yet George couldn't be faulted because he appeared to be trying so hard.

Now it would be Carson's turn. George was still finishing up, taking questions from reporters. There would be a short news update and a few minutes of local station activity. Carson walked to the makeup room where they brushed her hair quickly and put the finishing touches on her face. Malcolm Kremm was waiting for her there.

"You have any idea what you're going to say?" he asked.

"Yes."

"Would you mind telling me?" He had a clipboard ready to take notes.

"You'll just have to wait with the rest of the nation," she said with a deadpan expression.

His nostrils flared. "This isn't standard procedure," he said. "We have to know where to break, and we also have to

414

know if what you're about to say is within management guidelines. You know how careful we have to be during a crisis."

"I'll signal the director when he can break. As for the rest of it, go censor your asshole if you want to censor something."

"Damn it, Carson, this is no time for you to get weird on me!"

"But with ninety million viewers waiting, you're not going to do anything about it, are you?"

He looked at her for a moment. "No," he said at last, "I guess I'm not."

"Then why don't you go get lost?" she said.

He started out the door, then stopped suddenly and turned to her. "You're not on anything, are you?"

"I'm high, all right, but it's not dope. No, it's something quite different."

The director knocked on her door a few minutes later. Carson had butterflies in her stomach. When was the last time she had butterflies? She stood up. She seemed to be floating. At last she was coming into her own; finally she could drop her mask. Now the *real* Carson would emerge!

She walked down the hall and into the studio. The usual people were there: the sound people, the cameramen, the director, and all the assistants. The producer was up in the control booth. She liked to give her commentaries sitting on a tall stool on a barren stage, usually holding a notebook. Today, she preferred to stand. She told the cameramen to come in slowly.

"One minute, Carson," the director said. A digital clock over the control booth clicked down. Her legs felt heavy and the butterflies seemed to have increased their activity. The number one camera moved in close and turned on. Carson paused for a moment, then stiffened and said:

"Ladies and gentlemen, friends. It is with great trepidation that I greet you this afternoon. As you know, these past several days I have been covering the current crisis in the financial world—a crisis which worsens by the hour if not by the minute. After studying every facet of the crisis, and having spoken to experts of every stripe, I feel it is my moral duty to give this warning: the assurances given to you today by the administration that the government is backing every bank deposit in the country is a smoke screen. The truth of the matter is, there are plans afoot at this very moment to pay back only ten percent on the dollar now, and ten percent in ninety days, to depositors of defunct banks, and nothing thereafter. There is not enough cash in existence to back up every dollar unless dollars are printed on toilet paper. I myself went to my bank today and drew out every cent. I feel it is my duty as an honest observer to tell you this, and I hope each and every one of my viewers will act to save what they can for themselves and their families."

There was a general hubbub off camera and the producer in the booth cut off the broadcast. He came running out of the booth screaming, "Do you know what you've done? Our network will be ruined! The country will be ruined!"

Carson Black said, "Just telling it like it is, Malcolm, telling it like it is . . ."

George Corbett thought he'd performed rather well for the TV cameras, looking something like a general facing defeat in war trying to put on a brave front. Back in his apartment with Svetlana Popov he watched clips from the show which were being replayed on all four networks. The clips were followed by shots of fires burning in several sections of New York, Watts, Chicago's West Side, Cincinnati, and Detroit, and a gun battle at a Memphis police station. Bombs were going off all over the nation, and everywhere there were protest marches and riots.

The networks did not show clips of Carson Black's

speech; all they would say was that she had "inadvertently" triggered mass rioting and looting. Governors of sixteen states had declared martial law. College campuses were being closed everywhere, airline flights shut down due to bomb scares, trains derailed. Power lines were being hit all over the country. Half the phones were out. On the West Coast terrorists had blown up bridges and attacked a National Guard armory in San Francisco.

George poured some brandy for Svetlana Popov and himself. They smiled at each other and danced around the room arm in arm. George had never felt so much joy in his life. They were toasting and dancing, then suddenly he was kissing her, sliding his hands down her back . . .

George stopped suddenly. Was he crazy? This woman was a KGB lieutenant, his link to Moscow Central. This was not the person to get amorous with.

"I have done something wrong?" Svetlana asked, her big filmy blue eyes looking up at him.

"This is craziness," he said.

"Isn't it?" she said, putting her arms around his neck and kissing him deeply. He felt a charge of electricity clear down to his toes.

"Craziness and stupid," he said, kissing her back.

"I agree completely, Comrade General," she said.

Somehow he had lifted her up. She was like a feather, and he was kissing her, and then they drifted into the bedroom.

"What the hell are we doing here?" Rudolf asked.

"I told you already, Rudolf," his mother said.

"Tell me again, I'm thick."

"Your father says with all this turmoil he wants us to be safe."

They were at the cottage in the Catskills, accompanied by two heavily armed men from the Weston Security Service

417

Company. One entire bedroom was full of food and survival gear, including two rifles and ammunition, kerosene stoves, a portable generator, and warm clothing. And it looked as if they would be needing all of it, because the entire Northeast had been blacked out since Monday noon. It was now later Tuesday. The Niagra power transmission lines had been blown up.

Rudolf said, "What the hell does he want us safe from?"

"I've explained it as best I can, Rudolf." Linda went back to the kitchen to rearrange the cupboards.

Rudolf wandered over to the window and looked out on the lake, half covered with ice. It was gray and gloomy, and a thin covering of snow lay dirty on the ground. Most of the cottages around were occupied now, as more and more people were abandoning the cities. Rudolf, though, had found things in the city exciting. Before his mother had come with the two security guys and taken him out of school, he'd been planning to go along with a couple of friends to do a little roaming around the streets; maybe somebody'd leave a door open they shouldn't have. And now what? He was stuck here with two dumb-ass security guards and his mother. What a drag.

"Okay if I go for a little walk?" he asked.

"One of the men will go with you."

Rudolf put on a sweater and a windbreaker and a pair of boots. He'd just had his hair frizzed out so his head looked like cotton candy. His mother had taken one look and called him an idiot.

Rudolf started down the trail that led around the lake; it was well beaten down with footprints. It was sunny and the snow was melting. Rudolf considered himself a city guy. He lit a cigarette. He didn't like to smoke around his mother, didn't like her staring at him like a goddamn criminal.

God, he wished he had some grass or a toot of snow.

He came around a bend in the trail and found a woman sitting on a bench. She was not bad-looking for maybe

418

thirty-five or forty. Dark brown hair. She looked up and smiled at him.

"You're George Corbett's boy, aren't you?"

"Who are you?"

"Name's Cat. Mind if I walk along with you, Rudolf?"

He glanced back at the security man, who was lagging behind by about thirty yards, watching them with a bored expression. The guard's brown uniform coat was unbuttoned, and his pot belly was folded over his belt. He was armed with a large revolver worn high on his right hip.

Catlyn walked beside Rudolf, her hands in the pockets of her slacks. She was wearing a kerchief and a red car coat. They passed a few cottages by the lake. Some men were arguing on a porch. A couple of them had shotguns.

"Your friends call you 'Shuck,' don't they?" Catlyn said.

"Yes, how did you know? My parents don't even know that."

"I know quite a bit about you."

"I don't think I've ever seen you around here before."

"I've done some business with your father."

"Dear old dad." Rudolf kicked a chunk of snow.

Catlyn took a deep breath of fresh air. "Can I ask you something, Rudolf?"

"Were you waiting for me back there?"

"As a matter of fact, I was."

"How come you didn't come up to the cabin?"

"I didn't want your mother to see me."

He looked back at the guard. He was still there, strolling along with his hands in his pockets and the big gun on his hip.

"I ain't done nothing," Rudolf said.

"I'm not the police or anything, Rudolf. I'm just a friend who has a favor to ask you." They were walking up a small hill, where the trail left the lake and went through an orchard. The trees were barren and, Rudolf thought, forlorn-looking. There were no more cabins for half a mile or so.

Catlyn continued. "I want to ask you something very important, both to you and to your country."

"What are you talking about?"

"This nation has never before faced a panic like this one. It's very severe. You can help your country get out of this mess, Rudolf."

"I can? How?"

"By coming with me and pretending to be kidnapped."

"How's that going to help anything?"

"I'll tell you straight out. Your father is involved with the people who have brought about this crisis."

He glared at her. "Listen lady, you're cuckoo in the head. My father is chairman of the friggin' Federal Reserve Board. He's a big muckety-muck in the government. What the hell you trying to pull?"

He glanced back; the security man was gone. Disappeared. There was another man standing in his place.

"That's Oscar," Catlyn said. "He didn't hurt the guard. He knocked him out with a drug."

"What the fuck's going down?" There was fear in his voice now.

"Since Carson Black, the newswoman, announced that the banks weren't safe, panic has hit every community in the country. I have reason to believe she is working for your father."

"You're really nutso, know that, lady?"

"I'm afraid, Rudolf, you're going to have to come along and help us whether you want to or not."

He glanced back at Oscar. "You gonna hurt me?"

"We aren't going to hurt you, Rudolf. If you're with us, your father will stop trying to hurt this country and he'll come over to our side."

"Hey, wait a minute here. How the hell do I know you're not just giving me an ole ring-a-ding jobby here? How the fuck do I know *you* ain't with the fucking bad guys?"

"We wouldn't need you, Rudolf, the country's already shot to hell."

He looked at her, bewildered for a moment, then said, "Wait'll the kids at school hear about I've been kidnapped, it'll blow their fucking minds to the fucking max!"

THIRTY

Telephone service at Fed headquarters was sporadic and getting worse. Military communications people were installing microwave transmitters aimed at the White House, the Emergency Riot Control Center, and the Treasury, but they weren't yet in service. George kept exhorting everyone to keep money flowing out as quickly as possible, but the panic that gripped the country had gripped everyone at the Fed as well, and things were a shambles. Most of the staff were not coming to work, and the rest were exhausted from working nearly around the clock. George had successfully sabotaged the computer system which had been doing all transfers of funds, and now they had to be done by hand, an almost impossible task. Armored trucks carrying cash from central depositories were escorted by tanks, and still they were held up by angry mobs.

As the situation worsened hourly, the messages from the White House and the Treasury became more and more confused and contradictory. As far as anyone could tell, George was doing everything he could to comply, but there was nothing that anyone could do. That was obvious. The entire financial structure of the so-called Free World was crumbling, and all anyone could do now was sit back and watch it crumble.

Throughout most of Wednesday, the Fed headquarters building was ringed by protesters, who hurled rocks and bottles intermittently, then regrouped and made speeches through bullhorns. A few hundred riot-equipped policemen kept them at bay, but the crowd was growing, and their mood was getting angrier. They were waving large red banners and George's spirit soared when he saw them, even though he kept muttering "Goddamn Communists" whenever anyone was in his office.

The mob was finally dispersed by Army units which showed up at three in the afternoon and drove them back three blocks, past Jefferson Drive, on the other side of the Smithsonian. Most of the Fed employees watched from the windows and clapped and cheered.

At five that evening, George went back to his apartment accompanied by two armed bodyguards. The sky was black with smoke. A block away he could see a long column of tanks heading north, toward Baltimore, where it was rumored the rioting was intense. There were only a few cars on the streets, no buses. Army and National Guard vehicles were everywhere. He had to wait for two groups of marchers on their way to the White House. They were accompanied by long lines of National Guardsmen wearing face and chest protectors, and carrying clubs.

At George's apartment, the power flickered on and off. From the window he could see fires up the Potomac. He guessed it might be an oil refinery. The flames were leaping almost half a mile into the sky. A few dozen men with a few gallons of gasoline and a pack of matches could cause a hell of a lot of destruction, he thought. He could feel the warmth of the fire in his soul.

George poured himself a little cognac, sat down in his easy chair, and watched the TV flicker on and off. He wished Svetlana Popov could be with him, but all consular staff people were ordered to their embassies. Two TV and two radio stations had been taken over by "liberation forces," and were proclaiming a "people's republic," and so far the Army and police swat teams hadn't been able to recapture the stations. Rebel announcers were calling for the President to turn the country over to a revolutionary council, which included Carson Black, a radical California lawyer, and a black preacher from Philadelphia—all three George's protégés. George was beaming.

George didn't think the government was ready to hand over power. But still, all this in just a couple of weeks! America was on her knees and bleeding. A few more blows would send her into death throes. Perhaps, he thought, if he persuaded the President that the only thing to do was to give in, that history had turned against them . . . Yes, he would go to the White House first thing in the morning. If the President just sat down and talked with the revolutionary council, it would legitimize their demands, and pitch the country into more delicious confusion.

A knock came at the door. He hoped it was Svetlana. He had discovered that morning that she was not only a great officer and true professional, but she was also the greatest piece of ass he had ever had. Not counting Esther, who was truly the greatest on earth. He went to the door and asked, "Who is it?"

"It's me, your wife."

"Linda!" He opened the door. She stood before him, pale and shaking. George said, "Come in, darling, what is it?"

"Rudolf's gone," she said.

"Hold on here, where did he go?"

"Kidnapped. They grabbed him at the lake yesterday. I tried to get you all day, but the phones have been out. I managed to get a police escort all the way. You can't imagine what's happening out there. Newark is burning. The tunnels are closed, the bridges are out. I had to come down the Jersey shore. Power poles down."

"Take it easy," he said. "Sit down, have a drink. I'm sure

Rudolf will be all right. He's probably just run off some-place again. He's not the most reliable person in the world—as you've been fond of telling me for years."

"No, George, you don't understand. Somebody drugged one of the guards, knocked him out with some kind of little dart."

Then it was true, George thought. He slumped down on the couch.

Linda poured herself some cognac, then she paced nervously up and down the room. George sat rubbing his face with his hands. He said, "Who's got him? Why'd they take Rudolf?"

"One of the kidnappers was a woman, the guard told me. She had dark brown hair, mid-thirties. She left no demands or anything. There must have been at least two of them. What do they want, George?"

"It must have something to do with my duties at the Federal Reserve, don't you think?" His thoughts were swimming around. It could be the Cavanaugh woman and the Israeli agent. But why would they kidnap Rudolf? That wouldn't get them anything. They wanted revenge, not ransom money. No, it had to be someone else.

An idea suddenly hit him. If drugged darts were used, it had to be somebody who knew what he was doing and had access to the equipment. The Israeli agent? The KGB? Had Moscow ordered Rudolf taken to ensure that George's mission would be fulfilled? If so, why hadn't they told him?

It had to be the KGB. They wanted insurance. They didn't trust him. He started to relax. They wouldn't hurt Rudolf. They would just hold him until the current crisis was played out to the last penny. It was typical of them to want additional guarantees. George began to feel a little better.

"What are you thinking, George?"

"I don't think Rudolf's in any danger. Not really. And I

can't say why I think so right at the moment."

Linda poured herself some more cognac.

Then the phone rang. But the phones were out. It would have to be someone in the building. George went to the phone, thinking: This must be Svetlana calling to say that Rudolf was all right. George promised himself that if she had anything to do with it, he would dedicate himself to ruining her career.

He picked up the receiver. "George Corbett."

A woman's voice said, "We have Rudolf."

It wasn't Svetlana. A sharp pain went through George's chest. "W-who is this?"

"Catlyn Cavanaugh—I'm sure you remember me. The assassin you sent to find me is dead. Now we have your son. If you don't do exactly as I tell you, we—we'll leave that to your imagination. It will not be pleasant."

George took a deep breath. The walls seemed to be floating. In his mind's eye he saw Rudolf being cut up with a chain saw and stuck in a garbage can, like Park had done to the woman who had worked in his office. A wave of nausea overcame him for a moment.

"You hear me, Mr. Corbett?"

"I hear you." George looked over at Linda, who was waiting expectantly. "It's going to be all right," he said to Linda. Then, into the phone, he said, "I remember who you are, but I don't know anything about an assassin."

"Time is very short, Mr. Corbett. Come downstairs, I'm waiting for you in the lobby."

George felt his throat close up. He looked over toward Linda again, who was standing still as a fence post, holding her breath.

To Catlyn, he said, "I, ah, don't know what you think I've done, but I assure you, I don't know anything about an assassin."

"All right, Mr. Corbett, play dumb. Your kid is dead."

"No . . . wait! All right, all right, I'll do what you say.

I'll be right down! Don't kill him, please!"

George hung up the phone. "Some very bad people have Rudolf," he said to Linda. He swallowed. "They intend to do very bad things to him unless I go with them." The room seemed to be pulsating. Sweat streamed down his neck.

Linda said, "You've got to tell me what's happening, George. Rudolf is my son, too." He looked at her. Strange, she didn't seem panicky.

"Don't worry," George said, "Rudolf will be all right." He wiped his forehead with a tissue. "The people who have kidnapped Rudolf, they . . . they want me to violate the oath I took when I joined the Fed. You see . . . you see, some Communist conspirators have taken Rudolf. The Communists are behind this catastrophic drop in the value of the dollar—"

Linda said, "Who's really taken him, George? I want an answer."

"I told you, Communists. Terrorists."

"I believe that like I believe you can shit gold bars."

He looked at her. He'd never heard her say anything like that before. "What's come over you?" he said.

"I know it is not terrorists who have taken Rudolf. I want to know who has. Come clean, George."

The phone rang again. For a moment, he didn't move.

"Get it, George," Linda said.

He shuffled over to the phone and picked it up. "This is George Corbett."

"Are you coming?"

"Yes, yes. One moment, please. My wife is here, I'm trying to explain."

"I'll give you three minutes."

George hung up the phone again. Linda was staring at him with cold eyes. She'd picked up her purse, and was clutching it tightly.

George's heart raced. He was light-headed. It was all going to come out now. They would force him to make a public confession. Everyone would know what he had done. He felt strangely ashamed. Terrified. After he made the confession, then what? Then, no doubt, they'd make him suffer a terrible death—yes, execution in some horrible gas chamber . . .

But then he thought, what did that matter so long as Rudolf was safe? Saving Rudolf, that had to come first.

"I—I've got to go now, Linda. I promise you, Rudolf will be all right."

"You aren't going anywhere until you tell me the truth, George."

"The terrorists in the streets have him. Radicals. Communists."

"Don't give me that fucking bull, you're the Communist."

He looked at her, puzzled. How could she possibly know that?

She said, "Your leader is General Kosnoff. You were born Gyorgi Vlahovich, your control was Mr. Peabody, you now report to Lieutenant Popov. Now I want you to tell me who's got Rudolf."

"I, ah . . ." His mind couldn't quite grasp this. "Linda, I . . . Please, I don't know anything . . ."

"Stop babbling, George. I know you went behind the Curtain when you were supposed to be staying in Switzerland. I know you just got promoted to brigadier. I know Peabody got recalled because he opposed your plan. I know you engineered the fall of the dollar. You see, George, all the goddamn time you thought of me just as your airhead wife, I've been reporting every goddamn move you've made. You knew I was in the movement when you married me. Did you think I just forgot my commitment?"

George walked into the kitchen and put his head under the tap, then dried it off with a towel. He'd never imagined, never thought . . . All these years, she'd been reporting his comings and goings. And he never once suspected. So that's

428

how Moscow Central knew about the secret fund for Rudolf in Switzerland. She was telling them everything.

He came back into the living room. Linda was finishing off her cognac. She no longer looked afraid for Rudolf, he thought. She looked like a determined woman warrior, ready for battle, shoulders square, lips pressed tightly against her teeth.

"I hope you'll forgive me," George said, "for not taking you fully into my confidence, but I had my orders and I obeyed them."

"And I had mine," she said. "Now tell me, who has Rudolf?"

"Catlyn Cavanaugh."

"Damian Carter's girlfriend?"

"Yes."

"A goddamn civilian. Is she working with that Israeli? He's a joke."

"Yes, I think they're in it together. She had employed a large black man, too, but Park killed him—they killed each other. I've got to go now, my time is up."

"She makes her living playing cards, did you know that?"

"Yes."

"High stakes poker. She's a pro at bluffing. She's bluffing you, George. You don't have to go anywhere with her. She won't hurt Rudolf. It isn't in her to hurt Rudolf."

"She isn't bluffing. She knows I killed Damian. I know when someone means it. She means it. She'll cut Rudolf up into small pieces."

"She's making a fool of you. Okay, there's a slim chance she might go through with it. We'll have to stall her. But you can't go with her. Moscow Central wants your role in this kept secret. Those are your orders. Your plan is working better than even you expected. This country may have a People's Republic before the week is out, and then we can deal with Rudolf's kidnappers."

George started for the door. "I'm going to save Rudolf, Linda."

"Wait, George," Linda said. "Here, look at this."

He turned around. She had a gun in her hand, a snub-nosed revolver. "Come back here, sit-down."

"Your son is going to meet a horrible death—"

"Listen to me, George. When we signed on years and years ago, we pledged our lives to the movement. We were willing to give everything and anything to see our dreams brought to reality. Your life's work is on the line. I doubt they will harm Rudolf, but if they do, then Rudolf must give his life for the movement."

"He's your son!"

"Yes. And I love him. But he has been called on to make a sacrifice for the cause and he must make it!"

"What does he know about the cause? He doesn't know Karl Marx from Groucho Marx." He inched toward her, but she backed away, keeping the distance between them constant.

"Just sit down, George. We'll just sit here and wait."

"We're talking about Rudolf, Linda! Little Rudolf. You used to cuddle him and read him stories. The Three Bears. Remember how he smushed his oatmeal into his hair when he was a baby? We taught him to swim at Virginia Beach— you almost drowned pulling him out of a wave. He's our son! Our flesh and blood! How can you just let him suffer and die?"

Tears welled up in her eyes, but she raised the gun and pointed it at George's face. "Other boys have died. Others are dying all over the world in plagues that the capitalists force on the world. If we must give our son, we must give him. He never was much. He was never bright. This is one way perhaps he can make a difference in the world."

George looked at the clock on the wall. How many minutes had elapsed? Five, ten? Would she still be waiting?

"I intend to shoot you, George, if you don't sit down now." The gun was shaking in her hand.

"Listen to me," he said. "What Catlyn Cavanaugh wants me to do, I don't know. Confess, probably. Say I go, and tell them everything—hear me out, please—what can they do? If the people hear that the chairman of the Fed is an agent it will further destroy their trust. Don't you see? It's already too late to *do* anything. I don't have to admit I'm KGB. I'll deny that. I'll say I'm just a committed Marxist. I've knocked the legs out from under the economy already, the whole structure is teetering. It will fall by the force of gravity!"

"Don't talk anymore George, just sit. Sit down! I won't hear it. You'll do nothing, understand? You'll just sit down or so help me I'll shoot you dead!"

George took a deep breath and studied her. She was trembling with fear. Her eyes were resolute, but her lower lip was quivering. "No you won't, Linda. I'm your husband." He spoke as calmly as he could. "I'm the father of your child. Okay, the movement means a lot to you. It means a lot to me, but we don't have to let Rudolf die to prove it. Just toss the gun down on the chair there."

He stepped closer to her, careful not to be threatening. She cocked the gun. "Back up, George. This isn't a cigarette lighter in my hand." He raised his hands in a gesture of surrender, but he took one more step closer. She fired.

The bullet hit him low on the left side, just above his belt. He staggered a few steps forward. "Son of a bitch," he said.

He moved his hand to show her the blood. She lowered her eyes. "You made me . . ." she started to say, horrified.

He lunged for her, grabbing her wrist. The gun went off again, the bullet whizzing past his ear.

He had hold of her tightly now, snapping her wrist, shaking the gun loose. Linda cried out, but then George

431

had her by the throat, choking off the air. She grabbed his wrists and dug her fingernails into them, but he didn't let go. He squeezed harder. Her face turned red, then a deep purple, as it bloated up, then her eyes became fixed and he saw the light go out of them.

He dropped her to the floor.

He stumbled into the bathroom. He raised his shirt. The hole was just above his belt, about two inches in. There was blood flowing, but not gushing. He figured she hadn't hit an artery. Good. He felt sweaty for a moment and sat on the toilet seat. No time to get squeamish, he told himself.

He felt around in back. The bullet had gone clean through. He got a bath towel out and tore it into strips, then put washcloths over the entry hole and the exit hole and wrapped the strips of towel around him. He went into the bedroom and put a belt around his waist and cinched it tight, which made it hard to breathe. His guts burned, but for the moment at least he still had his strength.

He put on a clean shirt and a sport coat, got his wallet and car keys, and went into the living room. Linda was lying twisted on the floor, her neck at an oblique angle, her arm flopped behind her back. As he looked down at her, he felt profoundly sad, yet proud she had been his wife. She was committed to the highest ideals, and he greatly admired that.

"I forgive you for everything, Comrade," he said.

He went down the three flights of stairs to the lobby and through the security gate. Catlyn Cavanaugh and Oscar Feldman were waiting for him.

Oscar patted him down for weapons. He felt the towel. "What's this?"

"My wife . . . she shot me. Never mind why. How's Rudolf, is he all right?"

"He's all right," Catlyn said.

George said, "I'm sorry I had to have Damian killed. I liked him, I really did. It was a matter of duty. I want you

432

to know that. I held no enmity for the man."

"And we hold no enmity for Rudolf," Catlyn said. "Now, this way, Mr. Corbett. We've got a car waiting outside."

"Where are we going?"

"To fulfill your destiny."

BOOK III

THIRTY-ONE

A White House limousine with an American flag on the right front fender was waiting just outside the front door. The limousine was surrounded by a half dozen police officers on motorcycles and two National Guard armored personnel carriers.

"What's going on?" George asked.

Catlyn said, "We thought if we stormed in with a lot of police, you might do something rash. We're taking you to see the President."

"I—I don't want to see him."

"This isn't an invitation to a cocktail party, Mr. Corbett," Catlyn said. "You don't get to R.S.V.P." George glanced at the two burly police officers standing nearby and decided not to argue the point. Catlyn, George, and Oscar got into the backseat of the limousine and the motorcade started off, sirens blaring.

Catlyn took out a small notebook and a pen from the pocket of her leather car coat and said, "You've got a lot of questions to answer, Mr. Corbett, and if you don't answer them promptly and honestly, you know what will happen—Rudolf will suffer." Her tone was firm, and there was a half-crazy look in her eye.

George thought: she means it. She would make him die a

horrible, hideous death.

"I intend to cooperate," George said, images of a mutilated Rudolf floating through his head. But he was careful not to show fear. He had been well trained never to show fear. Nor would he grovel. He was caught; they had Rudolf, so he had to go along with them, but he wasn't going to show the least remorse or regret. He was a KGB general and he had his dignity. "Before you begin your interrogation, might I ask why you're taking me to see the President?"

"You're going to restore order," Catlyn said.

"It can't be done," he scoffed. "You can't unscramble an egg. A financial panic like this has a force of its own. Once it gains momentum, it must run its course. There is no stopping it."

"You'll find a way. I have complete confidence in you. So does Rudolf."

George felt momentarily dizzy. There was no way he'd save Rudolf if miracles had to be worked. "Listen to me, please," he said. "What you're asking is just not possible. The economy has been shot through the heart."

Catlyn glared at him in the dim light with an intense madwoman-look in her eye that said it all. Too bad for Rudolf. George turned to Oscar, perhaps he was sane. "You may be making a horrible mistake. If the newspeople find out I am who I am, it will only make matters worse. You've found me out, I can't go back to the Fed. I'm finished. What good is it going to do to take me to the President? There'll be reporters there, television people. Word will get out and the panic will get worse."

"He has got a point, Cat," Oscar said.

"This country was founded on the idea that the public is entitled to hear the truth."

George leaned back, trying to collect his thoughts. He was in the hands of a vicious and vengeful woman, no doubt about that. There was no reasoning with her. She wanted him to suffer, no matter the cost. Perhaps he would die at her hands, some slow, painful, and grisly death. He thought: as long as they spare Rudolf I can endure anything. I *will* endure anything.

"We have a lot of questions," Catlyn said. "Sit up."

"Let me have a moment to get my breath. I'm in pain."

"First you tell us who's in this with you," Catlyn said.

George was rather surprised by the question. Didn't they know? "Who do you think is in it with me?"

"We're asking the questions," Catlyn said.

Oscar said, "You might as well tell us, Mr. Corbett. I'm sure you know how few men can resist modern techniques of persuasion."

"Are you threatening me with torture?"

"I'm just telling you the obvious facts of your situation."

They were in the light of a searchlight at that moment, and George caught a look on Oscar's face. His eyes were narrowed and his lips were drawn tight, but there was no real hardness in the man. Could he torture someone? Extremely doubtful. Drugs, perhaps, but nothing terrible.

"I'm waiting," Catlyn said. "Who's in this with you?"

George was looking at her now. Was she putting on an act as well? Was she just real good at playing the mad-woman? One of the first things one must do in espionage is evaluate the opposition and their intentions. Had he been conned by a couple of amateurs? He felt suddenly stupid. It was pretty clear he had been. He said, "I will admit my involvement in return for Rudolf's life, but I will not compromise my associates. Period."

Catlyn said, "It will cost Rudolf one finger for every hour you do not tell us."

He could feel her body stiffen as she said it. Her voice had a metallic hardness to it; it was convincing, but not quite *totally* convincing, he thought. He'd give her an A but not an A +.

"She's telling you the truth," Oscar said as if he'd caught

on to George's suspicions.

George glanced at him. His tough guy impersonation was thin. Rudolf was in no danger from these people. How, George thought, could he have been such a fool? Linda had given her life for nothing!

He felt a momentary pang of grief, but he pushed it out of his mind. He had to keep his mind on his predicament, he told himself, he could weep for the dead later.

George eased back in the seat and tried to steady himself. His wound was burning, but he was not too uncomfortable. A strange thought crossed his mind. It was a quote from a famous American baseball player, one of many sayings he had been made to learn during his training. The quote was from Yogi Berra: *The game ain't over until it's over.* And the game, George thought, certainly isn't over. He was caught. They had Rudolf. But George still had his wits and his nerve, he thought, and what the Jews called *chutzpah*. Perhaps all was not lost.

They'd gone down Massachusetts to Thomas Circle and headed down Vermont toward 15th Street where they would intersect Pennsylvania Avenue. The streets were almost deserted. Everywhere there was litter and debris and burned-out cars left by rioters. Some store windows were boarded up, others had been smashed. Smoke permeated the strangely quiet city like a fog, dense and stinking. To the south and east the sky was bright orange where large sections of the city were on fire. Now and then, off in the distance, the quiet was broken by the clatter of automatic weapons fire. Chaos, George thought, beautiful chaos!

A TV news truck passed them, then two armored personnel carriers, heading north. Circuses everywhere.

"We're still waiting, Mr. Corbett," Catlyn said.

"Waiting?"

"Your partners . . . who's in this with you?"

"Sorry," George said. "I'd like to hear your theories." George folded his arms across his chest.

440

"A consortium of billionaires, who could make even more billions in gold speculating. That was your plan, wasn't it? But once things got steamrolling, it got completely out of hand."

"That's a pretty good theory," George said.

"Rudolf will soon be missing a finger," Catlyn said.

George said, "Rudolf doesn't do anything with his fingers but get into trouble, anyway. He'd no doubt be better off without them."

Catlyn turned to George. He knew she was trying to read his face. Then she settled back into her seat. He'd taken the axe she was holding over his head right out of her hand. Who the hell did she think she was playing with, a ninny?

They were nearing McPherson Square. George saw a huge red banner between two telephone poles. On it was an American flag with a hammer and sickle where the stars should be. George felt a thrill. He thought: The revolution is here!

When he'd first proposed the idea of crashing the economy, he had envisioned a limping, wounded America sinking slowly into the mud of history. But he saw now that Lenin had been a better forecaster than he. *Debauch the currency, and capitalism will collapse*, Lenin had said—and here it was, collapsing right before his eyes!

A feeling of excitement began to well up in him. He was stopped, but the fire he had started was now a blaze, and would soon be a conflagration!

They were passing Lafayette Square now, where the police and National Guardsmen had fought pitched battles with protesters that afternoon. The statues had been smashed, the trees and shrubs torn up.

"Look!" George cried, "see how thin the veneer of law and order was in America, how quickly it cracked open. Isn't it remarkable?"

Catlyn and Oscar were silent.

On the other side of Lafayette Square, there was a

441

barricade of wire and tank traps, and a row of tanks. Helicopter gunships hovered overhead. Searchlights aimed outward from behind the barricade made it difficult to look in that direction. Across the street in front of the White House perhaps a thousand protesters huddled under the watchful eyes of a few hundred soldiers with automatic weapons.

The sawhorses and coiled barbed wire were moved aside to let the motorcade enter. There were armored personnel carriers and dozens of tanks and hundreds of soldiers in jeeps waiting along the side of the driveway heading up to the White House. The limousine went on from there without escort. It pulled up to the West Portico. The spotlights that usually illuminated the White House and the grounds had been turned off. It was dark and eerie.

An Army officer opened the door. "Mr. Corbett? The President is waiting."

Catlyn turned to George and said, "Every great man has his moment on the stage of history. This, Mr. Corbett, is yours." George thought: She's right. Two minutes with Jerome Hustead and I'll have him believing black is white and up is down.

An aide took them inside where they were passed through a metal detector. He took them down a hallway crowded with civilian and Armed Forces personnel. Nearly every room was full of telephones and computer screens and telex machines clacking away. In general, things seemed chaotic. There was a lot of hurrying around and loud talking, but most everyone looked frantic and confused.

They took an elevator to the third floor, to the President's private rooms, and entered a living room lined with books and crowded with staffers and military people. James A. Preston, the President's chief economist, glared at George, but said nothing.

Catlyn, George, and Oscar were met by the First Lady: "George, I'm so glad you've come! Jerome's in a terrible

442

tate. Have you heard? Detroit is on fire! National Guard
nits have refused to fire on civilians. Some Army units
ave refused to leave their barracks!"

Obviously she hadn't heard of his change of status,
'eorge thought. "It's a night we shall never forget,"
'eorge said, patting the First Lady's hand.

"Jerome wants to see you right away—he's in his study."
She showed George, Catlyn, and Oscar into the room
ith the rolltop desk and the fireplace, where George had
pent so many evenings drinking with the President. The
irst Lady excused herself, closing the door softly behind
er.

The President swung around in his chair, looked at
'eorge and said, "I want you to tell me, George, that what
've been hearing just isn't so."

George eased himself into a chair near the President.
You've known me to be a man with a strong will and high
rinciples, and if you've heard differently, Jerome, you've
een lied to. What specific charges have been leveled
gainst me?"

"Malfeasance in office, dereliction of duty, deliberate
abotage."

George nodded and said, "I guess that would depend on
our point of view. But let's not argue over semantics. I've
ome to cooperate, sir. I hope that will be taken into
onsideration. I think I'm entitled to have a lawyer present
uring questioning, am I not?"

"I think the circumstances merit a suspension of the
sual rules." The President turned to Catlyn. "You're the
oman who phoned my staff earlier—Miss Cavanaugh?
nd this man with you must be Oscar Feldman, is that
ight? Both of you, pull up a chair, let's get to it. The
sraeli ambassador has told me you've uncovered the roots
f our current crisis, but he didn't have all the details."

"Thank you, Mr. President." She was looking him over
arefully, trying not to be obvious about it. She'd seen

many men in a state of inner turmoil when losing the last of their fortunes at cards; they'd tremble, their eyes would roll, they'd sweat. Such men would toss the last of their chips on the table without even looking at what they held in their hands. She could see no such symptoms in the President and she was glad of that. He had deep circles under his eyes, and his shoulders seemed stooped, but he had a determined look in his eye. He was, she concluded, weary but not defeated.

"Now then," the President said to Oscar, "I know you're an agent for the Israeli secret service. Your ambassador told me that much." Then to Catlyn he said, "But I don't know exactly who you are or how you became involved in all this."

"I was a friend of Damian Carter," Catlyn said. "I was with him when he was killed by a man named Robert Park. Mr. Park was an associate of Mr. Corbett's, and killed Mr. Carter on Mr. Corbett's order."

The President looked at George.

"You better have a drink, Jerome."

The President said, "I've been getting one shocking piece of news after another all day. There's nothing you could possibly say that would faze me, I assure you."

"I, ah think this just might faze you a little," George said. "It's true, Jerome. Miss Cavanaugh was Damian Carter's friend. She was with him the night he was killed. She tracked down the killer. I don't know how she did it, but she did. But that's history now. Perhaps if I told you my real name, you'd apprehend the situation. I am Gyorgy Andreyevitch Vlahovich, and I am a brigadier general in the Committee of State Security of the Union of Soviet Socialist Republics."

The President looked at him with his head cocked to one side, as if he hadn't heard what George had said. Then his mouth came open.

"What the hell do you mean, the Committee of State

444

Security. What bullshit is this?"

"It's true," George said. "I went undetected for thirty-one years." He smiled a small, prideful smile. "I've been compromised now, but it doesn't really matter, my mission is complete." He looked at Catlyn and then at Oscar. They both looked dumbfounded. He said, "I am a brigadier general, and I expect to be given all courtesy my rank is entitled to."

The President shook his head. "I just don't believe it. George, is this some kind of plan you've come up with to shock the nation back into its senses? It would never work in a million years. Would someone please tell me what the hell is going on here?"

George said to Catlyn, "You see how good I was. I was very good. Had you not kidnapped Rudolf—" He turned again toward the President. "If they hadn't resorted to kidnapping my only son, I would not be here telling you this, Jerome. You might as well hear all of it, the FBI will surely uncover all my activities anyway. You know how we did it? We bid the dollar up. The Fed and the International Monetary Fund did not intervene like it should have as the dollar was rising, because I was there to make sure it didn't. I gave speeches against it, but let it rise, way way up, to twice, almost three times its value. And then we started selling off dollars and the slide started. Once a slide starts the Fed is supposed to keep it from getting out of hand. I made sure it didn't. And then banks began to fail. I let them. Americans are slow to panic, but once they do, they go into the streets. The panic is in full fury now and there is no stopping it."

The President had pushed his chair back away from George. He was staring at him coldly, his hands grasped tightly to his chair. "You played me for a complete fool."

"I was doing my job."

"Who recruited you? When, where?"

"Recruited me? Oh—I get it. You think I'm an Ameri-

445

can. I'm not. Never was. I was recruited when I was just a kid in the Soviet Union. I'm a career officer."

The President wiped his face again. He looked pale. "I thought honest to God you were becoming one of my most trusted friends." His voice cracked.

"And I can still be your friend, Jerome. Listen to me. You want to know something about yourself? You trust not just me, you trust people. It's an odd American failing. You Americans even trust the Japanese and they've been skinning you for years. Listen, Jerome, what's happening now—this is a good thing. I mean the collapse. It helps a nation's character to suffer. America has never suffered. Twenty million we Russians lost in the Great War of Liberation. We know suffering intimately." He leaned forward in his chair. "Now, we've smashed your economy. Your cities are burning. Your troops are deserting. Radio and TV stations are in the hands of rebels. You are barricaded in here like a bandit in his hideout — No, let me finish, Miss Cavanaugh. Jerome, there's nothing that can save America—except one thing. Turn your government over to a revolutionary council. You could come to terms with them. I would help you. I would have a lot of say in what they decide to do—a coalition could be formed . . ."

The President's round face was flushed now, and swollen with anger. "It seems, George, you not only have provided us with the goddamn crisis, but its solution as well."

George said, "You must be realistic, Jerome. The destruction of the American economy is a fait accompli. It's over. I only wish to offer my services as a mediator. That's all." He opened his coat to show the President the blood seeping through his shirt. "You see this? A bullet went in here and out the back. I'm in critical condition, probably. But still, I offer my services in the name of humanity. What is one life, when a nation's fate is in the balance? Ask any one of your economic advisers and they will tell you the money system in the country is now defunct. The dollar is

446

irtually worthless on all world markets. The banking
ystem will not recover for another fifty years, if then.
Inless America accepts a Revolutionary People's Democ-
acy, it will suffer severe hardship. It may never recover. I
Deg you, Mr. President, accede to the demands made by
he provisional revolutionary government. At least open
negotiations . . ."

The President stared at George. "What would that make
ne? The most cowardly villain in history. The man who
ended freedom on this planet."

"That's just an abstraction, a platitude. Freedom in
America is freedom for the rich and you know it. Think
about it, Jerome, and you'll see. You *must* accept a
People's Revolutionary Council. You have no choice. It's
either capitulation, or order your army to start machine-
gunning civilians in the street. Friday, the banks will not
open. No store in the country will accept—Jesus, my
belly's aching—a million dollars in exchange for a crust of
bread. I'm telling you the truth, Jerome, either you accept
the reality of the situation or you make war on your own
people. Even Ferdinand Marcos and Baby Doc Duvalier
refused to do that. At least let me open negotiations with
the council, Jerome, at least get things started."

The President seemed frozen. He just sat and stared. It
looked, Catlyn thought, as if he might be in shock. Catlyn
lit a cigarette. "Mr. President," she said softly. "May Oscar
and I speak to you privately for a few minutes? There may
be a way out of this mess the country's in yet."

The President nodded blankly.

George said, "Save the country, Jerome, save yourself.
Don't listen to her. What does she know? Let me talk to
you alone, Jerome, please. There's no telling what the
people might do tomorrow. It's Thanksgiving and everything will be closed. Millions of terrified workers will swell
the ranks of the protesters." The President didn't answer
him; he pushed a button under his desk and a Secret

447

Serviceman appeared.

"Take this man out, but keep him handy."

George said, "This isn't really necessary, Jerome. I'm not about to run away."

"Get him out of my sight!" the President said.

As he was going out the door, George said, "I can save a million lives if you'll let me!"

After he was gone, the President sat still for a long moment. Then he said, "The head of the Fed is a KGB agent . . . suddenly it all makes sense." He reached in his desk and took out a bottle of whiskey and three glasses. "Well," he said, "I've heard the KGB's solution, now what's yours?"

Catlyn said, "Did you ever play poker, Mr. President?"

THIRTY-TWO

George was taken to a small emergency medical clinic in the basement and given four units of whole blood and two hypodermics of antibiotics by a young Navy surgeon. George refused painkillers. He didn't want any drugs clouding his judgment. Besides, so far at least, the pain wasn't any worse than a bad stomachache.

The surgeon told him that it was bound to get worse. The bullet had passed through the bowel. Acids and bacteria were escaping into the abdominal cavity, he said. In a few hours he was going to be damn sick. If he had surgery quickly, he'd probably make it.

"How long have I got?"

"Somewhere between four and five hours, maybe. Depends on what the bullet penetrated. I'd have to get in there and look around, to tell you for sure."

"How soon can you operate?"

"I guess as soon as the President says okay."

When the doctor was through with him a Secret Service-man told George the President wanted to see him. The Secret Serviceman escorted George back up to the President's private suite of rooms. An aide at the door to the President's study told them to wait. George insisted he had no time. The aide said the President had been advised of his medical condition. George was given a chair by the window. The Secret Serviceman stood by, like a soldier at parade rest.

An admiral, followed by two generals, arrived and went directly into the study. By the fruit salad on their chests, George assumed they were high-ranking men. George asked the Secret Serviceman what was going on.

"Wouldn't know. They want me to know something, they tell me." The Secret Serviceman had the dull-eyed expression of a functionary. George didn't think much of functionaries.

There was movement suddenly on the grounds outside the White House. George looked out the window. Lines of staffers were boarding buses and military transports. A helicopter was warming up. George tried to get to his feet to get a better look, but the Secret Serviceman pushed him gently back into his seat. "There's nothing out there that's any of our business, now, is there?"

George sat back, thinking something was going on. Then he began to wonder: How come they aren't interrogating me about the underground groups we supplied— where the arms are stashed, the safe houses, the codes, the networks? Strange. His belly was hurting more now. It was feeling like a furnace someone was stoking hot coals into.

A young Air Force warrant officer with a briefcase chained to his wrist came into the room; an aide showed him into the study.

"You know who that was?" George asked the Secret Serviceman.

"I know, but I'm not saying."

"What do you bet it was the nuclear attack code carrier? He's always with the President. They have a code that changes every day—what the hell do they want with him?"

"I wouldn't know."

An aide came out of the study and told George the President was ready to see him. George walked into the President's study holding himself as upright as possible. The room was already crowded with generals and Cabinet officers, who were all standing. The President was the only one seated. Oscar and Catlyn were still there, standing behind him by the fireplace. George was ushered to the front of the room to face the President. Except for a few hushed whispers, the room was quiet. Everyone seemed tense. George glanced at all of them one at a time, trying to get some clue as to what might be going on. There was a lot of fear in the room; it reeked of it.

George was given a chair near the President. George eased himself into his seat, holding his side where he'd been shot.

The President had a clipboard on his lap. He glanced at it and said, "Mr. Corbett, it seems that your ambassador is nowhere to be found." His voice sounded brittle. The muscles around his mouth were drawn tight, and he addressed George without looking at him. He continued. "When the rioting broke out this afternoon, your ambassador fled, along with most of his senior staff members, and has taken refuge at some unnamed location in the Virginia countryside. So what I would have said to him, I'll say to you."

George said, "If you wish to transfer power to a People's Revolutionary Council, my government stands ready to assist you in any way we can." George knew that wasn't what he had been called there for, but he wanted to say it anyway, just for the satisfaction. He noticed the President's cheeks color slightly. The generals and Cabinet officers murmured among themselves.

The President cleared his throat and gestured for silence. Then he said, "I'm only going to say this once, Mr. Corbett, so listen. I have talked it over with members of my administration and members of the Congress. We, together, agree that what you and your country have done constitutes an act of war against the United States, just as certain and just as terrible as an act of war involving troops or bombs or missiles—"

George interrupted. "I totally disagree with that, sir! All of you, listen. What has happened to your country is a result of your nation's greed and reliance on international banking—your own selfish, imperialistic design."

The President said to the Secret Serviceman, "He speaks again before I've finished, shove a gag in his mouth."

The Secret Serviceman took a handkerchief out of his pocket to keep it handy. George fell silent.

"Here is what we want," the President said, his voice growing stronger. "One. The Soviet government will immediately declare that the fall of the dollar has been a deliberate conspiracy instigated by them, with the object of destroying the economy of the West. Two. The Soviet government will immediately begin to buy back dollars on every currency exchange throughout the world as fast as funds can be transferred. The buyback will continue until the dollar reaches parity to its value on September 1. Three. The Soviet government will recall each and every deep penetration agent in the West, not only in the United States, but in every country outside of the Warsaw Pact. And if they refuse these demands, the direst of consequences will result." The President handed him a piece of paper. "We've written it down for you. You'll be given access to the hot line. They have until midnight, that's three hours from now, to make up their minds. Any questions?"

George stared at the President for a long moment, looked around at Catlyn and Oscar, and then at the Cabinet members and the military leaders. He began to chuckle, then he laughed out loud.

"This is the dumbest thing I've ever heard, Jerome. Do

452

you think you're dealing with a bunch of children?"

"Will you deliver the message or not?"

"I'll deliver the message, but I'll tell you the answer right now: *Nyet.*"

"Then you'd better convince your superiors that very terrible things will happen. I'm talking here about the very real possibility of war."

George glanced at Catlyn. This, he thought, was her stupid idea. Poker Queen. Faced with a growing disaster, there was nothing else to do but bluff. And the President had invested her with his complete confidence, the confidence and trust he used to give to George, the idiot. George got slowly to his feet. "I'll communicate your demands exactly as you have stated them, Jerome."

As he was heading down the hall with a Presidential aide and the Secret Serviceman, he remembered that at his training school they'd taught the cadets to play poker. He never liked the game, but he studied it intensely, because he'd been told you had to know poker if you were to understand the American character. One of the first rules was: *Never try to bluff when your opponent has a superior hand and knows it.*

At the moment, he figured, he held all the aces.

They took George to a small communications room used by translators down the hall from the Oval Office on the first floor. The room and hallways were nearly empty now. Even though he was certain no one in the Kremlin would listen to the President's silly ultimatum, George would communicate it to Moscow Central as a matter of form. What else could he do? He would tell them and he would bring the answer back to the President, who would do what? Nothing. He certainly was not going to order an attack against the Soviet Union because of a financial panic.

Jerome Hustead was not a madman.

George sat in the chair behind the desk and picked up the phone. "Hello," he said in Russian. "To whom am I speaking? This is General Gyorgi Andreyevitch Vlahovich, of the Committee for State Security."

"This is Deputy Director Androlin of the KGB. Greetings, General Vlahovich. We have been informed your cover has been compromised."

"*Da*. At this moment I am under guard, but they have asked me to deliver a message—more than a message. A sort of ultimatum. This would be handled by the ambassador, except that he has taken refuge away from the embassy and cannot be located. I think I should give the message directly to the premier. It is directed to him, from the President."

"I am hearing you and will speak to the premier, if you will hold the line."

"Thank you, Comrade Director."

The line was quiet for a few moments. The same voice came back. "The premier is in conference at the moment and wishes me to take down what is the ultimatum."

George read it in English exactly as it was written for him. He would have translated it but he was not that good a translator and he didn't want any mistakes. Not that it mattered. The voice came back on the line. "The premier said he wishes to study the ultimatum."

"The Americans are demanding an answer in three hours' time."

"I will pass that along. Nice speaking to you, Comrade. Good day."

The line went dead.

George looked to the presidential aide who had been listening in. "They always have to study everything," he said. "May I go to the hospital now?"

"That is up to the President."

George sat in the chair and waited while the aide

reported to the President that the Russians were considering the ultimatum. George didn't want to look too at ease; after all, he was still a prisoner. But so far, since his cover had been blown, things had not been going at all badly. The Americans were in a state of total disorganization. This ultimatum was just so much gas. In two or three days perhaps, depending how things went, the rioters might be welded into revolutionary cadres. If there were enough of them, who knows, they might win. Then he would surely be released and decorated as a hero by the American Soviet State.

In the meantime, he had better get the hole in his belly fixed. The coal fire was getting hot enough to melt steel.

The President paced back and forth with a drink in his hand.

He was alone once again with Catlyn and Oscar. He'd sent the military men down into the command posts in the bunkers beneath the White House office building across the street, along with his key civilian advisers. He'd heard what they had to say, then he'd made up his mind to do what he was going to do. That was enough. He didn't want to listen to any more opinions.

Still he had his doubts.

"I think we're playing it the only way we can play it," Catlyn said as if she could read his mind. He stopped pacing and looked at her.

She said, "What are your other choices? A Soviet America?"

"God, I'd rather die."

"A civil war?"

"We've damn near got that now."

"Listen, Mr. President," Catlyn said. "We played our card and made our bet, now just let's wait and see."

"Easy to say, hard to do."

"Let me tell you how people in my profession play this sort of thing."

"All right."

"You play always as if you have what you need and are going to raise and keep raising."

"It's done that way in international diplomacy, too. Sure."

"Okay, then. If you want to make your opponent believe you are going to push things to the limit, you first have to convince yourself that you're holding a winning hand. I've seen guys bet a hundred thousand dollars on a full house, and when they turn their hands over, they're amazed to find they only had a pair of fours. But they won! They won because they were willing to create a winning situation for themselves by their own damn bravado."

The President smiled, at least he tried to smile. "After this is over, how would you like to be Secretary of something or other?"

"Sorry, Mr. President, but I can't type."

The President chuckled. He turned to Oscar. "I never did hear what you thought of all this."

"I don't think you want to hear it, either. The Russians will not like being given an ultimatum. I'm sorry, Cat. I'm scared."

"I am, too," she said.

They took George back to the clinic and gave him two more units of blood. This time George took a shot of something to cool the pain. The doctor said he was running a temperature. The blood loss wasn't bad, but there seemed to be quite a bit of internal hemorrhaging which he couldn't do anything about. After the doctor left, George slept for a while. A Presidential aide woke him up at 11:48 and, accompanied by the Secret Serviceman, took him back to the communications room where

456

KGB Deputy Director Androlin was waiting on the phone.

"This is General Vlahovich speaking."

"You may tell the Americans that the premier wants more time to study the ultimatum. He is meeting now with Party officials. We regret that three hours' time is not enough, but with all due respect we cannot have an answer any sooner than twenty-four-hours—it's just not possible. Explain to them how these things work here, General."

"I will relay the message, and I will explain."

The aide and the Secret Serviceman accompanied George to the elevator and took him up to the first floor to the Oval Office. The painkiller was making George a little light-headed. The President was sitting in a large swivel chair behind his desk. There was nothing on the desk but a pen and pencil set, a telephone, and something that looked like a small electric typewriter. Off to the right, Oscar and Catlyn sat looking on, and the Air Force warrant officer with the nuclear assault codes stood by the window. The only other person in the room was sitting in a chair to the President's right. It was Admiral Kroner, the head of the Joint Chiefs of Staff. Kroner was well past retirement age, a gaunt, white-haired man with a humorless disposition. George had met the man but once. All he could remember about him was how stiff he seemed when he moved.

George was deposited in a chair facing the President. The President nodded to the Secret Serviceman to leave the room, which he did. George looked up at the clock on the wall. It was 12:09.

"Well, George?" the President asked.

"Your people were listening in, you must know what the answer is."

The President said, "We are not prepared to wait twenty-four hours. An act of war has been initiated by the

Soviet Union against the United States. If they are unwilling to take immediate and direct action to nullify what they've done, by all means at their disposal, to admit their duplicity to the world, and recall all of their deep penetration agents, then we have no choice. The honor and integrity of our nation is at stake."

"Hold on a minute here, Jerome," George said. "You're speaking like a wronged party. Not quite the right way to look at all this. The United States has deep cover agents working in our country. You've been sabotaging the Soviet State any way you can for years—that is an undeniable fact of history. You've fought a covert war with us, and now you've lost. It's as simple as that. Now then, you have two courses open to you. You may fight a war with your own citizens—which you will no doubt lose eventually—or you may negotiate with the Revolutionary Council." He sat back in his seat. "As I said, I would be more than happy to act as an intermediary in handling the transfer of power."

The President dismissed that with a wave of his hand. "I told you, if you did not agree to our terms, what the consequences would be." He gestured for the warrant officer to open the briefcase chained to his wrist. The young warrant officer paused for a moment. Then he stiffly walked over to the desk, put the briefcase down, took a key from his pocket, and opened it. Inside there was another case, with a combination lock.

"Three, sixteen, twelve," the President said, glancing at George.

The warrant officer spun the dial; a compartment opened. Inside were three smaller compartments, marked "A," "B," and "C."

"A 6—9—5."

The warrant officer spun the combination and opened the first compartment. Inside was an envelope.

"Open it," the President said.

The warrant officer opened the envelope and handed im the 3" x 5" card inside. On it was a number: A-6074. The warrant officer removed his briefcase from the resident's desk. George had been watching him closely; ere was a thin line of sweat across the top of his brow. hen George looked at the admiral, whose face was ashen ray.

"Okay, Jerome, you've got out your codes," George id. "But it doesn't change a thing."

The President said, "There are few things worth dying r, George. I think honor is one of them. Since you are ot a man of honor, I don't suppose you'd understand at."

"I'm a man of honor as much as you or anyone."

"Needless to debate the point, since you sit there in isgrace. You listen now, traitor, I'll explain it to you. Our ation has suffered a crippling blow. Honor demands that ther the nation that inflicted that blow compensate us r our damage, or we deal a crippling blow to them."

He reached for the machine that looked like a type-riter, and opened the top. Then he took the telephone ceiver and put it into a cradle in the machine. So it asn't a typewriter. It was some kind of telecommunica-ons device. The President switched it on. There was a uzz, then the machine dialed a number, there was a lick, and on a sort of screen on the inside of the top a ord appeared:

READY.

The President put his palm against a glass plate on the ont of the machine. The machine responded with:

VERIFIED.

The President slowly punched in the numbers from the " x 5" card, slowly, one at a time. A-1-6-0-7-4.

The screen read:

CODE VERIFIED

The President typed in GO. The screen read:

LAUNCH COMMAND STATUS GO.

The President put his palm against the glass; the screen flashed:

LAUNCH COMMAND STATUS GO VERIFIED

The President turned a switch on top of the machine; buzzer sounded.

COMMAND LAUNCH ON READINESS VERI FIED

The President typed GO.

Nothing happened. The admiral said, "It needs another palm read."

The President put his palm against the glass. The machine read:

ATTACK STATUS

Oscar suddenly bolted from the room. George looked at Catlyn; she hadn't moved, hadn't even breathed. Her expression was cold, sure of herself.

The President typed:

GO

A buzzer sounded. The screen read:

WAR STATUS

The President turned off the machine and put the telephone back.

George said, "I know, and you know, perfectly well even if you have given the order, it can still be called back."

"You're right, George, that's perfectly true. How much time do we have, Admiral?"

"I'll check with the war room, just a moment." The admiral left the room. No one said anything. George leaned back in his chair and folded his hands. What did they think, he was some kind of idiot? He kept his eyes on the President; he was looking down at his hands on his desk.

The Admiral returned. He said, "3:42 is the last possible moment a recall order can be given. After that, the missiles will be airborne and no power on earth can stop them."

The President said, "Your bosses, George, have until 3:42 to accept the terms of our ultimatum."

George stood up. "I get it. Now that I've witnessed this little drama, you want me to get on the phone and see if I can't scare the hell out of them, convince them that you're really serious about all this."

"I think he is serious," Catlyn said.

George said, "But there's nothing I can do about it. If you don't mind, Jerome, there's a surgeon waiting to cut on me."

"He'll have to wait a little longer. I don't want you sending any messages to your masters right at the moment. They'll find out what we've done soon enough. When we know they've been informed, then you can go get surgery."

George sat back down. "This is going to be interesting. We're really playing with fire, aren't we now, children? If you did order an attack, Jerome, I guess there's nothing to do but sit here and see how close we can get to 3:42 before you shit your pants."

"Or you shit yours," Catlyn said.

Air Force Spec Sergeant Frank Pendergast thought of himself as having the most boring job in the world. Twelve-hour days sitting on his ass in an underground "launch unit" for Peacekeeper missiles. He was twenty-eight, black, loved to play basketball with the guys, considered himself a very funny man at a party, irresistible to a certain kind of woman—the kind that loved to have fun—and couldn't wait until his hitch was up. This was his second four-year stint and he just couldn't take it anymore. Even if the economy was going down the shithole, he figured it was better to be a civilian bum than a well-fed, well-paid, sit-on-your-ass Air Force flunky.

What the hell was there to do but read books, shoot the shit with Lieutenant Margolian or Private Marcy Wain, who was so goddamn one-hundred percent military she'd faint if she got a grease spot on her goddamn dress blues. She even filled out her damn daily log with every word spelled correctly, in perfect goddamn penmanship. Never late, never messy, never nothing but perfect.

He'd heard some white women were like that, but he'd never met one before.

The lieutenant, he was no winner either. He didn't like cars, girls, sports. He was into his goddamn garden. Hot topic of the night: how to make the best mulch on earth.

Neither of them ever seemed to read a goddamn newspaper or watch the goddamn news on television. The banks closed, rioting. Shit. The two of them just came to work like, hey, another day, another dollar. The Air Force, he was sure, was going to turn him into a people hater.

The fueling order came at 12:17 EST.

Okay, Frank Pendergast thought, with all the shit going on, they want to make sure we're still ready. Just another drill. Thanksgiving day, people got their minds on turkey and Aunt Agnes coming over, they ain't got their mind on business. Good day for a drill. Keep everybody sharp.

He got out his fail-safe codex card and checked his number: 887. Then he punched up his number on his screen: 887. So the alarm hadn't gone off by accident. Okay, we got some action here.

He looked over at Private Wain, sitting at a launch station identical to his. She had punched her code numbers in, which were displayed on a separate fail-safe board. She said, "Verified fueling order." Frank turned to the lieutenant and said, "Same here, sir: verified fueling order." The lieutenant's launch station had a few extra buttons and switches. A faint smile appeared on the lieutenant's little-boy face. "I've got a verified fueling order as well."

Frank had gone through four actual fueling drills, and twice had received "launch orders." Tests were never announced in advance. A test and the real thing were handled the same way, so there was no way to know. Still, he was getting a queasy feeling in his stomach. He always did, no matter how hard he tried to tell himself it was a matter of duty, that the decisions weren't his, that he was just doing a dumb-ass job.

The fueling control valve box took two keys. The lieutenant had one to open the top lock; Frank and Private Wain each had a key to the lower one. The lieutenant opened his first. A small green light appeared above the lock. Frank used his key for the second lock. It hung up for a moment, then turned. A second small green light came on. The lieutenant opened a small door like a wall safe. Inside was a ten-digit key pad. The lieutenant punched in his code, then Frank punched in his, then Private Wain punched in hers. A buzzer sounded.

The lieutenant went back to his launch station and pushed the GO button; a second buzzer sounded and red lights began to flash. Nearby, in three silos deep in the ground, liquid oxygen and hydrogen were beginning to be pumped into the missile booster tanks of three massive Peacekeepr ICBMs. The process would take two hours, fifty-eight minutes. When fueling was complete, Lieutenant Margolian would send a signal to Missile Launch Command and he'd receive a "test complete defuel" or "launch on readiness" message.

A launch-on-readiness command might still be a test, Frank knew. The two previous times they'd given a launch-on-readiness command after fueling there had been no launch. They had been personnel tests. He figured that's what this was. Had to be.

For the moment, there was nothing to do but wait. Wait and think about the millions of Russians they might be ordered to kill.

Private Wain said, "My boyfriend asked me to marry him." She said it right out of the blue, as if there was nothing else on her mind.

"That's really great," Frank said. But he felt a pang for the poor slob.

Captain Raymond Fort drove through the gates at Travis Air Force Base in northern California. He'd left only three hours before, after returning from a routine flight to the border of Siberia. SAC, the Strategic Air Command, had been flying these fully armed missions for more than forty years and never once had a squadron crossed into Soviet territory.

Something was strange.

Usually there was a single gate guard, a stiff-faced MP who did the routine job in a stiff-faced mechanical way. Now there were ten of them. And they checked the trunk of his car. Nobody, not in ten years, had ever checked the trunk of his car when he came on base.

He figured it had to do with the trouble they were having in Oakland and Richmond with the roving gangs and the terrorists. Goddamn anarchists. Okay, so if he had to be searched, he had to be searched, he wasn't going to put up a beef.

He drove his new Camaro down the main drive past the hangars. There were spotlights on all over the place. Every hangar was lit up. All the maintenance sheds. Holy shit, he thought, they were rolling out every B-1, B-52, and support fighter they had. What the hell was going on? Defensive missiles and cruise missiles were being loaded under the wings. Holy shit, was somebody getting serious?

Captain Raymond Fort found himself grinning. He was a career man, and he'd been flying up to the Siberian border for eleven years and always turning back. He wondered what it'd be like to go over that line. To finally have a GO order and get it over with once and for all.

He remembered the time they'd gotten some mixed-up orders. It was when he was green, a co-pilot, and he thought they were going in. He remembered getting a hard-on. A real one. He thought at the time how strange it was to get a stiff cock at the very thought of battle. The sensation of sex and the threat of death and unleashing all that destruction had inflamed his loins. He still remembered it. If it had been real, he'd have come in his pants right then and there.

Guys were always talking about if it came right down to a nuclear exchange, could they really go through with it? He'd always said, hell yes! And now it was coming down to it. It looked like it might just be the real thing.

He knew there'd be a counter punch, that America, too, would suffer severe damage. That gave him a momentary tingle of fear. But what the hell, that's war, there has to be casualties.

James Baltimore was on duty in the radio room of the SSBN *Harry S Truman*, a fleet ballistic missile submarine, when the coded message came through. They were cruising at twenty fathoms under the choppy waters of the North Sea off the coast of Scotland. Captain Cushing was in the sick bay with a fever of 102, so the radioman, James Baltimore, brought the message to the Executive Officer. The Exec opened it, then looked in his code book and decoded the message.

He pressed the button on the PA system.

"Attention crew. We've received a launch readiness order. This is not a drill. Status alert. Helmsman, maneuver to slip surveillance. Take us down to 42 fathoms. All personnel report to fire control stations on the double—

that is all."

He turned to the radioman and handed him back the message. "What's the matter, sailor, you look a little green about the gills."

"Must be something I ate, sir."

In Belesebaden, West Germany, it was six in the morning.

Vlad Gunderhausen was washing the breakfast dishes in the enlisted men's club at the Gretal Army Base. He had a good view of the small freight depot and the entrance to the underground facilities where German nationals were forbidden to go.

Cartloads of weapons were being loaded on trucks. This had been going on for over an hour. MP's were everywhere. Men in battle dress and full packs were starting to mill around the parade grounds while trucks were coming over from the motor pool.

Vlad could not tell what kind of weapons were being loaded. There was something going on, but what?

Usually the place was packed with bright-eyed young men, stuffing themselves with wienerschnitzel and beer. Today there were only a few. Vlad asked Mr. Rappaport, the American civilian who ran the club, what was going on.

"Maneuvers of some kind." Then he winked and said, "I heard they're going to take the dogs for a walk."

Vlad nodded. Deep in the ground in old Hitlerite bunkers were stored intermediate-range Pershing and cruise missiles, whose atomic warheads could reach any city in Europe, including Moscow and Leningrad. Whenever the soldiers took the missiles out for maneuvers they said they were taking the dogs for a walk. Sometimes the missiles were just dummies. At least the men were told they were dummies.

Never before had all the units gone on maneuvers. No, this was different. Usually the soldiers acted like Boy Scouts going camping. But not this time. The men loading the trucks looked grim and serious.

"No business today, eh?" he said. "Maybe I go home. I don't feel zat goot anyvay."

"Sure, take off," Rappaport said. "You got sick leave coming, you might as well use it."

When he got to the gate he wasn't allowed to pass. "No one in or out today. We got an alert on."

The young MP's name was Peterson; Vlad knew him from when he worked the bar at the club. He gave him free beers when Peterson was short, and then "forgot" to collect when payday came around. Vlad said, "I been sick today, I got to go home, sleep. Come on, Peterson, give me a favor."

Peterson talked to his sergeant for a moment, then said, "Don't let nobody see you."

Vlad walked across the street, bent over and shuffling, as if he had a pain in his stomach. He turned down a side street, found a pay phone, and called a number in Bad Holstein. When a woman answered he said in German, "I'd like to order a new bicycle."

"You have the wrong number."

The woman at the other end of the line was Helga Moyer, who knew that "I'd like to order a new bicycle" meant that the base was on alert status. She forwarded the message through a microwave transmitter via a Volga IV communications satellite to Moscow Central.

467

THIRTY-THREE

The clock on the wall read 2:45, over two hours since the launch order was given. George had not said a word. He simply sat in the chair and watched, the ache in his belly growing worse. Shooting pains were going down into his legs and up his back. His stomach was tight and pumping bile up into the back of his throat, but he didn't complain, and he didn't let it show on his face.

He was still convinced that the launch order was a charade. They wanted him to buy into it so he would plead with Moscow Central to cave in to the ultimatum. Simple as that. They were playing liars' poker. He was insulted that they'd try such a stupid thing with him. He was, after all, the greatest, most cunning, most daring espionage agent in the history of the world. And they thought he'd go for something like this. How foolish.

He figured all he had to do was wait; the alleged deadline would pass and that would be that. Game over. In the morning the riots would resume, and it would soon be clear that America was finished. This phony war posturing was merely the last gasp.

The President and Catlyn had spent the past hour or so sipping whiskey and playing poker, using matches for chips. How appropriate, George thought. The admiral had left almost immediately after the charade was acted out. Then the Israeli, Oscar What's-His-Name, had returned and was now spending his time pacing by the windows, putting his hands in his pockets and taking them out again. George didn't quite know what to make of him. He was obviously intelligent, knew economics, world politics, and seemed sane. Surely, George thought, he knew it was extremely risky to try to pull some fakery with nuclear weapons. George figured he might even use him to try to talk sense into the others.

At 2:30, George said, "Jerome, may I say something?"

"What is it?"

"This gambit will seriously backfire. This is no time to anger the men who run the Kremlin. You will need them later when you're trying to rebuild your shattered economy. The new government will call them in for technical assistance."

"There isn't going to be any new government, George. There's going to be the old government, or there's going to be war."

"I don't believe you're serious about this, Jerome."

"Then just sit and watch, you'll see how damn serious I am."

George fell silent again. It looked as if the President was determined to carry the charade out to the bitter end; there was nothing George could do about it. Admiral Kroner returned. The President looked up from his cards. The admiral said, "We've received intelligence reports that the Soviets are fuelling their SS20s, 22s, and 30s, and have mobilized their intermediate range missile strike force. Their naval code transmissions indicate their seagoing nuclear strike force has gone to alert status." His raspy voice had risen to a slightly higher register.

The President nodded, as if the news was expected.

Oscar said, "Have they gone into launch mode?"

"Not that we can tell," the admiral said. "But it's expected they will." Then he said to the President, "Should I have your chopper warmed up?"

The President looked at the clock. "I'm expecting a call

on the hot line from Premier Krukov."

"They can patch it through to you at the Command Center."

"That patching through business can be a problem. We'll wait a little longer."

"We've also had a report of a fuel dump being blown up near Pute Re, the Netherlands. Possible sabotage. Big flash reported, may have been a tactical nuclear device, but not confirmed. Two of our Beamstar satellites are out, possibly due to enemy action. Our NATO partners have been informed of the opening of hostilities, full mobilization is in progress."

George had been studying the old admiral's face. It looked hard as marble. The admiral said he'd keep the President informed of further developments, and left. A shiver went through George. The old admiral wasn't bluffing, he was talking war.

George looked at the President, who seemed to have gone rigid, his face pale, his eyes fixed. The President poured himself another drink and downed it quickly. So a launch was under way. It wasn't purely a charade. George imagined the grim-faced men in the Nuclear Strike Force Control Center deep in the Urals. Buttons being pushed. Orders going out. Missiles being readied.

For a moment Rudolf appeared in George's mind, his clothing burned off, his skin blackened with radiation burns. George thought maybe he ought to rethink this. All right, the Americans were bluffing. But the Soviets weren't! Once they got to pushing buttons they couldn't stop things quite so easily.

George, careful to keep control of his voice, said, "A bluff is fine, Jerome. All right, I admire your courage. But it didn't work. The premier hasn't called. And he won't. I know him. He's a stubborn, prideful man. Now call it off before things go too far. You don't know the people on the other side. I do. They are *dangerous* people. They will not shrink from what they see is their duty—even if it means killing every damn person on the face of the earth."

"Is it possible they will strike first?" Oscar asked.

"Yes," the President said, "they may strike first. It's possible but not likely. It takes them time to fuel their rockets and load their planes, the same as it does for us." He shuffled the deck, struggling clumsily to keep the cards from falling out. "Whose deal is it, Cat, yours or mine?"

"Mine," Catlyn said, taking the deck from his hand.

George said, "It takes *no* time to fuel a solid fuel rocket, they are already fueled. The Soviet Navy has subs right off the coast. Maybe right in the goddamn Chesapeake Bay." The terror was coming through his voice now, he couldn't hold it in. "They may try to take out your SAC bases—are you listening to me, Jerome? They believe in 'launch on warning.' " The President wasn't looking at him, he was studying his cards. George got up out of his seat. His legs were cramped and it took him a moment to steady himself. He approached Oscar. "She talked him into this, didn't she?" Without waiting for an answer, George turned to the President. "That's the way you are, Jerome, you trust people. You're a goddamn fool! You trusted me and look at what I did to you and the country. And now you trust her—you go fooling around with nuclear strikes and Krukov will hit you first!"

The President said, "Got openers, Cat?"

"Nope."

"You better listen, Jerome!" George was shouting now. "I'm telling you how things are!"

"I guess you haven't been listening, Corbett," the President said in a sudden burst of anger. "Let me tell you how things are. This nation is in a shambles, caused by an act of economic sabotage perpetrated by the Soviets. That economic sabotage *is* an act of war. The only way to prevent our just retaliation is for the goddamn Soviets to back the dollar and withdraw their deep penetration agents. If they do not, then at 3:42 A.M. we are launching an all-out strike against their miserable fucking country with all our land, naval, air, missile, and space forces. You got that?"

George just shook his head. "Economic maneuvering an act of war? That isn't the way the Soviet leaders see things, Jerome. They don't see they have committed any act of aggression. It is you who are committing the aggression. Listen to me. I know you fully intend to call this strike back. I know you and I know you are not intending to go through with this. This stupid woman here talked you into this. The boys who run the Kremlin, they don't understand Americans very well. They will strike first, don't you see? They don't play poker. They play *real*. You can't face such people down in the street with your six-gun."

The President said, "They will do what they will do, and I will do what I will do." He wiped the sweat off his brow with his sleeve and went back to playing cards with Catlyn.

George said to Oscar, "Looks like they're going to play these stupid games to the end. You're in espionage, you know what I'm saying is true. I've worked for these paranoics in the Kremlin for thirty years, I know how they think. They've been told all their lives that the West is out to get them, and now you've given them proof." He turned again toward the President. "They won't wait for you, Jerome, they will let loose. Listen to me, damn it!"

Oscar said, "He's telling you the truth, I think, Mr. President."

The President was studying his cards. He looked up after a moment and said, "I'll tell you what, George. Why don't you call your people—since they already know what we're doing—and convince *them* to agree to accede to our demands. We have ordered a launch. We will not call it back unless our demands are met. It's that damn simple."

"What can I say to convince them?"

Catlyn said, "You'll come up with something. You're good at convincing people."

472

George started for the door, then stopped. "They won't trust me if I call from here. I'll have to call from the Soviet Embassy on the scramble phone."

The President said, "Miss Cavanaugh, I'll see your four, and raise you two . . . All right, George, but you've only got until 3:42."

An Army sergeant drove George over to the Soviet Embassy in a station wagon with a squad of soldiers following in an armored personnel carrier. The streets were mostly deserted, except for the National Guard and Army units. The sky in the distance to the west and north was still glowing orange, but there was a breeze blowing now off the river and the air was clear of smoke. An eerie quiet had settled over the darkened city.

"Ever see anything like this?" the sergeant muttered. "People gone nuts, that's the truth."

"More nuts than you imagine," George said. He felt cold all over despite the fact that he was sweating. He'd never sweated under strain before. His belly was cramping now, and he found he had to lean over to relieve the pain. Whatever painkiller the doctor had given him had long since worn off.

They turned down Embassy Row. The power was out, but emergency generators had restored power to most of the embassies along both sides of the street. They pulled up in front of a gray brick building surrounded by a high-walled courtyard. The first-floor lights were on; the upper four stories were dark. The front gates had been sandbagged, and a squad of National Guardsmen were posted around the perimeter.

"Here she is," the sergeant said. "We got orders to wait until you come out if it takes till Chinese Christmas."

George got out. For a moment, the thought hit him that the fate of the whole world was up to him. His knees were

473

putty under him. How did this happen? When he'd started, he had it in mind to fight a bloodless war, a war of stealth and secrets, not nuclear bombs. Where did it go wrong?

He blamed Catlyn Cavanaugh. It was all her damn fault. Then he blamed himself for not telling Park to cut her damn throat while he was taking care of Damian Carter. One stupid mistake in thirty-one years.

He walked past the National Guardsmen. They were a sloppy bunch of soldiers, just standing around, smoking, talking. They must have heard he was coming, because they didn't ask to see his identity papers or ask any questions. They knocked on the gate. One yelled: "Hey, Ivan, you got company!" A Soviet soldier opened the gate and let him in.

On the other side of the heavy wooden door George found himself face to face with two Soviet soldiers carrying automatic weapons.

George said, "I am General Gyorgi Andreyevitch Vlahovich of the Committee for State Security, and I must make a communication with the premier immediately."

One of the soldiers said, "Have you identity papers, sir?"

"I have been working deep cover, so naturally I have no papers."

"We will have to take you to the lieutenant in charge tonight. Come this way."

The embassy inside was nearly deserted. They led George down a long, highly polished hallway to a large office, where Svetlana Popov was sitting behind the desk with her feet up and a large snifter of brandy in her hand. She dismissed the soldiers with a salute. Then she saluted George from behind the desk without getting up. She said, "The ambassador took his wife and children and fled. Most of the staff went with them. One of the assistant ambassadors is here, but I tell him what to do because he's a frightened little weasel. Well, we did it, didn't we?

America is finished. Let us celebrate." She pushed the bottle of brandy toward him with her foot.

"This is no time to be drunk, Svetlana. The Americans claim to have ordered a preemptive strike against the motherland. I must call the premier. I must try to convince him it is all a bluff."

"You don't look so good, George. There's blood on your shirt."

"Never mind that! Get up, Svetlana, show me where I can make the call."

"Let's go upstairs," Svetlana said. "The ambassador has a bed as big as the front yard—"

"The world is about to blow up, Svetlana, don't you give a damn?"

"We all knew it was going to happen someday. We have them out-gunned, out-thought, out-everything. We will die, but the Great Pig will die with us. Could anyone ask for more glory than that?"

George rubbed his forehead. It felt as if it was being ripped open. He leaned over the desk. "Listen, Svetlana, we must now act in a way which will benefit humanity. We cannot think only of the motherland. Hurry now!" He pushed her feet off the desk.

She looked at him with a scowl on her face. "If it is total war they want, I say give it to them. We will turn this miserable country into a pile of ashes."

"No, Svetlana, on your feet, there are only a few minutes left."

"To hell with it. Rejoice in the destruction of capitalism!"

"You talk like a schoolyard tough, Svetlana. You can help me. Verify that what I am telling them is true—that it is only a bluff."

"I would do nothing like that! I do not make policy. What has happened to you, General? Have they tortured you? Have you become a milksop?"

George, with a sudden burst of strength, hit her squarely in the face, knocking her backward over the chair.

She looked up at him with astonishment. "You will get up, you fool, and you will tell Moscow Central what I tell you to tell them, do you hear me?"

"Beat me to death if you will, I will not raise a finger to help you!"

George felt tears coming to his eyes. "What hope is there in a world full of fools?"

He went into the hallway and asked one of the soldiers to get him to a radio, he had to talk to Moscow Central immediately.

"Not without Lieutenant Popov's permission."

He hit the soldier, driving him back against the wall. Then he tried to grab the startled soldier's gun, but the young man pushed him away easily. George fell to his knees, gasping for breath. Pain from his wound shot through him in volleys.

Svetlana stood in the doorway, blood running from her mouth. "Looks like you're in trouble, Comrade."

George said to the soldier, "Call Moscow, they will tell you who I am. You must. Can't you see she's drunk! You do not have to obey an officer who's drunk, do you? There will be rockets falling on this city in twenty minutes if I do not convince them otherwise. Take a chance, what have you got to lose?"

The soldier looked George over for a long moment, then nodded. "If you are lying, you will be punished."

"All right, fine. Let's move."

Svetlana laughed, and called after them: "What difference does it make? Go ahead and call them, General, see what they say. You will not convince them of anything."

The soldier took George to the top floor where the microwave transmitter was located. It was a large room full

476

f gray transmitters placed in rows, separated by dividers, each with its own decoding device. Svetlana Popov followed them, the brandy bottle in her hand. The communications specialist put the call through for George, then handed him the phone.

"Moscow," the voice said in Russian.

George said, "This is Brigadier General Gyorgi Andreyvitch Vlahovich of the Committee for State Security. I order you to put me through to Premier Krukov, this is a class one state emergency."

"One moment, General."

The line went dead. Then, "The premier is otherwise occupied at the moment. I have instructions to take down your message."

"Does he know the whole goddamn world is about to blow up?"

"I have my orders, please give me your message, General."

"Damn your orders!"

"You may damn my orders, I cannot. Premier Krukov says you may speak with Comrade Batyushkin of the KGB."

"Fine, fine, put him on the line."

"It will take a few minutes to get him . . ."

"Hurry, damn it, you idiot!"

Svetlana said from the doorway, "Poor, poor George, no one will listen to him."

"They will listen."

"Greetings, Comrade Vlahovich, it is a terrible night, is it not?" George recognized Batyushkin's voice.

"Listen, Comrade Batyushkin. I have been at the White House. I was with the President of the United States not ten minutes ago. Listen to me, Comrade. There is no attack imminent. The United States is not making war, it is a bluff. I swear to you."

"What have you told the Americans about your role in

breaking their economy? You know the penalty for cooperation with the enemy."

"Comrade, please, this is no time to bother with that. Listen to me, damn it! The Americans are going to call off their attack before any missiles are launched. Their deadline is 3:42, Washington time. Believe me, no attack is going to be launched."

"What evidence can you give us?"

"You know I have been with Americans for thirty-one years. I know how they think. I was with the President when he gave the order. I know the woman—her name is Catlyn Cavanaugh—who talked him into doing this stupid thing. She's nothing but a cardplayer, but the President listens to her. This is her doing. You must believe me!"

There was a pause on the other end of the line, then Batyushkin said, "The premier should talk to you."

George looked toward Svetlana standing in the doorway, drinking from the brandy bottle. she said, "You are a despicable coward, General."

"And you are a fool."

There was a crackle on the line. "Comrade General? This is Premier Krukov. Tell me everything you know and how you know it . . ."

George told him how things were as he saw it. How the President of the United States had a disastrous tendency to put full trust and faith into his underlings, and at the moment seemed to be under the demonic influence of Catlyn Cavanaugh, who had no experience in world affairs but instead spent her life playing poker. He explained how they made a big show of ordering the attack with a communications device of some kind and secret codes to impress him, and how they were sitting in the Oval Office playing cards instead of running for a bomb shelter someplace. He ended by saying, "They know their country is on the ropes and they are desperately grabbing at straws. They will call off this phony launch. I could not be closer to this

478

situation, sir, and I know my estimate is correct."

The premier said, "When you called I was in the process of ordering an immediate, all-out attack on America." His voice, George thought, was remarkably calm.

George felt the sweat dripping from his chin.

The premier said, "I can understand how the President feels. Perhaps I, too, would be driven to a desperate gamble. How much time until the deadline?"

"It is now 3:14. Just a little under half an hour, Comrade Premier."

"Hold the line, I wish to speak to my advisers . . ."

George sat down in the chair. The room was rocking back and forth. The light seemed to be fading.

A few moments later the premier came back on the line. "General Vlahovich, we have decided some things. First, you are to be awarded the Order of Lenin, First Class, and we have authorized an immediate promotion to major general—and we are putting you in charge of all our operations in North America for the duration of this emergency."

"I feel unworthy, Comrade Premier." George noticed that Svetlana looked stunned. She dropped the phone she was listening with, turned, and disappeared down the hallway.

"Never mind thanking us," the premier said, "You are now fully responsible. Pay close attention, Major General. We have no other indication that what you say about the Americans is true. Reports of our satellites, and our networks from around the world indicate that the Americans are in the process of launching an attack. But I believe you. I trust you. Perhaps I believe you and trust you because I do not want to see a war. I have seen a war, and one is enough for any lifetime. You are in a unique position to know the truth, and that is another reason I believe you. Now then. You have said that 3:42 Washington time is the deadline. They will either go through with the attack, or call it back. We will not wait until that time. They already have planes in the air. We will wait until 3:30. Our submarines will fire their missiles at exactly 3:30 at Washington. At 3:35 or so Washington will vaporize. You tell them they have until 3:30 to call back their attack. Afterward we will discuss their protest with us, and any legitimate grievance they have, we will rectify."

"But, sir, the Americans are not going to launch. You don't have to do anything but wait and see. They will not launch. Damn it, you have to believe me!"

The response was cold. "You have your orders. Go and carry them out." The line went dead.

George stood up. The two communications specialists, who had also been listening in, stood up and saluted him. On his way out the door George said, "As soon as I'm gone, you're to have Lieutenant Popov thrown out of here. She is not to be admitted again, ever."

Outside, the sergeant and the squad in the armored personnel carrier were waiting for him. George got into the station wagon and said, "Back to the White House quickly. Drive as if the fate of the earth depended on it."

Spec Sergeant Frank Pendergast was no longer bored. He was watching the pressure gauges on the wall and he knew the rockets were nearly full. In fact the fueling sequence was a few minutes ahead of schedule. He knew the launch order was for 3:42.

He wasn't supposed to know, but when the lieutenant's digital message came in he saw the screen and he saw the time. So he knew it wouldn't be long. He thought maybe Private Wain knew it, too. She was knitting. The damn bitch was always knitting, but she was breathing heavy through her nose so he knew it was getting to her, too.

So once again it came down to pushing the button and seeing whether it was fucking for real.

He remembered the last test. He went through with it. He did his job. He had pushed the launch sequence buttons and waited for the roar of the rockets in the nearby silos. But then the buzzer went off, indicating a test rather than a launch. He remembered how he and Private Wain and the lieutenant—another lieutenant, Cooper, his name was—all jumped up and down. And when the shift was over the three of them went outside and made snowballs and played around like little kids. That was about the only time he'd ever seen Private Wain smile.

"We have to set telemetry," Lieutenant Margolian said.

Frank joined the lieutenant at his launch station. The lieutenant punched some keys; numbers appeared on the screen. Then he opened a fail-safe envelope; the numbers were the same. Frank looked away while the lieutenant entered his code number, then he verified the numbers with his code while the lieutenant looked away

The fate of a few million Soviet citizens was sealed.

Frank, of course, had no idea what cities the missiles were aimed at. What difference would it make to him anyway? He didn't know Moscow from Irkutsk. The only difference it made was how many people were in them. And what the hell difference did it make?

What was the difference between two million and ten million? If this was it, man, it wasn't going to make no difference to nobody. He looked at the clock; it was 3:21.

Then he wondered, just for a moment, *why*.

Captain Raymond Fort was airborne now, sitting beside his co-pilot who wasn't but maybe twenty-four years old and had, in Raymond Fort's opinion, shit for brains.

All the kid kept mumbling was, Humpty Dumpty sat on a wall, Humpty Dumpty had a great fall. . . .

"What the fuck you prattling about?" Fort asked.

"You're never going to put Humpty—this old world—

together again."

"You really think this is it?"

"I do."

Captain Raymond Fort looked down on the lights along the California coast in the distance beneath him. "This is the day we all been waiting for, ain't it?"

Captain Cushing of the *Harry S Truman* was back in the control room, despite his fever. He'd had his radioman busy for an hour confirming the message before he finally believed it and switched off all communications with land. He was forty-two years old, and for the first time in his life he was truly panicked.

It was now 03:22 hours, Washington time. He had to go into launch readiness mode. His hand was shaking. He had a wife and daughter back in Newport News and that's all he could think about.

His Exec said, "We have to get started with launch sequence, sir. Sonar reports we have slipped surface surveillance."

He looked up at his Exec. His name was Dawkins. He was a big man, with broad shoulders and deep blue eyes.

"This was going to be my last trip out," the captain said.

Dawkins said, "Maybe this is going to be everybody's last trip out."

THIRTY-FOUR

George fought to keep himself from passing out. The pain had him doubled over. He was weak, out of breath. It felt now as if there was a giant hand pulling on his bowels, tearing them out.

"Faster, driver, faster."

They had long since outdistanced their escort. At the corner of Massachusetts Avenue a shot rang out and a bullet crashed through the windshield. George sat up to take a look, but realized instantly what a stupid idea that was.

"Fucking snipers," the sergeant said

George's vision was blurred now, darkness closing in on him. Not yet, he told himself. A few more minutes and you can die. Not yet.

They were waved on through the barrier at the White House and George was helped out of the car and taken directly to the Oval Office. The clock on the wall read 3:24. Six minutes until the premier's deadline. It took George a moment to catch his breath, sitting down in a chair, still bent over. Then he said, "I spoke to the premier. He is willing to negotiate your grievances, Jerome. He does not reject your demands outright. Only he needs more time to settle things. Give him that time. Call off your attack, because if you don't, and I swear to you this is true—he's ordered an attack at 3:30. You have five minutes, and ah, forty seconds. This is not a bluff. Not a fake. This is real!'"

Catlyn blinked at him, then turned to the President and said, "It's your bet, Mr. President. I had openers. Are you in?" She fanned her cards in front of her.

The President looked at his cards and shoved three matches into the center of the table. "I'll take two." He looked at George, then at Catlyn, then at Oscar, then at the clock. George thought he seemed drunk or maybe dazed. There was a faraway look in the President's eyes.

George took a deep breath. "They will not give in to your demands. Even if they suspect you are bluffing, they cannot take the chance. But believe me, they are not bluffing. You have four minutes to decide if you want this world to die."

Catlyn said, "I'll see your two and raise you one," and pushed three matches into the pot.

The President looked at her as if he hadn't understood what she was saying.

"I said I'll raise you one match."

The President said, "I'll see your one, and raise you three."

Oscar got up out of his chair and touched George on the shoulder. "Will they agree to any of the President's demands?"

"They said they will discuss the grievances after the launch order has been canceled. They meant it, too, they are extremely disturbed by what's happening."

George suddenly started coughing, spitting up blood into his handkerchief. He felt himself sagging into unconsciousness for a moment, held his breath, and forced himself to hold on. "Hear me: The Soviet Union has at this moment four or five submarines right off the Atlantic coast. Five or ten minutes after 3:30 Washington will be gone."

"Ten minutes after that, Moscow will be gone," the

President said.

Catlyn said to George, "Better call them again, there isn't much time left." To the President, she said, "I'll see your three and raise you three more."

The President pushed the phone across his desk in George's direction. "Just pick it up, it's a direct line."

George reached for the phone. He looked at the clock. 3:27.

Catlyn said, "It'll cost you three to call, Mr. President."

The President took a bottle out of the desk and poured himself a drink. Catlyn nodded to him. "It's your bet," she said.

"Are you going to make the call or not, George?" the President asked.

"First, you have to call off the launch."

"Not unless your people agree to terms."

"I've told you what they said, they are going ahead with an attack in three minutes! They have agreed to negotiate. Now it's up to you. If you can't stop the launch, delay it."

The President looked at Catlyn, then at his cards, then he said, "No."

George shook his head. Neither side was going to listen, that's all there was to it. They were going to face each other down and blow the damn world up. He leaned on the desk and picked up the phone. A moment later a voice answered. It was Anatolin, the KGB Deputy Director he had spoken to before. George said, "This is Major General Gyorgi Andreyevitch Vlahovich."

"Yes, General."

"This is my last communication. The fool who is President of the United States refuses to cancel his attack orders until the last possible moment. The fool who is Premier of the Soviet Union is intent on attacking. No one can stop fools. We are a world full of fools who have fools for leaders. I therefore recommend that all nuclear strike forces of the great Soviet State be launched immediately against the

485

Americans and their allies. Long live the Revolution!"

He hung up the phone. He looked at Oscar, who was standing by the window, staring blankly into the night. George walked over to the door and said, "You know what Mussolini said when they took him out to shoot him—he wanted to die with the warmth of the sun on his face. I will die with the warmth of a thermo-nuclear explosion on mine."

He went out, closing the door behind him. Oscar walked over to Catlyn and kissed her on the cheek. "You pushed it as far as you could, but it's time to fold the hand."

"Never fold on your own raise."

The clock read 3:28.

The President put his hand on the hot line receiver. "I wish to hell now I'd lost the damn election. If two percent of California and four percent of Illinois had gone the other way, I'd be in Iowa now raising the best goddamn alfalfa in the state."

Oscar said, "Pick up the phone, Mr. President. I know in my heart George was telling the truth. I know the economy is gone, but the country can recover. Even if it takes half a century. From a nuclear holocaust, there is no recovery."

3:29.

"Cat?" the President asked. Sweat was streaming down his face. He bit hard on his lip. Blood trickled down his chin.

Catlyn said, "I think they're bluffing."

"Give me one good reason to think so."

"I'll give you two good reasons. One, my poker player's intuition."

"And two?"

"If they were going to attack, they would just do it, they wouldn't tell you about it first."

"What if you're wrong, Cat?" Oscar asked. "The entire planet . . ."

"I think she's right, Mr. Feldman," the President said. "They would have attacked already." He pulled back away from the phone.

The three of them watched the clock. The second hand was sweeping toward 3:30. The President poured Catlyn and Oscar a drink.

Catlyn said, "You ever see anything like that?" She held up her hand. It was trembling. "I used to think I was cool."

"Did I call you or did you call me?" the President asked, picking up his card.

"I don't remember." She laid down her cards. "I've got a pair of deuces."

The President laid down two pairs: kings and jacks. "That's only the second hand I've won from you." He scooped up the pile of matches from the pot.

"Perhaps you've had other things on your mind, Mr. President."

The clock on the wall said 3:30. The three of them watched it in silence for a moment.

"I think we have time for another hand," she said. "If they've launched."

Oscar walked back to the window and looked outside. "Clear night," he said. "Are you going down into the shelter?"

"I don't think so," she said.

"I don't think I will either," he said.

She started to shuffle. "Want to up the stakes? How about a two-matches ante?"

"What the hell, let's throw caution to the wind."

The President kept his eyes on the clock. Catlyn started to deal. The hot line phone rang.

The President said, "That may be Premier Krukov calling to tell me to kiss my ass good-bye. Why don't you get it?"

Catlyn picked up the receiver and said, "Hello, this is the Oval Office."

There was a crackle on the line. Then: "I am calling for Premier Krukov. Please tell the President the Soviet Union has agreed to each and every one of his demands . . ."

George was standing on the lawn with the Secret Serviceman looking up at the stars when they heard the cheering inside, and then some presidential aides burst out the door crying, "We did it! We did it! They've agreed to everything!"

George stared at them in disbelief, and then it began to sink in. The world was not going up in smoke, at least not now. George fell on his knees crying with joy.

He was still lying on the grass crying like a baby when, a few minutes later, two FBI agents came and put their hands on him.

EPILOGUE

The son of the don looked up from his cards. Sweat, in beads the size of watermelon seeds, dripped from his nose.

"Well, Mr. Crupiano?" Catlyn asked. "It's twenty-five thousand to you." She looked over at the Egyptian, who had already quit the game after losing what he claimed was enough money to buy the Statue of Liberty.

"I know you ain't got shit," the son of the don said.

"Then why don't you raise me again?"

He looked down at his meager pile of chips, and then at the pot. There was maybe four hundred thousand in the pot. And she'd already won twice that much; it was stacked in front of her like a mountain. Neat and tidy, not a chip out of place.

The son of the don leaned back and said, "What the fuck's another twenty-five G's." He shoved his remaining chips into the center of the table. "Show me."

Catlyn fanned a full house onto the green felt table. "Aces riding jacks."

"Fuck!" The son of the don threw down his cards.

"It has been fun, gentlemen," Catlyn said, scooping up the pot.

The Egyptian opened his gold cigarette case and took out a dark cigarette and put it in his mouth, lighting it with a gold lighter. "You are a marvel, Miss Cavanaugh. We ought to do this again sometime, if my accountant will permit it."

"Next time, it's my turn!" the son of the don said. "I got her once, I'll get her again."

He grabbed his coat and headed out the door.

The Egyptian said, "You're going to end up owning him, Miss Cavanaugh."

"I think I already do, Mr. el-Towik."

When she got back to her apartment, Oscar was waiting for her. He'd been in Israel for nearly a month and he looked tanned and fit. His bags were sitting in the middle of the living room.

She kissed him and hugged him. He seemed a little tentative, as if he had something to say and couldn't wait to get it out.

He said, "I found out something about you."

"That I'm not totally cured of my addiction to jelly doughnuts?"

"You aren't married," he said. "In fact, you never have been."

"You didn't buy the brain-dead husband story?"

"Nope. You send money out to Long Island every month all right, but it's for a school for homeless girls."

"Very good detective work there, Sherlock."

"In fact, everything you told me was pretty much a work of fiction. Your father was a New York real estate tycoon who went bankrupt when you were a kid. You've never been to any college in your life and you've been making a living playing cards since you were seventeen years old."

She tugged on his tie. "Okay," she said. "You got me. I perjured myself. Guilty. Now what are you going to do about it?"

"Well, I thought as long as you've never been married, maybe you'd like to try it out."

"Ooooo, you're asking at a very bad time. I had an

490

ceptionally good afternoon. Besides, what kind of a usband would you make, running around the world seducg women, getting cracked in the head. Stuff like that."

"I've resigned from the Mossad."

She felt a jolt. "But it meant so much to you."

"I'm going back to my original plan. Being a half-time armer and a half-time teacher of economics. I'm going to ve on a kibbutz—that is unless you strenuously object. We ould get an apartment in Haifa, maybe, near the beach. e'll have a garden. I've been thinking about writing a ook about economic espionage."

"I think," she said, "you're married to Israel. And I am arried to my game."

"Can it mean that much to you?" He put his arms round her waist.

She said, "There's a knot-headed son of a Mafia don at still has a couple hundred thousand dollars of my oney. Yes, it does mean that much. You know what appens inside you when you're on a streak? When a rtune rides on the turn of a single card? When you look a an in the eye and raise like hell into his little straight hen all you've got is guts? There's nothing like it . . . but u mean almost as much, Oscar. Honest."

"I think I've just been compared to a game of chance ad came up lacking."

"Oscar, I love you. Why can't we just love each other? hy do we have to build a nest?" She kissed him again. How long are you going to be in New York?"

"A few days."

"What do you say we rent a boat and spend your few ays bobbing out on Long Island Sound, eating strawberes, drinking champagne, and feeling each other up?"

Oscar said, "You sure do know how to plan a vacation."

At first, life for George in prison was pure misery. The

491

cell was cold, small, and damp. The food was terrible. The cot was lumpy. The itching of his healing wounds was driving him insane. They let him read newspapers, but the stories sickened him. The "miracle of the recovery," as they were calling it, dominated the news.

And his lawyer kept telling him there was little hope that he would get anything less than the death penalty.

They let Rudolf visit him, and George told him the unvarnished truth. Everything. How he grew up, how he was trained, how he came to America, how the KGB had helped him build his fortune. He even told how and why Linda had shot him, and that he had killed her. He had to, he said, to save America, and to save the world, which wasn't quite true, of course, but he didn't want the boy feeling guilt because his mother had been killed to save him.

Rudolf at least listened. He was cold, but he was not, George thought, *brutally* cold.

Rudolf was now living with Mattie, the Corbetts' former maid, and she didn't let him smoke dope or horse around. He had gotten a sensible haircut. She had him doing schoolwork and playing basketball. Rudolf the athlete. Maybe something good came out of all this mess, George thought.

Then two days before Christmas, George made a deal with the FBI, the greatest deal of his life.

He agreed to tell the whole story in every detail in exchange for three things: the prosecution would not ask for the death penalty in his case, he would be allowed to write and sell his memoirs and his son could keep the proceeds; and, lastly, he would be allowed to serve his sentence (no doubt the rest of his life) in the new San Gabriel Correctional Facility in California, where they had a golf course, tennis courts, and the inmates could have female guests visit them in their "housing units" from time to time.

He had Esther in mind.

He knew the Soviets already regarded him as a traitor, so what difference did it make if he cooperated with the FBI? Besides, something had happened to him that night when it looked as if the world might blow up, when he'd called both the President of the United States and the Premier of the Soviet Union fools. He changed. He lost his faith. He no longer cared for the triumph of international socialism, or any other *ism*, for that matter. He now believed only in himself and his family.

In the meantime, now that he was cooperating, the accommodations provided at the Washington, D.C., jail were made less horrible. He was given a larger cell, a nicer cot, a color TV, two extra blankets, three meals a week brought in from an outside restaurant. His lawyers were arranging for him to plead guilty to two hundred counts of espionage, conspiracy, murder, and the like. This would all net him something in the neighborhood of thirty-one life sentences plus a few hundred-odd extra years for miscellaneous felonies and infractions. That was of course *pro forma*. As soon as the paperwork was taken care of, he'd be in sunny California, getting a tan, pumping a little iron, working on his backstroke, and catching up on his reading.

So life wouldn't be that bad, he figured. Tolerable anyway. And, as he told a reporter from *The New York Times* who interviewed him:

"Life has infinite possibilities for the man of imagination."

The reporter scoffed. "Even in here, you still think of yourself as having infinite possibilities?"

"Why not?" George asked. "Am I not a man of infinite imagination?"